'By opening up to the drama[...] Thorne has added a dimension to his [...] better for it' Alfred Hickling, *Guardian*

'*Child Star* is a sharp social comedy'
Hugo Barnacle, *Sunday Times* Culture

'A skilful, funny and moving evocation of pubescence and a judicious stitch-up of the world of television soaps . . . [Matt Thorne has] carved out a territory that's uniquely his'
Tibor Fischer

'Matt Thorne's breezy, absorbing novel . . . this entertaining, atmospheric book . . . As *Child Star* illustrates with casual eloquence, fame is a new religion for people who no longer believe in God' William Cook, *Independent*

Matt Thorne conveys Gerald's angst in a fresh, insouciant style. His lively narrative never slackens . . . This is his best book so far' Charlie Campbell, *Literary Review*

'It is as a study of a single character that *Child Star* really excels . . . teasingly bittersweet'
Benji Wilson, *Independent on Sunday*

'This sparky, witty novel examines the consequences of fame at an early age' *Evening Herald (Dublin)*

'An interesting novel, with some strong social themes . . . a sharp polemical edge' Julia Flynn, *Daily Telegraph*

'A hatful of modern preoccupations are explored . . . His lucid, unadorned prose is well suited to exposing the pretensions of celebrity culture, and Thorne details the lives of his dysfunctional moderns with compassion'
Oliver Robinson, *Observer*

Matt Thorne was born in 1974. He is the author of *Tourist* (1998), *Eight Minutes Idle* (Winner of an Encore Prize, 1999), *Dreaming of Strangers* (2000) and *Pictures of You* (2001). He also co-edited the anthology *All Hail the New Puritans* (2000).

By Matt Thorne

Tourist
Eight Minutes Idle
Dreaming of Strangers
All Hail the New Puritans (*as co-editor*)
Pictures of You
Child Star

child star

MATT THORNE

PHOENIX

A PHOENIX PAPERBACK

First published in Great Britain in 2003
by Weidenfeld & Nicolson
This paperback edition published in 2004
by Phoenix,
an imprint of Orion Books Ltd,
Orion House, 5 Upper St Martin's Lane,
London WC2H 9EA

A CIP catalogue record for this book
is available from the British Library.

ISBN 0 75381 753 5

Typeset by Deltatype Ltd, Birkenhead, Merseyside

Printed in Great Britain by Clays Ltd, St Ives plc

For my sister

Acknowledgements

Lesley Shaw, Michele Hutchison, Rose Gaete, Katie White, Susan Lamb, Alice Chasey, Kate Shearman, Richard Milner, Mark Rusher, Jin Auh, Marion Mazuaric, Anne Guerand, Kaye Thorne, Sarah Ballard, Alexandra Heminsley, Kate Le Vann, Fleur Darkin, Nicholas Blincoe, Leila Sansour, Ben Richards, Rossana Leal, Toby Litt, Leigh Wilson, Jim, Jamie and Catherine Shaw, Anju Desai, Richard Thomas, John Rush, Neil Taylor, Sarah Harris, Sarah Waters, Lana Citron, Tibor Fischer, Borivoj Radakovic, Drazen Kokanovic, Ivo Caput, everyone at FMCM, Dan Gunn and Toni D'Amelio.

I would also like to thank Nick Guyatt, Steve Merchant, Huda Abuzeid and David Thorne for furnishing me with various bits of information needed to complete this novel. Any mistakes are, of course, entirely their fault.

PART I

★

1

I hope this doesn't sound horrible, but I always prefer my friends when they're single. I don't like it when they've been out of love for ages and they get all depressed, but there's definitely something bewitching about being around someone when they're disburdening themselves of a dead relationship.

When my friend Sally broke up with her last partner, a group of us went out for the evening. Sally and I have been friends for a while. Neither of us is especially emotionally expressive, but over the years we've learnt how to take care of each other. I was the one she came to whenever a man let her down, and after I broke up with Ellen, Sally moved into my flat and slept in my bed for two weeks. This time I'd gone out with Sally and a group of her female friends and the conversation turned to sex. Half the table was arguing that they could do without it; the rest disagreed violently. Then Sally said something that sounds trivial, but I think sums up the whole thing for a lot of people. What she said was:

'I don't feel that I want to have sex this minute, but I hate thinking that I might never have it again. It's like wanting to be naked and holding someone versus wanting a relationship. Maybe it would be better if we could have the first thing without the second.'

I knew what she meant. Some of my happiest nights happened during those two weeks when she moved into my bed. Just being beside someone and knowing that's enough.

I've been in a relationship with a woman called Sophie for almost two years. Before that I went out with Ellen. I dated Ellen from when I was fifteen until I was twenty-three. She broke up with me. I'll explain why later, but for now all you need to know is that from the moment I met her I knew I was ready for the whole shebang (marriage, babies, the works).

With Sophie, it's the other way around. She's definitely in it for the long haul, and now I'm the one who's not sure. It's not that I don't love her. In fact, she's the most loveable person I've ever met. Spot the evasion in that last sentence. Nah, I'm just playing. I'll tell you exactly how I feel soon enough. But there are a few other things I want to get out the way first.

Let's start with my sister.

2

My sister is a psychopath. She's a nice psychopath, though. Or at least, she is now. As a child, she was a nightmare. My mother and I like to joke that her brain is powered by a hamster who turns a wheel inside her head. The hamster is old and lazy, and easily distracted. If you ask my sister a hard question and then listen to her skull, you can hear the clunking as his fat body struggles to get the wheel round one more revolution.

My earliest memory of my sister is her digging her fingernails into my cheek. She was going for my eyes, so I guess I got off lightly. Since then, our relationship has rivalled Itchy and Scratchy's. It wasn't hard to get the better of her, but that meant living in fear until the next violent retribution. I realise I'm turning my sister into an exaggerated lunatic, but that's how she seemed to me. With other people she could be different. On family holidays, she was the one who befriended other children, while I sat with a coat over my head to hide from the sun. And as long as they didn't question Erica's authority, most of these kids escaped unscathed.

At the moment my sister is in Vietnam, the latest stop on her round-the-world trip. Erica is the only traveller in our family. Dad once spent a few weeks in Africa and my grandfather once went on a Caribbean cruise, but apart from that, the Wedmore clan has spent much of the last two hundred years in the UK. Maybe even longer, but that's as far back as I can be bothered to trace. (Although, actually, now I come to think of it, we did have a weird uncle who used to go on strange trips to Silicon Valley and come back with loads of boring slides of empty terrain.)

My journeys have mostly been internal.

3

Between ten and thirteen, I went to a hundred and thirty-seven auditions. The procedure was always the same. Dad would pick me up after school, drive me to whatever big hotel the producers happened to be using, stand me in a line of two hundred show-off kids, wait till I'd done my piece, and then console me in the car afterwards as I complained bitterly about being asked to take out my brace and ditch my specs and read from a script without spitting or slurping.

But I knew from the start that the *All Right Now!* audition was different. Usually by the time I got into the hotel room, the three people facing me had long since burnt out. They'd made their decision hours ago, and were just seeing through the last few children out of a sense of duty. The room would smell of thwarted ambition. A coffee table would be covered with empty bottles and cans, but rarely would they offer me anything. Today my audience was alert, a woman handed me a drink the moment I walked in, and before I had chance to open the copy of *Death of a Salesman* I always read a speech from even though it'd brought me no luck so far, the producers stopped me and said they'd prefer to ask me a few questions instead. This time when they made me take out my brace I knew they weren't trying to embarrass me. The woman controlling the video camera stopped and looked up, then came across, gripped my head, and peered into my mouth. Looking back at her partner, she said, 'There's an operation to fix this, right?'

'What?'

'The gap. His mouth.'

He nodded. She wrote something on her clipboard and

released me. They asked me to read again, then told me to stay behind until they'd auditioned all the other kids.

I went back outside and found my father.

'How'd it go?' he asked, mouth ready to twitch into disappointment.

'They want me to stay behind.'

'Really? That's great.'

All the other kids in the queue immediately looked round. The attention embarrassed Dad and he took my shoulder and led me to the lift. We got in and went down to reception. As we walked across the polished marble floor to the bar, Dad turned and asked, 'Do you want to call Mum?'

'Let's not jinx it.'

'OK.' He smiled. 'How about a Coke?'

Some of the other kids who'd already auditioned were sitting with their parents. Usually Dad was strict about making sure we kept our distance from the competition, but today he seemed more relaxed. As he returned with his whisky and my Coke, he asked, 'Want to sit with the others?'

I shrugged, embarrassed by the fact that most of them were girls. We walked across.

'Hi,' he said to the small cluster, 'I'm John and this is Gerald.'

The girls looked at me for a second and then turned their eyes away. Even at thirteen I was used to this kind of reception. The mothers were usually kinder.

'Have you been up yet?' Dad asked the mothers, taking a sip from his whisky.

They nodded. 'Yeah,' answered one. 'We were asked to stay behind.'

'Us too,' he said, motioning at me.

I looked round at the four girls and one boy. Although I didn't know it yet, they represented half my future co-stars. Wendy, Lucy, Sheryl, Perdita and Pete. I drank my Coke.

'Do you do this sort of thing regularly?' Dad asked them.

Everyone nodded. Then Wendy and Lucy's mum said,

'The set-up seems a bit more elaborate than usual today, don't you think?'

'That's because it's a series,' observed Pete's mum. 'They make more of an effort.'

'Really?' Dad asked. 'I would've thought the opposite was true. After all, there's more money in a movie, surely?'

'Yeah, but then they usually only want the kids for a bit part, so it's not as important. But with this series, the kids are going to be stars.'

'Do you think they're going to give them any training?' Perdita's mum asked. 'I thought they usually used children from theatre schools.'

'No,' Pete's mum replied, 'that's the whole point. They want to take a whole load of normal kids and give them a chance to be on TV.'

'But they're not just going straight on TV, are they? They've got people to help them out.'

'I think they said there's going to be a dramaturge working with them.'

Everyone looked at Dad, shocked by the unusual word. But none of the other mothers wanted to admit their ignorance, and the conversation was closed when Wendy's mum said, 'Yeah, that's what I heard too.'

4

The night I split up with Ellen, Sally took me to a gay bar. I'm not homophobic, but neither am I bisexual, no matter how many drinks I sink. I knew Sally didn't go for girls, which left me doubly confused about her choice of venue. Surely we should be out there living it up, pretending we were a couple and using each other to help pull people.

'No,' said Sally, 'that's not what you need tonight. If we go to a straight bar you'll end up going home with someone completely inappropriate, having meaningless sex and waking up feeling completely wretched.'

It was at this point that I began to reconsider the wisdom of having a female best friend.

'So what do you want me to do? Go home with a man?'

'No, I don't want you to go home with anyone. I want to take you somewhere where lots of people will fancy you so your self-esteem goes back up, but where there's no danger of you acting on your instincts.'

'But I don't want to be alone tonight.'

She gave me a cryptic smile. 'You won't be.'

'How come?'

'I'll come home with you.'

'Will you sleep in my bed?' I asked her.

She nodded. 'If that's what you want.'

'Will you fuck me?'

'No, of course not.'

Sally was right about the gay bar. If we'd gone somewhere straight for a drink I would have felt overcome with desperation, and no doubt failed to find even the meaningless sex that Sally thought would be bad for me. But within seconds of going into the gay bar I remembered how great it must be to be a woman. I'm not saying that the way a gay man looks at another man is the same way that a straight man looks at a woman, but there is something about how men do it that announces itself in a way that female attention rarely does. Unless you're a Chippendale, George Clooney or the Diet Coke man, I suppose.

When we first arrived at the bar it was only seven o'clock and neither of us got any attention. The bar was relatively empty, populated only by a few clumps of businessmen here straight from work, and a group of tall, attractive women gathered around a pinball table. The businessmen interested me more than the lesbians as most of the gay men I'd met had been either artistic types or quite isolated, closeted individuals. I realise I'm stereotyping wildly here, but I was genuinely intrigued as to whether all the men worked in the same office, whether they were all gay or only some of them, and whether they felt separate from or accepted by their colleagues. I suppose what caught my interest was, as usual with me, the idea of an enticing world from which I was clearly excluded.

'Stop staring,' Sally hissed at me.

I nodded, and looked down at my menu. Still running on nerves, I felt anxious to get at least a sandwich inside me before I started drinking. It was only an hour since Ellen had ended our eight-year relationship and although I was holding up so far, I knew alcohol on an empty stomach was liable to send me spiralling into despair. Ellen had chosen to tell me she no longer loved me outside Waterloo station, and rather than argue, I'd told her that was fine and got on my mobile to Sally before Ellen was even out of earshot. I didn't want to make her jealous (although she'd never been pleased that I often had more fun on my nights out with my best friend than with her), but I did want Ellen to understand her bombshell hadn't fazed me and I was able to make Friday night plans as casually as if all she'd done was cancel an evening dinner date.

Thank fuck Sally was home.

The cover of the menu was a black-and-white photograph of a man's penis. It was an unappetising image, and I wondered whether I could bear to eat there. I know this sounds like more homophobia, but I'd have felt just as uncertain if the cover of the menu was a full-frontal of a woman's front passage.

'Order for me,' I told Sally, pushing back my chair.

5

It took two hours to get through the rest of the kids. By this time Dad had downed five whiskies and I worried one of the mothers would tell him he shouldn't drive. Dad's an excellent drinker: it's one of the things I admire most about him. Sure, he sticks to shorts, but can put away half a bottle before it has any effect. Although few of the mothers were drinking, the group had relaxed, and we were on the verge of forgetting what we'd come for when the video lady returned to collect us.

I'd kept quiet for much of the previous two hours, aside from answering a few questions from Sheryl. I'd already decided Sheryl was the most embarrassing member of our group, and felt reluctant to align myself with her. But Wendy and Perdita hummed with unassailable brunette confidence and had no interest in talking to the likes of me. Watching Wendy and Perdita size each other up, I sensed that Wendy would be the dominant of these two girls. She seemed to take it for granted that she would be the coolest member of any group, while Perdita looked pleased to have found someone who would let her be her deputy.

I did feel a small advantage over the other half of our number; the ones sitting in pairs with their parents and scattered around the bar area. They'd yet to make even the most basic of bonds with our dominant group, and were already at a disadvantage. The next time we reconvened, I could feel unembarrassed about going to stand with these four girls and Pete, and maybe Sheryl's constant chatter would even wear down the other two into accepting us.

As we followed the video lady back up to the suite, I tried to get the measure of Pete, who'd said almost as little as I had while we were waiting. He was younger than me, shorter but with the same dark hair. He didn't have braces or glasses, but his teeth were goofier than mine. I could tell he too disliked Sheryl (kids are quick to blackball, and once a decision's been made it's usually irreversible), but felt less sure why he hadn't tried to befriend me. *I* wasn't talking to Pete because five years earlier my mother had decided that my father was a bad influence, separated from him, and taken me and my sister to a feminist commune where a group of like-minded women were attempting to raise their children away from the unnecessary influence of men. This episode hadn't lasted long and within a year my mother had returned to my father, but at this age I still felt uneasy about my masculinity, even though there had been other boy

8

children in the women's commune. It was shame that also made me awkward around girls, although I found it especially difficult to connect with other children of my gender. But it seemed unlikely Pete had experienced a similar childhood, and I was forced to conclude that either he didn't like me, or that he was one of those drama boys who only ever wanted to spend time with the opposite sex.

I was expecting a second-round audition, the sort of thing I'd experienced several times in my previous one hundred and thirty-seven auditions, but that had never led to anything before. Usually, I was brought back to do a more complicated screen test or perform a duologue with another kid. But today the parents were called into the hotel room while we were asked to wait outside. The group was uncertain whether this was a good thing or not, but previous close calls warned me not to get too excited. I chose not to share this with the others, worried it'd give them a bad opinion of me. Even if we were getting close to being the final group, I still couldn't believe I'd actually be chosen for this programme.

Pete pushed himself forward and pressed his ear against the door, but was unable to hear what was going on inside. He jumped back as the parents emerged, all of whom looked at me with sympathy in their eyes before passing on to their own kids. It seemed obvious that I was the one who hadn't made it, and although I wasn't surprised or especially upset, I did think they were mean to make me stay behind if I was the only one they had doubts about using.

I knew whatever had been said must have been serious, as the parents quickly gathered their kids and left the hotel. Sheryl was the only child to say goodbye to me, adding that she hoped we would meet up again. On the way to the car I asked Dad what the video lady had said.

'I'm sorry, Ger. I want to wait until I've talked to your mother.'

His reply baffled me, so I pressed him further. 'I'm not in, am I?'

He didn't answer, going round to the driver's side and opening the door.

Dad had been given a sheaf of printed pages that he dropped on the back seat. I picked it up and looked at the top sheet.

ALL RIGHT NOW!
A Six-Part Improvisational Drama Series
<u>Outline</u>

All Right Now! is an exciting new development in television drama. Eight children from average educational and social backgrounds will be given the opportunity to create a soap opera from the normal day-to-day events of their lives.

I put the pages back on the seat, too excited to read any further.

6

I suppose I should put in a disclaimer somewhere, to prevent anyone buying this book under false pretences. This isn't the usual story. It's not the song-driven memoirs of a Jack Wild (the Artful Dodger) or Aileen Quinn (Annie). I didn't follow the usual route to my minor, short-lived fame. No terms at Sylvia Young's, no pushy parents, no serious problems with drink or drugs. This isn't *Gerald Wedmore: the Alcohol Years*. And I suppose my story lacks some of the punch of Drew Barrymore's, although that's more to do with the difference between England and America, and between film and television. You could put this book back on the shelf and take home a proper celebrity story instead, if that's what you're after.

Most celebrity bios are the result of someone talking into a tape-recorder. And this always gives the narratives a weird, fragmented quality. The celebrity in question always believes they know exactly what the readers are interested in. Even the structure is always the same. Rags to riches, hello drink and drugs. Downhill from there, with either a black screen or a tentative comeback at the end. What they all fail to realise is that the bits they think we're interested in (the debauchery) are, in fact, often the least compelling. After all, that's when a celebrity becomes ordinary. We already know enough drunks. What we want to know is what they were thinking when they were on screen. Did they love their co-stars? Were those relationships real? And, in spite of what they think, we don't really want to know the tawdry truth. This book isn't a sob story, it's a tale of my experience of being on television, and the effect that that's had on my life. I'm not famous enough for most of you to buy my book on the strength of my celebrity, so instead I'm going to offer you the truth.

Somehow that seems more honest.

7

Sally and I left the gay bar at nine. So far she'd been sincere and sympathetic, but wary about letting the conversation get serious. I wasn't sure whether she'd stick to this surface-only approach when we were no longer in public, but judging from the way she usually behaved with me, I thought she probably viewed making me better as a long-term project, and the flippancy that had so far characterised her response would give way to understanding when we were alone.

At that time I was living at the Oval with four friends. Mickey, the most efficient of our small gang, had found the house. Although he could occasionally flip out or behave in an unexpected manner, most of the time we could rely on Mickey for this sort of thing. He was brilliant at working out bills, paying the television licence fee, and handling everything needed to keep our household going. When he first told us what this house was like, it sounded so strange that Lorraine, Tom and I dispatched Stan with his video equipment to get a recording. His tape showed Mickey was telling the truth. Each room in the three-storey house (apart

from the kitchen and bathroom) was decorated with a
different bird as its main wallpaper motif. So the rooms
looked like this:

Ground Floor
hallway: blue pigeon
lounge: red penguin
pantry/Mickey's room: yellow eagle
shower room: no birds

First Floor
Tom's room: grey canary
My room: purple ostrich
secret room: unknown
bathroom: no birds

Second Floor
kitchen: no birds
bathroom: no birds
Lorraine's room: pink owl
Stan's room: black emu

A couple of things need explanation here. We didn't make
Mickey sleep in the pantry: the lounge was actually two
rooms with a closeable double dividing-door, and we
suggested he should take one of these, but he didn't think the
doors would provide adequate sound-proofing and elected
to live in the pantry instead. Also, the reason the kitchen was
on the third floor was that before we moved in, the house
had belonged to an incapacitated old lady who confined
herself to the top level. Stan's room had originally been a
second lounge. I was extremely amused by the prospect of
having an upside-down house, and tried to persuade the
others that we should keep this arrangement and put Stan
and Mickey in the downstairs room, but was voted down by
the others, who wanted somewhere to flop on the ground
floor. As it turned out, we usually found ourselves convening

in the third-floor kitchen, which was the largest room in the house and, especially during the summer months, the most pleasant place to sit. I'll explain about the secret room later.

My housemates didn't go out that often, and spent most Friday nights in the kitchen with a few bottles of wine. As I only had a small single bed and Ellen suffered from a bad back, she rarely stayed over, and I knew my friends would be surprised to see me with Sally. I took her up to the third floor and found them sitting round finishing up plates of pizza. Tom and Mickey smiled as I came in, and Stan, who though extremely tall and thin was always hungry, took advantage of their distraction to steal another slice. I looked up at Lorraine, who was perched on the counter with her feet in the sink, a sauce-smeared plate and empty wineglass beside her.

'Who hasn't met Sally?' I asked.

'Me,' said Lorraine. 'Ger, you'll never guess what the neighbours are up to.'

Our neighbours were a great source of entertainment. The Oval must be the best area in London for voyeurism. Almost every house is designed to overlook another, as if the whole neighbourhood originated as the pet project of a perverted architect. From the front of the house we could look directly into the bedrooms of our over-the-road neighbours; the people next door had a prime view of our bathroom, and from the kitchen we could see the garden of the house behind us. These were the neighbours Lorraine referred to: five men who were always doing something weird. Tonight, they'd surpassed themselves. Dressed only in striped shirts, black socks and boxer shorts, they appeared to be dancing a quadrille. I watched them until the music ended, at which point Lorraine began to whoop and whistle. This aroused their attention, and we jumped back from the window.

'Lorraine, this is Sally,' I said, motioning to my friend. 'She's going to be staying with me for a while.'

13

Lorraine picked at her toes. 'What happened to your bird?'

'We broke up.'

We joined the others at the table and Tom passed Sally a large slab of pizza. He was trying to be charming. Tom had once been our most likely candidate for future acting success, but frustration had set in, and he'd started to let himself go. But he still fancied himself a ladies' man, and enjoyed his increasingly rare opportunities to practise his act.

'What do you reckon they do?' Lorraine asked the group. 'The neighbours.'

This was a conversation we'd had many times, but I always enjoyed it, amused by each new suggestion.

'I reckon they're merchant bankers,' said Stan. 'They all work at the same company and see themselves as a secret society because they live together. They're really into science fiction and detective novels and have secret code-names when they're at home.'

'A religious sect,' Mickey suggested. 'One of those ones that wear suits and have plastic name-tags.'

'Gerald?'

'Television comedy writers. The dancing they're doing now is merely a practice for some hilarious routine that we're all going to think is brilliant when we see it on screen.'

'Speaking of which,' said Tom, '*Frasier*'s about to start.'

Lorraine walked across to the small kitchen television and turned it on. I hated *Frasier*, finding the faux-sophistication as annoying as the forced slapstick, but as I seemed to be one of the few people in the world with that opinion, I refrained from sharing it with others and kept quiet as we listened to the familiar theme tune.

'What are you afraid of?' I asked Sally later that evening. I realised as I said it that it sounded as if I was referring to our current situation, and quickly added, 'I mean, in general. You know, morbid fears.'

Sally looked at my bed. 'I'm afraid we're not both going to fit in there together.'

'I know it looks small,' I told her, 'but I can make it bigger by pulling the mattress to the side and putting two of the old lady's bolsters in the gap.'

Sally gave me a sceptical look. 'If I'm going to stay here with you for any length of time we're going to get you a new bed in the morning.'

'Just for tonight, though, it's OK, isn't it? I'll make myself as small as possible.'

She laughed. 'Do you have something for me to sleep in?'

I walked across to my wardrobe and looked inside. 'T-shirt OK?'

'Yes.'

I brought her one. She unfolded it and squinted at the writing and image on the front. 'Who the fuck are Royal Trux?'

'A band I like. Is that OK? Is it long enough?'

She smirked. 'I'm keeping my knickers on, I hope you realise that.'

I looked away, embarrassed. 'So, come on, you haven't answered my question. What are you afraid of?'

'I don't think I'm afraid of anything,' she said, starting to undress.

'Everyone's afraid of something. You're not afraid of fire, of drowning? Of ageing? Or death?'

'Fat,' she replied. 'I'm afraid of getting fat.'

'That's it?' I asked. 'That's all you're afraid of?'

She smiled. 'I wouldn't like to be fat.'

I'm still getting used to telling my story, but already I can feel the pressure to record events in an entertaining way pushing me in dangerous directions. I keep hearing the instructions of our dramaturge, Nicholas Pennington, with his stupid rules on how to turn real life into drama. I've introduced you to Sally, explained the closeness of our friendship, and the simplest way of proceeding would be to forget about attempting to calibrate the subtle fluctuations in it. It's a question of chronology, a fairly straightforward one. Basically, at university, Sally and I were best friends. She had an absent boyfriend; I had an absent girlfriend: it made everything easy. And after the two weeks we spent sharing a bed, we became close again. But at this moment in time, we didn't know each other as well as we once had. We still had great nights out, but there were blank spots in our understanding of each other. She barely knew my housemates; I had only met Darla, the woman she lived with, on a couple of occasions.

Sally and I were equally matched looks-wise: not head-turningly attractive, but definitely above average. Still, she'd felt as unloved as I had during adolescence and it had left us both cautious. With women, I don't feel I have a type, but there are certain looks I just don't go for. And I didn't like Sally's hair. It was too controlled, a nest of tight blonde curls rising in a crescent over her forehead. Beneath her hair her features were fine – light blue eyes, a wide, full smile – but I couldn't see past her hair whenever I considered her as someone I might want.

I feel guilty writing this, aware that it's the only time my friend is likely to be described in print. Other men have loved her hair, and I'm sure if she wrote a book in which I appeared there'd be some similar detail that stopped her fancying me. I imagine it would probably be the way I inhabit my body. I have conventional good looks, but somehow forget this when I'm with attractive women, trying too hard to impress. And, to be honest, I think the hair thing is only a little trick my brain is using to stop me destroying the friendship. It's a boy thing, probably. If I was a girl and Sally was a boy I could say, 'We're friends. Sex isn't an issue.'

The reason I've gone through this here is, of course, to stop myself looking bad. For the truth is, in spite of my friend's incredible generosity, at this moment, I was pissed off with her. I couldn't understand why she was deflecting my attempt to open an intimate conversation. In a way, I would have preferred an emotional proximity to a physical one, and as we finished undressing and got into bed together, I felt cross at her. Sally was right about the size of my bed, and it was hard for us to get comfortable. I was behind Sally, against the wall, propped up on one of the old lady's ghastly bolsters and trying to keep my erection away from her buttocks. I had the arm problem, and it was extra difficult as it didn't seem appropriate to embrace her. After a moment, Sally's voice emerged from the darkness.

'Shall we establish some rules?'

'OK.'

'You know better than to try it on with me, right?'

'Of course.'

'Well, in that case I don't think we need to be embarrassed about any intimacies between us.' She turned over. 'And given the size of the bed, I think things would be a lot easier if you held me.'

'OK,' I replied, wrapping my arms around her. 'Yes, that feels a lot better.'

I moved tentatively towards Sally, and was pleased to find her wriggling back into my arms. I felt shocked at how different her body felt now that we were lying down together, and said,

'Would you like a drink?'

'What?'

'Some water or something? My throat's dry.'

'OK.'

She moved her legs round to give me space to get out. I was naked apart from my boxer shorts, and had to go into the kitchen, but as a household we didn't worry about that sort of thing. I went upstairs to the kitchen. The others were engrossed in some late-night filth on Channel Five and didn't say anything. Apart from Lorraine, who asked,

'Getting ready to join the neighbours, are you?'

I ignored her and filled two glasses with water, taking them back to Sally. She was already asleep, so I placed her glass on my bedside table, and got in behind her, feeling depressed that there would be no further conversation this evening.

8

By the way, that audition wasn't my first show-business success. There's a prehistory to all this: a story I've got to get out of the way now because I was too young to remember it. It is important, though, inasmuch as it was how this started, and it proves that although my father ferried me around during my early teenage years, it was my mother who initiated the whole thing in the first place.

Mum's easily bored. So when she took two years off to look after me, she soon found herself looking for ways to make the experience more exciting. And when she saw a programme on television about baby models, she decided this was something we should explore. Being the product of two attractive parents, I was a pretty baby, and my mother made sure I was always clean and wearing laundered clothes. To begin with, we spent most of our time doing mother-and-baby shoots for catalogues and magazines. Mum loved this, and kept it up until I was a toddler. By this time, most of the work being offered was for me alone.

Mum didn't mind being sidelined. She had got pregnant again, and was hoping to relive the whole cycle with my sister. Unfortunately, although Erica grew up to be an extremely attractive adult, she was the ugliest baby anyone had ever seen. Eleven pounds, with a face that would shame a Garbage Pail Kid, she made people yelp whenever they caught sight of her.

Mum was so depressed by my sister's appearance that she immediately returned to the community centre where she worked, making my father take time off work to chauffeur me. Before long, he grew tired of this, and as I was no longer making much money, the first stage of my acting career came to a premature end. There is one last thing, though, something significant. My sister and I did appear on a record sleeve together: my face on the front, hers on the back, representing good and evil. The album was called *Eyes of a Child* and the band was named Colosseum.

Don't worry. You aren't supposed to have heard of them.

9

This is going to sound weird, but throughout my early childhood my father would leave me (or me and my sister, or just my sister) alone in the family car in the street outside his mistress's house while he was inside with her. I suppose he can't have been having sex every time he visited, as sometimes he was only absent for a matter of minutes, but often we would be left in the car for hours, growing psychopathic with boredom.

I didn't mind being alone in the car. I suppose this was probably the beginning of me developing coping strategies, as I did everything I could to make the inside of that car interesting. We were never a tidy family, but our car (a Princess) was a particular disgrace. This meant that as well as my mess (books, comics, magazines), there was my sister's (banana skins, second-hand shoes, hairbrushes), my mother's (cassettes, business papers, make-up) and my father's (empty whisky bottles, casino chips, full-scale maps). I tried to keep my mess fresh, knowing a new book or magazine could salvage a whole afternoon, but sometimes I was reduced to plotting imaginary journeys, combing my hair, or reading the side of my mother's eye-liner.

It was always more difficult when I was trapped in the car with my sister. Incapable of entertaining herself, her only way of passing the time was to pick fights with me. Everyone in my family is cursed with a wicked tongue, and within minutes I had always provoked Erica into launching her violence onto me. On those occasions I could do nothing except pray Dad returned before I passed out.

On the day of my audition Dad stopped at a payphone to tell my mother what'd happened so far. Then he lied and said we'd be detained for a further two hours. My heart sank when I heard him say this, knowing I only had twenty pages left of my current book. Dad looked at me as he finished his call, and, as if reading my mind, said, 'Shall we buy you a new book?'

'Thanks, Dad.'

'You deserve one anyway, after what happened today.'

'What did happen today?'

He smiled. 'I already told you, Ger. I can't tell you anything until I've talked to Mum.'

'But you just talked to her.'

'Not properly. Don't be impatient.'

I nodded, and we walked back to the car.

My father always bought me books from the WHSmith in Kingston. Although I wasn't sure whether I had got a part in *All Right Now!* I felt in a theatrical mood and decided that today I would begin reading Shakespeare. A teacher at school had been trying to get me interested in *Macbeth* or *Romeo and Juliet*, but as I already knew the stories to those plays, I wanted to try something different. Going through the selection, I decided on *Troilus and Cressida* and took a copy to my Dad.

Dad drove to his mistress's house, turned to check I was all right, and then got out of the car. You don't think about stuff that seems normal, but looking back, his inscrutability seems astonishing. It served as a kind of black magic; an ability to draw curtains across parts of his life and convince people that there wasn't anything interesting behind them.

It seems extraordinary now that neither my sister nor I ever said anything to my mother. I think there were probably two reasons for our collusion. Most importantly, Mum couldn't drive, and as our father was so keen to get out and visit his mistress, he was prepared to drive us anywhere, wait any length of time, and ignore anything untoward we might be getting up to. Also, both my sister and I had a keen recollection of how unpleasant some of the other children in the women's commune had been, and were therefore eager not to do anything that would encourage her to take us away again.

I took out my book and started reading.

10

Sally wasn't in my bed when I woke up. I was worried, remembering her fidgeting throughout the night and feeling scared she might have given up on me and gone home. I took a sip from the glass beside my bed, ignoring the overnight aeration.

I looked at my alarm clock. 10.15. Getting out of bed, I pulled a pair of jeans over my boxer shorts and went looking for Sally. She was sitting in the kitchen with Tom. Usually Tom happily slobbed about in a manky green dressing-gown and dirty moccasins until mid-afternoon, but today he was wearing his best T-shirt and a clean pair of jeans. His honey-coloured hair was wet, and scraped back.

Sally had her back to me, but noticed Tom looking over her shoulder and turned round.

'All right?' she asked. 'Ready to buy that bed?'

'Yeah. Just let me have a quick shower.'

'The shower's broken,' said Tom. 'Mickey did it.'

'How can you break a shower?'

'Well, I'm not sure if it's the actual shower that's broken. But he's done something weird to the electrics and doesn't think it's safe for anyone else to go in there. He says it's a death trap.'

'And you've just had a bath?'

He nodded.

'So there's no hot water. OK, Sally, let's go.'

It was warm outside. Sally was still wearing the T-shirt I'd lent her last night. When we reached the end of my road, she stopped and pulled it straight.

'This is an OK T-shirt to be wearing, isn't it? People won't think I'm weird?'

'Put it this way. Royal Trux aren't the sort of band people have opinions about. The only people who know about the band are the people who like them.'

She nodded. We started walking towards Brixton. I've never understood people who don't like South London. To me it seems by far the best area to live in. I know one of the arguments is that there are fewer trendy bars and meeting places, but I'm a kid from the suburbs: it all seems exciting to me. And South London doesn't force a lifestyle onto you. You can do whatever you want, unobserved. There are no thirtysomethings eyeballing you for inspiration for their latest TV show or advert. When Lorraine was living in West London, she said this got so bad that she started wearing really embarrassing ugly clothes and trainers, waiting till she sparked a revival in some style magazine.

I'd never bought a bed, having spent the last few years in fully furnished flats. I hadn't even been inside a furniture store since my childhood, when my family had found excuses to visit one almost as often as they went to the supermarket.

It didn't occur to me that there would be a element of choice involved in this expedition. I thought we'd go in and ask for a bed and they'd point one out and we'd ask if they had free delivery and then go home. But instead Sally wanted me to sit with her on almost every one, testing the bounce as if it was something I was qualified to judge.

'You do have enough money for this, don't you?' she asked.

'Yeah.' I swallowed. 'Well, I've got a card I can risk.'

'Good. Now I didn't like to mention this earlier, but your bedding is pretty disgusting. While you're here you might as well replace it.'

I looked back at Sally, shocked by her frankness. This was

the sort of thing Ellen would never have said to me, although no doubt it was something she thought, and probably as much a reason as the size of my bed and her bad back for why she didn't stay over at my place.

Ellen had told me that she would send her father round on Monday with the stuff I'd left in her house. Now that I'd had time to think about it, her announcement didn't seem so much of a surprise. I'm one of those people who doesn't like to think of himself as a bad person. I realise that almost everyone is like that, but we all have different coping strategies. Religion is the most obvious, but that's never helped me. I am a Christian, but of the most non-denominational kind. My Christ is an adult one, a bearded friend in a dark blue tracksuit from whom it would be embarrassing to beg forgiveness. But neither can I allow myself the truth that I am probably – like most people – a good person who sometimes does bad things. I have to fool myself that I do not have the weaknesses I clearly do suffer from. And not only that but I also refuse to countenance the possibility that I have the capacity for certain failings.

Like the state of my bedding.

11

My sister was in the lounge, watching a programme she'd taped from last night's television. It was a documentary closely observing a heart-bypass operation, with lots of bloody close-ups. When we walked in, the screen was almost entirely red, the camera focused on what looked like a squishy scarlet cushion.

'Jenny?' Dad called, standing at the foot of the stairs.

'What?'

'I need to have a word with you.'

'I'll be down in a minute.'

'No. Not in front of the kids.'

'Come up then. What's the matter with you?'

I looked at my sister, who was loaded up with a Dracula's

Blood soda-stream and a tub of Choc-Dips, and decided to risk sitting next to her.

'Where have you been?'

'Didn't Mum tell you? An audition.'

She nodded, and looked back at the TV.

'How can you watch this, Erica? It's disgusting.'

'You're disgusting,' she replied, and turned up the volume.

I didn't find out what my parents were talking about until the following morning. Over breakfast, before school, Mum explained that the video lady had told Dad that I could be in *All Right Now!* as long as I had an operation to reduce the gap between my two front teeth. The operation would involve cutting a small flap of skin between the teeth and stitching it up. My parents were against the idea of me having any kind of cosmetic treatment, especially for a television programme that was supposed to feature normal kids, but they knew how important this was to me, and had decided to leave the final decision in my hands.

'If I have the operation, can I definitely be in the show?'

'That was what the woman said.'

'And it'll definitely happen?'

He sighed. 'You know what these TV shows are like, Gerald. Nothing's definite until it's on air.'

It was true. There had been several auditions I'd failed for programmes that never actually materialised.

'When do I have to decide?'

'End of the day.'

I nodded, feeling scared about the potential operation and wanting more time. 'Can we call them when I get back from school?'

12

Outside the furniture store, Sally told me she wanted to go back to her flat to pick up some clothes. I said I'd come with her and we walked to Brixton tube.

'Why did you ask me what I'm afraid of?' Sally asked.

I stared at the passenger opposite me, a suited, dark-haired man with a childish face and a briefcase balanced on his lap.

'Because I thought I wanted to talk about stuff.'

'What stuff?'

'Stuff I hadn't told you before.'

'Like?'

'Oh . . .' I swallowed. 'Don't you think it's too soon to start being disloyal?'

'Ger . . . not everything you think was hidden was actually hidden, if you know what I mean.'

'No, I don't know. Explain.'

'You think that because you didn't say anything and Ellen never really got intimate with us we don't know what it was like between you. But sometimes you don't have to talk about that stuff. I mean, every time the two of you came out with us one of the girls heard her crying in a toilet cubicle.'

'OK,' I said, 'but if I start talking properly, that means that's it, doesn't it? I'll have broken something irreparably.'

'Gerald . . . you can trust me.'

'It's nothing to do with you. At the moment, in my head, I can still see Ellen and me getting back together. Neither of us has done anything wrong. OK, she's broken up with me, but that's the sort of thing that could be forgiven. If she called me tomorrow and said she'd made a mistake, that she'd changed her mind . . .'

'It wouldn't make any difference.'

'Why?'

'Because I'm not going to let the two of you get back together. You're my friend, Gerald, my best friend. I don't want to dismiss your relationship with Ellen – I understand that the two of you have been together longer than some marriages – but trust me, it's a good thing it's over.'

The tube stopped. Sally walked out through the open doors. I was grateful for the interruption to our conversation, not wanting to risk getting annoyed with the one person willing to help me. I knew Sally was only trying to be a good friend, but I did feel resentful that she was encouraging me to accept my relationship with Ellen was over. We'd talked intimately before and I knew she didn't fancy me, but she had been single for a while and it seemed obvious that she was eager to make our friendship a more important part of her life. At the moment, it seemed she was being selfish. Later I would realise exactly what she'd done for me.

I followed her. We didn't speak again until we'd walked the short distance from the tube to her home. As we walked up the steps of her flat, she said, 'God, I hope Darla's home.'

'Don't you have a key?'

She shook her head. 'Darla needed to get a replacement cut. But she should be in.'

The door opened. Darla's face appeared in the gap, one eye squinting. Her scruffy black hair looked recently dyed. I'd only met her a couple of times before, a face in a group at Sally's birthdays or on trips to the pub, and assumed she was probably as surprised to see me here as my housemates had been when I brought Sally home. But she smiled warmly as she said hello, remembering my name.

We went inside. 'Now, Darla, you have to be nice to Gerald.'

She looked at me. 'Why?'

'My girlfriend left me.'

'So you're single? Great.' She twirled, pulled her dress straight, and looked me in the eye. 'Would you like to go out with me?'

'What happened to Loz?' Sally asked, surprised.

'He shagged someone else.'

'Anyone we know?'

'How d'you guess? My sister.'

'God,' I said. 'I'm sorry.'

Sally moved further down the corridor. 'Can you make Gerald a coffee, Darla? I'm just going to pick up some clothes.'

'What d'you need clothes for?'

'I'm staying with Gerald for a while. Till he feels OK again.'

'What about me?' she said in a petulant voice. 'I need you to help me get over Loz.'

'I'm sorry, Darla, I think Gerald's situation is a little more serious.'

'Why?'

Sally put her hand on her hip. 'How long have you been going out with Loz?'

'Three weeks.'

I laughed.

Darla turned to me. 'Why? How long had you been going out with your girlfriend?'

'Eight years.'

'Oh.'

'See,' said Sally, walking away from us.

'Why did your girlfriend leave you?' Darla asked me.

'She said she didn't love me any more.'

Darla was silent for a moment. Then she asked, 'Would you like a coffee?'

'If you're having one.'

'OK. Come through with me.' She took my hand and pulled me behind her. I felt slightly shocked by the contact, but let myself be led. In the kitchen, she sat me down at an extremely basic table that looked more like an ironing-board than a piece of furniture. I stared at her back as she reached up into a high cupboard for the coffee.

'So how come you didn't argue with her? Everyone must go through patches like that in an eight-year relationship.'

'Well, then she said something else.'

'What?'

'That she'd started fancying other men.'

'So?' she said, sounding cross. 'After eight years that's only to be expected. Don't you fancy other women?'

'Of course. Sometimes. But it's more complicated than that. Ellen takes things very seriously. If she says she fancies other men, she doesn't just mean she fancies other men, she means she wants to sleep with other men. And she's going to act on that instinct.'

'So fidelity's a big issue for you?'

'Isn't it for everyone?'

'Not necessarily,' she said in a knowing tone.

'What about you and your boyfriend?'

'That's different. He slept with my sister.'

'So you wouldn't have minded if he'd betrayed you with someone else?'

'God, you're serious, aren't you? Were you planning to marry this woman?'

'She didn't want to marry me.'

I realised my voice had suddenly become very tight, and worried I was going to start crying in front of Darla. Something about the way she was talking to me brought back all sorts of memories of the *All Right Now!* girls, and the way they'd always seemed so much older and wiser than me.

Darla noticed my silence and turned round to check on me. 'You OK?'

I shook my head.

13

We should have been latch-key kids. But because my mother was quite paranoid, and my sister was so dangerous, we spent our afternoons at a succession of different friends' homes. We lived in a very suburban area, and at that time a lot of people's mothers were happy being housewives. Most of them thought our parents were stupid to pay them to look after us along with their own kids, but were happy to take their money. At least until Erica spoilt everything by acting like a lunatic.

By the time I was thirteen we'd been banned from all of Erica's friends' homes and most of mine. So we spent every afternoon at Reggel's house. They were the only family that seemed able to cope with Erica's mischief. This was partly because Reggel's parents were almost as odd as Erica was, but mostly because both mother and father were out of work and prepared to put up with more for the money.

Reggel's father had a glass eye, having lost his real one in a car accident. His gearstick had lacked a protective bulb and, after a crash, gained one from his eye-socket. He had a variety of medical complaints which, he claimed, made it impossible for him to work. Mrs Reggel had worked at most of the shops in the high street, but had been sacked from every one for failing to show up on time. Mr Reggel came from a poor background, but Mrs Reggel's parents were wealthy, and in spite of their dislike of their daughter's husband and the family's lifestyle, kept both adults afloat by paying their mortgage and giving them a cash contribution every month. (By the way, the family name was Regal, not Reggel, but they had adopted the latter as a joke some time in the early Seventies and used it in almost all circumstances ever since, even though they'd long forgotten why it was funny.)

Reggel was a little overweight, but nowhere near as grotesque as his sister Sandy, who had inherited her mother's laziness and half of her father's obscure complaints. Erica hated her, but they were sort of friends, mainly because Sandy was prepared to endure all my sister's most evil tricks. The worst thing Erica did was to play Strawberry Patch with her almost every day, so the wounds on her hand never had chance to heal. Those of you who don't know what Strawberry Patch is should count yourselves lucky and pray you never run into my sister.

When we started going over to Reggel's house, he had a crush on my sister for about three weeks. Then she pushed him through a window. After this, Reggel steered clear of her and we stayed downstairs watching children's television with Reggel's parents, while Erica and Sandy got up to God knows what in her room.

Part of the deal with Reggel's parents was that they were supposed to give us a meal as well as looking after us from four to six. Mrs Reggel was a terrible cook, and stuck to a fixed food order each week (Monday: Sausages, beans and chips; Tuesday: Ham, peas and chips; Wednesday: Faggots, peas and chips; Thursday: Fish fingers and chips; Friday: Fish and chips). But they allowed us to eat our meals off trays on our laps in front of the television and didn't mind if we left food uneaten. This probably doesn't sound like such a big deal, but Erica and I had encountered all kinds of weirdos on our suburban odyssey through our friends' parents' homes, and our biggest problem was over-passionate advocates of the Clean Plate Club.

Usually, I had no problem coping with the two hours until Dad came to pick us up. Mr Reggel seemed to enjoy my company, and was happy to play computer games with his son and me. I'd asked Reggel not to tell his parents about my audition and so far he'd kept quiet, but I was bursting to talk about it and wasn't sure if I could last until six o'clock.

Thankfully, today, for once, Dad was early.

14

Darla was giving me a consoling hug when Sally came back downstairs. I looked up just in time to see Sally shoot Darla an angry look, and then felt Darla raise her shoulders in response.

'What's that T-shirt you're wearing?' Darla asked Sally.

She pulled it straight again. 'Gerald lent it to me. It's some band he likes.'

'Royal Trux? What kind of music do they play?'

I smiled, grateful for the distraction. 'Scuzzy rock and roll. It's a man and a woman and they used to be junkies and they're clean now, but they still play like they're fucked up.'

'So it's indie?'

'No,' said Sally sternly.

I looked at her, surprised. I thought she'd never heard of them before. 'It is a bit indie, I suppose. The sort of band that'd be called alternative in America. Have you heard of Pussy Galore?'

'No.'

'John Spencer Blues Explosion?'

'Of course.'

'Well, John Spencer used to be in Pussy Galore with Royal Trux. Only Royal Trux have stayed a little bit more underground. Well, not really, not properly underground, but you know what I mean.'

'No,' said Sally again, 'I wasn't answering her question. I was just telling her to forget the plan she's forming.'

'Sally . . . He'd like it . . . and it'd be a good way of us all staying together. I've already told you I don't feel up to being on my own.'

'What would I like?' I asked.

'Darklands. It's sort of a club, although it's in an art gallery instead of a club space, and it's mainly indie music. They don't really advertise – it's basically just friends and whoever they invite, and it's the first Saturday of every month.'

'Which is tonight.'

'Exactly. So, what d'you reckon? Do you want to come?'

She smiled expectantly at me. I didn't want to upset Sally, but this sounded like a fun plan. And I was grateful that neither of them had made a fuss about me getting upset. Darla was the first person in ages whom I'd instinctively liked. And not only that, but I didn't fancy her either, so there wouldn't be any complications. Unless she fancied me, which, in spite of her initial joking, seemed unlikely.

'OK,' I told Darla, 'that sounds great.'

15

It was always a relief to get out of the Reggel household. Our car may have been disgusting, but it still felt great to climb into it and be driven home.

'I've decided,' I told my Dad. 'I'm going to have the operation.'

Erica's eyes lit up. 'What operation?'

'Gerald has to have an operation on his mouth,' Dad told my sister. 'To bring his two front teeth together.'

'Will there be lots of blood?' she asked, trying to sound innocent.

'A little, I expect,' Dad said in an emotionless tone.

She couldn't restrain herself any longer. 'Can I come?'

'Erica, your brother probably doesn't want you to watch him having the skin extracted from between his teeth.'

She considered this. 'Can you video it then?'

'We don't have a camera.'

'I can borrow one. From Mr Hendrix at school.'

Dad didn't reply, keeping his eyes on the road ahead.

Dad waited until Mum had come home before making the phone call. I knew he was worried I'd change my mind and Mum would make him get me out of it, but I was determined. My life was so boring, and the memory of my audition had remained bright in my mind. Even if Wendy and Perdita weren't interested in me, the prospect of sharing proper female company (and with nice girls, not the kind of nutters who'd been predominant at the women's commune) was intoxicating. And the added attraction of regularly appearing on television made the whole thing even more exciting.

It was my mother who started taking me to auditions. But I definitely had certain childhood habits that are common among serious celebrities. Ever since I could remember, I'd imagined my life was continuously broadcast on a pretend television station. I didn't do anything without believing there was an audience out there watching, so when, for example, my Dad asked me for help with decorating, it became 'Gerald and Gerald's Dad's Decoration Day' on GerTV. My parents didn't seem to mind this, although I think that taking me to auditions was their way of helping me get it out of my system, so I wouldn't end up like my sister.

What I didn't realise back then was that as well as being the lead actor I was also the camera, only what I was recording would come out several years later on paper instead of immediately appearing on screen. So I suppose all those years of fantasising were worth it.

16

'Do you reckon your housemates would like to come to Darklands?' Sally asked.

'I doubt it. Stan, maybe, but the others are always moaning they don't have any money.'

'I thought TEFL teaching paid OK.'

'Only really in the Summer months. The rest of the year we're sharing four people's employment between five of us.'

Sally nodded. 'What about Lorraine, though? She seems the clubbing type.'

'She is. But she wouldn't be seen dead in an indie club. It's all speed-garage for her.'

The tube reached our stop. The bag Sally had brought back with her was huge, making me optimistic she was planning a long stay.

'Maybe Tom'll come too . . . if you work on him. And if you persuade Tom and Stan, Mickey won't want to be left out.'

'OK. It'll be much more fun if there's a gang of us.'

We got off the train and walked towards the escalators. I asked Sally if she wanted to have lunch in the Lavender.

'Don't you have anything at home?'

I shook my head. 'Tom's the only one who keeps food in the house. Oh, and Stan, but he has weird stuff.'

'What weird stuff?'

'I don't know. The sort of food you'd buy with ration books. Powdered egg. Pickled onions. Fish paste.'

Sally squinted at me, unsure whether I was winding her up. I wasn't: Stan did eat that sort of thing, all the time, feeding his obsession with the past. We walked past the huge red building with the golden entrance that had once been a children's hospital and then an asylum before being turned into prohibitively expensive flats. I'd long harboured a fantasy to move into there, although no doubt the ghosts were especially scary. I wasn't usually worried about the supernatural, but Stan got so edgy whenever anyone mentioned the secret room that I'd absorbed some of his sensitivity.

'OK,' said Sally, 'lunch sounds nice. Shall I dump my bag first?'

'Nah,' I replied, 'no need.'

17

I couldn't understand why so many people were scared of my sister: she was only eleven. And yet almost everyone was so afraid to stand up to her. Her teachers let her get away with whatever she wanted. My parents stayed out of her way. Which meant that the only person who risked restricting her was me.

So when she came home from school with Mr Hendrix's video camera, I knew I had to get someone else to take my side. I really didn't want Erica to record my operation. It wasn't that I was ashamed of having my pain preserved on videotape, more that I was frightened the dentist would be amused by her filming and start showing off, digging into my gums to produce ever more elaborate arcs of blood.

My father understood my fear. So Erica went to my mother. It seemed obvious a good parent should say 'No, stop being a psychopath,' and confiscate the camera. But Mum was afraid to risk this, telling Erica that if she really wanted to record my operation she should explain her reasons to me and I'd come round.

I didn't come round. Erica's reasons were stupid. So what if she'd seen a lot of operations on television and always wanted to film one herself? It was a sick ambition, and to encourage her was macabre.

The dentist, at least, turned out to be a sensible man, perplexed when this mini-documentarian followed my father and me into the operating room. Blocking her passage with his white-clad body, he leaned down and asked, 'And who might you be?'

'That's Erica, Gerald's sister,' Dad explained, 'she wants to record the operation.'

'For a school project?'

'Oh no,' I replied, 'her own amusement.'

The dentist looked Erica in the lens. 'Well, I'm sorry, little lady, but I can't allow you to film in here.'

Erica lowered her camera. 'But Dad said . . .'

'Your Dad's not the dentist. I'm sorry, dear, but if you wait in the waiting-room, I'll happily consent to an interview after I've finished with your brother.'

The dentist was clearly quite a narcissistic man, so well-groomed I can still remember the finer details of his appearance all these years later. White-haired, with expensive glasses, a neatly clipped beard and moustache, he was the kind of man who always intimidated my father. It was obvious that he regarded giving my sister an interview an incredible generosity, and was shocked when she muttered, 'I don't want a fucking interview. I want to film his operation.'

As a family, we weren't that bothered by profanity. Mum swore all the time, and told people 'bollocks' was her favourite word. Dad didn't swear quite as much, but always took amusement in scatological references. Erica's bad language had, on several previous occasions, been the source of some embarrassment, but today Dad just laughed.

'Well, that's it, little girl,' said the dentist, 'no interview for you.'

Before I had chance to savour my triumph, the dentist's nurse, who Erica had been making sad eyes at throughout this exchange, spoke up.

'Oh, come on, Derek, surely it won't do any harm if she just sits in the corner.'

Derek looked at the nurse. Even at thirteen, I could pick up on illicit connections between people, and immediately realised the argument was over.

Erica would be filming my operation.

18

It was good to be having lunch with Sally. I went to the Lavender quite often, but usually alone, and on nights when I wasn't seeing Ellen.

'I should warn you now, Gerald, that I'm not going to let you fall in love with Darla.'

I smiled. 'Why not? She's lonely. I'm lonely. Besides, she already asked me to be her boyfriend.'

'She says that to everyone, it doesn't mean anything.'

'Sally, I just broke down in tears in front of her. I hardly think that's the sort of thing that's going to make her interested in me.'

'Don't.'

'What?'

'Don't ask me for reassurance that Darla fancies you.'

'But I thought you said her fancying me doesn't mean anything.'

'It doesn't.' She sighed. 'Do you have to be so relentless? Can't you just accept stuff sometimes? I'm telling you, on this occasion, you have to be the adult. No matter what Darla does, or says, to you, keep your distance, OK?'

'Why do I have to keep my distance? Why can't we just be friends? I like her. She's nice.'

Sally stared at me. Her gaze made me feel guilty. And alive. I didn't think she was making a big deal out of this for my benefit, but her protectiveness towards her friend had also become a gift to me. She was creating a romantic intrigue, reinvesting me with the ability to attract.

'I can trust you, can't I, Gerald?'

'Of course. I'm surprised you think this is a big deal. I'm not going to make a pass at your friend.'

'What if she makes a pass at you?'

'Ah, well, that's different.' I laughed. 'No, I promise, if she makes a pass at me, no matter how flattered I am, I won't do anything . . .'

Sally seemed satisfied with this, and returned her attention to her salad. Her cheeks and neck had reddened during our conversation, and as I watched her chew her food, I felt she was holding something back. It seemed obvious why she wouldn't want me to get involved with her friend. She had taken it upon herself to look after me, and that would be complicated if I had any romantic interaction with her housemate, especially if what happened between Darla and me was trivial and left us embarrassed with each other. Most friends would probably advise me that I needed a few one-night stands before getting involved with anyone else after ending an eight-year relationship, and I could see why Sally would prefer I didn't do that with someone she lived with. But as well as this obvious reasoning, there seemed something hidden, as if she thought Darla and me getting together would be in some way dangerous. But maybe this too was just a friend thing, or a perfectly acceptable minor jealousy: a fear of Darla and me getting together and casting her out, so that she'd lose her two best friends at once.

'Besides,' I said finally, 'I don't fancy her.'

After lunch, we went back to my house. Stan and Lorraine were sitting in the downstairs lounge, watching a video. By the look of it, the film was something from Stan's strange collection, which was made up entirely of black-and-white films connected to World War II.

I leaned round the corner and asked, 'What's this?'

'*The More The Merrier*. Jean Arthur and Joel McCrea.'

This meant nothing to me. 'Is Tom still in?'

'Yeah, he's doing modal verbs with Mickey.'

I nodded and left them to it, following Sally upstairs. The furniture store had promised to deliver our bed between three and five, and I was curious to see whether it would show up.

Sally dumped her bag. 'I take it your shower's still broken?'

'I expect so. It wouldn't really be like the others to get something fixed.'

'Can I have a bath instead?'

'Of course. There should be hot water by now. Just let me go check.'

I turned round and ran past Tom's room, the secret room and up the stairs to the bathroom. Opening the hinged wooden door, I wondered how long I had to clear up the mess before Sally worried where I'd gone and came after me. One of our short-lived arrangements when we first moved into this house en masse was that we'd all have one area each to keep clean. I took the shower room; Mickey the kitchen; Tom the downstairs lounge, and Stan (always the joker) opted for the secret room. At the time we didn't know Lorraine that well and thought it was good that a girl was in charge of the bathroom. Shortly afterwards, however, we discovered that Lorraine was the messiest of us and giving her that responsibility was a terrible mistake.

There was no time to attempt anything major. Opening the window, I dumped the contents of the bathroom dustbin into next door's garden. Then I shoved Stan's beloved collection of *Force* magazines behind the loose panel on the side of the bath. I ran all the plastic toys under the tap long enough to remove the dirty coating, then chucked them together in the pink raffia basket that was one of the few feminine touches Lorraine had brought to the room. Deciding this was as good as I was going to get it, I ran the tap, checked the water was hot and put the plug in.

'You did want the bath now?' I said to Sally as I returned downstairs.

'Yes,' she said, 'if that's OK.'

'Of course. I've started running it for you.'

'Thank you,' she smiled, and returned to her unpacking.

19

When I stopped crying, Dad took me to WHSmith's. Today he didn't let me choose my own book, but pushed three Minster Classics into my hands, saying, 'You don't have these, do you?'

I looked at the books. *Huckleberry Finn*. *The Adventures of Tom Sawyer*. *Tom Sawyer Abroad & Tom Sawyer Detective* (in one volume), *The Turn of the Screw & Daisy Miller* (in one volume) and *White Fang*. I knew these were the sort of thing he'd read at my age, and that he wanted me to read them. Surprised by his urgency, I thanked my father and went with him up to the till.

'I'm sorry about today,' he told me as we waited to be served.

'That's OK,' I told him, 'I wanted to have it done. Now I get to be on television.'

'No, I mean letting Erica come. I didn't want to. Your mother ...' he tailed off, and looked away.

I'd never seen my father like this. He seemed genuinely moved by my pain, which after my sobbing session in the car, was now more an irritation than a serious agony. He was always a hard person to have a conversation with. I enjoyed talking to him, but it was too one-sided, as he rarely listened to me for long, and hardly ever volunteered anything in response. He didn't like talking about himself, and didn't have any real interests. Well, not ones he could share with me, as he most enjoyed drinking, gambling, and afternoons with his mistress (whom I'd never met). He did occasionally try to interest me in another of his hobbies, the stock market, and even lent me his prized copies of *Investor's Chronicle*, but I found the figures too hard to follow on my own.

'Is it your birthday?' the woman on the till asked me.

'No,' my Dad replied, 'it's just a treat. He's been very brave today.'

'Oh yeah?' she said. 'What did you do?'

'Had an operation on my mouth,' I mumbled.

She bagged up the books. 'That is brave. I hate going to the dentist.'

Dad laughed. 'I think Gerald will too. From now on.'

He was right. After my stitches were removed, I hardly ever went again.

20

I opened my wardrobe and looked inside. Sally had thrown away the old lady's stinking mothballs and filled all the empty space. She'd brought enough clothes to stay for ages, and I felt touched to see them hanging up next to my few suits. Not wanting to snoop, I closed the wardrobe and went downstairs.

The film had finished. Lorraine jumped up from the sofa and announced that she was going to the supermarket.

'Oh, hang on,' said Stan, 'I'll come with you.'

'OK,' she said, 'I'll be back down in a minute. I just need to use the toilet.'

'Sally's in there.'

'Then I'll use the shower room.'

'You can't.'

'Why not?'

'Mickey's turned it into a death trap.'

'It's true,' said Stan, 'he's fucked up the electrics.'

'Don't be ridiculous. Going to the toilet's got nothing to do with the electrics.' She stood up and left the lounge. I sat down next to Stan.

'All right?' I asked.

He eyed me suspiciously. 'I'm not doing your shopping.'

'I don't want you to.'

'I mean, I don't mind picking up a few things for you . . .'

'Stan, it's OK, I had lunch with Sally.'

'Then what do you want?'

Stan was always like this. He was the only one of my housemates I'd known before moving in, and we had a complicated history. He'd gone to my school, but had been in the year below me. He was even more eccentric as a child, at one time even making himself a suit out of newspaper and wearing it to class. Even Reggel and Francis thought he was weird, so I kept my distance, until we reached the sixth form. In our school, the number of kids who stayed on for A Levels was so small that the lower and upper sixth often had to have classes together. By this time, Stan had mellowed, and Reggel and Francis had left school to find jobs. He was still strange, but I decided to take an interest in him. There's a short story by Flannery O'Connor, her most famous one, I think, where an extended family are planning to drive down to Florida together. The grandmother doesn't want to go to Florida, and tries to dissuade her son from making this trip by telling him that there have been stories in the newspaper about a serial killer called the Misfit who's escaped from prison and is heading towards Florida. The son ignores her and the next day they begin their journey. Along the way, they have an accident and, while stuck, are discovered by the Misfit and his criminal gang. The Misfit's gang kills every member of the family, and then the Misfit shoots the grandmother. Up until this point, the grandmother has been pleading for her life, and after she's dead, one of the henchmen says to the Misfit that he thought the old lady talked too much. The Misfit replies that the grandmother might have been a good woman, if only there had been somebody there to shoot her every minute of her life.

The way the Misfit felt about the old lady was the same way I felt about Stan. He might become a good person, but only if I was there to shoot him every minute. I didn't literally shoot him, of course, but every time he expressed an opinion I told him why he was wrong and explained what he should think instead. For the twelve months we were in the sixth form together I did a fairly decent job of shaping him into a more stylish individual, and when I went off to university he did well in his exams and enjoyed a new degree of personal popularity. But then he got into a different university from me and fell in with Mickey and Tom, who had gone through their school lives without anyone around to shoot them, and had ended up becoming two rather peculiar individuals whose tastes were exactly the same as Stan's before I put him through a self-improvement programme. This led him to question my teachings and by the time he graduated he was back to square one.

Since leaving university, I had had an empty twelve months, working at a call-centre and leading an impoverished existence. The first few months had been OK, with Ellen and I enjoying the excitement of living together, even if we were only able to afford a one-bedroom flat between us. But then, on the night of Ellen's audition for drama school, my father was arrested and I ended up spending most of the night at a police station sorting things out. Unable to sleep, she lay awake worrying, and was in no fit state to perform the following day. She didn't get in, and our relationship deteriorated to the point where the only way for us to survive as a couple was to stop living together. She returned to her parents' house and I carried on renting our place alone. I couldn't afford to do this for long, and remembered Stan telling me there were jobs going at the language school where he was employed. A few months earlier I had turned down this offer, not wanting to accept that his life was progressing more smoothly than mine. Now, though, I reconsidered. Stan was still living with his parents, although for a while he had been planning to rent somewhere with Tom and Mickey, who had also taken a job at the language school. He said I was welcome to move in with them, and by the time we had found somewhere Lorraine had also joined our group. So I was in Stan's debt, grateful to him for finding me a home and a job. This meant I was unable to give him a hard time in the way I used to do, and our relationship had become a lot less fun.

'What are you doing tonight?' I asked him.

'Watching television. Why?'

'Would you even consider coming out?'

'Coming out where?'

'Sally's got this friend.'

'I don't want to be fixed up, Gerald.'

'I'm not talking about fixing you up. But she knows about this club. And I thought you might like to come along.'

He considered this. 'What sort of music?'

'Indie, I think.'

'What sort of indie? Nice, fun stuff like Happy Mondays and New Order, or your horrible weird noisy shit?'

'Fun stuff.'

He laughed. 'Are you telling the truth?'

'Of course.'

'Let me think about it.'

I nodded, and sat back. 'I'm going to get Sally to persuade Tom.'

'You'll never get Tom to come out.'

'Oh, I don't know. He might do. If Sally asks him.'

Stan looked at me. 'So there really isn't anything between you and her?'

'She's my friend, that's all. I told you that last night.'

'Yeah, I know,' he said, lifting one long leg over the other and leaning forward again, 'but I didn't believe you.'

'Why not? You know Sally's a friend of mine.'

'Yeah, but . . .'

'But what?'

'You're sharing the same bed. And she seems interested in you.'

If anyone else had said this to me, I would have given the possibility serious consideration. I think all romances, even great ones, have that this-might-or-might-not-exist Schrodinger's cat moment at the beginning. By this, I mean that love for me has always been preceded by the knowledge that I could or could not go for them (or they could or could not go for me). I'm not a very experienced man, having had only two major relationships and a few little things before and in between, but I do believe that everyone has this moment early on, when they decide whether to bother. Sometimes this stage lasts a few seconds; in other cases, it can last for years. But because it was Stan, I didn't pay attention to him, replying, 'She is interested in me. As a friend.'

21

Erica sat in the back of the car, her head against the window. She looked sad, and I almost felt sorry for her. She was a creature of appetite, my sister, and I suppose it wasn't her fault her appetites were so strange. I knew part of the reason she got so angry with me was because I wouldn't unite with her against our strange parents. She wanted a crazy playmate, and I wouldn't co-operate.

She noticed my large bag of books but, uncharacteristically, didn't complain that she hadn't been given anything. Wanting to cheer her up, I asked, 'Is there a way of watching what you filmed on that camera?'

She nodded, and handed it to me. 'Press Play and look through the eyehole.'

'Viewfinder,' Dad corrected. I looked up at him, surprised at this intervention. He wasn't the kind of father who usually picked up our verbal infelicities, and I was surprised that my operation was still making him act out of character. Today was the sort of trip where he'd usually try to swing by his mistress's place on the way home, but instead he drove us straight back.

As he drove, I watched myself on screen. It seemed harrowing to me, and I felt like a voyeur even though I was the one being tortured. No wonder Erica was shaken out of her psychopathic complacency. Irritated again, I handed back the camera and turned away.

Mum was working at the commune, so Dad made us some dinner, three microwave meals which he heated up for us. I put my plastic plate on a metal tray and sat down with my sister in front of the television as she searched for something violent to watch, finally happy when she found *Monkey* on BBC2.

22

The men with the bed showed up at six. I hadn't considered it might be hard to get a double bed up the narrow stairs, but the old lady had managed to move all her furniture into the top of the house so it couldn't be that difficult. The men looked reluctant to stick around, so I gave them a fiver each and asked if they'd be prepared to give me just a little more help.

What looked awkward to me proved no problem to them, and they just flipped the bed on its side and powered it up the stairs. Sally had been successful in her attempt to persuade Tom to come out with us, and as I'd predicted, fear of a night home without us prompted Mickey to come too, even though he usually wasn't interested in any music which didn't sound like robots fucking. Surprisingly, Lorraine had also decided to join us. The only explanation I could see for this was that she was quite proprietorial towards Tom and Mickey, and probably wanted to make sure they didn't get too friendly with this new female interloper.

As soon as the bed was installed, Sally happily jumped onto the mattress.

'It's nice this, isn't it,' she said, 'having a new bed.'

'What shall I do with the old one?'

'Turn it on its side and put it against the wall. It'll be useful if you have anyone else to stay.'

'I'm not turning the place into a guest house. There are more than enough people here already.'

'I was going to ask you about that,' she said. 'Do you think I should offer the others some money for letting me stay here?'

'Don't be ridiculous. You're doing me a favour. If anyone should pay it should be me, but I'm not going to. The others have all had friends to stay here before. Stan had a Chinese friend who slept under the kitchen table for almost a year. Relax. It'll be fine.'

'And you're sure the others don't mind?'

'Well, Tom, Stan and Mickey certainly don't. Lorraine you might have a bit of trouble with, but that's only because she's used to being queen of the ranch. But you don't have to worry about her making you do household stuff – she doesn't believe in all that.'

'I can see. How can you live like this?'

'I'm not sure. We do tidy up sometimes. Every now and again it all gets a bit much for Mickey and he makes us spend a Sunday getting rid of the worst of it.'

'Do you think he'll want you to do that tomorrow?'

'Probably. Who knows, maybe I'll initiate it. Now, come on, help me sort out my bedding.'

23

When I was thirteen, before I started work on *All Right Now!*, I had no idea what a social life might entail. Maybe I'm misremembering this, but as far as I can recall, I don't think I even had any real conception of what a nightclub might be like. I must have done, though, right? Surely I'd seen enough nightclub scenes in television programmes and films? At that age I'm fairly certain I'd bought my first Prince and Madonna albums, although everything that happened on them seemed to take place in a fantasy world far removed from my own. I knew about the local youth club, but had never gone, considering it a scarier version of school that took place at night. If school was a daytime soap opera, with incidents and mini-crises that always got resolved without serious horror, youth club was a post-watershed programme with lax restrictions. Hearing about what had happened in youth club was like being told the gory highlights of a programme that was on too late and you were secretly relieved you didn't have to watch. Not that my parents laid down any restrictions: I had to pretend this was the case and hope Erica didn't blow my cover. And even if I knew about nightclubs I had no desire to visit one; no sense that these would be the places I'd be going to on a regular basis when I got older. No, at that age, I could imagine no greater excitement than going to bed early with a new pile of books and my stereo. I don't remember feeling lonely, either, not at night. During the day I'd often experience a sense of isolation, but at night I was safe on my own, happy to read and listen to music.

I can still remember that night after my operation more clearly than any night from the last two years. That's not because of drugs. It might be because of drink. I don't drink that much, but it does usually play a part in most of what should be my most memorable evenings. But I think the main reason I can remember that night is probably because it was the last time I happily enjoyed a state of almost total innocence. It wasn't until a few days later that I went to the first *All Right Now!* meeting, but those nights I can't recall because I was too excited: not reading, not doing anything. Just going to bed early and lying there trying to will myself into the world awaiting me; a world of women and television.

That night, though, that night was important. I went to bed with my books, a mug of Coca-Cola, a packet of crisps, and a copy of *Sign o' the Times* on my stereo, trying to work out the night's programming on GerTV. The music was essential: I listened to that record so many times that year, and it took me, if not from innocence to experience, then at least from innocence to inexperience.

By the way, I have to add here, lest you start feeling sorry for me, that my bedroom was not your standard boy's bedroom. When Mum returned from the women's commune, she insisted that we all had to make a fresh start. She had never liked our standard suburban home and wanted to look for something a little different. So we moved into a new place that had once been a conventional three-bedroom house, but had had all these weird bits and pieces added to

47

the top, sides and back, stretching the house to the very limits of planning permission. Because I was the one who seemed to have been the most adversely affected by the previous year's upheavals, I was given the loft conversion at the top of the house, which was a giant space, almost twenty-five feet square. It had a separate staircase and a lockable door that divided the room from the rest of the house, so I could pretend it was my own private penthouse.

No, it was a more than fitting studio from which to broadcast my life. Especially when my life started to get interesting.

24

Darla arrived two hours before we planned to leave, presumably under the mistaken impression that my four flatmates would be fun people with whom to spend the early part of the evening. Lorraine answered the door in her usual surly manner ('Who the fuck are you?') and looked even more concerned at the arrival of a second attractive woman.

'Hi, Darla,' I shouted downstairs, 'd'you want to come up to my room?'

I heard her run up the stairs, and stood to move the chair out from beside the computer so she wouldn't feel she had to sit with me on the bed.

Darla came into my room. She was wearing a fawn duffle coat over a pink shirt and a pair of dark blue jeans. She'd put a pink slide in her black hair and was wearing red lipstick. I gestured for her to sit down.

'Thanks,' she said, unbuttoning her coat. 'Who's that girl downstairs?'

'Lorraine.'

'Is she always like that?'

'That's why I have a private phone line.'

'What are the rest of your housemates like?'

'All right, actually,' Sally told her. 'There's one guy I think you'll especially like.'

48

'Who?' I asked.

'Stan.'

'Stan?' I repeated, incredulous. 'Why would she like Stan? Is she a freak? No. Is she obsessed with the Second World War? No. Does she like grotesquely tall, weird-looking men?'

'Sometimes,' Darla threw in. 'I admit the other stuff sounds strange, but as long as he's tall.'

'You don't really think she'll be interested in Stan, do you?' I asked Sally. 'You're just saying that to wind me up.'

'Well, partly,' she admitted, 'but I don't know. She might well like him. What do you think, Darla?'

The door opened.

'Is this him?'

'No,' said Sally, 'that's Tom.'

Tom looked startled. He seemed to have had another bath since this morning and his hair was still damp. He looked much less miserable than usual and had changed again for the evening. Tom didn't come into my room that often, and he looked wary. I enjoyed having Sally and Darla there to lure him, but wasn't about to encourage his advances. Letting him stand there, I waited until he got fed up and came across and sat with me on my bed.

'You smell strange,' I told him.

He turned to me. 'I know. I tried to wash it off but it won't go.'

'What is it? Something from last Christmas?'

'Oh, no, I found it in the bathroom. It was an odd-shaped bottle with no label. I thought it was Mickey's, but now I'm worried it was the old lady's.'

'Have you eaten, Darla?' I asked.

'No,' she said, 'but you don't need to go to any trouble. Just some toast or a piece of fruit would be fine.'

'They don't have any food,' Sally told her.

'But there's a takeaway around the corner. I can get you something there.'

'OK,' she said, 'thanks.'

'I'll go fetch a menu,' said Tom, getting up from the bed and leaving my room.

Darla smiled at Sally. 'He seems nice.'

I snorted. 'Just you wait.'

PART II

★

25

I was not a well-dressed thirteen-year-old. Is anyone? At that age, my parents were still buying my clothes, so I think a serious proportion of the blame lies with my father. These days, he doesn't dress so badly, but back then, he was a serious fan of labels. Not proper labels, though, like Levi's or Nike. No, my father was a connoisseur of the nasty knock-off. He liked them because they were cheap, but that wasn't the only reason. No, he seemed to take a sincere pleasure in walking round wearing Taurus jeans and PowerMad trainers. I knew I didn't want to dress like him, so, not being allowed enough money to buy clothes with recognisable logos (and, most of the time, being prohibited from the shops where such items are sold), I chose instead to go for items without any identifying brand-names. This would have been fine, if I hadn't succumbed to my father's other major weakness: choosing clothes that were garishly coloured. Again, the main reason for this selection was the price. Almost every shop – from Burton's to Concept Man to River Island – had a rack of reduced clothes in colours so horrific that only a madman would wear them. Dad seized on these items with such enthusiasm that I felt encouraged to join in with the joke, and soon my wardrobe looked as ridiculous as his did.

I didn't really have any criteria for my clothes selection. There were certain items I owned that I liked more than others, although as I rarely received any compliments on my clothes, there was no real rationale behind these choices.

For my first night of *All Right Now!* rehearsals, I decided to wear silver-and-grey-flecked trousers and a jumper with alternate stripes of light and dark green. I took my pot of congealed hair gel and slicked back my hair. Then I sat waiting for the television company's car.

Erica knew I was excited, and didn't bother hiding her jealousy. She'd played up to both my parents for the past two weeks, who sensibly figured that favouring her with treats was preferable to preparing for a delayed tantrum. Today she came across to where I was sitting and said, 'You should get ready. You'll have to go soon.'

'I am ready.'

'What about your hair?'

This sort of direct attack was unusual from Erica. On an average day, she could start a fight without saying anything. She'd just sit there doing something insanely annoying, and then the moment I complained, she'd go crazy. I should have learnt not to say anything, but the tension was usually more unbearable than the eventual outburst. Today she could see I didn't want to engage with her, and she also knew it wouldn't be long before the car arrived to transport me to my new life. I knew she was afraid of how I might change once I got away from her, and that made her hunger for one last fight all the more keen.

'My hair is fine.'

'Aren't you going to wear deodorant?'

The doorbell rang. I gripped my sister's head, and, for the first time ever, kissed her on the cheek.

'Goodbye, Erica.'

26

We joined the back of the queue. If the way the crowd was dressed was any indication, it looked like this evening was going to be fun. Darla seemed to know everyone, receiving smiles and kisses from the crowd around her.

The punters reminded me of clubs I'd gone to in my adolescence, mainly in the year before I started seeing Ellen. I didn't know these sorts of places still existed, imagining they'd gone overground with the explosion of Britpop and then died out. My taste in music swung back and forth, usually dictated by my friends or the music press. This was the time when it was embarrassing to pronounce yourself a fan of indie music, and I'd assumed there wasn't enough genuinely alternative music to sustain this sort of night-life. It still meant something (this is 1998, remember), but this was around the time that former fans started proclaiming themselves devotees of anything but indie music, switching allegiance to everything from reggae to big beat, 70s rock to soul. I shared this embarrassment, and in polite company I'd probably play up my interest in hip-hop, but tonight, standing with this crowd of people who dressed like me, I felt happy and at home.

The doors of the gallery opened and the crowd swarmed inside. No matter how laid back everyone seemed, I was surprised they'd left the art-work up on the walls. I mentioned this to Darla and she said, 'Even on normal nights the gallery's more of a party place. When we get inside I'll introduce you to Ronnie.'

'Who's Ronnie?'

'He owns this place. Don't worry, you'll like him, he's not up himself.'

I nodded, and looked back at my housemates. Lorraine had dressed up in her standard clubbing gear, which, as she favoured heavyweight, all-night outdoor raving wear, didn't look too inappropriate. Mickey also fitted in, his long, shaggy black hair, blue top with a thick red stripe running down each arm, blue jeans and deliberately inexpensive trainers making him look much like everybody else pushing into the artspace. Sally was maybe slightly too elegant, lacking the studenty disrespect for her clothing that characterised the dress of the rest of the crowd. Tom and Stan didn't quite fit in either, but this was because they always maintained a distance from their surroundings.

There wasn't a proper bar, just four people serving cold beers out of ice-packed black bins from behind a trestle table. Darla grabbed my arm and pulled me across to meet Ronnie. I knew it was him because he was wearing a suit and had a happy, proud smile.

'Ronnie,' said Darla, 'I'd like you to meet a friend of mine. A new friend. His name's Gerald. It's his first time here.'

Ronnie nodded, but looked distracted. 'So what do you think, Gerald?'

'It's great.'

Ronnie shrugged. 'It's an experiment. We'll see how it works out.' He looked at me again, and his expression became more serious. 'Have I met you before, Gerald?'

I shook my head.

'Are you sure?'

'I think so.'

'What do you do then? Are you a comedian?'

'No. I'm a teacher.'

'Are you sure you haven't been on television? Maybe on an advert or something?'

'I was on television once,' I told him, 'for a while, actually. But it was a long time ago.'

27

It's hard to describe the excitement I experienced six weeks after my operation, when I went out through my front door and saw a large, smartly dressed (but shaggy-haired) man standing next to the television company's car, waiting for me to get in. Everyone has a moment of escape some time in their life, I suppose: it's just that mine had come at exactly the right moment. I walked down the garden path, tongued the no longer sore spot between my two front teeth, and took my seat in the back.

The driver started the engine. 'I've got two other people I need to pick up on the way.'

'OK,' I replied, as if he had been asking my permission. I wanted to ask him who the two other people were, desperately hoping we would be driving to Wendy and Perdita's, but felt too shy. The driver didn't say anything else to me, and I kept quiet, looking out of the window until we pulled up outside a suburban house that was very much like my own.

The driver went up to the front door. After a few seconds, it opened and a girl to whom I had yet to be introduced emerged. She had brown hair cut in an unflattering, heavy style that made her face look extremely serious. Her clothes didn't help matters, and the dress she was wearing over her large body looked better suited to a middle-aged woman. She didn't smile at me as she walked down to the car. She got in next to me and announced, 'Jane.' I ignored her.

Maybe it would have been different if she'd been someone I could get interested in. Then I might have made an effort. But instead I just stayed silent until the driver picked up Robert, the other child who lived near me. I found Robert immediately intimidating, for several reasons. There was his age: sixteen, I would find out later, making him the oldest member of our group; his clothing, which didn't look especially smart or expensive, just suited him, and suggested that he had started to think of buying clothing as a pleasure rather than a chore; his haircut, which was so precise it gave the impression that he never had to get it cut, or styled, or in any way maintained, and, most of all, his intimidating sexuality, which was already beginning to work on Jane. I knew boys like him at school, mainly from years above me, and didn't like the way girls changed when they were around, knowing I'd never be able to have that effect on them.

We didn't talk. Jane and I were too shy, and Robert didn't seem in the mood for conversation. The journey took longer than I expected and when we reached our destination two women pulled open the back doors of the car.

'What's wrong?' the driver asked.

'Nicholas is waiting.'

28

Ronnie seemed fascinated by my story, and invited Darla and me to join him for a drink in his private office. Although I was worried about Sally and my housemates, I told myself that there was a group of them and they could look after themselves. I was intrigued by Ronnie and didn't want to pass up this opportunity for an intimate conversation. He didn't seem much older than Darla or me, but had a sophisticated ease with himself that seemed far removed from my daily struggle. When I quit acting, I accepted that a lot of my fantasies were over, and from now on I would be living the life of a 'civilian', as Liz Hurley would have it. Not that I ever experienced genuine fame, but my simulacrum was intoxicating enough, for lots of different reasons. And it seemed less painful to give it all up in one go than carry on going to auditions as an adult in the hope that someone would still see something in me.

Which isn't to say it didn't still hurt, and one of the most distressing things about the loss was that the reality of my life and my fantasy world were separate again. Reading celebrity autobiographies was especially painful (but compulsive: I slept with a copy of Geri Halliwell's *If Only* on my bedside table for several months), as I identified with everything in the childhood sections, especially if – like Geri – they were around the same age as me (when I read in Geri's diary entry for Wednesday, 23rd July 1986 that she'd been reading the novelisation of *Desperately Seeking Susan*, I wondered whether I'd been doing the same thing on that evening, although, unlike her, I'd been reading the book because I failed to get into the film, something Geri achieved by putting on her friend Natalie's sexy dress, and a bra filled with her brother Max's football socks), and felt slightly superior when the celebrity reached their teenage years and had yet to achieve a fame transformation. Then as they blossomed and started meeting up with other celebrities and passed fully into that glamorous world, all I had left were memories. Biographies and autobiographies of older celebrities were fine, especially when their careers ended in ignominy or disease, but I still wished I had something more substantial in my creative life than one series of *All Right Now!*

Sometimes, when I watched programmes about proper former child actors who had gone on to pursue alternative, but still exciting, careers, I wondered whether there was still time for my own life to change direction. I have to admit that, secretly, since the end of *All Right Now!* I'd started to see myself as a bit of a failure. It wasn't that I was unhappy with my life, just that it had been a long time since I'd done anything fun. I'd tried to make the slide from student life to gainful employment as painless as possible, and as a result it was only now I realised I was beginning to get stuck in a rut. Ellen leaving had a lot to do with this new awareness. But perhaps I wouldn't end up driving a taxi like Geoffrey from *Rainbow*. Maybe one day an opportunity would present itself to me and change my life for ever. Who knew? That might be about to happen right now.

'You both drink whisky, right?'

I nodded. Darla didn't say anything. I felt less intimidated by Ronnie now we were in his private office. It was stylish enough, but it also revealed that perfect taste is hard to develop in under thirty years. The room owed too much to fantasies gleaned from films about what an art gallery owner's office should be like. Ronnie was clearly caught up in his own dream-vision, and there was still some distance between who he was and who he wanted to be.

He gave us our drinks and sat down behind a big desk. 'I'm still trying to remember if I ever saw your show. I used to love children's programmes, and you're around the same age as me so I must've watched it. I just can't remember the idea, and it seems like one of those ideas that would definitely stick in your mind. I remember *Press Gang*. You remember *Press Gang*, don't you? I think that was one of the greatest television programmes they ever made, for kids or adults.'

'*Press Gang* was great,' I replied quietly.

He looked at his computer. 'Are you on the net? You must be on the imdb, right? Everyone's on the imdb.'

'Yeah,' I said, 'but there's also a fan-site.'

'A fan-site,' he said, astonished. 'For something that long ago?'

'Yeah,' I replied, 'it's not that surprising. There are fan-sites for almost anything you can think of on the web. They've even started a campaign to release the whole series on DVD.'

'The power of nostalgia, huh?'

'Well, it's not just that. Andy Medhurst wrote an article about the programme in *Sight & Sound*, citing it as one of the great achievements of Eighties sociological television, and it picked up a whole load of new interest.'

Ronnie sipped his whisky. 'It does sound like it was very original. Has there ever been anything else like it?'

'There was something a bit like it on Channel Four some time around the mid-nineties. I don't think it was just children, though. I didn't watch it, but I think it was whole families, and it wasn't a series like us, it was just a one-off, or a two-parter or something, but I think Nicholas was involved.'

'Nicholas?'

'The dramaturge. The guy who helped us with our stories.'

Ronnie leaned forward and placed a hand on his keyboard. 'What's the address for the web-site?'

'*All Right Now* dot com. With an exclamation mark after Now.'

There was a scuttling sound as he typed this in. 'Oh yeah,' he said, surprisingly quickly. 'Which one's you?'

I got up, carefully placing my tumbler of whisky on the

edge of his big desk, and walked round behind him. There was a time when I visited this web-site almost every night, hungry just to see the j-pegs of these friends I no longer had contact with, and intrigued to read the surprisingly passionate recollections of watching the programme written by people on the message-board. Ronnie was right about the site initially being a nostalgia exercise – *hey guys, remember this?* like it was *Metal Mickey* or something – but it seemed to have grown more serious while it was up, especially when people realised that some of the other actors and actresses on *All Right Now!* had gone on to more well-known programmes. At first, I had wondered whether it was one of my forgotten co-stars who had created the site, but when I did a domain-search I found it was registered to a woman called Michelle Onions, a name that meant nothing to me.

I don't know if everyone feels like this, but I think there's something really sad about the internet. And I mean sad as in upsetting. For a long time, I didn't really use computers, and even when I first started accessing sites, it took me a long time before I started any personal digging. I know that sounds unlike me, but seriously, it was months before I fed my own name into a search-engine. That was when I found the *All Right Now!* site, but it wasn't the end of my investigation. When I grew tired of going back there, I tried a few more names: Nicholas Pennington, Perdita Dawkins, and so on. Nicholas's site was the most depressing, offering himself up as a dramaturge for hire. But some of the others weren't far behind, including the guy who'd composed the music for our show.

'That's me,' I said, pointing to the lanky figure with messy hair in the corner of the picture. 'This is the first publicity photograph we ever had taken.'

'What else is on the site? Anything interesting?'

'There are some topless pictures of Perdita in murky light, taken from some terrible Canadian film she was in.'

'What's Perdita's surname?'

'Dawkins.'

'I recognise that name.'

'She's been in some television stuff you might have seen. Big stuff on ITV. If you go on to the next page and then click on her name.'

He did so. A few seconds later he said, 'She was in *When, Voyager?*'

'What's *When, Voyager?*'

'Oh, nothing,' he said quickly.

This caught Darla's interest, and she sat up. 'No, come on, Ronnie, what is it?'

'No, forget it, I'm embarrassed I mentioned it.'

We both waited for him to continue. Neither of us understood what he was talking about. Grinning, he asked Darla, 'Can you shut the door, please?'

She got up. 'It is shut.'

'I mean, go across and lock it. There's a key there.' He waited. 'See it?'

'Yeah,' she said, twisting the key and rattling the door. 'It's locked.'

'Good.' He unlocked his desk drawer and lifted a small tray onto the desk. Then he reached into his suit jacket for his wallet. 'You two like this, don't you?'

Darla answered, 'Yes,' before I had chance to say anything.

He started unwrapping a small packet. Someone from outside tried the office door and, finding it locked, started to pound heavily against it.

'I'm busy,' Ronnie called out.

'It's important,' a female voice replied.

'Fuck,' said Ronnie, opening his desk drawer and putting the tray back again, 'Darla, can you?'

She went to the door and unlocked it. A twentysomething woman appeared behind it.

'Sorry to interrupt, Ronnie, but have you got a minute?'

'What's up?'

'I need to talk to you in private.'

'OK, hang on.' He turned to us. 'You two are all right here on your own for a moment, aren't you?'

Darla nodded. 'We're fine.'

29

He stood in the centre of the room. We formed a circle around him. Six foot tall, bald with a white goatee, he was dressed in jeans and a dark blue shirt. Unlike everyone else I had met while getting involved in this enterprise, he radiated a sense of supreme seriousness.

'Welcome,' he said in a deep voice. 'Before we start, there are a few things I want to make clear. Is that OK?'

We murmured agreement.

'Good. My name is Nicholas Pennington and I am a dramaturge. This is not the same thing as a teacher. I am not a teacher. Neither am I a youth club leader, nor are you children. Some of you may already be actors, most probably are not. Be that as it may, I am not interested in you as actors, at least not yet. You have not come here to play parts in a play. You have not come here to make faces on TV. You have come here, whether you know it or not, to take part in a kind of transubstantiation. It will be a difficult and painful process. But,' he pulled out a ball from behind his back, 'it begins easily.'

He squeezed the ball. 'When someone throws you the ball, say your name, your full complete name, Christian, middle and family names. And if you have one you're prepared to share with the group, your nickname. I'll start. My name is Nicholas Pennington. I do not have a nickname, although sometimes people I am close to have used my family name as a form of familiarity. You are not permitted to do so.'

The yellow ball came through the air.

'Gerald Wedmore. Sorry. Gerald John Wedmore. I don't have a nickname, really, although my friend Reggel sometimes calls me Spider because Wedmore sounds a bit like Webmore.'

'Good. Throw the ball.'

I looked round the room. This was my first chance to appraise the full assembled cast. Although I was only just thirteen, and a young thirteen, without any real sexual feelings or serious frustrations of desire, I was looking more for female friends than male ones. And, I suppose, while I knew it was an ambition I was unlikely to fulfil, a possible girlfriend. What should have been a simple motion was complicated by all sorts of difficult questions. First, I had to decide whether I would continue trying to form an exclusive group with the children I'd met at the audition. If I went with that option, should I throw the ball directly to the girl I liked the most (Perdita), the one I wasn't interested in at all (Sheryl), or a boy (Pete)? I quickly checked out the girls I hadn't met yet. Did any of them seem nice? Too innocent to have any real scheme, I let instinct lead me and tossed the ball to Perdita. My aim wasn't great, but she caught it, holding it back against her blue *Bodytalk* top.

'Perdita Jane Dawkins. Sometimes people call me Perdy. Or Purry. But that's it.'

Perdita was tall and lean, her brown hair pulled into a ponytail and kept together with a blue hair-band. She was definitely the girl I most wanted to be friends with. She seemed sharper than Wendy, somehow more exciting. The ball went from her to a girl with dark colouring and long black hair. Oddly, the girl, who looked small and young, was wearing ballet clothes. She had a slight lisp.

'Lola Doll,' she said, her theatrical manner making us laugh. 'I suppose I get Baby Doll the most. Because I'm small.'

Lola twirled and let the ball rise from her hand and sail across to a girl whose clothes looked slightly more suburban than the rest of us. She was the only child here who could be considered mature. She reminded me of the mothers of my friends, the ones Erica and I had encountered on our after-school odyssey, only slightly reduced in size. She had neat, almost fifties-style brown shoulder-length hair, red, made-up lips, and was significantly taller than the rest of the girls. She wore brown sandals, blue jeans and a blue and red checked shirt. As she caught the ball, she said, 'Amy Brown. Amy Angela Brown. I don't have a nickname. Just Amy. My Dad calls me Sweet Bonnie Brown, but whenever he does that my Mum gets really cross. I don't know why.'

She threw the ball to Sheryl, who was standing alongside me. Sheryl caught the ball awkwardly and had to wiggle to stop it falling to the floor.

'Sheryl Claire Casement. The girls at school call me Headcase.'

Nicholas laughed. 'That's nice. I like that.'

Sheryl threw the ball to one of the boys I hadn't met yet. I wondered if she fancied him. Although Perdita had ducked the issue by throwing to a girl, I sensed Sheryl would be as obvious as me.

The boy was clearly a sportsman, something of a surprise in these circles. He caught the ball with a neat click as it came against his hand.

'Robert Buckpit. No middle name. My nickname is too rude to share.'

'Wrong,' shouted Nicholas, 'nothing is too rude to share. I told you already, you are not children. What is your nickname?'

'Fuckpit. The kids in school call me Fuckpit.'

'Good. Throw the ball.'

He tossed it to Wendy, who was standing on the other side of me.

'Wendy Sparks,' she said, 'Wendy Claire Sparks. My nickname is Sparky, or lightbulb, or anything along those lines really.'

Fuckpit smiled at this. His attention made me turn to take another look at Wendy, who was the girl I second-most fancied in the group. She seemed slightly more approachable now than she had on the day of the auditions, although I knew if she had to choose between Fuckpit and me he'd definitely win. She was shorter than Perdita or Amy, and while not overweight, had large breasts (so noticeable that it wasn't only Robert and me, but also most of the girls who looked at them) and a big bum. She had a nest of brown curly hair, much less neat than Amy's, and a kind, round face, with a small nose, blue eyes and a small but not thin mouth.

The ball went from Wendy's hand back across to Pete. Was that who she fancied, or did she throw it to him because he was the only boy left?

'Peter Chris Crook. All my nicknames come from my surname. Crook, Crooky, Crooked, Burglar, Thief, Teef, Tea-leaf, along those lines. Although, yeah, sometimes people call me Peter Cook instead of Crook.'

He threw the ball to Lucy, Wendy's sister. She caught it and said, 'Lucy Sparks. My middle name is Louise. I get the same nicknames as Wendy.'

She smiled and threw it in a straight line to Jane, the last person in our group.

'Joey Deacon,' she said, and everyone laughed. 'That's my nickname. Sorry, I shouldn't have said that first, should I? My name's not Joey Deacon, obviously, that's my nickname. My name is Jane Clair Smith. Isn't that funny? I'm the third person in the group whose middle name is Claire. Although mine's without an "e". What about you two?'

'With an "e",' they both said quickly.

Nicholas seemed to realise that he was in danger of losing the group's attention to Jane, who had grown much more talkative and friendly than she'd been in the car with me, and walked across to take the ball from her.

'OK, everyone, thanks. Now in order to cement that into everyone's memories I want you to say the name of the person you're throwing the ball to as you throw it. OK? I'll start.'

He threw the ball to Fuckpit. I felt a sudden embarrassment that I could no longer remember his real name. Oh well, that didn't matter for the minute, as long as I didn't throw the ball to him. The ball went back and forth among the members of the group, circling among the same few people, clearly the ones who had made the biggest impression. The circuit was mainly Perdita, Peter, Wendy and

66

Sheryl, who (although I was still certain no one liked her) was certainly memorable. In fairness to Sheryl, Jane was probably more embarrassing, but somehow she seemed less over-eager. Sheryl was like a lolloping dog; Jane was uncool, but not embarrassing. The sort of girl most people would ignore, but who no doubt had enough friends of her own in school. After the ball had been passing between us for a while, Nicholas stepped back in and said:

'Good. That's a start. Now, I don't know how much any of you know about acting, but any experienced performer, especially one adept at improvisation, will tell you that drama is all about energy. It's not always about creating energy, but conducting and controlling it. Good acting is about the passage of energy, moving between people in the way that ball went from one of you to the other to the other. I have another way of showing it. Everyone hold hands. In your circle. Come on.'

This, again, was fraught with complications. I didn't often get chance to hold girls' hands, and wished I had ignored my earlier nerves and stood next to Perdita. I was so innocent back then, even holding her hand would have been enough. It was almost as exciting to be holding hands with Wendy, but the pleasure was slightly diminished by having to connect myself to Sheryl at the same time.

'OK,' said Nicholas, 'at the moment I don't want any of you to create your own energy. What I'm about to say now may sound strange and I don't want any of you professors of physics to tell me what I'm describing is impossible. This is an exercise in imagination as much as anything else. But what I'm going to do is create a pulse. I'm going to create this pulse from my body's energy and then I'm going to pass it on to Robert. Now, Robert, when you receive my pulse I want you to carry it through your body without adding any of your own energy to it. This is important. I will pass the pulse from my body into your hand and I want you to let the pulse pass up your arm, across your shoulders, down your other arm and into your hand. Then I want you to pass the pulse from your hand into Lucy's hand, making sure you are passing exactly the same amount of energy that I passed on to you. Then, Lucy, I want you to do the same thing, passing the energy on to your sister and so on and so on until the energy has returned to me. OK . . . Robert, are you ready?'

He nodded.

The pulse quickly came round to me and although the whole exercise struck me as silly, I tried to pretend that I felt the energy going from Wendy's hand into mine, up round my body and on to Sheryl. I certainly felt excited when Wendy squeezed my hand, but that seemed to do with a different kind of energy, an energy that was in danger of diverting down my body.

'Good,' said Nicholas as the pulse returned to him. 'Now, this time, I want you to let the pulse pass round the circle several times, then, when you feel ready, I want one of you to reverse the direction of the pulse. It doesn't matter who does it, but it can only happen once, do you understand?'

We understood. He started the pulse and when it reached me I passed it on to Sheryl. I was excited about the possibility of passing the pulse back to Wendy and waited for the direction to change. The group followed Nicholas's instructions, allowing the pulse to go round several times before doing anything. Each time the pulse passed through me I looked onwards to the others, mentally picturing the pulse moving through each person and simultaneously counting forward and back so I'd be able to work out who was daring enough to reverse the current.

Maybe it was only because my eyes were drawn to her, but it definitely seemed to be Perdita who made the switch. When I received the pulse from Sheryl, I held my breath and passed it back to Wendy, then waited until it got back to Nicholas. When it did, he smiled and said:

'Well done, everybody. I think this proves the group is in harmony and we'll be able to work together. Now, before we go on to the next part of this exercise, I'm afraid I have to give you a little lecture. I know there is a difference in ages among the members of this group, and some of you will inevitably be more mature than others, but I need to repeat my earlier insistence that this is not like school. Or a youth club. The reason I asked you all to say your nicknames as well as your real names was to give you a kind of test. A test you all passed admirably. You didn't make up cool nicknames for yourselves, but revealed your real ones, even when they were embarrassing. And that takes trust. But for trust to work, you need to watch out for each other. There can be no bullying, no making fun. I don't know what your normal lives are like, but I would imagine that at least some of you' – he looked at me – 'get a hard time at school. That will not happen here. This will be your sanctuary. You all have a long way to go, but by the end of this experience, we will have a television series and you will have skills that'll stand you in good stead for life. Now, can I have a volunteer, please?'

Jane put up her hand.

'Great,' said Nicholas, coming across and pulling her into the centre of the circle. 'Now, it may seem that I'm taking things a little bit slowly this evening, but that's because these first few meetings are about building up trust. Once we get started we'll soon get to the meat of things and you'll understand why these exercises are a necessary beginning. OK, Jane, this exercise is a game and it's supposed to be fun, so don't take it too seriously. The object is to see if you can pick up on the energy that's being passed round the group. Everyone else is going to repeat the last exercise, only this time they can switch and reverse the direction of the current whenever they want to. You have to watch the others, trying to see if there are any changes in the faces of the group when they receive the pulse. OK?'

Jane nodded, looking upset that she had volunteered for an exercise that would make her the outsider. It seemed to me that this game would be quite hard to win, especially when Nicholas told her she had to close her eyes until the pulse had gone round a couple of times.

'OK,' he said, 'now.'

The pulse was moving faster than before, as if everyone really was afraid of being caught with it. Jane moved closer to look at the faces of the people in the circle, her serious expression making them laugh. Jane turned back to Nicholas and asked, 'How do I catch them out?'

'Just point to the person who you think has the pulse. This is a trust exercise, and you can rely on them to be honest.'

'OK,' she said, pointing at me.

I didn't have the pulse, and shook my head. Jane looked irritated, but tried again. After two more incorrect guesses, she caught Pete, and they swapped places.

30

I met a friend last night and told him that I was writing about my childhood experiences and had come up against a problem that I wasn't sure how to resolve. I'm writing a book about childhood, essentially from an adult perspective, and that's fine when I'm talking about myself, but what happens when I present my childhood self interacting with other children? This is a narrative, so I have to keep some stuff hidden, and show how my understanding of certain people changed over time, but am I allowed to offer my adolescent self a small degree of protection? My friend laughed at me and said, 'I don't mean to belittle your problem, but it does seem a little bit like Jack London trying to decide whether to write Call of the Wild from the perspective of the dog.' And then he laughed and looked all smug. I couldn't even remember if Call of the Wild was from the perspective of the dog (the only Jack London novel I have is that copy of White Fang my father bought me after the operation on my mouth), and didn't understand what he meant, but the conversation moved on and I felt I couldn't challenge him. I thought this exchange might make more sense written down, but its meaning still eludes me, so this is what I've decided to do. I'm going to give my childhood self a slightly better ability to characterise people, but apart from that, let him take his own chances. And if he occasionally looks at scenes with too adult an eye, you'll know there's a reason for it and forgive me.

Or throw the book across the room in disgust.

31

I didn't notice how dark it was in Ronnie's office until he left me alone with Darla. She had retaken her seat, and I found myself staring at her dimly lit face and wondering why she looked so mischievous.

'So what do you think of him?'

'Yeah,' I said, 'he's all right.'

She pushed her black hair behind her small right ear. 'You never told me you were a celebrity.'

'Oh,' I laughed, 'I don't think that's the right word. I appeared on TV a few times when I was a kid, that's all.'

'But still,' she said, 'Ronnie seems impressed.'

'I get the impression that Ronnie is very easily impressed.'

'I thought you liked him.'

'I did. It's just when you've got money I imagine you always have to be nice to everyone.'

Darla shook her head. 'No,' she said, 'usually he's very careful to keep people at a distance. He genuinely liked you.'

'Because I used to be on TV, or because you vouched for me?'

She didn't reply. I felt guilty about being churlish, but didn't know how to apologise without making things worse. Before I had chance, Darla glanced towards the desk.

'I think he'd want us to help ourselves.'

'No thanks.'

She raised an eyebrow.

'I don't take drugs.'

'What d'you mean, you don't take drugs? Everyone takes drugs.'

'Not me.'

'Come on, Gerald, for nostalgia's sake. Pretend you're eighteen again.'

'I didn't take drugs when I was eighteen.'

'Twenty then.'

'Or twenty. I've never taken drugs. My sister handles that side of things in our family.'

This gave Darla pause. I could tell she was trying to work out if my sister had died of a heroin overdose. I didn't want to let her off the hook, so I kept quiet. I know this makes me sound like an uptight cunt, but I was disappointed in Darla. I liked her, and wanted to be her friend, but have always been extremely wary around people who use anything other than the softest of soft drugs.

'Come on, Gerald, please keep me company. It's no fun on my own.'

I considered her offer. If I was going to start hanging out with people like Ronnie, I would have to learn not to be so strict on myself. And, besides, there was something magic about tonight that made me certain that I wouldn't come to any harm no matter what I did.

'OK,' I told Darla, 'I'll do it.'

She smiled, and sat behind the desk.

32

After we'd finished playing the pulse-game, Nicholas Pennington returned to the centre of the circle.

'OK,' he said, 'I told you before that I am not yet interested in you as actors. That's because of the very special and unique qualities of this project. In order for you to understand your relationship with me, I have to tell you about myself. I am a dramaturge. Does anyone know what that is?'

Perdita had prepared for this question. 'A specialist in theatrical production?'

'Well, yes, well done, that's the dictionary definition. But can anyone tell me what being a dramaturge might entail?'

I shrugged. 'You're going to teach us how to tell stories?'

'Good, Gerald, that's an excellent start. But I'm not going

to teach you how to pluck stories out of the air. I'm here to help you become recording angels, and then once we've mastered that I'm going to show you how to use that raw material to create something incredible. Can you split into two groups of five?'

I turned to look at Wendy, but she had already begun walking over to Perdita. Sheryl was eagerly sticking to my side. I nodded at her and made us both move across to Wendy and Perdita. Perdita nodded her consent and the four of us stood together. Amy was the only one not swallowed up by the other group, and she slowly edged towards us.

'Move slightly further apart,' Nicholas advised us, as he picked up two chairs. Placing one at the centre of each circle, he stood back and said, 'I know it probably seems strange to you that I keep emphasising the importance of trust, especially as at your age it means little to you outside of the odd playground squabble, but I do have to stress this again as we will not be able to create anything if you are not honest and open with each other. These two groups you've formed now, these will be your groups for all future exercises. Within your groups, I'd like you to split into one pair and one three.'

It was no use looking at Perdita. She and Wendy had already traded arm-pats. But maybe I could get Amy into our group instead of theirs. I could tell she wanted to go with Perdita and Wendy, but I didn't give her chance, grabbing her shoulder. She turned back to Sheryl and me, trying to look enthusiastic.

'And now everything is sorted,' said Nicholas Pennington. 'Can one person from each group sit in the centre of the circle?'

Perdita took the seat. In the other group, Lucy was the volunteer.

'What I want you to do now is for the four people left in each group to try to get a sense of the person sitting in the chair. Keep your questions general for the moment. Find out about the person, their likes and dislikes, that sort of thing. And be aware, just as important as finding out this information is being able to remember it. I want you to ask questions that will allow you to get a fixed sense of the person in the chair. Think about what details will turn this person from a relative stranger into someone you can feel something towards.'

I didn't need personal details to feel something for Perdita. But I did like the idea of the group taking over the small talk I had no idea how to make. Nicholas Pennington was beginning to look tired, the strain of his performance evident from the dark stain climbing up the back of his shirt. He seemed eager for us to take over, so I asked Perdita, 'Do you have any pets?'

Everyone laughed. I wasn't sure why. But Perdita smiled and told me, 'Yes. I have a black cat called Suzy.'

'Come on,' Nicholas Pennington shouted at the other group, 'start asking Lucy questions.'

They did. I returned my attention to Perdita, looking at the two wisps of brown hair she'd allowed to curl loose in front of each ear.

Sheryl asked, 'What do your parents do?'

'My dad's an engineer and my mum's a playwright.'

This caught our dramaturge's attention. Turning back from the window, he walked back towards Perdita, asking, 'Is she famous?'

'No.'

'But she's a professional?'

'What do you mean by professional?' Perdita asked, encouraged by the attention.

'Are her plays performed?'

'Oh . . . yes.'

'In what sort of theatres?'

'Proper ones. Sometimes big ones in London, other times in different places.'

We were all watching Nicholas Pennington, unsure whether to carry on with our own questions. He seemed quite distressed by hearing about Perdita's mum's job, and flinched when Sheryl asked, 'Are you a playwright, Mr Pennington?'

'Nicholas,' he snapped, 'I am not a teacher. Don't call me Mr Pennington.'

'But are you a playwright?'

'No,' he said quietly, 'a dramaturge is quite different from a playwright.'

He looked back to the window. Everyone stared at Sheryl, who at least seemed aware that she had said something insensitive. Trying to relieve the situation, she asked him, 'Have you always worked in television?'

'Not always,' he said, perking up, 'but for the lion's share of my career.'

'What's the most famous programme you've worked on?'

'The most famous?' He pretended to consider her question. 'I suppose that would have to be *Coronation Street*.'

All credit to the man. He must have known how this would transform him in our eyes. Just as we were beginning to forget what we were here for, and about to start worrying that this soap opera might not be the showbiz heaven we'd imagined, he tells us that he'd worked on the most famous television programme of them all.

And, suddenly, Perdita's playwright mother didn't seem anywhere near as exciting.

33

Darla reacted so swiftly to my advances that I couldn't help wondering if drugs were a regular part of her seduction technique. I started by noticing her shoes, which were much sexier than the rest of her outfit and looked slightly odd sticking out from beneath her jeans. I was surprised I hadn't noticed them before, especially as they were exactly the same kind of black leather shoes with a raised heel and thin strap that Ellen always looked best in. Wrapping my fingers around her ankles, I said, 'You were too good for him.'

'Who?'

'That man, Rufus or whatever, the man who shagged your sister.'

She laughed. 'Loz.'

'Yeah. Him.'

'Come here,' she said, pulling me upright, 'my feet aren't that interesting.'

I sat up.

'Aw,' she cooed, looking at me, 'are you OK?'

'Can I have a cuddle?'

'Of course.'

I was too enthusiastic, almost knocking her off her chair.

'Hang on,' she told me, 'let's move onto Ronnie's couch. We'll be more comfortable there.'

She pointed to the couch in the dark corner on the opposite side of the room. I walked across and let myself drop down onto it, putting my legs up and moving aside so she had space to lie alongside me. Darla took off her shoes and then loosened the laces on mine, pulling them from my feet. Then she got on the couch and looked at me. I immediately pulled her into my arms, nuzzling my face against her small breasts.

'Oh,' she said, 'you need a lot of love, don't you?'

I looked up at her, shocked at the truth in what she was saying. How did she know? I did need a lot of love. At that exact moment, I felt as though I needed all the love in the world. I moved up and started kissing her. She seemed receptive, and we snogged for I don't know how long. Then I pushed her away and said, 'Oops.'

'What's wrong?'

'Sally,' I told her, 'my promise to her. I can't have sex with you.'

'We're not going to have sex, Gerald.'

'But I shouldn't even be kissing you.'

'It's OK, you're lonely. It doesn't mean anything.'

'What you said just now, about me needing a lot of love?'

'Yes?'

'How did you know that?'

'Everyone needs a lot of love, Gerald.'

'Yeah, but the way you said it, like it was specific to me. Has Sally talked to you about me?'

'She said you laugh too loud in the cinema.'

I considered this. 'No, but did she say anything about me and Ellen?'

Darla moved round on the couch, and I realised I'd been squashing her. 'That's your ex-girlfriend?'

'Yeah.'

'The one who left you because she'd started fancying other men?'

'How do you know that?'

'You told me this morning.'

'Did I? Oh yeah.'

She was staring at me. I decided I wanted to kiss her again, and put my arms around her. After we'd been kissing for a while, I realised I'd started pawing her breasts and, self-conscious again, stopped and looked up at her.

'Are you sure you don't mind this?'

'No,' she said, 'it's nice, I like it. Don't you?'

'Yeah, but . . .'

'Don't worry, Gerald, tonight's a night off. Don't you feel you deserve it?'

'Definitely. I'm just not used . . .' My voice croaked. 'I'm not used to people being nice to me. I mean, first Sally, now you . . .'

She smiled. 'This woman you used to go out with. It sounds like she was really tough on you.'

'No,' I said, shaking my head emphatically, 'she wasn't tough on me. I mean, not deliberately. She had a lot of troubles of her own.'

'And you looked after her?'

'Not really. It's hard to look after someone when you're in love with them.'

'Why?'

'Love makes you judgemental.'

She looked at me. I got the impression she didn't want me to carry on talking, and I felt happy to shut up. We continued kissing, and I groped her breasts. Darla didn't touch me apart from stroking my hair, and I was careful not

77

to try to intensify our intimacy. When we next broke apart, I asked her, 'Can we get Stan in here?'

'Is he into . . . ?'

'No, he's like me, he never has. But I want him to share the experience.'

'I'm not lying on this couch with Stan.'

'No, no, I didn't mean that. I just want . . .'

'Him to share the experience. You already said that. OK, but let's be quiet about this. I don't want to upset Ronnie.'

'Why would Ronnie get upset?'

'He has to be careful . . . He doesn't want to draw too much attention to this place. The wrong sort of rumours . . .'

'It's OK, I'll get Stan away from the others before I tell him.'

'Well,' she said, 'it's not just Stan. You be careful too. Don't draw attention to yourself.'

'Why would I draw attention to myself?'

She laughed.

'Relax, Darla, I'm fine.' I struggled to get up. 'Come with me, though. I need your help to find the others.'

She put her arm around me and we left the office.

34

Sheryl was the last one into the chair. Wendy had answered every question we asked without revealing anything about herself. The only details that stuck with me were that she was fifteen – two years older than me – and had a boyfriend called Andrew who was seventeen. She may have been the girl I second-most fancied, but these two details effectively put her completely out of my league, and led me to turn my romantic attention solely to Perdita, who was only fourteen, and, she'd said (with a giggle at using an inappropriately adult word), single.

Sheryl grinned at us, awaiting her first question. She looked stupid, her coarse blonde hair pulled into two pigtails, a style that didn't suit her and made her look immature next to Wendy and Perdita. Her green dungarees were too boyish, and her green and red flower-print sweatshirt was excessively ugly. I knew she wanted to be friends with me, and, more embarrassing still, everyone else (in both groups) had already decided I liked her and were waiting for me to ask her something.

I gave in. 'How old are you?'

'Twelve and a half.'

That helped explain it. After Lucy, Wendy's sister, who was only eleven, and Lola Doll (twelve) she was the youngest in the group. A year or two's age difference might not matter when you're an adult, but I was used to school, where the only person below my age whom I had any dealings with was my sister. I knew Wendy and Perdita probably looked down on me in the same way I looked down upon Sheryl, but I wasn't going to give up trying to be connected to them instead of her.

'Where do you live?' Perdita asked her.

'Carshalton.'

'Any brothers or sisters?'

She shook her head, plaits swishing over both shoulders.

'What do your parents do?'

'My Dad works in a factory, and my Mum's a librarian.'

Nicholas didn't seem as interested in Sheryl, and had moved across to the other group, where Fuckpit was the one answering questions. He sat with his back straight and his hands clasped behind him as if his interrogation was something he wasn't enjoying. I felt so pleased I'd got into this group, feeling privileged to be the only boy in a quintet with three attractive girls (and Sheryl). I couldn't imagine Pete or Fuckpit being attracted to Lucy (too young) or Jane (too embarrassing) and sensed I would soon have to fend off their challenges for Amy, Wendy and Perdita's attentions. But just doing exercises with these girls was exciting enough for the moment, and I decided not to get too tense about potential future problems.

'OK, everybody,' said Nicholas, a few questions later, 'that's a good start. The next stage of our research period is a little bit complicated, and if your parents have a problem with it, can you tell them to call the production office? Transport won't be a problem, and once you've made the arrangements with each other, we can arrange for cars to take you across and bring you back. Basically, what I want you to do is, in your groups, each of you has to go to the other four persons' houses. Do you understand what I mean by that? It's quite straightforward. For example, Perdita, you have to visit Gerald, Wendy, Amy and ... sorry, yeah, Sheryl's house, and also let Gerald, Wendy, Amy and Sheryl come visit you. Now, I'll leave you to make the arrangements for this among yourselves, but I need you to get this done some time in the next fortnight, because, as you know, after that we have our weekend away on the Yorkshire Moors, and by that time we need for you to have collected all your raw material so we can start thinking about how we're going to put together our stories.' Nicholas stopped, looking round at the production assistant who had tapped him on the shoulder. 'Oh, yeah, and there's lemonade for anyone who wants it.'

There was a collective sigh of relief as we realised the formal part of the session was over. I could see Wendy and Perdita wanted to talk, and it had been strange to experience such a restricted introduction to each other. Of course, if it wasn't for the television programme we were all involved in creating, I never would have talked to any of these girls. Except maybe Sheryl. Although in my day-to-day life I had almost no social contact with the opposite sex, there had been other occasions when slightly nerdy girls had sought me out. One of the most embarrassing had been on a family holiday the previous year when I had been playing backgammon with my father (he'd been suffering from withdrawal from gambling, and until the third night – when he took us all to a casino – this was as close as he could get) and a fourteen-year-old girl had come across to ask if she could give me a game. My parents thought this was hilarious, especially when she started touching my knees in an attempt to put me off my dice-rolling. Usually my psychopathic sister was the one who pulled my essentially antisocial parents into holiday friendships with other families, and they were extremely amused by this change in the natural order of things, making friends with the girl's parents and enjoying my embarrassment throughout the rest of our time away. The worst moment came on the final night when I had to hide in the toilets to avoid dancing with her at the end-of-holiday disco. Sheryl wasn't that different from the holiday girl, and I could see how that might present a later problem. Usually I would have cut this off by being horrible to her now, but Nicholas's words remained firmly in my mind, and I didn't want to shame myself by behaving badly.

Sheryl walked across to the counter and brought back two plastic cups of lemonade. 'When do you want to come to my house then?'

'I don't know.'

'Well, I think it might be the best idea if you come tomorrow or Sunday, because then my parents will be home and you can talk to them too.'

'Your parents?' I asked.

'Yes. We're supposed to use our families for stories, aren't we?'

I considered this. Things like this made my mother very, very angry. She didn't even like it when my sister and I had to write 'what I did on my weekend' pieces (admittedly because Erica used to submit gory fantasies about her and Dad going on killing sprees that had, on one memorable occasion, resulted in a supply teacher sending the police to our home). But, aside from that, Mum was a genuinely private person, and I couldn't see her agreeing to this. Indeed, I was unsure whether she'd even let Sheryl, Wendy, Amy and Perdita visit me. It occurred to me that one possibility was to sneak them in when both my parents were at work, but that would probably prove too difficult as I wasn't supposed to be home alone, and didn't have my own front door key. No, it looked as if I'd have to fight my corner on this one.

'So,' she said, 'is Sunday all right then?'

'Yes. Although, Sheryl . . .'

'Yes?'

'I don't know whether you'll be able to talk to my parents. You know, when you come to my house.'

'That's OK, Gerald, you can tell me stories about them. And show me photograph albums.'

I nodded, not wanting to tell her that Dad had burnt all our family photo albums after an argument with my mother. She finished her plastic cup of lemonade and belched loudly. Embarrassed, I said, 'Shall we sort things out with the others too?'

'Yeah,' she said eagerly, 'that's a good idea.'

I took another small swig from my cup of lemonade and we walked across the green-carpeted floor to the small wooden counter in the far left-hand corner. Perdita was sitting on the counter, engaged in conversation with Wendy and Amy. I let Sheryl interrupt them, staring at Perdita's black boots as she tapped them together. The look they gave us made me realise that they weren't exactly excited about coming round to our homes.

'Gerald and I were just wondering . . . Do you want to sort out times for our visits?'

'Do we have to do it now?'

'I thought we were supposed to, yes,' Sheryl replied, standing her ground.

'Look, Sheryl,' said Perdita in a slow, careful voice, 'why don't you find a pen?'

'I've got one,' she said excitedly, 'I brought one in my bag.'

'OK,' Perdita said, 'go get your pen.'

Sheryl nodded and went out into the cloakroom that was adjacent to the rehearsal space. I stayed where I was, feeling embarrassed when they carried on talking as if I wasn't there. I looked round for someone else to speak to, but there was no one who wasn't already involved in conversation. So I had no choice but to wait for Sheryl to return with her pen.

When she did, Perdita ignored her for a moment and then said, 'Do you have any paper?'

Sheryl nodded.

'Rip off a piece for Gerald too.'

She did so.

'OK,' said Perdita, 'this is my phone number.'

She gave us her number. Sheryl wrote it down, then handed me the pen so I could do the same.

'So we should call you then?' Sheryl said hopefully.

'That's right, Sheryl.'

'What about you, Wendy?'

'Yeah, call me too.'

Wendy turned back to Perdita and started talking to her again. I could see Sheryl didn't appreciate the way we were being disregarded, and felt a secret admiration for her when she said stubbornly, 'And what's your number, Amy?'

'I'm in the book. My Dad's name is Eric.'

Perdita gave Amy a look of impressed admiration, as if recognising that she'd managed to treat us even more disdainfully than she had. I caught Sheryl's eye, and, trying to end our embarrassment, nodded in the direction of the opposite corner, where most of the other children were standing with Nicholas and the female production assistant. But she seemed unwilling to give in to the three girls' rudeness, and stayed where she was. I kept beside her, remembering my earlier hope that she might bludgeon them into accepting us.

Realising we weren't going to go away, Wendy looked at me and said, 'Do you like Madonna, Gerald?'

Perdita tried to cover her mouth as she exploded into sudden, shocked laughter. I didn't understand what was funny, but knew the joke was at my expense.

'Yes,' I replied, 'I do.'

'I thought as much.'

'Why?' I asked, confused. 'Don't you like Madonna?'

'Oh yeah,' said Wendy, 'I love Madonna. What about you, Amy?'

'Yeah, I like Madonna.'

'Sheryl?'

'Not really.'

I laughed then, thinking they would find it funny that Sheryl didn't like Madonna. But they remained straight-faced. I was the only one they wanted to laugh at. I didn't understand. They said they liked Madonna too, and the joke seemed more mysterious than the simple fact that I was a boy and they were girls. Besides, it was just as acceptable for boys to like Madonna as girls, wasn't it? I had to ask them, 'Are you laughing because I'm a boy and I like Madonna?'

'Oh no,' said Perdita, still chortling, 'it's not that.'

'But it is something?'

Wendy looked at me with an expression of mock-sympathy. 'No, Gerald, don't worry. It's nothing.'

35

Stan stared at me. I knew he knew something was up with me, but I also knew he didn't know what it was. The others were standing in a corner, looking uncomfortable. The only place to sit down was a long, padded black leather bench running down the left-hand side of the gallery, and there were already so many black-clad strangers on it that it looked like a negative exposure of polar bears on an iceberg. 'Cannonball' by the Breeders was playing over the speakers and I found it hard to resist the urge to dance. But first I had to get Stan involved in the evening's entertainment.

'What's up with you?'

'Nothing.' I moved from one foot to the other. 'Why?'

'You've got one of your weird faces on.'

I hated going through this process with Stan. It was so hard to get him to do anything, and I knew persuading him to give up his drugs virginity was going to be impossible. But I wanted him to join me. Partly because I thought it would be safer if we both did it, but also because now Darla had corrupted me, I was keen to do the same thing to him.

'Cannonball' segued into 'Sheela-Na-Gig'.

'Oh yeah,' I said, 'come on, Stan.'

He looked towards the others. Sally shrugged and followed me as I walked towards the small group of dancing strangers in the centre of the gallery. Stan, Darla and Tom came across too, leaving Lorraine and Mickey standing together by the wall. I felt at home on the dance floor, as the loose-limbed student shuffle is the only dance step I've ever mastered (apart from the Skim, and I don't think that counts as Reggel made it up).

'Stan . . .'

'Yeah?' he said, looking annoyed that I had distracted him from his extravagant dancing.

'I've taken something.'

'You don't say.'

'Would you like some too?'

'Some what?'

'Coke,' I said, feeling self-conscious.

'Gerald, I'm a teacher. Teachers aren't supposed to take drugs.'

'Oh, come on, Stan, that's no excuse. You're not even a real teacher. Most people who teach English as a Foreign Language only do it as an excuse to drink, take drugs and screw their way round the world. Just because we've decided to stay in England doesn't mean we should deny ourselves the odd adventure.'

Stan burst out laughing. 'You're so sad, Gerald.'

'Why?'

He didn't reply.

'Listen, Stan,' I said, putting my arm around him, 'I'm twenty-three and I've only ever had one girlfriend, I've never taken drugs – well, before tonight – and my students have more excitement in one weekend in England than I've had during my whole life here.'

Stan looked away. 'At least you've had a girlfriend.'

'You've had girlfriends.'

'I've had shags. I haven't had girlfriends. Not properly.'

'That's why you've got to do this. Look, remember when we were teenagers and you, me and Ellen used to go to clubs and the cinema and although we had a good time it never seemed as exciting for us as everyone else, because we kept ourselves in check, and . . .'

'If your sister could see you now.'

'Exactly. Just for one night, I want to be like her. And you know, in your heart, that you do too.'

Sally caught my shoulder as I stepped backwards. I turned to see what she wanted.

'What are you up to?'

'Nothing.'

She let me go and we continued dancing. The song changed. 'Been Caught Stealing'. How many times had I danced to this before? I remembered one club where this always came into the DJ's set at exactly midnight, destined to be followed week in week out by the Revolting Cocks squealing 'Beers, Steers & Queers', and then that Sheep on Drugs song about the Baby Jesus whose title I had never been interested enough to find out.

'All right,' said Stan, 'give it to me.'

'I don't have it. You have to come with me to Ronnie's office.'

He nodded. 'OK.'

36

No one said anything until we were out on the main road. Then Fuckpit whispered, 'You're a jammy bastard.'

'Why?'

'Going to Wendy's house.'

I didn't say anything, partly because I felt self-conscious in front of Jane, but also because I was unused to this sort of conversation.

Jane put on a serious tone. 'Don't be horrible to him.'

I looked at her, surprised she was sticking up for me, and beginning to worry that everyone saw me as an object of pity. I had felt a strong sense of reassurance when Nicholas had given us his lecture on how we were all in this together and shouldn't take the mickey out of anyone, but now I worried it would be even more embarrassing if the other kids kept stopping each other from picking on me. In fact, I felt more embarrassed by Jane than Fuckpit, wishing she hadn't intervened.

Wanting to recover some face, I said to him, 'Wendy's not that special.'

'What?' he squawked. 'Are you gay?'

'No. I just preferred Perdita.'

'*I just preferred Perdita*,' he repeated in a mincing tone. 'Bet she didn't prefer you.'

'You liked Sheryl, didn't you?' said Jane, sticking up for me again.

'No,' I replied. 'Sheryl's a dog.'

'Yes she is,' Fuckpit laughed. 'A dirty dog.'

'Sheryl's not a dog,' Jane intervened.

I wondered whether she realised that if she wasn't here we'd be calling her a dog as well. Fuckpit leaned forward and tapped on the sheet of clear Perspex that separated us from the driver.

'Yes?' he asked.

'Is it all right for us to smoke?'

The driver waved his hand at him, granting permission. Fuckpit smiled and took a packet of Benson and Hedges from his jacket pocket. He offered one to Jane. She hesitated, then took one. I did too, even though I'd never smoked before. But I'd watched Erica often enough to know how to do it, and I waited for Fuckpit to light my fag. After he did so, the atmosphere in the back of the car changed. As Fuckpit slouched deeper into his seat, Jane also became noticeably less tense. I'd found out earlier that she was also older than me, fifteen, although the fact that she seemed relatively straight and was much less attractive than Wendy and Perdita meant that I didn't feel nervous around her.

We smoked our cigarettes in silence for a while. Then the driver asked, 'Would you like the radio on?'

'Yeah,' said Fuckpit, 'that'd be all right.'

The driver nodded and turned on the radio. I recognised Mick Jagger's voice, but I didn't know what song he was singing. The Stones were very firmly one of my mum's bands. I found them impossible to take seriously, as every comedian on television had a Jagger impersonation. I looked across at Fuckpit, for some reason expecting him to respond to this music. But he barely seemed to notice it, dragging on his cigarette and staring out of the window.

My night had been so exciting that I knew I wouldn't be able to sleep when I got home. I wanted to tell Mum and Dad everything that had happened this evening. I knew Dad wouldn't like the sound of Nicholas. He'd call him a 'pseud', as he did anyone who had any kind of artistic or intellectual pretensions. Earlier I had been worried about how Mum would react when I told her I had to bring strangers into the family home, but maybe if I got the two of them together tonight and blasted them with my fresh enthusiasm, she wouldn't have the energy to argue.

After a while, I began to recognise my surroundings, and realised we were drawing closer to my home. We passed the rank of shops where Mrs Reggel had had her short-lived experience of paid employment, and the driver turned into my road. It was later than I thought – the dashboard clock said ten-thirty – and when we reached my house and there weren't any lights on, the driver assumed my family had gone to bed.

'No, no,' I told him, 'please wait. I'm not sure my family is home.'

'Is that a problem?'

'Yes. I don't have a key.'

37

I didn't know how to respond when Sally freaked out on me. It was much later in the evening and, somehow, I had persuaded Darla to hide with me behind the long black padded seat. We'd pulled some coats over us and were now necking in the same passionate way we'd been doing earlier in Ronnie's private room.

Stan had disappeared shortly after Darla had sorted him out. I wasn't worried, but Sally and the others had started to get anxious, and knew they were being left out of something significant. I'd kept them company for a while, and danced for over an hour, but now I was fed up and just wanted to snog Darla.

Sally pinched my shoulder hard as her arm came under the coats to hoist me out. In her next movement, she pulled back the other coat to reveal Darla, before turning back to me and shouting, 'You're making a fucking fool of yourself!'

There was genuine anger in her voice. I couldn't understand why she was so upset. OK, so I'd promised her I wouldn't do anything with Darla, but it wasn't really her business, when it came down to it.

'No, no,' I mumbled. 'It's OK, don't worry. It doesn't mean anything. We're having a night off.'

She was holding us both by our collars, as if we were a couple of naughty children she had to separate. I kept expecting her to release us, but her grip remained strong, and I realised her hands were trembling. I looked at Darla, wondering if she was as worried as I was. I don't know what I was afraid of – losing my friend, I suppose – but I suddenly felt incredibly guilty.

'A night off from what?'

'You know, responsibility. Anything that means anything. We're just having a nice friendly snog.'

'Darla,' said Sally, 'have you taken something?'

'Maybe,' she said sheepishly.

'Oh Jesus. The two of you deserve each other.'

She released us from her grip, and walked away. I looked at Darla, seeing her properly for the first time since we'd been left alone in Ronnie's private room. What we were doing suddenly seemed very wrong. It wasn't just the guilt. It had finally dawned on me that Sally had been keeping us apart for a reason, and that whatever she was trying to save us from was something that I should take seriously.

'What's wrong?' Darla asked me.

'I don't know. I feel bad.'

'Don't worry about Sally. She's just protective of me.'

'Do you need protecting?'

'Sally thinks so. Some other people do too.'

I nodded, wondering what I'd got myself into.

38

The driver was a decent man. It must have been a real pain for him still to be stuck with me at midnight. He'd parked in the road outside my house, rolled a cigarette, and turned the radio down so it wouldn't upset the neighbours. I always enjoyed talking to adults, and was doing my best to appear sociable, hoping to keep him here as long as possible.

'What's your name, by the way?'

'Shep.'

'Have you been doing this long?'

'Two years. Are you sure one of your neighbours couldn't look after you?'

'I don't expect they'll be long now,' I said hurriedly. 'I expect my dad's gone to the casino.'

He looked at me in the rear-view mirror. 'What about your mother?'

'I don't know. The thing that really puzzles me is my sister.'

'What about her?'

'Well, my mum doesn't like leaving her alone in the house. And she doesn't take her into work with her either. So she must be at a friend's house. But I can't imagine Mum not picking her up until midnight.'

'Maybe she's sleeping over somewhere.'

I laughed.

'What?' he asked.

'No one would let my sister stay in their house overnight.'

'Why not?'

'She's dangerous.'

This, as intended, caught his interest. He turned round

and faced me through the gap in the seats. 'What do you mean, dangerous?'

'Just not to be trusted. Around taps, matches, animals, other people . . .'

'She's accident prone.'

'Oh no. Malicious.'

Shep didn't reply. I watched him smoking his cigarette. I'd just begun to realise how uncomfortable he felt in his chauffeur's clothes, and asked him, 'Is this your only job?'

'Who are you? The taxman?'

'No,' I said, not really understanding, 'just curious.'

He looked out through the windscreen again. 'I work as a projectionist sometimes.'

'That sounds cool. Which cinema?'

'Not in the cinema. I work for a man who has his own screening room.'

'In his house?'

'Yeah. Now, listen, mate, I'm sorry, but I'm really going to have to go. You'll be all right waiting, won't you?'

It seemed easier to say yes. And part of me wanted to be left here alone. I often stayed up late, but rarely went outside after midnight. I was still at the age where the night seemed friendly and exciting, and just being in the dark was a thrill.

He rolled down his window. 'Bye then.'

Shep drove away. I walked down to the gate at the side of our house. We never locked this gate, and it allowed me into the back garden. Usually, everything here was overgrown and untidy, but last weekend Dad had done one of his extremely rare clean-up operations after complaints from neighbours on both sides. I rescued a garden chair that had fallen over and seated myself at our white metal table. So far I had yet to start worrying about my family, knowing that although something strange had happened, this wasn't unusual, and they were unlikely to be in any real danger.

Although I still believed this, I did wonder what was keeping them out so late. Dad had been known to stay at the casino until four in the morning if he was on a winning (or losing) streak, but Mum was usually reliable. I hoped something hadn't happened to her. For some reason it seemed more likely that she might be in trouble than my dad, and once I started worrying about that, being in the garden stopped being fun and I became desperate for my family to come home.

39

It wasn't until we were waiting for a taxi that we realised we'd lost Stan completely. I was the one who noticed as well, which was surprising given the emotional state I was in. Lorraine and Mickey seemed unconcerned by Stan's disappearance, but Tom was really worried, mainly, I suspected, because it meant he would have to get a separate taxi back on his own.

'We don't all have to get in the one cab,' said Lorraine. 'We could have three in each car.'

'That's not really the point,' I told her. 'We've lost our friend.'

'Oh, he'll be all right,' she said confidently, 'I'm sure he's just copped off with someone.'

We all considered this. Then started laughing.

'It's not impossible,' Mickey offered, 'it has happened before.'

Lorraine scowled. 'I don't know why you're all worrying. He can find his own way home. I mean, what do you think happened to him?'

'Gerald's worried because Darla gave him drugs,' Sally explained.

'What d'you mean, drugs? Who had drugs?'

'Ronnie gave me some coke,' said Darla, her tone apologetic.

'Who's Ronnie?' she demanded. 'And why didn't I get some?'

A black cab with its light on came down the road. Sally stuck her arm out. 'OK,' she said, 'how are we going to do this?'

Sally, Darla and I took the second cab, letting my housemates go on before us. It seemed fairer that way round, especially as I knew they wanted to bitch about me. Darla was still annoyed with Sally for interfering, and sat with her head slumped against the window. I lolled against the other door. Sally was perched between us, sitting up straight. I could tell she was feeling pleased with herself, and part of me wanted to rebel by dropping her at my house and staying on in the taxi with Darla.

Although I now understood why Sally wanted to stop Darla and me from getting involved with each other, I still wasn't sure of the exact nature of her friend's problem. I felt I had found out more about Sally than I had about Darla, and ungrateful as this sounds, I was now worried whether letting her look after me was a good idea. It struck me that one way of looking at this was that she was suffering from the same condition as me. I had wanted to rescue Ellen. Now Sally wanted to rescue me. And she was worried that I would want to rescue Darla.

Why? Because she wanted to save the pair of us.

40

I had been sitting in the garden for twenty minutes when I recognised the sound of my father's engine. Still worried about my mother, I ran across the garden and through the gate. There I saw my whole family, dressed up and climbing out of the car.

'Oh God, son,' said Dad, 'I'm so sorry. How long have you been waiting?'

'Hours. Where have you been?'

'We went to a Chinese restaurant at about seven o'clock. We thought we'd be back in plenty of time for you but then Erica told one of the waiters it was her birthday and they kept bringing her cakes and Chinese presents.'

'But it's not her birthday.'

'I know, but once she'd said it, it was too embarrassing to

tell them she'd lied. So we had to go along with the whole thing.'

I looked at my sister. She was wearing a purple ra-ra skirt with white knee-high socks and a white top. Her brown hair was pulled into plaits. In her left hand she carried a white plastic bag filled with booty. She didn't look like an evil genius, but that's what she was. Not wanting her to know she'd upset me, I turned away and waited for my father to unlock the door.

'Anyway, Gerald, how was it?' my mum asked, coming over and rubbing my shoulders. 'Did you do any filming?'

'No,' I replied, 'we won't be filming for ages.'

'What did you do then? Was it exciting?'

I was angry with my family, and didn't want to talk to them. The only reason I hadn't rushed upstairs to my bedroom was because then my sister would have won. But I wasn't going to share my feelings with them. It didn't matter that I needed my mum's permission to have the girls round to our house: if I tried to persuade her now I would get too angry if she put up any protests (as she inevitably would) and blow everything. No, if I played this properly, if I was just polite and went to bed, I could leave them feeling guilty, which would make Mum more likely to give in if I brought up the subject calmly some time tomorrow.

'Yeah,' I replied, 'it was exciting.'

Dad opened the door and we went inside. I could tell he was most embarrassed about not being there for me this evening (which seemed unusual, given his track record) and his whole body looked awkward inside his smart but, as always, oddly-coloured clothes. He knew Erica had hood-winked him, and hated taking sides with one of his children against the other.

'Well, come on, then,' he said, 'tell us all about it.'

'I'll tell you tomorrow, if that's OK. I'm really tired.'

'Of course. We'll talk about it then.'

'OK. Thanks. Goodnight.'

They stood there in silence as I went upstairs to my bedroom and closed the door. I waited a moment, congratulated myself on my self-control, and got into bed.

Part III

★

41

Last night I was talking to Sophie about whether she thought anyone would buy my book and she said people would always be interested in child stars. I asked her why she thought this and she said that as a nation we have always been fond of seeing people punished. And most of the time what we want to see people being punished for is celebrity and success. The most entertaining spectacle would be to watch Hollywood stars being beheaded. But as that isn't going to happen, the most we can hope for is to see them leading unhappy lives. Getting divorced and enduring miscarriages, going from blockbusters to a string of flops. And as the story of the average Hollywood celebrity is too long to get to the meaty bits, child stars offer us an acceptably accelerated version of what we want. Plus, as most people have unhappy childhoods, it seems even more annoying when someone achieves their success at an early age.

I didn't really agree with Sophie's analysis. I'm sure in broad terms it's psychologically accurate, but there has to be more to the phenomenon than sad *schadenfraude*. Personally, I think it's got to do with the continuing erosion of what constitutes celebrity. Everyone makes a big deal out of *Popstars* and *Big Brother*, but I think it can all be traced back to the Spice Girls who, like most people my age, got it from Madonna. Got what? The idea that you can will yourself to celebrity. All you need is front and the most mediocre talent and if you wish hard enough you can become a pop goddess. Or a film star. Or whatever you want. Did you see that documentary about Geri Halliwell, the one she made after she left the Spice Girls? I was truly spooked by that bit where she had a 'psychic shopping-list'.

If you missed it, basically what happened is that from an early age Geri would write lists of things she wanted and put the lists inside the back of a photograph frame. By doing this, she would magically make these things come true. By force of will, or the power of her unconscious mind, or whatever. Among her wishes was the desire to become friends with George Michael. The whole scene was uncannily similar to one in Nick Broomfield's documentary about Courtney Love. Courtney's wish-list included becoming friends with Michael Stipe instead of George Michael, but in many ways, as surrogate father/dream lover figures, those two are interchangeable. Both scenes revealed that for Courtney and Geri, there was never any possibility of failure. And it immediately became obvious that for both these women, desire completely outweighed talent. Now it may sound misogynistic to suggest that Geri and Courtney are without some artistic ability, and that's not what I'm saying, but put it this way: would you really care if you never heard their music again? Madonna seems slightly more talented, but that's becoming increasingly hard to remember.

How does child celebrity fit into all this? Well, it's the ultimate example of someone trying to get by without ability. I'm not talking about all of them (all of us): there's no denying that Charlotte Church has an incredible voice (so powerful that it seems obscene that it is hidden within her body), but take someone like Bonnie Langford. Watching her childhood performances you can see that she is powered solely by belief, and the only reason to keep watching is to marvel at how that never crumbles. The child celebrities we like are not the ones who underwent years of training, but the have-a-go types that remind us of ourselves. Karaoke has proved we can sing; all we want now is a chance to show we can act.

When I was a child and sleeping in an unfamiliar place, I would always wake feeling disorientated. I spoke to other people about this and found they experienced a similar sensation. But then, when I was about fifteen, it suddenly stopped. No matter where I was, I never felt that disconnection. Sleeping and waking were easy, even with a stranger in my bed. At least, until the night I snogged Darla.

The following morning I awoke screaming. Sally was terrified, especially when I shoved her onto the floor. In my dream things had been much the same as they'd been in real life, except for me feeling with absolute certainty that the fact that Ellen had left me would lead to my death.

It took me a long time to calm down. Sally waited for me to stop thrashing and then climbed back into my bed. As she did so, I remembered what had happened when we got home last night. We had had a terrible argument, with me demanding to know what gave Sally the right to interfere in my life. She had listened to all my crap, and then, when I had stopped ranting, hugged me as hard as she could. I hugged her back and tried to kiss her. She turned away. Upset by the rejection, I had remained silent until she fell asleep. I knew it was partly guilt about the way I had treated her that had prompted my nightmares, and also that I had some apologising to do.

'God,' I said, 'I bet you regret agreeing to look after me.'

'A bit,' she smiled.

'There's only one thing I don't understand.'

'What's that?'

'Why aren't you worried about Darla?'

'I am worried about Darla.'

'But isn't it a really big deal?'

'What?'

'That guy sleeping with her sister. I mean, if she's got all the problems you say she has, then surely that's the sort of thing that's going to drive her over the edge.'

She shook her head. 'It's happened before. Several times.'

'So when you said, "Anyone we know?" and she said, "How did you guess?" you were both talking about her sister?'

'Exactly. In fact, when a guy goes off with her sister it's usually a good thing.'

'I don't understand this at all.'

'Make me some breakfast and I'll explain.'

'We don't have any food, remember?'

'Oh God. Gerald, you really do have to sort yourself out.'

'I will do. We can go to the supermarket together this afternoon. The only thing is, you have to be aware that anything we might buy is likely to be stolen by the others. But for breakfast, on a Sunday, I usually go to the greasy spoon around the corner.'

'Then that'll have to do. Can I go for a wash without being electrocuted?'

'I think so. If you use the bathroom instead of the shower room.'

She nodded. 'OK.'

42

Saturday was a day of argument. I had actually underestimated my mother's response. She was so horrified by the idea of letting strangers into our home – and not only that, but also having to talk to them – that she insisted I drop out of the programme immediately. If my father hadn't been present, that would have been the end of my acting career right there and then.

'Hang on, Jenny, you can't make him do that.'

'Why not?'

'He's had his teeth done.'

'So? He needed his teeth fixed anyway. If the TV company want us to reimburse them for the money they've spent we can easily get it together.'

'It's not about the money. You weren't there. You didn't see what the boy went through.'

'So you're saying that you want to let strangers into our home? You want to sit there and let *strangers* grill you about your private life?'

He shrugged. 'They're only children.'

'Girls,' I added.

'What difference does that make?'

'Well,' I said, 'they won't cause trouble. And besides, they're not like normal girls. Everyone involved with this programme is really mature.'

My mother wasn't having it. She told me on Monday she would phone the television company and tell them I could no longer be involved with their programme. I was devastated, screaming at her and running upstairs to my room. Three sides of *Sign o' the Times* later, Dad knocked on my penthouse door. I went down my separate staircase and let him in.

'All right?' he asked.

'Yeah.'

'This going round to other people's houses business, when's that supposed to start?'

'Tomorrow.'

'You told people they could come round here tomorrow?' he asked, surprised.

I shook my head. 'No. I'm supposed to be going to a girl's house.'

'Well, look, I'll take you, OK? I'm still not sure if I'll be able to change your mother's mind, but maybe when she calls the television company they'll be able to come up with an alternative arrangement.'

I smiled. 'OK. Thanks, Dad.'

43

'There are a lot of disturbed men out there.'

Sally's breakfast was twice the size of mine, so big they had to bring it on a special plate. I ate a mouthful of dry toast and waited for her to continue.

'And Darla has a habit of finding them. I'm not her mother, I can't stop her having boyfriends. When she picks someone up and they end up dumping her for her sister, it's usually a relief. Because then I know that the main thing that's wrong with them is that they like to sleep around.'

'Still,' I said, 'that's a pretty big betrayal. And I don't think it's as normal as you're making out.'

'OK, Gerald, how do you think these men meet Darla's sister?'

'I don't know. She doesn't live with you?'

'No.'

'Maybe she visits a lot.'

Sally gave me a long look. 'Darla sets it up.'

'Right. So what you're saying is that Darla wants these men to sleep with her sister?'

'Do you know the Chinese Zodiac?'

'I know my sign.'

'But you don't know the characteristics of the other animals?'

'Not really.' I shrugged. 'Some of them.'

'Well, Darla's sister is a rabbit. Or a hare, whatever it is. And she takes her attributes very seriously. The big thing about being a rabbit is that you're very shy, and that . . .'

'Ellen's a rabbit,' I said suddenly, interrupting her.

'OK . . . They rely on other people for social interaction. Darla's sister is so shy that if it wasn't for her family and her very few friends, she'd never get to meet anyone.'

'So you're saying Darla pimps for her sister?'

'No, it's not as straightforward as that. But if Darla has someone she's really interested in, let's just say she won't introduce them to her sister.'

I decided to be difficult. 'But she'd have to, eventually, wouldn't she? I mean, at a family gathering or something.'

'Yes, OK, but she'd warn her sister not to go for them. The point is, they have a sort of arrangement.'

I finished my toast and stared at my plate. Although I had nowhere near as much food as Sally, I couldn't help feeling intimidated by the size of my breakfast, especially as my stomach still felt fragile after the indulgence of the night before. I sliced myself a small square of bacon and said, 'OK. It sounds strange, but I think I understand. But what happens with the men she doesn't introduce to her sister?'

'Trouble, mostly. You'd really be amazed at the depths of

perversity in even the most normal-seeming men. And something inside Darla gets off on that. In fact, once she finds a weirdo she locks onto him so tight that it . . . Well, it always ends messily.'

It was at this point that I remembered how I fitted into the story.

'So you think I'm a pervert?'

'What?'

'The kind of man that Darla needs to be kept away from?'

'No,' she said carefully, 'you fit into a different category.'

'Which is?'

'You've got a Marilyn complex, Gerald. There's no point in denying it.'

'I don't deny it. I don't even know what it is.'

'You like rescuing women. You think you can heal them.'

'Ah,' I said, 'I wondered when we'd get to this.'

'Come on, Gerald, you've told me this yourself. And every time you even heard about a girl having problems at university you were straight round to their room ready to lend a sympathetic ear. Besides, I can't imagine any other man being prepared to nurse his girlfriend for eight years.'

'Three things, OK? First, I didn't nurse Ellen. Second, there's nothing wrong with helping people. And third, what about you?'

'What about me?'

'You've got a much stronger Marilyn complex.'

'Women don't have Marilyn complexes, Gerald.'

'Well, whatever the female equivalent is. You're just as bad. I mean, you're protecting Darla, looking after me.'

'Yes, Gerald, but I don't fancy you and Darla. It's not a sex thing.'

'It's not?' I said, feigning a crestfallen expression.

'You know it's not. I'm just trying to be a good friend.'

'OK, I accept that. But going back to what you said about Darla, why would it be such a disaster if she and I had a little fling? You've already told me that she can have short-term affairs without any psychological damage. Then when she gets fed up of me she can pass me on to her sister. Is her sister pretty?'

'Gorgeous. But trust me, if you got involved with Darla it would not be a little fling. It would be another disastrous eight-year relationship.'

'Sally, I'm very grateful for everything you've done for me, but can you please stop being so rude about my relationship with Ellen? This is a very fresh wound you're making fun of.'

Sally laid down her cutlery. 'All right, fair enough. But I can't help it if I don't think you two would be good for each other. And, besides, this is the first single woman you've met since Ellen left you. Why don't you try waiting just a few more days before starting something new?'

I didn't reply. We finished our breakfasts and then Sally told me that she wanted to go home and check on Darla. I told her she had to be back by five if she still wanted us to visit the supermarket. She kissed me goodbye and I walked back to my house, mulling over the conversation. I realise that for a man who doesn't see much action I spend a lot of time worrying about women, but I can't help it. I knew Sally was right, and that there was something about me that was attracted to women in trouble. I also knew that although I was eager to have a one-night stand, just to prove I could do it, it would, ultimately, be impossible to do that with Darla. Not just because she was Sally's friend, or because Sally thought it was a bad idea, but also because Darla did have that same thing Ellen did, the quality that would make me want to make her happy so she would stay with me.

Before I could stop myself, I had started thinking about Ellen. It was Sally's fault, making that comment about rabbits and the Chinese Zodiac. Although as far as I knew, Ellen wasn't that interested in astrology, Chinese or otherwise, she did have a thing for rabbits.

I don't remember if she'd actually had one as a child or just always wanted one, but every time we passed a pet shop she stepped in to look at them. She had a fluffy toy rabbit she'd owned since she was a child, and was always having complicated dreams about this innocent animal. I had once made the mistake of taking her to see *Celia*, the Australian film by Ann Turner, having seen a trailer which made me think that part of the movie might address the friendship between a girl and her rabbit. The scene where Celia carries home her dead, waterlogged rabbit distressed her so much that we were asked to leave the cinema.

As well as liking rabbits, Ellen had other similar traits to Darla's sister. She wasn't shy, as such, but she did have a strong sense of reserve, which meant that she didn't have many friends she'd made herself, tending instead to build up relationships slowly with friends of mine, or my sister's. This tendency had made me do something bad, something I didn't tell you or Darla in my earlier accounts of my break-up. After our conversation, the one where she'd told me that she'd started fancying other men and I pretended not to care, I had spat one last spiteful remark, 'Just make sure you stay away from my friends.'

This had shocked her, as I'd intended. If she thought our break-up was going to be easy, she was mistaken. I wanted to remove all trace of her from my life.

44

Dad didn't tell Mum he was taking me to Sheryl's. Instead he pretended we were going to the cinema. This, of course, made Erica desperate to come with us, even more so when Dad said she couldn't come because he was going to sneak me into a film I was too young to see. But Mum managed to persuade Erica that she definitely wouldn't get in, and that it would be much more fun for her to stay home and watch television with her than wait for hours in Dad's car.

My father had taken a surprising degree of interest in my trip to Sheryl's, asking me several times exactly what Nicholas Pennington had instructed us to do. To my surprise, he didn't think the man sounded like a pseud after all, and said that he thought the programme seemed a more interesting exercise than he had originally imagined.

'But what about Mum?'

'Never mind Mum. I can't get anywhere with her, but I doubt the TV company are going to let her pull you out of the show.'

'How do you know?'

'I don't know. But let's just wait and see.'

Then he went into his bedroom and unlocked the large wooden box that he kept with the cacti and broken accordions in the space beneath his bed. I had never seen him open the box before. Its contents were a source of considerable interest to Erica and me, and we had spent several afternoons together attempting to pick its lock. This was one of only two activities my sister and I could pursue harmoniously, the other being searching the insides of the downstairs sofa for dropped change. Before I could see what else was in the box, my father had pulled out a Dictaphone. He waited until I came across and then handed it to me.

'If you're going to do this, you should do it properly.'

Although I was grateful for his interest and the present, at that age I rarely accepted anything from anyone without an argument. So I said, 'Isn't that cheating? Nicholas said the act of recording was as important as the information itself.'

'That's why I'm giving you the Dictaphone.'

'But he said we had to record. Ourselves. He said he wanted us to develop listening and interpretation skills. To understand our fellow actors by hearing their stories and thinking about the way they tell them.'

'OK, Gerald, but why not take this anyway? Record your conversation, and if you can get by without playing the tape, fine. If not, you have it as back-up.'

His open face made me reluctant to refuse his offer, even though I didn't really want to take the Dictaphone and doubted it would come in useful. I knew it would make the others feel awkward, and that they would either worry they ought to have one too, or think I was showing off.

I hid the Dictaphone under my jumper and went downstairs. I said goodbye to Mum and Erica and followed Dad out into the car. He seemed pleased that I now had a secret too, as if it made it even less likely that I would tell Mum about his mistress. I climbed into the passenger seat, and sat there feeling guilty while I waited for him to set off.

45

My housemates were waiting for me.

'What's wrong?' I asked, as they led me into the lounge.

'Stan still hasn't come home,' Tom explained.

'Oh,' I said, surprised. 'Well, I still don't think we should worry yet. If he did go home with someone, he's probably still with them.'

'Unlikely,' said Lorraine, as if she was the detective conducting this investigation. She was wearing a lumberjack shirt over a grey top, grey leggings, and a pair of tiger-stripe slippers. She knew how to dress down.

'Why's it unlikely? Just 'cause you always kick your one-nighters out as soon as they wake up doesn't mean . . .'

'What are we going to tell his parents?' said Tom, his voice taking on the slightly effeminate, camp tone it usually did when he was worried.

'Why do we have to tell his parents anything?'

'They're going to phone. They always phone on Sunday.'

'So? The phone's in my room. I'll deal with it. Or better still, I'll get Sally to talk to them. They'll be really thrown by a stranger in the house and it'll distract them into not worrying.'

Everyone turned to stare at me. I realised from their expressions that they thought I was to blame for all this. We were quite a conservative household really, and I knew I was the one acting out of character. I also knew that usually I would be on their side. The obvious answer was to demonise Sally, but I was still anxious not to let the others drive her out of our house.

'All right,' I said, 'I can see you're all upset, but I really think you're overreacting.'

'Does he know?' Tom asked Mickey.

'Know what?'

'It's happened before.'

46

My Dad came up to the door with me. The woman who opened it was immediately recognisable as Sheryl's mother. Sheryl stood a short distance behind her, observing us. I've always been freaked out by family resemblance. And I think it's worse when you're dealing with parents and youngish children, as it's likely that the adult will still be dressing their offspring, and probably according to their own taste. I'm sure my Dad and I were an equally unappetising vision, our potentially winning dark looks rendered useless by our clownish attire, but seeing Sheryl with her mother made me feel sorry for the pair of them.

'OK,' said Dad, 'when shall I pick him up?'

'I don't know,' she replied. 'Has he told you what they have to do?'

He nodded, and suggested, 'Three hours? Will that be long enough?'

She turned to Sheryl. 'Angel, what do you think? Is three hours enough?'

She smiled. 'Yes, Mum.'

'Right,' said my Dad, checking his watch, 'that should work out fine.' He turned round and walked back to his car. I went inside with Sheryl and her mother. As I did so, a bearded man came hurtling down the stairs, so fast that he only just managed to stop himself from crashing into me. He was wearing a dark blue tracksuit and a pair of trainers.

'Hi, Gerald,' he said brightly, 'I'm Mike. Sheryl's Dad.'

I nodded, and gave a vague half-smile.

'OK,' he said, 'where do you want us?'

Sheryl's mother could see I felt awkward. 'Why don't we all sit down at the table in the lounge?'

'Um . . .'

'Yes, Gerald?'

'It's just . . . I thought I'd talk to Sheryl alone first.'

Mike rubbed his hands together. 'Yes, Gerald, don't worry, you'll get your chance to talk to Sheryl. But Angela and I have to go out in half an hour, so we thought you could talk to us all together first, and then we'll leave you to do the in-depth stuff on your own.'

I stared at him, amazed. I had assumed Sheryl's parents would be stricter than mine, yet here they were, prepared not only to leave me alone in their house with their daughter, but also to sit and answer my questions. I thought of what my mother had said to my father – *'So you're saying you want to let strangers into our home? You want to sit there and let strangers grill you about your private life?'* – and it suddenly sounded much more sinister than it had at the time. What did my mother have to hide? I knew my father had a secret, but more than ever I couldn't understand Mum's overwhelming desire for privacy.

As I said earlier, you don't think about the stuff that seems normal, but now I was reflecting on it, there were lots of other events in my past that suddenly seemed strange. My mother's parents, for example, wouldn't let my father, or me and my sister, into their house. The explanation they offered was that their house was so messy they were ashamed for us to see it, but surely that can't have been the whole explanation? And yet my sister and I had never wondered about this, happily sitting with my father in their garden, drinking lemonade and waiting for Mum to be done. Was there another, more complicated, reason my mother was so nervous about letting people into our house? It surely couldn't only be because it was messy? But what did she have to hide? Apart from an unhappy marriage.

The Casements walked through their house to the lounge and sat at a large, glass-topped table. I followed, still feeling nervous, but not for the reasons I'd anticipated. Sheryl had said her father worked in a factory, and after hearing my father's horror stories about his few years of manual labour, I had anticipated that he would be dismissive of this enterprise and, possibly, aggressive towards me.

I took the Dictaphone out of my pocket, now feeling pleased that I had brought it with me. It seemed just the distraction I needed at this moment, buying me time to recover myself. I put it on the table and asked, 'You don't mind if I record this, do you?'

'No,' said Mike, 'we don't mind at all. In fact, it's a very good idea.'

I nodded and pressed Record. Then I said to Mike, 'Sheryl said you work in a factory.'

'That's right,' he told me. 'I'm a shop steward.'

'OK.'

'Do you know what that is?'

'Yes,' I lied.

'Do you?'

'Yes.'

'Then you are clever.' He stared at me. 'Don't you think you should check whether this thing of yours is recording?'

'It is recording. The red light is on.'

'But you want to make sure it's picking up our voices, don't you?' he asked, oddly insistent.

'OK.' I picked up the Dictaphone, rewound it, and pressed Play. But either I hadn't rewound it fully or the button wasn't working properly because after about a second of our recorded conversation the words were replaced by a deep rhythmic grunting. Embarrassed, I immediately switched it off. Mike and Angela were staring at me.

'Well, that didn't sound like us,' said Angela, allowing herself a giggle.

Her husband looked at her. I tried Rewind again, hoping to distract them. This time I could see the reels going round, and when I pressed Play it was Mike's voice on the tape. I waited until I heard myself saying 'OK', then immediately snapped it off. Then I pressed Record, attempting to resume the conversation as if nothing had happened.

'Mike, how did you and Angela first meet?'

'Well,' he said, looking at his wife, 'it was at a protest meeting. A group of rich people were trying to block the building of a comprehensive school in their area. I went along, even though at that time I didn't have any children – I was just doing my civic duty – and the woman running the meeting . . .'

'Was me,' Angela said, smiling. 'I didn't have any kids either. But it was the principle of the thing that upset me.'

They smiled at each other, and I felt slightly shocked, amazed to see a couple backing each other up instead of arguing. I couldn't imagine my parents agreeing on anything, and neither of them could tell the story about how they first met without wincing about everything that had come afterwards. I could tell Sheryl's parents embarrassed her, but I thought she was lucky, even if they did seem overbearing. I wouldn't want Mike or Angela for my parents, but at least they believed in aiding good causes, and in each other.

47

I sat down. Mickey was the quietest member of our household, but he was also the one who held us together in times of crisis. I would probably describe his influence as maternal, if that didn't sound so strange. He knew everything about the private lives of our household, mainly because, for all his peculiarities, there was something about him that encouraged confession. Probably, I suppose, because he was so quiet.

'Go on then,' I said, 'tell me what happened.'

'It was halfway through the first term of the second year . . .'

'Hang on. What's this story about?'

'A relationship Stan had.'

'Stan doesn't have relationships.'

'Yes he does. He just doesn't talk to you about his love life because you always make fun of him.'

'No, he told me last night. He said he'd had shags, but not a proper relationship.'

'This wasn't really a relationship,' Tom told me, 'but it's a story about a girl.'

'OK, Mickey, carry on.'

'There was a girl he'd fancied all term. It wasn't one of those unrequited love things, she was generally interested in him, but she was a first-year and quite straight. Religious.'

'We didn't take it seriously,' Tom interrupted, 'because there were people – girls – that we were both interested in as well, but this was the term of the Top Trumps Scandal, and we'd been ostracised by pretty much everyone in the university.'

'What was the Top Trumps Scandal?'

Mickey allowed himself a sneaky smile. This was clearly the part of the story he looked forward to telling.

'We spent three weeks making a ginormous set of trump cards featuring students from the university. It was supposed to be secret, but we were so proud of them that . . . well, other people found out.'

'I don't understand.'

Tom stood up and went over to one of the old lady's cupboards, which was much less well-made than the furniture in the upstairs section of the house. He took out a set of what looked like almost five hundred small cards wrapped in cellophane and brought them across to me. I unwrapped a small section and pulled out a handful of cards. The first one I looked at had an astonishingly intricate drawing of a woman in blue biro. Underneath the illustration, they had pasted on a small square of paper on which was typed:

```
Looks: 9
Promiscuity: 2
Intelligence: 6
Special Ability: Gymnastics
```

I flicked through a few more cards. They all had intricate

blue biro drawings, and similar lists of attributes. How could three people devote so much energy to such a pointless exercise? I could just picture them sitting together in one of their rooms (probably Mickey's) guffawing with laughter as they gave some nerdy guy a Promiscuity Rating of ten. What struck me as most disturbing was that they'd clearly taken this game seriously. It frightened me to think of one of them (again, probably Mickey) doing all these line drawings. And they weren't caricatures either, but looked so realistic that I assumed that he must have done them from some sort of annual or yearbook.

'So why were people angry?' I asked.

'Because they didn't agree with their ratings, of course. The people we'd given high marks for looks wanted high marks for intelligence, and vice versa. But the promiscuity rating was the one that got us into most trouble.'

'And you thought this woman wouldn't be interested in Stan because you'd given her a bad card?'

'No. She was fairly innocuous so we hadn't been rude about her. But the rest of our year had been so angry that they started all these nasty rumours and jokes about us. They said we all slept in the same bed together and were afraid of women.'

'Which is true,' observed Lorraine.

'Just because they're scared of you doesn't mean they're scared of women,' I told her. 'You are scary.' She kicked me.

'So no girl would go near us. But that didn't stop us encouraging Stan. We thought if he could make friends with this girl, it might be the first step in getting people to stop hating us. And there was this big party, to celebrate term being half over and all that. Things were going well for Stan and this girl, they'd danced together and she'd been amused rather than horrified by his comedy movements. Stan wasn't really looking for much, he knew she was religious, but he'd also heard that she'd had a couple of snogs with other guys in her year. That was all he was after. And from the body language between those two, it seemed likely it would happen before the end of the evening.'

Mickey looked around, clearly beginning to feel self-conscious. The rest of us had stopped interrupting him and I could tell he was embarrassed, although I wasn't sure whether this was because he was aware the others already knew this story, or because he felt awkward about betraying his friend's confidence.

'Anyway, some time in the evening, the two of them slipped away. Tom and I had got into an argument with some maths students about sit-coms and we didn't notice them go. We stayed at the party until quite late and then went for kebabs and when we got back to our floor – the three of us all had rooms next to each other . . .'

'Hence the rumour.'

'What?'

'That you all slept together in the same bed.'

'Right. Anyway, when we got back we could hear these terrible screams coming from Stan's room. We didn't really know what to do . . .'

'So I went up to the door,' Tom took over, 'and it was like a big, thick, like fire door or something, but it was just about possible to hear through it. The girl inside, it was the girl Stan had been talking to at the party, and she was really upset. I couldn't really understand what she was saying, but as she began to calm down, I realised Stan wasn't inside with her and she was locked in.'

'But that didn't make sense,' Mickey resumed, 'because the locks in the halls of residence could all be opened from the inside. Tom assumed that the girl had got a bit mixed up with all her emotion and tried to remind her that all she had to do was turn the lock. That was when the girl said something about nails and we both noticed all these bits of metal or whatever coming out through the door and going into the frame.'

'He'd nailed the door shut?' I asked, astonished. 'Hang on, guys, I may be gullible, but there are limits. None of this really happened, did it? Stan's not missing. He's upstairs eating pickled onions.'

Lorraine laughed. 'You're freaked out, aren't you? You

don't realise how weird these guys really are. They haven't even got to the good part yet. Go on, Mickey, tell him the rest of it.'

'OK. As you can imagine, having three rooms next to each other allowed us to get up to all sorts of mischief. Our favourite game was when one of us was being moody or wanted privacy, the other two would get out through our window and walk across the ledge to their room to make faces or spy on them through the window.'

Tom had started giggling. 'So I got through Mickey's window. And it wasn't as if it was totally terrifying ... It was only one floor up, but it was a bit dangerous. And I went across the ledge to Stan's room and got the girl to open the window from the inside and she put her arm around me, and I helped her across the two window-ledges and back into Mickey's room. She was still really distressed ... Mickey, do you remember the girl's name?'

'No.' He thought for a minute. 'Was it Hannah?'

'That's right. Hannah. So, she was still upset, but Mickey smoothed things out with his Mum routine.'

Mickey smiled, revealing his thin teeth. 'I made her a cup of tea.'

'After we'd given her a while to calm down, she told us what had happened. She and Stan had gone up to his room, and he'd been really drunk – I suppose when he realised his luck was in he stopped worrying about staying sober and really let loose – and they still hadn't snogged or anything, but it was going to happen, they were joking about it, when Stan started going on about trapping her in his room so she'd sleep with him . . .' Tom stopped, noticing that Mickey was looking away. 'This is right, isn't it?'

Mickey nodded. He didn't seem to mind that Tom had taken over the story, and sat down with Lorraine.

'And the weird thing was that the girl actually seemed really normal. The rumours had obviously been mean-spirited and she said she'd liked Stan back and been interested in him too. But then Stan started getting more and more exaggerated in his movements. She knew he was really only joking, but couldn't get him to calm down. That was when he got out the hammer . . .'

'And she flipped?' I guessed.

'No, even then she wasn't that bothered. She knew Stan had a reputation for being strange, and his behaviour, while weird, still seemed acceptably studenty, in a way . . .'

'I can't understand this.'

'I know,' he said impatiently, 'but she knew about what we got up to, the Trump Cards, the Break-the-Lift parties.'

'I don't even want to ask.'

'Jumping up and down in the lift until it breaks,' Mickey quickly explained. 'We did it every week for a year.'

'And she liked it. She liked us. I know you think we're just a bunch of nerds . . .'

'You said it,' Lorraine laughed.

'But some girls think that's cool. They admire our playful, clever, anti-authoritarian nature.'

'Jumping up and down in a lift?' I asked. 'That's what they admire you for?'

'For being different. Providing an alternative.'

'OK,' I said. 'Be that as it may, what did Stan do to upset the girl?'

'We don't know.'

'You don't know?'

'No. She wouldn't tell us. It could well have been her upsetting him. But whatever happened, ten minutes later, Stan jumped out of the window.'

'I thought you said it was high up.'

'Only one storey.'

'So he ran off and left the girl?'

'Precisely.'

'When did he come back?'

'Not until the end of term.'

'Did he say where he'd been?'

'Wait,' said Lorraine, 'you're missing a bit.'

'I'm getting to that,' Tom said. 'The thing is, Gerald, when he showed up, he was in a bit of a state.'

'What sort of state?'

They traded glances. 'We don't know what happened to him. He looked like he'd been sleeping rough, he was wearing the same clothes that he'd had on when he'd run away, and . . . Well, there was something wrong with him.'

'What?'

'He was scary,' Tom said quietly. 'It wasn't just that he pretended nothing had happened, it was more that he seemed like he'd had some strange, profound experience that he didn't want – or didn't know how – to share with us.'

'Did he talk to the girl again?'

'No. Not that term.'

Mickey sat up. 'It was end of term when he came back. There was only another day or so before we all went home, and then when we all came back everything was forgotten. Nothing happened with Stan and Hannah afterwards. There was no question of them getting into a proper relationship, and they weren't really friends, but they didn't seem awkward with each other. They could talk in the bar. And Stan was totally normal again.'

'Well, then, there you go,' I said. 'Yes, I accept that the situation you've described is peculiar, and I had no idea Stan was capable of being quite so weird, but it sounds like just a slightly more serious than usual studenty flip-out. Work pressure, girls, getting turned down by someone he really liked. I can see how that would upset him. There were loads of people at my university who went a bit strange, became alcoholics or speed-freaks and started spending every night in their rooms with a strobe-light turned up to epilepsy-level.'

'Gerald . . .' said Mickey gently.

I ignored him, carrying on. 'And if Stan was sleeping rough, no wonder he seemed strange when he came back . . . He was probably suffering from malnutrition, or tiredness, or maybe he just went weird from not talking to other people for a while.'

The three of them were staring at me. I knew I had become defensive, but I wasn't sure why. I did think Stan was likely to be OK, wherever he was, and couldn't see any real reason why he might have run away this time. All my life I had been surrounded by people whose behaviour was a little bit odd, from my sister onwards, and I had learnt how to deal with extremes of emotion. This was really turning into a morning for finding out about people. First Darla, now Stan. I did feel a little bit betrayed that Stan hadn't told me this tale himself, but at least hearing it from Tom and Mickey made me feel closer to them.

'Yeah,' said Mickey, 'what you're saying makes sense. Except there is one last bit of the story. During the holidays, Tom and I both got a phone call from Stan's dad. He told us that he knew what had happened to Stan, and although it wasn't a big deal, he said that Stan had had problems before and made us promise that if anything like this ever happened again, we had to get in contact with him immediately.'

I laughed, which startled them. 'Stan's got problems, all right, but no worse than you lot. You know he used to wear a newspaper suit to school?'

They stared at me, not really seeing my point. I couldn't blame them. 'What I'm saying is, he was strange, so people picked on him. But he didn't have a harder time than you two, I'm sure. Or me, for that matter. Stan's dad was probably just being overprotective. He's older, he doesn't know what happens to people at university.'

'So you're saying we shouldn't tell him?'

'I'm saying what I said at the beginning, that I'll handle it. And I promise you that you're worrying over nothing. Trust me. Stan'll be back any minute.'

48

Sheryl's parents were much more interested in answering questions than I was in asking them. Every response turned into an anecdote, usually ending with a joke I didn't understand. As they talked, I thought more about my own family than I did about the people in front of me. I had always assumed we didn't have that many friends because my parents were slightly strange, but this trio were much weirder (although not as scary as my sister), and yet from the sound of their stories they were friends with half of Carshalton. After half an hour, I stopped the tape.

'What's wrong?' Mike asked.

'It's three-thirty. You said you had to go out.'

'Oh,' said Angela, 'we're only going to my aunt's. There's no hurry. If you've got more questions . . .'

'Yeah,' said Mike, 'we were just getting started.'

Mike was opinionated. The kind of man who would frighten my father, and irritated me. He was like a teacher, always trying to draw you into conversations all the time. Suddenly, this exercise was beginning to feel more like a school project than something fun.

'Can I have a drink, please?' I asked Angela, hoping to distract them.

'Of course,' she replied. 'What would you like? Is orange squash OK?'

I nodded. 'Thanks.'

Angela got up and went to the kitchen. Mike picked up the Dictaphone and pressed Record. 'Come on then, ask me more questions.'

I really couldn't think of anything else I wanted to ask him. I didn't really understand what a shop steward was, but every time he started explaining I understood even less. Like most people who enjoy talking, he was extremely boring. I could tell he thought it was admirable to address children as if they were adults, but it didn't impress me. Realising I wasn't going to ask him anything else, he started talking anyway, but all I heard was a sound like the teacher makes in *Charlie Brown*. I noticed Sheryl looking at her mother over my shoulder.

'Maybe we should set off,' Angela said to Mike. 'She'll be waiting for us.'

Mike looked at her, then back at me. 'OK, I suppose you're right. Seeing as the boy seems to have run out of things to ask.'

His face was disappointed as he got up from the table.

Sheryl, however, smiled at me and seemed pleased that her parents were going. Angela put a blue plastic beaker full of orange squash down on the table in front of me. I sipped from it and watched Mike as he went out into the hallway to get his coat.

'Now,' said Angela, 'you two will be all right, won't you?'

Sheryl nodded. 'We'll just sit here and talk.'

'I'm sure we'll be back before Gerald's dad comes, but if not, make sure you invite him in for a cup of coffee.'

'Yes, Mum.'

Angela and Mike got ready and left the house. After a moment, Sheryl stood up and went to the window. As soon as she was sure her parents had gone, she came back and asked me, 'What was that noise on your tape?'

'I don't know.'

'Didn't you record it?'

'No.'

'Who did?'

I looked away. 'My dad.'

'Let's listen to it again.'

'We can't. Your dad talked all over that side of the tape.'

'What about the other side? Play the other side.'

I looked at Sheryl. She was dressed in slightly less ugly clothes today. Her grey pinafore might have been dowdy, but at least she looked like a girl. Although her dry hair and blotchy face still stopped me from feeling comfortable in her presence.

'I don't want to. You do it.'

I stood up.

'Where are you going?' she asked.

I went upstairs to their toilet. It was a normal suburban bathroom, with carpet on the floor, the way I liked it. I went to the toilet, then sat on the edge of the bath. I could guess what was on the tape. Sort of. I knew that noise was my dad, and that it had something to do with sex. I felt angry that he had put me in such an embarrassing situation, and didn't know how to stop Sheryl making a big deal out of it. I considered staying in the bathroom until Dad came to pick me up, but didn't want to act like a baby in front of Sheryl. Instead, I washed my hands and left the bathroom.

Sheryl was standing on the landing, holding the Dictaphone against her ear.

'Can you hear anything?'

'It sounds like someone arguing. But they're far away.'

'Give it to me.'

She hesitated, then handed it across. The tape was still playing, turned up to full volume. There were voices, but they were indistinct. I pressed the Dictaphone to my own ear. The woman wasn't my mother. I heard her mentioning my name, and my sister's, but couldn't make out the rest of the sentence.

I had never met my father's mistress. I'd seen her face once or twice, a flash at the window when Dad pulled up outside her house. It seems strange that I knew about the peculiarities of adults before I knew about the mechanics of sex. I had yet to discover masturbation, had never seen a woman's (or a girl's) genitals, not properly. But I already knew that there were strange things that happened between couples, unknown events that could drive a father to another woman's door.

'Don't worry,' said Sheryl, 'my parents argue too.'

I didn't reply.

'I'm not supposed to say that. But they do. They argue a lot.'

I turned off the Dictaphone. 'How do you think they want us to do this?'

'What?'

'The finding out about each other. Should I just write a list of stuff down about you and your parents?'

'Nicholas said we should think about the details that would change the person from a stranger into someone we like.'

'What do you like about your parents?'

She shifted uncomfortably. 'I don't just like my parents. I love them.'

'I know that. But what do you like about them?'

'Everything. They're my parents.'

'OK, Sheryl, I understand that. But is there something special about them?'

'They're special to me. But to other people too.'

'Why?'

'My dad helps people. People admire him. He has lots of friends where he works.'

'What about your mum?'

'She's very organised.'

Sheryl was biting her bottom lip. She seemed to have forgotten about the recording on the Dictaphone.

'Do you have any friends, Sheryl?'

'Yes,' she said, her voice too quick and eager.

'Why did you get involved with this TV thing?'

'My mum says if you wish hard enough you can have anything you want. They wouldn't let me be in plays in school, so I thought I wasn't any good, but Mum said that school wasn't important. And she was right, wasn't she, because now I have this.'

'Why won't they let you be in plays at school?'

'Do you want to see my bedroom?'

'Now?'

'You should probably look at it now. Before my parents come back.'

'Won't they be gone for ages?'

'Yeah, but . . . Just have a quick look. It will help you build up a picture of me.'

I had never had a conversation like this with a girl before. I think it was because I didn't find Sheryl attractive, and knew she was even less cool than I was. In a way I was glad I had come to her house first, rather than Perdita's or Wendy's. Maybe this was the way all boys learned how to talk to girls. Start off with someone unthreatening and then work up. For a while, at the women's commune, I had thought that I might have female friends, but then something went wrong and I ended up spending every afternoon on my own.

Since then I had remained wary of the opposite sex, and mostly avoided girls at school. Occasionally I had to work with them, but in things like dance lessons I hid behind the curtains until everyone had chosen so I could pair up with the teacher. It never occurred to me that talking to a girl of around my own age could be as easy as this.

We walked across the landing.

'There are lots of reasons why I can't be in plays at school,' she told me. 'The main one is that most of them are musicals and I'm no good at singing.'

I laughed.

'What?' she asked.

'I was thrown out of the school choir for being tone deaf.'

'Really?'

'Yeah.'

Sheryl was just sort of standing in the middle of the room, looking uncomfortable. It occurred to me that she might want me to say something about her bedroom – she seemed oddly proud of it, although it wasn't anything special, not like my private penthouse – but I couldn't see what I could compliment.

'I spend a lot of time here,' she said.

I nodded. 'It's nice.'

The room was very tidy, with a small desk, a dressing table, a wardrobe and a single bed. The only other girls' bedrooms I had been inside were Erica's and Reggel's sister's. Reggel's sister's room was more like a teenager's room than Sheryl's, who had clearly thrown away her childish things, but had yet to replace them with anything adult. Erica's room, unsurprisingly, was a hell-hole, packed full of all kinds of rubbish she had collected from around the house. Erica was a hoarder, not only of stuff you might expect someone to collect, but of weird things too.

As Sheryl stood there, not saying anything, I realised she was probably used to showing her room to adults, who would be impressed that she was such a tidy child. But I was confused, not understanding how she could think this would give me any further insight into her character. The two of us hovered there for a moment, avoiding each other's eye. Then she said, 'Seen enough?'

I nodded, and we went back downstairs.

49

I sat on my bed. Sometimes I feel that I have lived some of my life too swiftly, and need to relax back into my normal rhythm. I knew I'd been avoiding dealing with my break-up with Ellen, and that I couldn't continue dodging this reality. I'm not the kind of person who has any real secrets, and I usually make sure that my friends and family get regular updates about my existence. But that thing I'd said to Sally on the tube about worrying that once I started talking to people about Ellen leaving me it would definitely be the end of it was true, and I had felt especially reluctant to share this information with my parents.

Now, though, I decided it was time to tell them. Picking up my white telephone, I stretched the cable across to the bed and dialled my father's number. Surprisingly, he wasn't in. So I called Mum. She didn't answer her mobile so I tried her home number.

'Jenny Wedmore,' she replied, her tone brisk and business-like even though it was a Sunday.

'Mum?'

'Hi, Gerald, how are you?'

'Ellen broke up with me.'

She went quiet, and then said, 'Is this a definite thing?'

I laughed. 'I think so.'

'And how do you feel about it?'

'I don't know,' I said truthfully. 'I mean, I am sad.'

'It has been a long time.'

'Yeah.'

Mum wasn't much good in these sort of situations. Dad would have been better. His reaction, no doubt, would be strange, but I knew he really liked Ellen and that he would have understood that whatever I said to him, however I acted, this was a big deal. It wasn't that Mum didn't care, rather that she'd never believed relationships were the most important thing in life, and she'd always preferred it when I'd visited her alone rather than with my girlfriend.

'Is there anyone else in the picture?'

'No,' I told her, 'but Sally's looking after me.'

'Is that the girl you live with?'

'No,' I smiled, 'Lorraine's the girl I live with. I can't imagine her taking care of anyone. She's like Erica.'

'Don't be mean about your sister. She thinks the world of you. So who is this Sally?'

'You remember. You met her at my graduation.'

'No.' She thought for a moment. 'Oh, was she the one you really liked?'

'No, Mum, not in that way.'

She didn't say anything, but I could tell what she was thinking.

Talking to Mum left me feeling frustrated. I thought she'd help me get Ellen out of my mind, but instead I had remembered all the worst feelings I had experienced on Friday while waiting for Ellen to appear. My first thought when Ellen broke up with me was that she was no longer afraid of dying. We had had so many conversations about this subject, and I'd always taken her fears seriously. I listened to her talk after she recovered from every suicide attempt, telling her she wasn't an evil person because she wanted to end her existence. For a while I spent every Saturday night standing on a hospital floor awash with charcoal. And I never complained when she woke me up with her screaming in the early hours of the morning, telling me she'd had another dream about being in Hell. I may have been freaked out when she told me that she sometimes heard the voice of Satan and it sounded like a slowed-down record, but I tried not to let that show, telling her that it was fine to listen to the voice as long as she told me everything he said and didn't follow his instructions. I coped with all this because I believed that the fact that Ellen thought about such dark subjects proved she was a deep person, and that it was my duty to protect her. And to be honest, it was at these times that she sounded most like a proper actress. Angelina Jolie was always saying that sort of thing in interviews, after all. I believed I would be with Ellen until she died, whether that turned out to be one year later or fifty. But the fact that she could leave me so easily made me realise that our relationship wasn't the grand tragedy I believed it to be. It was just another bog-standard adolescent romance.

Usually I checked my e-mails every day. Since Friday I hadn't logged on once. That was probably one of the reasons I thought I had been living too fast. I needed to share what had happened to me over the last few days with someone. I didn't have to worry about there being a message on my machine from Ellen: she didn't have a computer at home and could only access her e-mail account from work. I loaded up AOL. Seven messages. I read through them all, then answered the fourth. It was from my friend Richard. He was someone I'd known at university, probably my closest friend after Sally, who had also liked him. The three of us had been a gang for a while. When we'd known him, he'd been quite straight, and therefore best in small doses, but since he'd moved to America last year he'd loosened up a lot. He was always inviting me to come out and visit him, but so far I had only accepted once. I knew he would want to know about Ellen, so I wrote him an e-mail explaining the situation.

I closed down the computer and returned to my new bed. I had been against buying it, but now that I had, I realised how uncomfortable the old lady's mattress had been. It hadn't occurred to me before, but maybe Sally had made me buy the double bed not just for her but for the women who would follow. After all, I could hardly have brought a woman home to my tiny single bed. Maybe my friend was more subtle than I realised, and helping me in ways I would only discover later on.

I took off my shirt and shoes and lay back on the mattress, not planning to sleep, but wanting to rest for a while. My housemates were annoying me and I was keen not to have another conversation about Stan. The exertion of the previous night had caught up on me, and after my troubled dreams had kept me awake for most of the night, I felt like catching up on a little more sleep. It wasn't as if I had anything to do until Sally returned, and I could trust my housemates to open the door and let her in. No, a few hours' rest was probably exactly what I needed.

50

I sat in the passenger seat, holding the Dictaphone. I felt furious at my father, but didn't want to tell him. I always tried not to argue with Dad. Not just because I was dependent on him for transport, but also because I always felt embarrassed when I got emotional in front of him. He was always so calm, and although I knew I could probably provoke him into shouting at me, that wouldn't really provide any satisfaction.

I was angry with him for embarrassing me, but more than that, I couldn't believe he'd been so stupid. How could anyone be that sloppy? I just couldn't imagine the chain of events that had led to my embarrassment in the Casements' lounge. What had he done? Forgotten he'd taped himself with his mistress? I hoped that was what had happened. The alternative was too disturbing. Surely Dad didn't want me to hear what was on the tape? He knew I knew he went off with a strange woman several times a week. I couldn't believe he wanted me to know what happened between them in her bedroom.

'How did it go?' he asked eventually.

'OK.'

'She seemed like a nice girl.'

I didn't reply.

'You didn't think so?'

'Some of the others . . .' I tailed off, not wanting to talk to him about girls.

'Are nicer?' he finished for me, smiling. 'Don't worry, Gerald, I'm sure this is something we'll be able to sort out. Your mother has things she gets uptight about, and at first it seems like there's no solution, but then it turns out to be easier to fix than she pretends. And I'm sure she doesn't really want you to give up your programme.'

I could tell he was looking at me in the rear-view mirror. I knew he expected me to feel grateful, but I wasn't. He was always over-optimistic, and he'd already told me he wasn't going to support my cause. Things with my mother were never easy to resolve, and, although, ultimately, I was hopeful I wouldn't have to abandon *All Right Now!*, I knew there would be more to this process than I currently realised.

'So what film did we see?'

'Huh?'

'They're probably going to ask us about it. Do you want to pretend we saw a real film or make one up?'

'Won't they know if we make one up?'

'Not if we say we went into London. There's hundreds of cinemas. And your Mum's hardly going to go through all the newspapers to catch us out.'

I looked at him. He was enjoying this.

'OK,' I said, 'let's make one up.'

'Good. What sort of film?'

'Well, we said it was an eighteen . . .'

'So it'll either have to be rude or violent. Do you want to make up a rude one?'

'No. Violent.'

'OK, then, a thriller?'

'A detective story.'

'Who's in it?'

'No one famous, that'll give us away.'

'Good point. OK, a detective story . . . with no one famous in it. Someone new. What's it called?'

'*Back Seat Driver.*'

He looked at me. 'You came up with that fast.'

'I wrote a story called that at school.'

'Oh. OK. I suppose that will do. It sounds like it might be

the title of a thriller. And what happens in *Back Seat Driver*?'

'Maybe the detective isn't a detective. Maybe he's just a man who drives a car.'

'Like a taxi driver?'

'No, more for people who employ him all the time.'

'A chauffeur?'

'Yeah, but he also has another job.'

'What's that?'

'He works as a projectionist.'

Dad laughed. 'In a cinema? That doesn't sound too thrilling.'

'No, he works for a man who has his own screening room. In his house.'

'OK,' said Dad, getting excited, 'I see where you're going. The man is a film producer, but he's also a gangster. And the chauffeur has to bring this woman to his house.'

That wasn't where I was going, but I enjoyed encouraging him, saying, 'She's an actress.'

'An actress. Good. No, she wants to be an actress. But she's really a prostitute.'

This suggestion embarrassed me. I tried not to show it. 'A prostitute who wants to be an actress.'

'Of course. He's been promising her a part for ages, even given her a minor role, but she wants more. He's been having an affair with her for years, but now she's too old and knows he's never going to let her star in a film. So, what does she do?'

'She threatens him.'

'Yeah, that's right, she says she'll go to his wife and tell her about the whole thing. So he decides he has to kill her. And the person he gets to do it . . .'

'Is the chauffeur.'

'Who's in love with her.'

'Of course. Because he's been driving her around.'

'But he can't do it, so he tells her, and they decide to kill the producer.'

'That's brilliant, Dad, it sounds like a real film.'

'It does, doesn't it? Maybe we should write a script, you and me.'

'Yeah.'

'Well, son, you concentrate on getting famous, and that's what we'll do.'

He smiled at me. In spite of myself, I realised I felt happy, and had forgiven him about the embarrassment with the Dictaphone. I knew we'd never get round to writing the script, but that didn't matter. Dad and I were friends again.

51

I hadn't realised how tired I was, and what started as a cat-nap soon turned into a deep sleep. I was so far under that when I started feeling fingers touching my hair I was convinced it was just a dream sensation. Slowly, however, I returned to the surface, and when I finally got my eyes open, I realised Sally was sitting beside me, stroking my hair. Feeling defenceless, I murmured, 'You came back.'

'Of course,' she laughed, 'did you think I wouldn't?'

I looked at Sally, surprised to notice she'd changed her clothes since this morning. This struck me as odd, especially as she'd brought so many outfits over to my place. But she looked good – if not really herself – in her cowboy boots, dark blue denim skirt and black polo neck.

'No,' I replied, waking up properly, 'of course I did. What time is it?'

She looked at her watch. 'Half past four.'

'Shit,' I said, sitting up, 'if you still want to go to the supermarket, we're going to have to leave right now.'

Sally followed me out onto the landing and we went downstairs. The others were still in the lounge, but I didn't check in on them, not wanting to get saddled with a long shopping list.

'Some bits of this house are really nice,' said Sally.

'Yeah,' I agreed. She was right. The front door was heavy

and thick with elegant stained-glass panels, and the black-and-white tiled floor and walls around the entrance to our house did look more stylish than the rest of the rooms, mainly because they weren't covered with bird wallpaper.

'Oh,' she said, 'Darla wanted me to tell you that Ronnie called her this morning.'

'That's good,' I replied. 'One missing person is more than enough.'

I opened the door and we went outside. Sally caught me looking through one of our neighbours' windows.

'You lot are obsessed with spying on people.'

'It's not me,' I told her. 'There's a woman in that house who sits there watching television from the moment she wakes up until four in the morning. We think she'd be perfect for Mickey.'

'And that's another thing. Why are you so obsessed with each other's love lives?'

'We're only having fun. And I keep the others normal. You should've seen the crap they wanted to put in the house when we first moved in.'

Sally looked pensive. 'Gerald, don't take this the wrong way . . .'

'Oh God . . . What?'

'I know you and Ellen had got fed up of living together, but didn't she worry about you being with these people?'

'She liked Stan. I don't know what she thought of the others.'

Sally nodded. 'And what did you do about food before I moved in? You can't have eaten out every night?'

'Pretty much.' I flicked my fringe out of my eyes. 'The others are more takeaway types.'

'Isn't Ellen's parents' place quite a way from here?'

I nodded.

'So you were leading fairly separate lives?'

I still wasn't sure why Sally was doing this. She seemed determined to make me think of my relationship with Ellen as a condition she could cure. I suppose she was trying to stop me considering the break-up as a recent, reversible thing. It was probably my fault for mentioning Ellen at breakfast.

'I thought you promised to lay off this subject.'

She shook her head. 'I said I wouldn't criticise Ellen. But I am interested in your relationship. I can't imagine being with someone for eight years.'

'You've gone out with someone for five.'

'Yeah, but eight's different from five.'

'No it's not. Nothing changes. I bet your five-year relationship wasn't that different from my eight-year one.'

'Except Ellen didn't cheat on you.'

'No.'

When we reached the supermarket, I realised another implication of what Sally had said. If Ellen and I didn't eat together, sleep together, or even see each other that often, it was no surprise our relationship had come to an end. And I knew this was true, but didn't want to acknowledge it because then I'd be forced to concede that Ellen had been lying to me.

We'd had a terrible fight when she told me she wanted to move out. I was angry with her because it seemed like an admission that our relationship was a failure. She said this wasn't true, that she just needed more support than I could give. I knew this had come about because of my father being arrested and her failing her audition for drama school, but didn't see why she was taking it out on me. I really wanted her to get a place at drama school, helping her practise for months leading up to the audition. My acting career might have been over, but that didn't mean I resented her having a shot. The incident with my father was just bad timing, and hardly my fault.

Sally started picking up produce the moment we got through the metal barriers, filling the bottom of the trolley with fruit. I felt slightly shocked that we were doing a proper shop, and worried about how the rest of my household would respond to having food in the cupboards. I was also intrigued, wondering what she would buy. It was a long time since I'd gone to a supermarket for anything more than a handful of essentials, and I was eager to learn how to be normal again.

52

I followed Dad into the lounge. Mum was sitting on the sofa. She looked nervous, guilty, and slightly crazed. Dad asked her what was wrong.

'I had to do something,' she said. 'It's your fault for leaving her with me.'

A loud bang sounded from the second floor. Dad looked back at Mum.

'You shouldn't have got her all over-excited,' she continued. 'You know what she gets like when she's not allowed to do something.'

'What have you done to her?' he asked, and from his face I realised he was genuinely afraid.

Another bang.

'It was the only way to get her to calm down.'

'She doesn't sound very calm to me.'

Dad turned round and went upstairs. I followed him. Mum stayed in the lounge. When we got to the landing, her bedroom door twanged again.

'Where's the key?' Dad shouted to Mum.

'On the floor.'

We waited until my sister went quiet and then unlocked the door, throwing it open just as she charged forward, head lowered. Dad jumped out of the way and, unable to stop herself, Erica pelted towards the wall at the end of the landing. Hitting it hard, she bounced back, and plopped onto the floor. Dad went straight across and scooped her up. Her forehead was red and lumpy.

'Leave her with me, Gerald,' he said. 'Go downstairs and talk to your mother.'

I did as I was told. Mum seemed pleased with me, which made me feel guilty. She asked me about the film and I described it as simply as possible, trying to stick to the plot we'd come up with in the car and worrying Dad wouldn't remember it. But Mum wasn't really interested. I could tell she regretted locking my sister in her room. When Dad returned, we both looked at him, wanting to hear what'd happened.

'I put her to bed,' he told us.

'And she didn't complain?' Mum asked.

'I think she'd worn herself out.'

Dad picked up the remote and turned up the volume on the television. I stayed up late that night, waiting until after Mum had gone to bed. When she did, Dad said to me, 'I don't know, Gerald. I want to sort this out for you, but if your sister keeps going crazy . . .'

I didn't say anything. He kept his eyes focused on the screen. I'd known he was going to say this, but didn't want to challenge him, knowing that losing his support would be fatal. He stood up, ready to go to bed.

'Look, don't worry about it for the moment, OK? I'll do what I can.'

I nodded.

'And don't take it out on your sister. That's not going to help.'

I laughed. He looked at me.

'I know, as if you would, right? I don't know where Erica gets her temper from.'

I let him put his hand on my shoulder as he turned out the light in the lounge. Dad always tried not to take sides, and I could tell this was as close as he'd come to criticising Erica. But it was reassuring to know that he understood that things were difficult for me, and I hoped this would make him help me out when he next talked to my mother. I followed him upstairs, and left him in the bathroom as I unlocked the door to my private penthouse and ran up the stairs.

PART IV

★

53

Monday mornings were always fun. The five of us all trying to wash, eat breakfast, and prepare lessons was a finely choreographed operation. Usually Lorraine was the first into the bathroom, and remained wrapped in a towel while she made herself breakfast, her dirty tiger-stripe slippers shuffling across the lino floor. Today, Mickey (who normally used the now-broken shower on the first floor) got in before her. Sally seemed to realise that it would be more politic to wait until the rest of the house had washed before sneaking in herself, and it was fortunate that she didn't have to get in to the advertising agency until ten-thirty.

At eight-thirty the five of us were out of the house and down to Oval tube station. It was a much more pleasant place to catch a tube than most of the other stations on the Northern Line, with a surprisingly low morning turn-out. Mickey and I were the only ones who wore suits and ties to work. Smart dress wasn't compulsory at the Jennifer Keane Language School, and Tom and Lorraine both favoured a casual look. It was always entertaining when a set of students left and they had to fill out report cards on their teachers. Almost invariably, the students' responses would be something like this:

Tom: Tom was an excellent teacher. He taught us many useful things about English culture.
Lorraine: Lorraine doesn't like French/Spanish/Italian/ German/Japanese people. She did not like me and would not give me the help I needed.
Stan: Stan taught us lots about World War II.
Mickey: Mickey was a good teacher, but not very friendly.
Gerald: Gerald was not a good teacher.

I don't know why they didn't like me. I tried to strike a balance between Mickey's reserve and Tom's blokeishness in the classroom, but it didn't seem to work. The Language School's main employees were people who'd recently been discharged from the army, and I think the school director only kept me on to cope with the occasional homesick girl or foppish boy. I did a lot more one-on-one teaching than anyone else, and excelled at this. I was also good with the older students, the ones who'd paid to do the course themselves. I got on well with them, able to adapt my teaching to their precise needs. The problem I had with teaching groups was that I found it hard to keep everyone satisfied. Aware that most of my class considered the course an excuse for a holiday in England, I made sure we played lots of games, but then got so into keeping score that I failed to make sure the more dedicated students were getting the vocab they craved.

My first lesson each morning was a one-on-one with a member of the French aristocracy named Lucien. It was a source of great embarrassment to Lucien's family that their son took so long to learn anything, especially foreign languages. They had decided to punish him by making him stay in England until he could speak the language fluently. During our first week of lessons together I was reduced to the most basic exercises, showing him flashcards of flamingos, gypsies and bicycles. After five days of this, he decided he could trust me and confessed, in perfect English, that he had no problem with the language, and was just eager to escape his family.

I had my lessons with Lucien on the top floor of the Jennifer Keane Language School. The building had six storeys. Lucien had discovered that it was possible to get out through the window and up onto the roof of the building. Now he made us do this every lesson. I didn't suffer from vertigo, but the climb onto the roof still scared me. I feared for my own safety, but also Lucien's. If he fell, I had no doubt his family would sue me for every penny I ever earned. Then there were the pigeons. Lucien loved them, letting them crawl all over his legs. But they freaked me out, and I had an aversion to birdshit that he didn't seem to share. I also knew that although the director of the language school never came up to the top floor, there was always the possibility that there might be a phone call for me, and if anyone discovered the empty classroom, my employment would be terminated.

Still, there was a good view of Central London from the rooftop, and when the pigeons weren't out in force, I did occasionally enjoy sitting up here. Lucien didn't need to learn anything, so the pair of us just chatted through first period, psychologically preparing for the rest of the day.

54

Mum came back into the lounge. She had gone into the hall to call the TV people and tell them I could no longer be in their programme. I was waiting for Dad to rescue me, but so far he'd kept quiet. Mum looked confused.

'What did they say?' Dad asked.

'They're coming this evening.'

He looked up from his cereal. 'Who are?'

'The producers. They said that before they can release Gerald they have to talk to all of us together. Apparently, you signed some sort of contract.'

'That's right,' he remembered, 'I did.'

'And you didn't show it to me?'

He shrugged. 'Sorry.'

Mum went to the cupboard and took out a box of Special K. Erica was still asleep: she always refused to eat breakfast, preferring to stay in bed until the last possible moment. As Erica's moods were always worst in the mornings, we were happy to let her lie in.

Dad winked at me. I knew I hadn't got my way yet, but sensed this was a positive development. After all, the fact that the TV people were coming to our house must mean they were going to tell my mother something she didn't want to hear.

'What time are they coming?'

'Eight o'clock. You'll have to be home early to help me tidy up.'

'OK,' said Dad, 'no problem.'

The producers arrived an hour early. This was unfortunate. Usually I was really lazy when it came to helping out around the house, but today, as I knew it was in my best interests, I became a cleaning demon. Midway through the operation, Dad and I were dispatched to buy coffee, teabags and biscuits from the supermarket. This was when the producers showed up. Mum panicked and shot upstairs to get changed, leaving Erica to answer the door.

My sister may have been annoying, but she could, when necessary, pass for normal, even charming. And although until now the mere mention of my television programme had been enough to send her into a jealous fury, she clearly realised that this was her chance to turn things around, and seized it. I don't know how long it took my mother to get ready, but it was long enough for my sister to destroy my current happiness completely. I didn't realise this at the time, not knowing that there was the possibility of a worse outcome to this meeting than Mum getting her way and forcing me to withdraw from *All Right Now!* After all, it never occurred to me that the producers would want my psychopathic sister to take part in their programme.

I wasn't allowed to witness the conversation between the producers and my parents, but Dad told me later that the moment our guests suggested that Erica could also be in *All Right Now!*, Mum's attitude changed completely. Dad wasn't sure why. I thought I knew. Mum had always been enormously upset by the way my sister and I didn't get on, and no doubt saw this as an opportunity for us to bond. She was also prouder of the two of us together than either of us individually, and the idea of both her babies on television was much more appealing than me becoming a star on my own. To her credit, however, she did point out to the producers that my sister couldn't take part in the visiting other people's houses part of the research.

'That's OK,' the producers apparently told her, 'she can have a minor role. As Gerald's sister.'

When my father told me the outcome of the meeting, I disappeared up to my penthouse, where he later discovered me crying my heart out.

'Come on,' he said, 'at least you still get to be in it.'

But I was inconsolable. As far as I was concerned, my dream was over.

55

Lorraine answered the door, expecting it to be the police. It wasn't, so she shouted for me. I came downstairs and saw Ellen and her father standing in the hallway, both carrying blue plastic containers.

I hadn't exactly forgotten that Ellen was coming round this evening, but I'd failed to prepare psychologically for seeing her again. The strongest emotion was incredible, irrational, anger. Ellen was wearing dark glasses. I didn't doubt she'd been crying, but this seemed such an actress-y way of hiding it. Besides, she didn't need to be here, she could have sent her dad alone. I was in no desperate hurry to get my stuff back, and doubted there was a single thing here I urgently needed. And she didn't need to be wearing dark glasses.

Ellen's father, Ed, shrugged at me. Lorraine went back into the lounge. We'd called the police two hours before and I could tell Lorraine was disappointed that they hadn't shown up yet.

'Where do you want this?' he asked.

'Bring it up to my bedroom. Is there anything else in the car?'

'No,' he told me, 'this is it.'

Ed came up the stairs first, with Ellen a short distance behind. I liked Ed: he was a decent man who worked hard at his job on the city council and always had interesting things to discuss. It was obvious he felt embarrassed about being here, as if he was also breaking up with me.

I opened the door to my bedroom. Sally was sitting on the bed.

'You remember Sally,' I said to Ellen.

Ellen didn't reply, putting the container down on the floor. Ed nodded in Sally's direction and set down the second container. A blue vase dropped out onto the floor, but didn't break. Oh, I thought, so we're giving back presents too. Ellen was wearing a baby-blue vest and a pair of thin grey cords. Her long brunette hair was loose.

'Well,' said Ed, 'I suppose that's everything.'

'You can't stay for coffee?' I asked.

He looked at Ellen, whose dark glasses were directed towards the double bed.

'No,' he said, 'I don't think so.'

'OK. Thanks for bringing this over.'

He shrugged and offered me his hand. 'See you around, Gerald.'

'You OK?' Sally asked me after they'd gone.

'I think so. Ellen seemed weird, didn't she?'

'She's just upset. It was probably a shock to see me here.'

'Good,' I said. 'I want her to think I'm not bothered by this at all.'

'Are you sure you're OK?'

'Positive.' I turned away. 'Do you mind if I check my e-mail?'

I sat at my computer and logged on. I was only really interested to see if my university friend, Richard, had written back to me. He had:

Dear G, Sorry to hear about Ellen, but it sounds like Sally's taking good care of you. And, let's be honest, Ellen and you was always

144

going to come to an end one day. But how are you fixed
holiday-wise? Does that pretend job of yours let you take time
off? Cause if you ask me it's a perfect time for you to come to
Princeton. Think about it before you say no, anyway. All the
best, R.

The doorbell rang.

'I'd better go downstairs,' I told her. 'I want to hear what
they tell the police.'

'Shall I come too?'

'Yeah, you'd better. Make sure they don't drop Darla in
it.'

'OK,' she said, and we went down together.

56

Perdita phoned on Tuesday evening. Since my sister had
been invited to take part in *All Right Now!* I no longer felt
anywhere near the same excitement about the project, and
had put off calling the other three girls whose homes I was
due to visit. Sheryl had phoned this morning, and my mother
– who now thought this whole thing was fantastic – told her
she should come round the following weekend. I was
nervous about using the phone anyway, and would have
been terrified to call Perdita. Even her voice intimidated –
and excited – me.

'Can I speak to Gerald please?'

'This is Gerald.'

'Oh, hi, it's Perdita.'

There was a pause while she waited for me to respond. I
used this time to wonder whether Perdita's house was like
mine. We only had two phones in our house, one in the hall
and the other in my parents' bedroom. But lots of the girls at
school had begun to have phones in their rooms, and I
assumed that as Perdita was a year older than me, she might
have one too.

'I'm sorry about Wendy's joke,' she said.

'What joke?'

'Oh ... nothing ... Never mind. I was wondering whether you wanted to come to my house tomorrow after school?'

'Where do you live again?'

'Wimbledon. You could catch an overground train.'

'Didn't the producers say they could arrange for a car to drive us?'

'You could do it that way.'

'Do you think it's too short notice for tomorrow?'

'Why don't you call them?'

'OK,' I agreed, even though I hated calling anyone, 'shall I phone back?'

'Only if there's a problem. Otherwise, I'll see you tomorrow. Five o'clock.'

I went downstairs to the kitchen. The piece of paper with important numbers on it was held to the fridge by a magnet. I took it down and called the production office on the phone in the hall. Getting no response, I tried one of the home numbers listed. The woman on the other end – Immi, short for Imogen – sounded irritated, and I almost hung up without saying anything. But then I forced myself to explain and she said she would sort it out. I went back into the lounge and my mother asked in a sarcastic voice, 'Finished all your private business?'

'Yes.'

'Come on then,' she told me, 'sit quietly with us and watch TV.'

57

There was something unsettling about having the police in our living room, as if they were television characters who'd crawled through the screen. The policeman was in his late twenties, blond and innocent, wearing his uniform as if it were fancy dress. I could tell Lorraine liked the look of him, and the two of them kept exchanging coy smiles. He left the conversation to the woman, who, although sexy, was not having the same effect on Mike or Tom, both of whom were terrified by authority figures.

'OK,' she said, 'when was the last time you saw Stan?'

'Saturday night,' said Mickey.

'And what happened on Saturday?'

Mickey explained, leaving out, as we'd agreed, any mention of drugs.

'So you didn't see him leave the gallery?'

'No.'

'Could he have left with someone?'

'Maybe,' said Mickey, 'but it's still strange that he hasn't come back by now.'

'Does he have a job?'

'Yes,' I said, 'we all work together, at a language school.'

'A relationship?'

'No.'

'Anything traumatic happen to him recently?'

'Not that we know of.'

'He's a bit of a loner,' I explained. Tom glared at me. 'Well, he is.'

'But he hasn't been depressed?'

'No more than the rest of us,' said Tom. 'We're all out-of-work actors. Or ex-actors. Those three have given up.'

The policewoman looked at her partner. He was still making eyes at Lorraine. Frustrated, she took out her notepad and made a note of everything we had said.

'What about his parents?'

'We've spoken to them. They'll tell us if he shows up.'

'Does he have any other close friends? Apart from you lot?'

After asking a few more questions, they left without giving any real indication of what would happen next. We went upstairs to the kitchen for coffee. Lorraine took the kettle and went to the sink.

'Hey,' she said, 'the neighbours . . .'

'What are they doing?' Tom asked.

I walked up behind her and looked through the window. One of the neighbours was dressed up as Saint Sebastian, with a white sheet wrapped around his waist and plastic arrows sticking out from his body. Three of the others sat with easels in front of canvases painting him.

'Jesus,' I said.

The others crowded behind me. Tom said, 'Do you reckon they think we're weird?'

'No,' said Lorraine, 'we don't do strange stuff in the garden.'

'Only because we don't have a garden.'

'I think we should get to know them,' suggested Lorraine.

'How? Go round and tell them, "You don't know us, but we spy on you all the time and think you're really peculiar"?'

'No. It's time for a party. Gerald, you need cheering up after breaking up with that dreary girlfriend of yours, and I need to get to know that policeman.'

'Don't forget the TV woman,' said Tom. 'We should invite her for Mickey.'

The kitchen light flickered. It was a brown plastic strip of spotlights that was slowly falling from the ceiling, pulling wires behind it.

'The electrics in this place are fucking dangerous,' I said.

'I've called them twice,' Mickey told me. 'They promised they'd send someone round.'

'Try again tomorrow.'

I couldn't get to sleep. After I'd tossed and turned for about an hour, Sally asked, 'What's wrong, Gerald?'

'I don't know. Everything feels strange. I know it's partly because I'm not used to breaking up with anyone – I'm sorry to keep going on about this, but I really did think I'd be with Ellen for ever – but it's something else too. I feel like I'm about to enter a dark period of my life, and I've got a terrible sense of foreboding, as if I've got no real conception of how bad things are going to get.'

'These are normal feelings, Gerald. But I promise you it's just a stage in your recovery.'

'You sound like my dad.'

The streetlight outside our house meant that my room was never properly dark. I could see Sally was smiling.

'Have you spoken to him about Ellen?'

'He's never in. But I meant you sound like the way he used to talk to me when I was little. He was always telling me how what I was feeling was normal and describing what I'd go through next. He was usually right, but I hated hearing it.'

'Do you want me to shut up?'

'No, I don't mind you saying it. Besides, I'm an adult now. Less sensitive.'

I hugged her. Her body felt good in my arms. She wasn't wearing her pyjamas tonight, but a T-shirt and a pair of soft, fitted French knickers. I held her tight, and closed my eyes.

'What about Stan?' I said. 'I promised the others he was OK. What if he's dead?'

'I don't think that's likely, Gerald. If it was a different sort of club then yeah, maybe. But Darklands isn't like that. People know each other.'

'What if he had some sort of strange reaction to the drugs?'

'You didn't, did you? And Darla's fine. I'm sure there's some other explanation.'

I released her and we moved around again, trying to get comfortable. Talking to Sally had helped, and it wasn't long before I was asleep.

58

Shep dropped me at Perdita's door. Her house was smaller than mine, but equally eccentric. It had two floors instead of three, but was designed in the same thin style.

Perdita's mother opened the door. She had a long, serious face, and her brown hair was in a ponytail like Perdita's had been last time I'd seen her. She looked like one of the teachers at my school, wearing a green Maid Marian dress with black tights.

'Yes?'

'I've come to see Perdita.'

She stared at me, and then said, in a solemn voice, 'I've met you before.'

'Yes.'

'You're the boy from the audition. The one with the attractive father.'

I didn't reply.

'Well, come on then, come in.' She turned away from me and shouted up the stairs. 'Perdita . . .'

Perdita appeared on the landing, looking down at us. Her mother seemed bored, asking, 'I can leave the two of you alone, can't I?'

I nodded. 'We'll be fine.'

Perdita smiled down at me. She was wearing powder-blue leggings with a big white T-shirt cut straight across the neck with a blue belt wrapped round it. I felt intimidated by her stylish clothes, especially as I was still in my school uniform.

I went upstairs. Perdita pointed to a room at the end of the landing, and I followed her. She held the door open for me after she'd gone inside.

Perdita's bedroom was much more stylish than Sheryl's had been. A large window filled the room with light. She had bean bags, a wicker chair suspended from the ceiling, a large red bed, and posters on the wall. I didn't recognise any of the people on them, apart from the Beatles.

'Do you like the Beatles?'

'Everyone likes the Beatles.'

'I don't. I hate them.'

She looked at me. 'How can you hate the Beatles?'

'They're our parents' music. I hate the way people always go on about the Sixties.'

'But the Sixties was one of the greatest times ever.' She paused. 'Apart from the Seventies.'

150

'What do you know about the Seventies? You were just a kid then.'

'Yeah, but I've watched every episode of *The Rock and Roll Years*.'

I laughed.

'What?'

'You can't know about a time from watching television.'

'Why not? People will know about us when they watch our programme.'

I pretended to be considering this, but really I was wondering what I was doing. I was talking to Perdita like she was Reggel, or worse still, Erica. I didn't know why I was arguing with someone I was so keen to befriend, and at that age I assumed differences of opinion were insurmountable. But, oddly, Perdita seemed to be enjoying our argument. Maybe because she was a year older than me, and more mature. I knew adults who were like that.

'Anyway,' she said, 'none of today's music is better than the Beatles.'

'Yes it is,' I protested.

'Like what?'

'Madonna.'

She laughed.

'Prince, then . . .'

'Prince is obsessed with the Beatles.'

'No he's not.'

'Then why did he make an album where he tried to copy them?'

'He didn't,' I said, although I wasn't really sure of myself. At that age I didn't have more than one album by anyone, preferring to discover new bands with my pocket money.

Perdita went to her door. 'Come on,' she said, 'I'll show you.'

We went downstairs and through her house to a conservatory in the back. Perdita's mother was sitting there among the greenery, working on a typewriter balanced on a length of wood between two plant pots. There was a bottle of whisky next to the typewriter and she was wearing a pair of small glasses attached to a thin purple ribbon around her neck. We had to wait for her to finish a sentence before she looked up.

'Yes?' she said impatiently.

'Can we go in your bedroom?'

Her mother raised her eyebrows. 'Whatever for?'

'I want to play Gerald a record.'

'Yes, yes, I suppose that's OK, but it's probably not a good idea to still be in there when your father gets home.'

'Gerald will be gone by then.'

'OK.' She looked back at her typewriter and noticed a mistake. 'Oh, blast . . .'

We left her to it and returned upstairs. Perdita took me into her parents' bedroom. She went back through to her own room and came back with two records and a copy of *The Face*, a magazine I'd looked at in shops but never had the courage to buy. She held up the two sleeves.

'See,' she said, 'even the covers are similar.'

In her left hand, she held a copy of *Sgt. Pepper's Lonely Hearts Club Band*, in the other, a copy of *Around the World in a Day*. They didn't look that alike, but I could tell she was right.

'Shall I put it on?'

'Yeah. I don't have this album.'

'Which albums have you got?'

'Only *Sign o' the Times*. But I've heard *Purple Rain* a lot on people's Walkmans at school.'

This wasn't entirely true. Reggel had it on his Walkman, but everyone else spat at him and told him he was gay for listening to it, which neither of us understood, as we were fairly sure most of the songs were about sex.

Perdita pulled the clear sleeve out of the cover. I still couldn't believe this was happening. There had been so many times, alone in my penthouse, when I'd put on *Sign o' the Times* and imagined what it might be like having a girl there with me. The odd thing about Prince's music – at least on that record – was that he always sounded so lonely. Even when he sang about going to nightclubs and meeting

152

women, somehow I never pictured the scenes he described, but imagined him sitting in the studio making it all up. The record did make me feel sexy, but in an unfocused, isolated way.

'I've never heard *Sign o' the Times*. Apart from the single.'

'Oh, it's brilliant. You must hear it. Maybe when you come to my place. Can I look at the label?'

'What?'

'The record label. I want to see if it's the same as *Sign o' the Times*.'

She showed it to me. 'See, it's all sylvan on this side.'

I didn't know what sylvan meant, but wasn't going to ask her. She had a playwright for a mother, no wonder she knew more words than me.

'And there's the sky on the back. I think the songs on the second side are supposed to be more about God and stuff.'

'There's a song about Jesus on *Sign o' the Times*. "The Cross".'

She nodded. 'Well, there's one on here like that too. "The Ladder". I think it's about a ladder to heaven.'

'Do you believe in God?' I asked her, surprising myself.

She looked at me. 'My mum says it's a load of crap. I think my dad would like to go to church. He used to, but Mum made him feel stupid for doing it. She says religion is for ignorant people.'

'But what do you believe?'

'I used to believe in God. When I was little.'

She lifted the needle onto the record, and then sat back on the floor with me. I was immediately entranced by the music, but also by Perdita's face. I watched her as the record played, trying to make her features stick in my memory. The last two times I had met Perdita I'd found it hard to remember her face after I was away from her. I remembered her ponytail and her clothes, but her features eluded me. I thought about Nicholas Pennington's instructions about turning people into characters, and wondered how I would describe her. One thing I had noticed was that on all three occasions I'd seen her, including this one, she seemed to have a slight cold.

I sniffed a lot too, but she was more elegant about it than me, making it look as if it was a sign of refinement.

Perdita was different today from how she'd been at the group meeting, and I wondered whether she'd change when we were back with the others. I knew she was more concerned about being friends with Wendy and Amy than me, and couldn't get that look out of my head – the impressed one she'd given Amy when Amy was rude to us. Girls were always different when they were in packs, and I'd sensed that Perdita felt guilty about the way she'd treated me then by the fact that she'd started her telephone call to me by apologising for the joke Wendy had made. I thought I knew which joke she was referring to now, and decided to test my suspicion.

'Perdita, why did you laugh when Wendy asked if I liked Madonna?'

She looked embarrassed. 'I'm sorry.'

'But what was the joke?'

She hesitated. I could tell she wished she hadn't said anything.

'It was your jumper.'

'My jumper?'

'Yeah, the stripey one. It was too short for you and when you put your arms up it showed your belly button. You know, like Madonna.'

Mortified by her admission, tears sprang to my eyes, and I had to ask Perdita directions to her bathroom as quickly as possible so I wouldn't have a crying fit in front of her. I felt furious at everyone: at my father, for buying me cheap clothes that didn't fit; at myself, for wearing these clothes and not complaining; at my mother, for not intervening. After all, she dressed my sister, and she never looked stupid. Most of all, though, I felt angry at Wendy for making fun at me, and at Perdita and Amy for joining in.

I sat on the edge of the bath, unable to stop the sobs. I was really gulping for air now, and worried I might throw up. Horrifyingly, Perdita was knocking at the door.

'Are you OK?'

'Yeah,' I said, gasping and trying to sound normal, 'just using the toilet.'

'Don't take it to heart, Gerald. It was only a stupid joke. I'm sorry I laughed.'

'Oh no, don't worry, I understand. It's funny.'

She went away. I stood by the sink, washing my face so the tears wouldn't show. When I'd stopped crying, I wiped my face with toilet paper and went back to Perdita's parents' bedroom.

59

I sat in the staff-room, waiting for Mickey, Tom and Lorraine to finish their classes. One of the other teachers was allergic to wasp stings and carried a large shot of adrenalin with him at all times. He sat at the end of the long staff-room table, reading a copy of *Guns and Ammo* and playing with this container as he finished his coffee. It was always a mistake to be in the staff-room too long, and I realised I was in trouble when the school director placed his hand on my shoulder. 'Gerald,' he said, 'just the man. I need someone to supervise Wednesday's club night.'

I sighed. Every Wednesday, two of the staff had to take a group of students to a nightclub. Most of the students went out every night anyway, and the ones who signed up for the organised club night were always a bit odd, and if they weren't used to drinking, often became a nuisance.

'OK,' I said.

'Good man. Do you think you might be able to persuade one of your housemates to go with you?'

'Lorraine might do it.'

'Lorraine might do what?'

I looked up. She was standing in the doorway with Mickey and Tom. The school director smiled.

'Ah,' he said, 'just the people. Does one of you three want to help Gerald do the student club night tomorrow?'

'Yeah, OK,' said Lorraine, 'that's fine by me.'

The three of us were walking down to the tube station when I broke off from the group, wanting to book my tickets to America. On the rare occasions I visited travel agents, I always felt out of place. My bookings were always much less adventurous than those of anyone else around me. They all seemed to be planning year-long jaunts around the world, seeking out the most dangerous routes imaginable. I couldn't understand what motivated them. My life was boring, but it had to be preferable to being stuck in a jungle. Didn't it?

I got back to the house at seven-thirty. Sally wasn't home yet, so I e-mailed Richard and told him my travel plans. Just as I logged off, the telephone rang. I ran over to answer it. It was Erica. Mum had told her what'd happened and she wanted to check I was OK. I asked her if she wanted to meet up and we agreed to see each other on the following Thursday. I hung up feeling happy that my family were concerned for me, and looking forward to catching up with my sister.

60

Perdita didn't talk much when we went back into her bedroom. I kept asking questions that might reveal details I could later weave into an interesting plot, but the only significant thing she said was that she'd recently started going to a teens-only nightclub with some girls from her school. She stopped short of asking me if I'd like to go there with her, but I would have turned her down anyway. Just before Shep arrived, she asked me if I'd like to borrow her Prince album.

'Are you sure?' I asked, surprised by her generosity.

'Definitely. Then maybe when I come to your house I can borrow *Sign o' the Times*.'

'OK,' I said, 'thank you.'

She smiled, as if pleased to have made me happy again.

I went upstairs to my penthouse, put *Around the World in a Day* on the stereo, and sat at my desk. I'd written up my session with Sheryl and her parents into a school exercise book, and I started Perdita's entry on the page after Sheryl's. Turning the music down so I could hear the Dictaphone, I rewound the tape, ready to start taking notes. I still felt horribly embarrassed every time I heard my recorded voice, and couldn't understand why I sounded like a rambling drunk.

When I was eight, I'd had a few sessions with a speech therapist. At the end of our time together she told me my voice was fixed and she didn't need to see me again. And yet on tape I still sounded as if I lacked even elementary control of my alveolar ridge.

Still, I was surprised at the similarities between Perdita's voice and mine on the tape. She sounded much more in control, of course, but there we shared a certain intonation, as well as a tentative way of speaking. Listening to the conversation, it sounded as if we were equals, as if I wasn't in awe of her. I still cringed every time I heard myself stumbling over words, but there were moments when Perdita was equally inarticulate.

Halfway through the transcription, I started feeling angry again. Oddly, the anger eradicated my fear of Wendy, and I decided I would call her and organise a time to go over to her house straight away. I didn't care if she didn't want me there. After all, why should I feel ashamed?

61

Lorraine and I took the students to Bar Rumba, a reliable club on Shaftesbury Avenue. It wasn't my favourite venue, but at least you could sit at the bar and drink if you didn't like the drum and bass. The students liked it too, especially the shy ones, as you could guarantee that everyone would get chatted up at least once during the course of the evening. Lorraine left me at the bar with the two French students, Nadine and Lucien, and took Tatjana, Stefan and Junko onto the dance floor.

The music was loud enough for me to pretend to be engrossed, and I sat there slowly sipping my pint and wondering how long I would have to stay. The rule was supposed to be that at least one teacher remained present until the last student had gone home, but the director had told me as long as things looked safe he was happy for us to slip away at midnight. I checked my watch. Ten-thirty. I doubted whether I could last even that long.

I sat there until I'd finished my pint. Then I got up to go to the toilet. Before I had chance, Lorraine bounced up and grabbed my hand.

'Come and have a dance,' she told me.

I don't know if you've seen the Wim Wenders film *Until the End of the World*. It's not a particularly respected film and it was made during a period when people agreed he'd lost his way, but, as with many films that don't work, there are a few scenes from it that seem better than anything in any of his more acclaimed pictures. The main one is where William Hurt goes to a disco with, I think, Solveig Dommartin, and she tries to persuade him to dance. Hurt responds by shaking his head and raising his hands as if the idea is utterly abhorrent to him. Then, in the same movement, he breaks into fifties-style jiving. The scene is utterly winning, mainly because in that one gesture your opinion of the character changes completely. When he seems like he's refusing to dance, you think 'yes, that fits in with my sense of this person, he wouldn't like rock music,' and then, as he starts twisting, you think 'he has hidden depths, he's not pompous, maybe it wouldn't be so hard to be friends with this man.' Every time someone asks me to dance, I remember that scene. Sometimes I even attempt to imitate it, but tonight I just let Lorraine lead me to where the others were waiting.

Junko and Stefan seemed excited, eagerly getting into the music. Tatjana had already been dragged away from the group and was dancing with two men in the far corner of the dance floor. Lorraine's face was pink and part of her fringe was stuck to her forehead with sweat.

'Aren't you going to thank me for rescuing you?' she shouted over the music.

'From what?'

'You looked bored out of your mind.'

I shrugged. 'Not my sort of music.'

She stepped back away from me. I carried on dancing, looking at a small group behind Lorraine. A tall, sexy blonde woman in a shimmering black top and jeans was dancing with a man whose black hair stuck out in three points like a jester's hat, and a fat man in his fifties who was wearing a brown suit. The man was also wearing a brown trilby, and although he was clearly enjoying the music, it seemed strange that someone like him was here. I knew this place had a reputation for being a good place to pull, but I couldn't believe that either of these men had a chance with the girl.

Lorraine noticed me staring and looked over her shoulder.

'Do you want me to help?'

'What?'

'I could go join that group. You look after Stefan and Junko, and when we head to the bar, follow us.'

Lorraine smiled and artfully managed to dance her way back into the trio. I watched the two men, curious to see how they would react. I thought they'd be grateful to have another woman dancing with them, but they both looked irritated. Maybe the three of them were all involved in the same relationship.

Stefan and Junko seemed concerned that Lorraine had left us. I nodded and grinned at them, trying to maintain the illusion that we were all having a good time. Lucien got up from his seat, came over and told me, 'I'm going to go now.'

'Are you sure? How about another drink?'

He shook his head, and turned his back on me. I noticed Lorraine leading the threesome to the bar. Following her instructions, I asked Stefan and Junko if they wanted a drink and went across myself.

'Gerald,' she called out, 'come say hello. Guys, this is my friend Gerald. Gerald, this is Sophie, Don, and Uncle C.'

I shook hands with all three, feeling vaguely disturbed. Sophie was even more attractive close up.

'Tell them about the party, Gerald,' Lorraine instructed.

'Oh, yeah, right, we're having a party this weekend. You don't have to worry about not knowing anyone, we're a really friendly house and there'll be literally hundreds of people.' Feeling a bit desperate, I looked frantically back and forth between the three of them. 'Does anyone have a pen?'

Uncle C reached into his inside pocket and took out a black biro. I picked up a serviette from the bar and wrote down our address. I tried to hand it to Sophie, but Uncle C took the serviette back with the pen and squinted at the address I'd scrawled for them.

'So you'll come?'

'We'll see,' said Uncle C.

We left the club at two, and walked to Trafalgar Square. The bus took a long time to come, but the journey back wasn't too bad. It was almost full, but we managed to get the priority seats next to the stairs, satisfied we were unlikely to encounter elderly people or pregnant women this early in the morning. Lorraine rested her head on my shoulder and immediately fell asleep.

We got off when we reached Brixton Road, and walked down to our street. It was always hard to open the front door quietly, and I worried about waking Mickey. Lorraine mumbled something at me and darted up the stairs, clearly keen to get into the bathroom first. I waited for her to finish, then washed my face and cleaned my teeth. I really felt like having a bath, but didn't want to wake up the rest of the household. Cursing Lorraine for keeping me up so late, I went downstairs to my bedroom and tried to undress in the dark.

'I'm not asleep,' said Sally. 'You can put the light on.'

I flipped the switch. 'How come you're still awake?'

'I don't know,' she said, and then, in a quieter voice, 'it felt odd not having you here.'

'I'm sorry,' I told her, 'I didn't mean to stay out so late.'

She turned away from me and hugged a pillow.

62

I must be too young for nostalgia, surely. And it's worse than that. Regrets. It's probably a side-effect of writing. I looked at Nicholas Pennington's web-site again last night. As well as offering his services as a dramaturge, he's provided short plays you can access. I started reading one – all about a sadomasochistic female politician – but found it too depressing. I haven't shown you how Nicholas made us construct our stories yet, but he was always encouraging us to force drama out of reality. For someone like me, who tries to avoid confrontation, this was difficult. In order to create these dramas, Nicholas told us to define ourselves as characters, to take our individual traits and make them into strengths or weaknesses. If he was getting me to make a story out of my relationship with Sally (and romantic interaction ended up being a major part of *All Right Now!*), he'd probably ask me to explain why I had such a lack of sexual rapaciousness. When I was attempting an earlier version of this narrative, talking to a friend on a plane, she stopped me when I got to the bit about Sally and me sharing a bed and said, 'But weren't you even interested in the fact that you had another human body beside you? How could you sleep and resist the opportunity to explore?' And I looked at this friend and realised that even though she and I had gone through a similar situation ourselves, there was a fundamental difference between us, and what's more, that I was the weird one. I used to think that my character had been shaped by my childhood and family (at the commune, the women talked about sexual desire as if it was the thing that made men inferior to women), but now I think each person gets a different amount of desire, like brains or good looks. So many people seem powerless in the face of their libido, their whole life reduced to a series of sexual encounters.

It's not that I was horrified by the idea of having sex with Sally, but it felt extraordinary that we could be this close as friends, and I had a strong instinct that rather than strengthening our relationship, that kind of intimacy would destroy it. This did, occasionally, make our time together feel awkward. Soon we would start feeling like a normal couple, except without the sexual benefits, spending every night fighting for space in a bed easily big enough for the pair of us. And the problem wouldn't be repressed desire, but that we didn't have any way of resolving our occasional frustrations with each other. I couldn't shake the sense that I was disappointing Sally in some way, and when we bickered we couldn't calm things down by kissing or whispering 'I love you' into each other's ear. In eight years, Ellen and I had reached the point where we expected to be accepted no matter how we acted; Sally and I remained on our best behaviour, which became increasingly draining the longer we spent in each other's company.

63

It hadn't taken much persuasion to get my father to pick me up at lunchtime. He loved doing anything illicit, and using me as an excuse to skip work for an afternoon clearly appealed to him. My comprehensive was big enough for pupils to truant all the time without being noticed, and I knew no one would bother to check on me. I walked out into the car park just after midday and was pleased to see him already waiting.

'Now,' he said, as I got into the car, 'I'm prepared to do this for you, but I want you to understand that I'm not just giving you this money – I'm paying you.'

'What for?'

'Your loyalty.' My father took out his wallet. 'When you get a few years older, you'll probably start having strange feelings about me.'

'Why? What are you going to do?'

He laughed. 'Nothing. It's just what happens to boys when they reach a certain age. I understand that, and I know how things must look, but trust me, you don't know the full story. There are things I promised not to talk about, and I'm going to keep that promise for the sake of the family, but one day, you'll realise that I'm not . . . I'm not a bad man.'

He handed me three fifty pound notes and asked, 'Where do you want me to drive you?'

I had been considering this question. The first thing I thought I needed was some black 501s. If I was going to buy clothes with labels, they weren't going to be Taurus jeans or PowerMad trainers. So I told Dad to drive me to the jeans shop in Kingston, which seemed the best place to start.

I felt much more excited about going to Wendy's house than Perdita's. Even though Perdita was the one I fancied, I knew I wouldn't be able to get anywhere with any of the other girls until I had convinced Wendy to like me. I still felt angry at Wendy for making the joke about me and Madonna, but now I had my new clothes I felt much more confident, and the anger had taken on a strange, almost sexual quality.

I knew Dad would get cross when he saw the clothes I wanted to buy. I'd tried to persuade him to stay in the car, but one of Dad's biggest flaws is that he's convinced he can help with everything. He didn't mind me going into the jeans shop, but couldn't believe I was going to spend forty pounds on a pair of trousers.

'You could get five pairs of Taurus jeans for that amount

of money. You're not paying for quality, you're paying for the label.'

'Fine. Let me pay for the label. I'm fed up of people laughing at me.'

'People don't laugh at you.'

'Yes, Dad, they do. That's the whole reason I wanted new clothes in the first place.'

Dad had this look he gave me when he wasn't sure if I was telling the truth. I was prone to exaggeration, although oddly the times he didn't believe me were usually when I wasn't embellishing. He seemed to realise I was being honest, and this made him look miserable, as if he remembered what I was experiencing from his own childhood. After this, he became helpful, going through the piles to help me find the right size.

Wendy opened her front door and stared at me. She was wearing her school uniform, but still managed to look cooler than me. She had the same black moccasins that all the hardest girls at our school wore, with the requisite thick cream socks. Her black skirt was as short as possible and she wore a burgundy cardigan over her white blouse. I glared back at her until she let me in.

I followed Wendy into her living room, swaggering a little and feeling protected in my new clothes. Wendy's mother, and her sister, Lucy, sat on the sofa. Wendy's mother was only wearing a bra without a shirt, but didn't seem embarrassed, even though it wasn't really that hot. Her breasts looked even larger than her daughter's. I tried not to stare, feeling awkward. In the corner of the room, an overweight older boy sat in an armchair. They were all watching television.

'You ready, Andrew?' Wendy asked the older boy.

'OK,' said Andrew, tossing his car keys in the air and catching them in his palm.

'Let me come,' begged Lucy.

'Tell her, Mum.'

'Doesn't she need to go, isn't that part of it?'

'It's not that serious, Mum. She doesn't need to be with us.'

'But if she wants to go . . .'

I watched the four of them working things out, wondering what was being decided. I hadn't imagined that I'd have to talk to Wendy in the company of her boyfriend, although as their house was quite small, I could see why they wanted to go to the park. But Wendy's boyfriend seemed intimidating, and unlikely to indulge me for long. This made me nervous, even in my new clothes.

'OK,' said Andrew, 'I suppose it doesn't matter.'

Wendy glared at her boyfriend, and then said to Lucy, 'You have to behave.'

'She'll behave,' said her mother. 'Won't you, Lucy?'

Lucy nodded and got up. Andrew went out into the hall and through to the front door. We followed him. His car was parked outside the house, an orange Marina. I was surprised he had such unstylish transport, and assumed the car must belong to someone else, either his parents or Wendy's. Wendy and Andrew went ahead of us, climbing into the front seats. Lucy and I got in the back.

Looking back, I suppose the sensible, strategic thing would have been to make friends with Lucy. She obviously didn't like Andrew, and would probably have become a useful ally. But the idea of befriending someone younger than me was not an appealing one, and I still saw Wendy as the only useful source of power.

Andrew started the engine. The radio came on, at full volume. I tried to wind down the window, but it got stuck halfway. I jiggled the handle and got it working again, winding it straight back up.

There were lots of other people in school uniform at the park. Andrew and Wendy headed straight for the play-ground area, the two of them sitting on a roundabout and waiting for us to get on. Although I was worried about when I'd get to ask Wendy my questions, I felt pleased to be in their company, as it felt cooler to be hanging out with them than someone like Reggel or any of my other friends from school.

'OK?' asked Andrew, checking we were all safely on.

'Yeah.'

'Good.' He stepped down onto the tarmac and started to rotate the roundabout. When he'd got it up to a steady speed, he grabbed hold of a bar and jumped on. Then he reached inside his jacket and brought out a bottle of Southern Comfort. He took a long slurp and handed it to Wendy. After she'd had her gulp, she passed it to me. I was so keen for Wendy to like me that I took a drink and was about to hand the bottle to Lucy when Andrew reached out and stopped me.

'She's not old enough.'

I nodded and gave him back the bottle.

'So what is it that you have to do?' he asked Wendy.

'Gerald's got to ask me questions. About my family.'

Andrew rocked backwards and looked at me. I could tell he thought this was stupid, and that he was amazed Wendy had got involved. But I also sensed that he was worried. He clearly didn't see me as a threat, although the fact he was here showed he was suspicious. I took my Dictaphone out of my pocket.

'You're not going to record me,' said Wendy.

'Nah,' agreed Andrew, 'fuck that.'

'But I didn't bring any paper.'

'You don't need paper. You're supposed to remember what I say.'

'Let him use his Dictaphone,' Lucy told them.

I thought her intervention would definitely decide him against the idea, but, surprisingly, after a moment's silence, Andrew nodded his consent.

'All right,' said Wendy, 'but if I say anything I don't want to say you have to rewind the tape.'

I agreed, and held the Dictaphone in their general direction, wondering whether the turning of the roundabout would affect the way the words were recorded. Andrew handed Wendy the bottle again. I waited until she'd drunk from it, then asked, 'So how did you two meet?'

'No,' said Andrew.

'You didn't meet?'

'No questions about me,' he insisted, as if he was a Hollywood celebrity instead of an overweight teenager. Normally I would have caved in immediately, but having just won the Dictaphone argument, I felt confident enough to reply, 'But you're part of Wendy's story.'

'Just leave Andrew out of it,' she told me.

'What about Lucy? Can I ask you about her?'

'Why don't you ask me?' said Lucy.

I ignored her, saying to Wendy, 'How do you feel about your sister being involved in this project?'

'Our parents wanted us to do it together. It wasn't my idea.'

I nodded. 'I know what you mean. My sister's got involved now.'

'What d'you mean, got involved?'

I told her the story. She passed me the Southern Comfort.

'Do your parents have a happy marriage?'

Andrew sat up again. 'You can't ask her that. What business is it of yours?'

'You know,' I said, the drink making me strangely reckless, 'this would be a lot easier if you didn't keep interrupting.'

'You little shit,' he said, snatching the bottle back from me. 'I wouldn't have to interrupt if you didn't ask such impertinent questions.'

I was surprised he knew what 'impertinent' meant.

'I'm not sure if this is such a good idea,' I said. 'Maybe we can do it some other time.'

'Look,' said Wendy, 'let's forget it, Gerald, OK?'

That night, when I sat down with the notebook into which I had transcribed all my conversations with Sheryl and Perdita, I found that although I only had a few minutes' worth of recorded information, there were plenty of things I could write about Wendy, and in some ways, she was the person I understood as a character best of all. Her overbearing boyfriend, her relationship with her sister, the parents who had allowed their daughter to accept this dominating man into her life. I could see several stories waiting to be explored in our soap opera, and in spite of Andrew's threats, I felt eager to start constructing them.

64

There weren't many other people in the Italian restaurant, and we didn't have a problem getting a table. My sister seemed surprised that I wasn't more upset about Ellen, and I could tell she was suspicious about my relationship with Sally. It took her a while to work round to asking me about it, but after we'd finished our starters, she said, 'Ellen is a lovely girl, but I think it's good that you've broken up with her.'

'See,' said Sally, 'your sister agrees.'

'Do you think so too?' Erica asked her.

'Definitely. She made him so miserable.'

The two of them looked at me with a similar fondness in their eyes. I felt the familiar awkwardness I always experience when women are making a fuss of me. I knew they were trying to be nice, but this sort of talk just made me feel protective of Ellen, and I wanted to protest that neither of them knew her well enough to make these judgements. So they thought Ellen made me miserable? Well, she did, but that was part of our relationship. She went down low, but you find things in those depths, stuff that stays with you for ever. It was a love affair, the first proper one for both of us, more important in some ways than a marriage. How could my sister understand that? She and Sally had such a different approach to love, living in a cheerful, sunny world so unlike my own.

My sister was watching me. I had the strange sense that

she knew what I was thinking, especially when she said, 'You weren't like this when you were little, you know.'

'What?'

'Before you met Ellen you were always so hopeful.'

'That's not true.'

'Yes it is. Don't you remember all those silly, mystical, metaphysical conversations you used to have with Perdita?'

'Those weren't hopeful conversations!' I exclaimed. 'We always talked about how alienated we felt and how we hoped that when we died there would be another world to go to because we felt so miserable in this one.'

'Yeah, but that was just teenage introspection. And your strange way of flirting. Nutcases, the pair of you. But you and Perdita were proper soulmates. You really shouldn't have been so shy with her. Ellen was so . . .' she searched for the right adjective, 'earthbound. I've always thought that my brother needs a woman who's prepared to fly to the moon with him.'

I looked at Sally. She avoided my eye, and then signalled to the waiter for another bottle of water.

Later that evening, after Erica had gone home, Sally and I were lying in bed together, and she asked, 'Do you think your sister sees me as that kind of woman?'

'What kind?'

'The kind who'd fly to the moon with you. Someone who's not earthbound.'

'I told her that you and I were just friends. She knows there's nothing going on between us.'

'I know . . . But if things were different. Say we'd both been single when we first met.'

'Sally, we've discussed this. It would've been a disaster.'

'You're not getting my point. What I'm asking is, irrespective of how long we would have lasted or whether it would've been a good idea, if you'd introduced me to your sister in that context, would she have thought I was that kind of woman?'

'I think the fact that you're seeing me through this proves that, doesn't it?'

I looked at her, my expression sincere. She smiled and kissed me, the relief evident on her face.

'Thanks, Gerald. That's all I needed to know.'

65

Amy wasn't home when I arrived. Fortunately, her mother was friendly, inviting me into the lounge and saying her daughter had probably been given another detention.

'She didn't strike me as the type of girl to get detentions,' I said, more thinking aloud than attempting to ingratiate myself.

Amy's mother laughed loudly. 'You don't know my daughter very well, do you?'

'No,' I admitted, 'I didn't get much chance to talk to her at the first meeting.'

'Did she scare you?' Amy's mother asked, giving me a smile I didn't really understand. Ever since my mother had taken me to the women's commune, I had found that, on certain occasions, I was able to communicate with adult women in a way that was unusual for a boy of my age. But it was always the women who started it, because, I believe, they saw something interesting in me.

'A bit. She seemed more mature than the other girls.'

Amy's mother laughed and slapped her thigh. The theatrical gesture scared me. 'Mature? Good heavens, that's the last word I'd use to describe Amy.'

I didn't explain that the reason I thought she looked mature was because I'd assumed her mother had dressed her in too-adult clothes. Looking at Amy's mother now, I realised my assumption had been wrong. Amy's mother seemed arty, although in a different way from Perdita's mother. Her hair wasn't the same colour as Amy's, but had been dyed an artificial reddish shade. She had very white skin, and looked much less wholesome than her daughter.

She was wearing a purple jacket with purple trousers, flat brown shoes, and a black vest with a silver moon and stars embroidered on it. She reminded me of women at the commune, and I suddenly realised that Amy was the way she was because her mother embarrassed her. It reminded me of the way I would sometimes pretend I wasn't related to my parents, and looked forward to the day when I would no longer be introduced as someone's son.

'I'm sorry,' she said, 'I don't remember your name.'

'Gerald.'

'I'm Madeline.' She reached out and stroked my hair. I recoiled, but she held my gaze. 'Would you like a free haircut, Gerald? I'm trying to teach myself and I could do with the practice.'

'What about Amy?'

She looked at her watch. 'If she's in detention, which I'm sure she is, she won't be back for at least another forty minutes.'

'OK,' I said, 'as long as you don't cut it too short.'

'I promise. Don't you like it short?'

I shook my head. 'Every time I go to the hairdresser, the woman asks me what I want and I tell her, and then my mother goes behind her back and makes her do a really short cut.'

Madeline clucked sympathetically. 'It's hard being a child, isn't it? Do you know what Philip Larkin said about being a child?'

'Who's Philip Larkin?'

'A poet.'

'No. What did he say?'

'He said that when he was a child he thought he hated everybody, but when he grew up he realised it was just children he didn't like.'

'I like other children,' I said quickly. 'I'm not saying that.'

'I know, love. You weren't saying anything about other children at all. I'm sorry, it wasn't a relevant quotation. I just thought it expressed some of the . . . frustration you were talking about.'

'Do you know Perdita's mum?'

'Who's Perdita? One of the other girls?'

'Yeah.'

'That's a nice name too.'

'It's from Shakespeare.'

'Is it? Well, I probably met her during those auditions, but I don't know her. Why d'you ask?'

'No reason. I just thought you'd probably like her. She's a playwright.'

Madeline smiled. 'Is she? That's nice. I don't really do anything creative. I tried painting for a while, but I just found myself painting the same . . .' She stopped, shook her head, and laughed. I knew what'd happened. She'd suddenly remembered she was talking to a child, and realised what she was about to say was inappropriate. I'd learned that the best way to resolve these situations was to become an adult.

'Go on,' I said.

She looked at me and giggled. 'The same . . . I don't know . . . creatures. Have you ever seen any paintings by Francis Bacon?'

'Yes.'

'Really?' she asked, surprised.

'In books, I mean. My dad has some art books.'

'Well,' she went on, 'these creatures, they were female versions of the creatures in Bacon's paintings. The famous paintings. My husband thought they were disgusting.'

She laughed again. I took out my Dictaphone.

'What's that?' she asked. 'Do you want to record me?'

'It's part of the project.'

She looked worried. 'But Amy doesn't have a Dictaphone.'

'No, I know, it's not required. But I find it helpful. My dad gave it to me,' I explained quickly.

'Oh,' she said, 'so who's going to listen to your recording?'

'Just me. When I make notes about Amy and you. What does your husband do?'

'He's a policeman.' She looked at me. 'Would you like your hair cut now?'

'OK.'

'You'll have to come into the kitchen with me. I'll need to wash it first.'

I followed her. She said, 'I'll use a towel, but it'll make it a lot easier if you take your shirt off.'

It wasn't as if I'd never taken my shirt off in front of an adult before, but I didn't do it lightly. It took a full holiday's persuasion and intense heat before I would go bare-chested on our last day away, and I avoided showers and changing rooms. I didn't dislike my body – in fact, I was quite proud of it – I just wasn't ready to start showing it off. Madeline noticed my hesitation, and said quickly, 'Maybe I could just do it with the towel.'

'No,' I said, not wanting to seem like a wimp, 'it's OK.'

I was wearing one of the three black shirts I'd bought when I went shopping with my father the day before. I'd never worn a vest, ever since I'd overheard my mother making a joke to one of the women at the commune about my father wearing one. Madeline looked away as I unbuttoned my shirt.

'Just hang it over the chair there,' she told me, 'and come and stand over the sink. You don't want to tape me while I'm washing your hair, do you?'

'I suppose not.'

'Good. Now lean your head right down.'

I took my glasses off and put them on the counter. She pushed the rubber teat of the shower attachment over the tap and started running the water, testing it with her fingers until she'd got it to a suitable temperature. Then she held the attachment above my head, letting the water gently cascade onto my hair. It ran for a while and then she squeezed some shampoo onto her fingers and began massaging it into my scalp. Her fingers felt hard and bony and she rubbed vigorously. She stopped to adjust the towel over my shoulders and then rinsed the shampoo away.

She moved me across to a stool, and told me to wait there

while she brought a long mirror down from upstairs. I offered to help, but she said she was fine.

I hated having my hair cut at the best of times, mainly because I had to take my glasses off and couldn't see what they were doing. I didn't mind Madeline doing this when it felt like something between us, but now she was bossing me about I felt much less keen on the idea. I couldn't back out, though, and closed my eyes as she started snipping.

'Doesn't Amy call when she's got a detention?'

'They don't let her. That's supposed to be part of the punishment. It's meant to annoy the parents, so they get cross with their child as well. But I just feel angry with the school.'

'What about Amy's dad?'

'What about him?'

'Doesn't he get cross about her having detentions?'

'We don't tell him. He doesn't need to know.'

I could hear something in her voice. It was the same something Perdita's mother had in her voice when she talked about her husband. It reminded me of the women in the commune, and the way all the fun stopped when they talked, or thought, about the men they were in the process of leaving behind. My mother had never fully fitted in with them because she wasn't afraid of my father, and although she could happily list his flaws all day long, it was obvious he didn't reign in terror like the other husbands.

She continued snipping and she talked to me about school. Then I asked her, 'Where did you meet your husband?'

'My husband?' She laughed. 'In the fourth form.'

'And he's strict?'

'He's got stricter,' she admitted. 'But he really loves Amy. It's incredible. He loves her in such a good way. I love her too, of course. She's my daughter. But sometimes it's as if he gave birth to her instead of me.'

I wasn't sure I wanted to hear this.

'I'm sorry, Gerald, I shouldn't be confiding in you. There aren't that many people to talk to round here. Most of our friends . . . Well, the police force is like a family.'

Time to become adult again. 'It's OK.'

'Is it?' she said, her voice trembling as she brought her hand up to her face to stop the tears.

'You can talk to me.'

'You're a child.'

'A teenager.'

'Barely.'

I ignored this. 'I can cope.'

She closed her eyes and exhaled heavily. 'I need a cigarette.'

'Have one.'

'My husband's a policeman,' she said, a note of desperation entering her voice. 'I don't have any hiding places.'

'He doesn't let you smoke?'

She shook her head. 'It's OK, I shouldn't anyway. Gerald, if I tell you something, do you promise not to tell Amy I said it?'

'I promise.'

'The year after Amy was born, William had an accident. It wasn't serious, but he had to take a long break from work. He had cover, money was coming in, but it seemed silly for us both to be at home. He had to be there, he couldn't do anything else, but I didn't. So I went out and got a temporary position. It was only for about six months, but during that time something crucial happened. I suppose it must've been a natural part of her development, but while I was working, Amy transferred all her affection from me to William. And although I spent much more time with her after that, and I was the one who brought her up, she still loves him much more than me.'

There was a clatter and the front door opened. Without my glasses, I couldn't see her, but I knew it was Amy. She shouted hello and then came through to the kitchen. When she saw me, she said, 'Shit.'

'Amy,' her mother said quietly.

'Sorry. But I completely forgot he was coming here today.'

She was standing close to me. From her blurry movements, I realised she was taking her shoes off.

'Didn't you have a detention?' her mother asked.

'Detention? No, I was just talking . . . We stayed behind in the playground. Did he say you could cut his hair?'

'Of course. I didn't just grab him.'

'I'm gonna go upstairs and get changed. Are you going to be much longer?'

'A while, yes. But you two can talk while I cut his hair.'

'You're very brave, Gerald,' said Amy. 'She did such a bad job on me that she had to take me straight to the hairdresser to have it sorted out.'

'That was months ago. I've really come on since then.'

'How do you know? You haven't cut anyone else's hair.'

'I did your father's.'

She sniggered. 'Yeah, well, there's not much that could go wrong there.'

'Go and get changed,' Madeline snapped. 'Let me get on with Gerald's haircut.'

Amy did as she was told. As soon as she'd gone, Madeline said, 'You will keep what I said secret, won't you? I wouldn't be able to cope if you said anything to Amy.'

'Of course. I promise.'

Amy took a long time getting changed, and when she came back downstairs Madeline had almost finished. Amy moved past the pair of us, asking me if I wanted a drink of squash and some biscuits.

'Yes please,' I told her.

The two of them chatted while Madeline tried a last few snips, only occasionally involving me in the conversation. When it was done, she handed me back my glasses and said, 'I don't have two mirrors so I can't show you the back.'

To my surprise, she'd done an excellent job. My hair was always a mess, and the kind of hairdresser my mother took me to never worried about shaping or styling my mop. Madeline was the first person who'd made me look presentable. Especially with my new clothes and fixed teeth.

'Thank you,' I told her, 'I really like it.'

Amy stared at me. 'You look much better without your glasses.'

'Oh, Amy,' said Madeline, 'that's a horrible thing to say.'

'Why? It was a compliment.'

'But he can't help being short-sighted. He has to wear glasses. It's not a fashion choice.'

'He could wear contacts.'

'His glasses make him look very distinguished. He looks more like fifteen than thirteen.'

'Better to be cool than distinguished. You should definitely get contacts, Gerald.'

I didn't reply. A while ago, a comment like this would have really upset me. But now I'd got used to other people's criticism, I'd started to value it, deciding that self-improvement didn't have to be a bad thing. I'd never really thought about contact lenses before, but if it was another way of getting the girls to accept me, I was prepared to investigate the possibility.

Madeline removed the towel from around my shoulders. 'Why don't you two do your interview in the lounge?'

I put the Dictaphone on the table and pointed it in her direction.

'That's my dad's chair.'

'I'm sorry, I'll move.'

'No, no, it's OK. It just feels weird having you there. It's like I'm being interrogated by my dad.'

'Does that happen often?'

Amy crossed her legs. 'He's strict sometimes.' She paused. 'But only because he loves me.'

I nodded. 'You can talk to him, though.'

'Of course I can talk to him. He's my dad.'

'I mean about personal stuff. Private things.'

'Why would I want to talk to him about private things?'

'Problems, then.'

'He's brilliant at fixing things.'

'But what if things weren't going well? You'd go to him instead of your mum?'

The door opened and Madeline came in. At that moment, Amy said defensively, 'I love both my parents equally.'

Madeline stared at me, as if amazed that I'd managed to betray her so swiftly. I wanted to signal to her that I hadn't revealed anything, only picked up on things Amy had said. But there was no way of doing this. Madeline sat down and gave me a disappointed look, as if realising she'd been foolish to trust a child. I was embarrassed, and took several minutes to think of another question.

Madeline said, 'I'm still not sure I understand exactly what you're supposed to be doing.'

'Gathering information,' I told her. 'It's for when we go away to the Yorkshire Moors.'

'Yes, but what are you supposed to be doing with the information?'

My father was like this. Although I'd already explained everything countless times, and he'd accompanied me to the auditions where he'd been given several information sheets, he still failed to understand what *All Right Now!* was about. I think this was because if he really thought about the concept, he'd be forced to take it seriously. And if he did that, he'd see the dangers my mother had already foreseen. In a calm, patient voice, I told Madeline, 'The dramaturge, Nicholas Pennington, said we had to gather raw material to begin with, and then, when we go away, that's when we start turning it into stories.'

'Yes, but how?'

'He said we've got to learn how to see each other as characters,' Amy told her mother. 'Discover the details that make us real to an audience.'

'Are you all going to have parents?' asked Madeline. 'What I mean is, will they feature in the story? Because the action could be set in a youth club, say, or a boarding school.'

'I think they're going to employ professional actors for those parts. But, like I said, there will be a lot of changes. Perhaps some of us won't have parents.'

'Maybe you don't need parents, Amy,' Madeline said quickly. 'Your character can be an orphan. You know how much you like *Annie*.'

Amy looked embarrassed. 'I used to like it. When I was a kid. Not any more.'

'And if you were an orphan, your whole character would be different. So all these questions Gerald is asking would be irrelevant.'

'Mum,' said Amy, 'could you leave us alone, please? Gerald and I have to do this, and you're really not helping with all these interruptions.'

Madeline looked hurt, but nevertheless got up from her chair, and left us alone in the lounge. I was surprised Amy had stood up to her mother, and noticed that she seemed to have changed since she'd detected how suspicious her mother was of this questioning process. She became more conspiratorial than before, leaning in towards me with a friendly smile. I didn't fancy Amy, because she intimidated me, but I realised I was enjoying this session more than my time with Wendy or Perdita. I grew bolder with each question, impressed that she kept answering with no hint of embarrassment. I even got up enough courage to ask her whether she had a boyfriend. She shook her head, but there was no self-pity in the movement. It was more as if she considered herself above such trivialities.

The session ended when Shep returned to pick me up. Madeline knocked on the door before she came into the lounge, clearly still cross about being asked to leave. I'd hoped for a moment alone with her to smooth things over, but Amy stayed with us until I'd left the house.

'How'd it go?' Shep asked, as we walked back to his car.

'OK,' I told him.

He nodded. 'That's good. Hey, did they do something to your hair?'

I laughed. 'Yeah. Does it look OK?'

'Not bad,' he said, opening the passenger door for me. 'Who did it, the girl?'

'Her mother.'

'Weird,' he said, and started the engine. I smiled and listened to the radio as he drove me home.

66

Although my housemates were a peculiar bunch of misfits, they had no trouble summoning a huge crowd every time we had a party. Mickey had remained in contact with what seemed like the whole of Chelmsford, his home town, including three respected DJs who spent Saturday afternoon setting up a terrifying sound-system in our lounge. Tom knew every out-of-work actor in London, all of whom were always up for a party if they could get together enough money for a bus ticket and a bottle of wine. Lorraine pulled in a contingent of slightly crazed people she'd met in clubs. And I went into invitation overdrive, pulling out old address books and calling up everyone I knew.

Lorraine had gone round to the neighbours on Friday, returning with an assurance that they would definitely show up. We'd taken a group decision not to invite any students from the language school. Sally asked Darla, who said she'd be happy to come as long as my housemates weren't horrible to her. Mickey was nervous about the TV woman appearing, although this wasn't because he considered her a possible partner but because he knew we'd do our best to get the two of them together.

After seeing us avoid housework for so long, Sally was amazed at the operation mounted in preparation for the party. We filled fifteen bin bags, washed every surface, vacuumed all the carpets, and redistributed the furniture so that the whole downstairs area could become a dance floor.

'Are you going to do this again after the party?' asked Sally.

Mickey looked at Tom. 'How long did we leave it last time?'

He shrugged. 'About two weeks.'

'We'll get round to it eventually.'

Sally scowled, and walked away.

I'd told my sister to show up early, hating that boring period before a party really gets going, and not wanting to endure it alone. Erica showed up with six friends from home, including, astonishingly, Reggel. I hadn't seen him since I was sixteen, when he decided not to stay on for the sixth form. He'd put on weight and lost all his hair. It was strange to see someone in his early twenties who'd gone bald, but it didn't surprise me. Slightly more disturbing was the state of his teeth, which were seriously discoloured. We sat on the stairs and talked. I asked him what he did for a living and he told me he worked in a building society.

'I'm doing business with your dad,' he said happily.

This worried me. I thought he would've learnt his lesson after the arrest, but if he was up to something I didn't like the idea of Reggel getting mixed up in his mischief.

It wasn't until eleven that our house started to get really packed. I'd moved upstairs to my bedroom, which, now it had two sofas in it as well as my new bed, had become the main conversation area. Earlier in the evening I'd gone to the off-licence and bought several bottles of spirits that I'd secreted in various hiding places around the room. The idea was to have easy access to enough drink to get me and my friends through the whole night, although as we were already on our third bottle, it now seemed unlikely that it would last that long.

Reggel seemed overwhelmed by the party, but nevertheless eager to show how much he was enjoying it. He had adopted an open posture and kept smiling at everybody. I was surprised at how easy I found it to talk to him, even after all this time. He told me he was married to someone from our school. His wife was a girl who'd always avoided us in the playground, but had apparently come to work in the building society two years after Reggel and things had developed from there.

Darla was much calmer than she'd been the last time I saw her, seemingly happy just to be my friend. She'd said at the time that our night at Darklands was a once-only thing – an evening off from our usual responsibility – but I didn't believe her until she showed up acting normal tonight. I still had warm feelings towards her, and was pleased to have her sitting on the sofa with me, every drink making me feel more at home with my friends.

The music downstairs was getting increasingly manic and my sister said, 'Don't you mind them destroying your house?'

'Nah, not tonight. And besides, Mickey'll sort everything out. He's paranoid about losing his deposit.'

'Gerald.'

I looked up. Lorraine was standing in the doorway.

'You have to see this.'

I handed Reggel the bottle and got up from the sofa. Everyone looked up at me, curious whether I wanted them to follow. I held out my hands, advising them to stay seated. Lorraine had already gone and I went after her. The landing was packed with people and as I looked through Tom's doorway I saw a dark-haired girl laying out Tarot cards on the table while the rest of the room watched. I pushed past and went downstairs. Lorraine was making her way through to the pantry, and I stopped to marvel at the size of the crowd dancing in the lounge.

Lorraine came back to grab me. 'Come on.'

I went into the pantry with her. The room was crowded, but I realised immediately what Lorraine wanted me to witness: the pasty-faced TV woman making out with Mickey on the corner of his bed. It was a miracle, and I couldn't help laughing out loud. Lorraine turned round and pushed me out of the room, not wanting us to distract them. As she did so, I noticed a woman lying on the floor of the shower room. I went in to check on her and saw she was being sick into the shower's plastic tray. I reached up and turned the shower on. A hot spray splashed over her head and began to wash the vomity water down the plughole. Not knowing what to do, I started rubbing her back.

'You'll be OK,' I told her. 'Would you like some water?'

'No thanks,' she said, 'I think that's what triggered it.'

'Let me take you outside then. Fresh air always helps.'

She nodded, and put her hand on my shoulder. The girl was much more elegantly dressed than anyone else at the party, and although she was clearly very drunk she didn't have any problem walking on her high heels. As we made our way outside, I saw Lorraine's policeman coming in with a plastic bag of beer. Our front door was open and lots of people from the party were standing outside in the street. This worried me, as although we'd invited a few of our neighbours, there were others who'd be bound to complain. I sat the girl on our front wall and rubbed her back while she vomited again.

'Gerald,' said a familiar voice.

I looked up.

It was Stan.

67

Mum had said that if the four girls were going to come round to talk to her, she wanted to get it all over with in one weekend. It took some persuasion, but eventually I got everybody to agree to the following arrangement:

Saturday	Sunday
2pm Amy	2pm Perdita
4pm Wendy	4pm Sheryl

Dad was looking to escape the interrogation, but Mum told him that seeing as he'd been so keen for me to be involved in this, he had to stay. Although my mother hated having people in her house, on the rare occasions that she was forced to entertain, she always took the responsibility seriously, and today she sent my father and me to the supermarket to buy squash, soft drinks and several different flavours of Soda Stream in case the girls fancied a homemade fizzy drink.

In the supermarket, I asked Dad about contact lenses. He responded by lifting my glasses from the end of my nose and cleaning them with a corner of his shirt.

'Oh, Gerald, you know how dangerous they are. I had a friend who got his stuck round the back of his eyeball.'

This sounded horrible. 'How did they get it out?'

'They couldn't. But it punctured something round the back of his socket and they had to wait until it produced enough pus to push it out.'

'Ugh. Does that happen often?'

'All the time. Unless you're very, very careful and scrupulously clean.' He put the glasses back on my nose. 'Which you're not.'

I couldn't really argue. But Amy's compliment remained in my mind, and although I didn't want an eye-socket full of pus, perhaps if I had something I knew I had to keep clean, I'd be able to manage it. Dad noticed I was serious about this and said, 'Maybe when I've got more money, OK?'

There was a reason I'd scheduled Amy to visit first. I knew it was important to get my mother's approval quickly, and felt certain Amy was the one who'd impress her the most. Wendy could only do Saturday afternoon, which was a worry, as I knew Mum would find her rough, or common, or just too full of life. I didn't really understand Mum's class distinctions, especially as our own ranking seemed to change according to the situation. I had heard my parents describe us as both working class and middle class, depending whom they were talking to. Dad told us we should feel proud of our 'humble origins', but when we were in restaurants my parents always vetted my order in case I chose something that made people think we weren't middle class.

For some reason I didn't really understand, Mum, Dad and Erica had set up an interview spot in the back garden. They'd carted Dad's wallpaper-table out onto the lawn, and now all three of them sat behind it. I showed Amy through, and fetched her a drink. She seemed to have decided to take this seriously, and had brought a folder and a notepad.

'Hello,' said my mother, 'so you're Amy? I'm Mrs Wedmore.'

My father sighed. 'Let her call you by your Christian name, Jenny.'

'Why?'

'It's OK,' said Amy, 'I don't mind. Mrs Wedmore, can you tell me more about your job? It sounds fascinating.'

My mother loved this, and immediately launched into a long explanation of her job at the commune. I could tell Amy had asked this because she didn't want to end up being a housewife like her mother, and as she continued her questions, she almost completely ignored my father.

Amy stayed just over an hour, but the car that came to pick her up also delivered Wendy.

'What's going on?' I asked the driver, who wasn't Shep.

'The production office didn't want to send two separate cars.'

I nodded. He walked to the car with Amy. I smiled at Wendy, and invited her inside. In spite of the way she'd mocked me before, I found myself feeling sorry for her. It was no fun facing my mother's disapproval, and it wasn't as if Wendy was doing anything to invite it. For instance, she'd clearly made a real effort with her appearance. She was wearing a light blue blouse and a smart skirt, earrings and make-up. But I knew my mother would look at her and see only someone she wouldn't want me to associate with.

'Can you just wait a minute?' I asked her. 'My parents didn't know you were coming now and they're probably not ready.'

I left her there and went out to the back garden. My family had got up from the table and were making their way indoors.

'Hang on, hang on . . . ' I said quickly.

'Why?' Erica asked.

'The driver brought the other girl with him. I know she's early, but . . . '

'Fucking hell,' said Mum, 'we don't have to do all that over again right now, do we?'

'You can do it quickly.'

'You lot do it,' said Dad, 'I'm going inside for a nap.'

'Don't you dare,' Mum told him. 'If I have to do this, you do too.'

They continued to grumble, but retook their seats. I picked up their cups to refresh their drinks, hoping this might quell their irritation. Erica was enjoying having me wait on her, the usual psychopathic grin replaced with a more benign merriment. I went out and fetched Wendy, bringing her through to face my family.

She looked nervous as she sat down on a white garden chair and my freakish folks surveyed her from behind their wallpaper-table. I could tell from Mum's expression that she wasn't impressed with this girl, and once Wendy realised she was being appraised, she became even less interested in the exercise. I could tell my mother saw in Wendy a type of girl she'd never liked: a housewife-in-training, brought up by straight-talking parents.

'I like your earrings,' Mum told Wendy.

Wendy touched her earlobes, perhaps sensing there was an undercurrent to this compliment. She crossed her legs and asked my sister, 'Erica . . . is Gerald a nice brother?'

'No,' she replied, 'he's horrible.'

'Oh, Erica,' said Mum, 'you know you don't mean that. These two love to pretend they hate each other, but really they're as close as a brother and sister can be.'

I couldn't believe my mother was saying this. She often pursued this line when talking to another adult, who had no way of telling how we really felt about each other, but Wendy would soon be spending a weekend with my sister and me and would probably witness us at our worst.

'Oh,' she said, 'that's nice. My sister hates me.'

Mum pursed her lips. After that, every question Wendy asked her was met with a clipped, cold response. Erica and my father were kinder. Wendy wasn't stupid: she could tell my mother didn't like her, and directed most of her questions to the other two members of my family. They were both over-excited by all the attention, and answered Wendy's half-hearted questions in great detail. Soon Wendy stopped asking questions altogether, but Dad carried on talking, until my mother said, 'John, I'm sure the girl doesn't want to know all your personal details.'

Even this didn't stop him, and he carried on babbling. Just as I was wondering whether I could take this any longer, the doorbell rang. It was the driver, thank God, who winked at me and whispered, 'I thought your parents might be tired.'

I smiled at him. Wendy had already come through to the hall. She said goodbye to me and left. I went outside and listened to my mother make all the judgements I'd been anticipating.

'Well,' said my Dad, after she'd finished, 'I thought she was nice.'

'That's because you're an idiot,' she snapped, and Erica laughed until she threw up.

68

Stan was wearing a suit. I'd never seen him in smart clothes before – like Tom and Lorraine, he dressed casually for work at the Language School. He'd also either lost or abandoned his glasses, and as he came closer, I realised he was wearing make-up.

'Fucking hell, Stan, where have you been? We called the police, told your parents, everything . . . '

Stan looked at the woman on the wall beside me, who made an anguished noise before vomiting again.

'I met someone,' he said. I noticed he was holding several carrier-bags, the paper kind that come from expensive clothes shops.

'And you couldn't call? I don't want to act like your dad, but the others were really worried.'

He smiled. 'Unlike you, right?'

'Well, of course I was . . . All I mean is . . . '

'It's OK,' he said, 'and I'm sorry. It's hard to explain. It's kind of your fault though.'

'I thought it might be. Don't tell the others that, OK?'

'Were they blaming you?'

'Me and Darla. For giving you drugs.'

Hearing this, the vomiting woman righted herself, and grabbing hold of my shirt, implored me, 'Please, do you have anything?'

'Drugs? No. And how's that going to help you?'

She slumped down and maliciously vomited a few centimetres from my shoes.

'Oh, that's lovely,' I said, putting my arm around her and moving her down to the end of the wall. 'You just sit over there.'

I turned back to Stan, who said, 'No, it wasn't the drugs. Well, yes, that was part of it, but it was mainly your pep talk.'

'I knew that was a mistake. So what exactly happened? We didn't see you leave.'

'After Darla gave me the coke, I saw this girl. And I thought about what you said about all those nights in clubs and cinemas when we kept ourselves in check, and I thought, just once I'm going to go up to someone I find attractive and tell them I fancy them. I mean, what's the worst that can happen?'

'And what did happen?'

Just as he was about to answer me, I looked up and saw Sophie, the tall blonde woman from Bar Rumba. She was wearing a black top with a scarlet skirt and a pair of black leather sandals with a thick sole. Behind her were the two clowns she'd had with her the last time we'd met: Don, the man with the jester's hat hair, and her Uncle C, who wore a suit and trilby just like before, only this time both articles of clothing were dark blue. Stan didn't realise I knew this trio and continued talking. But I ignored him, unable to stop staring at Sophie.

'Hey,' I said, 'thanks for coming.'

'Don't thank me,' said Sophie, 'it was Uncle C's idea. He's got some pills he wants to sell.'

The vomit girl immediately sat up. 'I'll buy one.'

'Me too,' said Stan.

I didn't want to seem conservative in front of Sophie, but felt I had to intervene. 'Hang on a minute. Neither of you is in any fit state to take drugs.' I pointed at the girl. 'You've been vomiting solidly for the last fifteen minutes, and as for you,' I said, gesturing at Stan, 'well, you've only just returned from your last adventure.'

Uncle C, however, had spotted a business opportunity, and was quick to take advantage. The vomit girl already had her cash ready, and although this was the first time Stan had bought drugs and didn't know how much to pay, Uncle C quickly advised him.

'Can we go back inside?' I asked in a petulant voice. 'And you should all be careful. There's a policeman at this party.'

Uncle C looked panicked, and I smiled, pleased to have worried him.

69

My family didn't usually eat lunch on Sundays until at least three o'clock, as we had a cooker that took several hours to roast anything, and neither my mother nor my father enjoyed rising early at weekends. Today, with Perdita due at two, Mum decided to send Dad to the Kentucky Fried Chicken.

'You'd best get something for the girl as well,' Mum told him.

'But it'll be cold by the time she gets here.'

'That doesn't matter. We can bung it in the microwave.'

'Mum, I don't think Perdita's the type of girl to eat Kentucky Fried Chicken.'

'What are you talking about? Whyever not?'

'Well, she's a bit . . . '

'A bit what?'

'I don't know. Arty. Posh. Middle class. Her mother's a playwright.'

Mum laughed. 'Middle-class people still eat Kentucky Fried Chicken.'

Dad looked uncertain. 'I'm not sure they do, Jenny.'

'Oh,' said Mum, 'I've had enough of this. If she's middle class, she'll be polite. And if she's polite, she'll eat whatever we offer her.'

Perdita didn't eat the Kentucky Fried Chicken. She declined the offer politely, saying she'd had her Sunday lunch before coming out, but my father still smirked, pleased to be proved right. I could understand why Perdita didn't want the reheated fried food, but I worried about the way she was appearing to my family, as I really wanted them to approve of her.

Nevertheless, Perdita didn't take long to grasp that my mother required the same careful handling as her own, and quickly altered her behaviour, becoming quiet and deferential. Mum noticed this and clearly approved, going easy on her from then on. Dad and Erica were much less interested in Perdita than they'd been in yesterday's visitors, and toned down their usual performances. It didn't take them long to stop talking completely, and the conversation gathered slightly more weight as my mother fenced with Perdita. I could tell Mum was still riled by the suggestion that Perdita's parents were posher than us, and for every question Perdita asked, Mum sent one back, trying to find out more about our guest's background.

'Her father's an engineer,' Mum said triumphantly after the car had come to take Perdita away.

'So?' asked Dad, whose father was an electrician.

'Well, that means we're definitely a cut above them.'

'Oh, Jenny,' he replied, the disappointment clear in his voice, 'sometimes you can be so . . .'

'So what?'

'Snobbish. And petty. Who cares about stuff like that?'

'I care. It's important.'

'No it's not. It makes me sad that you think it is.'

My father's emotional temperature was much harder to gauge than my mother's. He was so self-contained that most of the time we assumed he was ticking along fine. This meant that we often didn't notice when he got upset, which was guaranteed to drive him into a rage. His anger, when provoked, always seemed much more violent than the situation warranted, and I always got worried when my mother didn't take him seriously. Now she said, 'You don't understand because you've got no pride. If it was up to you, this family would never do anything to improve itself.'

'That's self-improvement, is it? Looking down on others?'

'We're not looking down. We're just acknowledging that they're different from us.'

'Inferior.'

'If that's how you want to put it. I just think people should know their place.'

My mother didn't mean any of this, not in the way it sounds. Her family were probably more middle class than my father's, but she was estranged from them, and the main reason for this sort of talk was that she wanted our family to have a dignity that she believed would come from personal pride. It wasn't that she was really antisocial; she just needed to feel important. I could tell she was resentful Perdita's mother was a playwright, and she felt the need to compete, that's all.

My father, however, didn't understand any of this, and, rather than continue the argument, disappeared upstairs in a huff.

70

As we were going back upstairs to my bedroom, we passed Lorraine and her policeman. They were standing by the door to the secret room.

'Look,' said Lorraine, 'Steve's picked the lock. Don't you want to look inside?'

Stan, who was standing behind me, started freaking out. 'Oh shit,' he said, 'oh fucking hell, this is terrible.'

'Relax,' I told him, and turned to the policeman. 'You can lock it up again, can't you?'

He nodded.

'No,' said Stan, 'you don't understand. It's the secret room.'

'So? Look, all your superstitions about the secret room, they're entirely your invention. All they said when they showed us the place was that we weren't allowed to go in there. Nothing about ghosts, or the old lady's presence, or anything at all that should worry us. I'm sure the only reason they didn't want us to go in there is because the family are using it as storage space. That's all.'

The room wasn't being used as storage space. Behind the door was an adolescent boy's bedroom. It was tidy with a small single bed on one side of the room, two plastic clothes-hampers (one empty, the other filled with what looked like electronic toys), and a small, wooden desk. On the wall above the bed was a poster for the film *Street Fighter*.

'When did that come out?' I asked Stan.

'What?'

I pointed at the poster.

'Who cares?' he said. 'Let's get out of here.'

I turned and looked at him. The fear in his expression seemed so exaggerated that I thought it had to be a joke. But when I put my hand on his arm, I realised he was actually trembling.

'OK,' I said to Steve, 'I'm sorry, but this is really upsetting him. Can you shut it up again, please?'

The policeman looked perplexed, but did as he was told, closing the door and fiddling with the keyhole until the room was locked.

'Your housemates are strange,' he told Lorraine.

'Believe me,' she said, 'I know.'

71

In some ways it was a relief that Sheryl was the last girl to come to our house. She may have been embarrassing, but at least she was also endearing, and posed no threat to my mother. Although my father usually managed to pass through life without remembering the simplest details about the people surrounding him, he had registered that Sheryl embarrassed me, and, worse still, as soon as she entered the house, he seemed to realise why.

My family had drifted off around the house since Perdita's interrogation, and now I had to reassemble them. This meant leaving Sheryl with my father while I went upstairs. He was lounging on the sofa, half watching TV (he rarely gave anything other than a roulette wheel his full attention). Sheryl stood by the door, looking shy and scared.

Dad sat up. 'Make yourself at home,' he told her.

She remained where she was. Dad patted the cushion next to him and she reluctantly went across. I ran upstairs to Mum's study.

'Sheryl's here,' I told her.

'Can I just finish what I'm doing?'

'Mum,' I said, 'Dad's talking to her.'

She looked up, amused by the stress I'd put on these words. But she still seemed to accept my concern and got up from her desk.

'Where's Erica?' I asked.

'Oh, Gerald, she's not really interested. She's done really well so far and I don't think it's worth forcing her to take part.'

'OK,' I said, 'maybe Sheryl can ask you questions about her instead.'

We went downstairs. It had started to rain, so my parents didn't bother going out to the garden. Mum got Dad to turn the television off and brought a chair across from the dining table so Sheryl could sit opposite us. She reached into the pocket of her yellow plastic jacket and brought out a Dictaphone. Noticing my expression, she smiled and said, 'My dad bought it for me.'

Placing the device on the table, she angled the microphone towards my father and asked, 'How would you feel if Gerald brought a girlfriend home?'

Dad loved this question. 'I often wonder why he hasn't already. I think the boy's shy.'

'In general,' Mum interrupted, 'we don't encourage our children to bring their friends home.'

'Why's that? I mean, is there a particular reason?'

'Well, obviously if we know the child's family, that's different. But a lot of the kids at Gerald's school are quite rough, and they might cause trouble.'

Sheryl nodded. 'That makes sense.'

Both my parents quickly warmed to Sheryl, and I could tell she was the girl they liked the most. I knew they'd be happy if she became my girlfriend, and they started making jokes about her obvious affection for me the moment she left our house. It was like the girl from our holiday all over again, except that Sheryl had a rabbity innocence that made her sweeter than my previous tormentor. The only good thing was that Erica hadn't witnessed this, and I spent the rest of the afternoon fending off jokes and doing my best not to get annoyed, knowing this would only increase their amusement.

72

It was four in the morning. The party showed no sign of slowing down, and the only person who'd gone to sleep (in our bathtub) was Reggel. I'd gone up to the kitchen, where Sophie sat with her Uncle C and their friend Don. Standing by the window was one of the neighbours, listening while

Lorraine explained how we spied on them. I'd spoken to most of the neighbours earlier. They were a group of actors improvising a new show about the lives of various religious figures. I'd had a drunken conversation with one of them about *All Right Now!* and he kept insisting that he'd watched it, although I wasn't sure I believed him.

I still fancied Sophie, but I'd had enough of her peculiar accomplices. Don didn't seem to do anything apart from occasionally groaning and rubbing his forehead, while Uncle C seemed a thoroughly disturbing character.

'Are you really her Uncle?'

He nodded. 'She's my favourite niece.'

'Uh huh. And you're a drug dealer?'

'Hey,' he said, looking hurt, 'I thought this was supposed to be a party.'

'I'm not judging you,' I said quickly, 'I just don't know many uncles who hang out with their nieces.'

He gave me a long, hard stare, his expression suggesting he pitied me. 'The problem with people like you is that you have to put a label on everyone. You call me a drug dealer because I try to liven up your party, then say I can't spend time with my relations. What business is it of yours what I do? I hang out with my niece because she's a nice person. She doesn't judge me, I benefit from her company, and she benefits from the wisdom of my experience.'

I snorted. Uncle C got up from his chair. 'Come on, guys, we're not welcome here.'

'I didn't say that,' I said quickly, 'you're very welcome. I'm sorry, I was being a twat.'

But they didn't pay any attention, all standing up together and walking out of the kitchen. I ran after them, and Don stopped and took a small notepad from his inside pocket. He scribbled something onto a leaf, tore it off, and tossed it at me.

'What's that?' I asked.

'Sophie's number. That's all you wanted, isn't it?'

I didn't reply. He sneered at me and followed his friends downstairs.

PART V

★

73

My father was agitated. 'Are you sure they didn't give you a list?'

I nodded. My mother came in from the kitchen and told him, 'He's not going on an Outward Bound mission. He'll be with all those television types. They're hardly going to make do without their luxuries.'

'Yes, Jenny, but the Yorkshire Moors is still the Yorkshire Moors. What if they go on a midnight walk and he gets separated from the group?'

'They didn't mention anything about midnight walks.'

'And he has to protect his sister. Gerald, come upstairs with me.'

He led me out of the lounge and upstairs to his bedroom. I waited while he went under the bed and brought out his box. Keeping it carefully angled on the mattress so I couldn't see inside, he began to go through its contents.

'Right. The first thing you need is a compass. I've got an old Scout one here. It's basic, but it does the job.'

I took it from him. 'How does it work?'

'The magnet always points north. You start with it pointing away from you, and the arrow will show you where you are.'

'So if I get lost on the moors I can find my way back to the accommodation?'

'Well, you need to know your co-ordinates. If you've got your co-ordinates, you can find your way back from anywhere.'

I didn't understand any of this, but nodded anyway. My father reached into the box again and brought out a torch.

'Torch.'

'Thanks.'

'Matches.'

'Great.'

'Candles. Condoms.'

'Dad, I won't need condoms.'

'Yes you will. They're the best water-carriers you can find. Say you're in a situation where you're lost and you come across a stream or a tap – actually, I've got some water-purifying tablets somewhere, so it won't even matter if the water's dirty – and you don't know when you'll get chance to find water again, you can fill the condom and that might even turn out to save your life.'

He looked serious. I felt embarrassed, but took the condoms, knowing that if I didn't I would inevitably get stranded in a freak accident where I'd desperately need some means of transporting water. I waited while he had another look inside his box.

'I think that's it, everything you need. Mum's sorted you out with shampoo and biscuits and a mug and stuff, right?'

I nodded. He put the box back under the mattress and sat on the bed. He patted the space alongside him and I sat down.

'Gerald, I know you're a responsible boy. Much more so than I was at your age. I also know that this is going to be really exciting for you. Going away with girls like that, well, it's got to be great. And I realise it's going to cramp your style having Erica with you. Your mum's got her reasons for wanting that – she loves you both equally and wants Erica to be a part of what's obviously going to be something special – but I can understand why you might feel resentful. So I'm going to ask you to be an adult here, and overcome that resentment, and help your sister cope with being away from home. The way she behaves with us . . . Maybe it was a mistake, but once your mother and I realised what kind of girl she was, we decided to let her have her head, and that's gone on since she was really little, so she doesn't understand the rules outside her own kingdom. You'll have to watch her with the other kids, stick up for her, but also stop her being violent. I know it's going to be a pain, but if you do it properly, it'll make the girls like you more, not less, and when you look back on this weekend as an adult, you'll feel proud of yourself and realise that having your sister there was part of what made it wonderful.'

This sounded like nonsense to me, but my father's face was enlivened by an expression of such sincerity that all I could do in response was smile and nod. What you have to understand about my father is that he was an only child, and spent a lot of his youth dreaming about having a sister. Anyone with a sibling will understand how such dreams have no relation to reality. The only thing he'd said which interested me was that the other girls might be impressed by seeing me care for my sister, which I thought was extremely unlikely, but as I didn't really understand how the female mind worked, I was prepared to be surprised.

'OK, Dad,' I told him, 'I'll do my best.'

'Good chap,' he said, opening his wallet. 'Now, how much money do you think you should take? Will a hundred pounds be enough?'

After my talk with my father, I went downstairs to finish packing and endure a similar conversation with my mother, who was also worried about my sister and wanted me to take special care of her. I made the required promises and went upstairs to my private penthouse, too excited to sleep, but too eager for morning to come to do anything else.

74

Shep arrived at five o'clock the following morning. He was only driving us to the meeting point in Edgware Road, where we'd get on a minibus with the other children, ready for the long drive up the M1 to Leeds. Erica was quiet in the car, astonished to be awake at this hour. Every time I closed my eyes I felt the gentle pull of sleep. But I stayed awake, asking Shep, 'What time did you go to bed last night?'

'I haven't gone yet, actually, Gerald. My boss had a party and after the film finished he wanted me to serve drinks.

Things didn't grind down until four, so I just came straight over.'

'Wow. Aren't you tired?'

'A bit. But once I've delivered you I've got the whole weekend free. I'll sleep today, stay out late tonight, and it shouldn't take me long to get back to normal.'

He reached out and turned the radio on. 'You don't mind, do you? I just want to hear if there are any roadworks. Figure out the best way to go.'

Shep also had to pick up Jane and Fuckpit. Since Nicholas Pennington had split us into two groups I had completely forgotten about the other quintet and hoped that we'd continue to be separated from them. I liked working with four girls, even if some of them were mean to me, and didn't like the idea of the other two boys, Fuckpit and Pete, getting to spend time with our group. I didn't have anything against Lola Doll, or Wendy's sister Lucy, apart from them being too young for me (maybe, it occurred to me now, Erica could be friends with them), but I really didn't like Jane. Sheryl was geeky but sweet; Jane was just unpleasant. I know this sounds unkind, but like most children, I was quick to make judgements, and it wasn't as if Jane gave a shit what I thought of her.

Shep parked outside Jane's house and walked up the garden path. Jane emerged seconds later, red-faced and struggling with a suitcase that was far bigger than she needed. I wanted Shep to tell her to go back inside and pack properly. Or just pick up the suitcase and fling it into the neighbour's garden. Instead, he carried it to the car.

Jane climbed in alongside Erica and me. She looked at Erica.

'My sister,' I mouthed.

'So what are you doing on this weekend away?' Shep asked.

'Getting the stories together,' I replied.

'Writing the script?'

'Not yet,' I told him, 'and we're not doing that bit

anyway. We give our stories to the dramaturge and he writes it up.'

'I don't think it's as simple as that, Gerald,' Jane said in a knowing tone.

Erica looked at Jane. She wasn't usually loyal, but I could tell she didn't like this girl criticising her brother. I patted her shoulder, and when she looked back at me, shook my head. Jane didn't notice any of this, gazing forward the whole time.

Robert's father came to the door. He was bald with a brown moustache, and wearing a dressing-gown over a yellowing vest and a pair of pyjama bottoms. Although it was hard to tell from this distance, he seemed annoyed, and then startled as his son pushed past him clutching a sports bag.

'That's Fuckpit,' I told my sister, who laughed loudly.

'Gerald,' said Jane, 'that's not a nice thing to say in front of your sister.'

'Who gives a shit,' Erica shot back. 'We don't care about swearing in our family.'

Jane exhaled through her front teeth, but didn't reply. Fuckpit opened the passenger door and climbed in. Shep also got in, and said, 'So I guess you didn't tell your Dad you were going away?'

Fuckpit ignored him and took a packet of Benson and Hedges from his jacket pocket. He leaned round and offered one to us. We all took one.

'Isn't she too young to smoke?' asked Jane.

'She's too young to do a lot of things. As you'll soon discover, that doesn't make a blind bit of difference.'

Shep got us to the meeting-point early. Everyone was still grumpy from lack of sleep, and he looked relieved when two of the producers, Immi and Carolyn, arrived and he was allowed to go. Immi had short red hair. She was wearing long metal earrings, black sandals, a red batik top, and a pair of beige trousers. Carolyn was blonde and smartly dressed, wearing a black cardigan over a white blouse. After they'd dismissed Shep, Carolyn said to Immi, 'Are you going to park in the NCP then?'

'Yeah.'

'And you're not worried about leaving it there all weekend?'

'No. Should I be? I don't think so. No, I'm sure it'll be fine.' Immi looked back at us. She smiled warmly at my sister. 'Hi, Erica.'

So she was the one my sister had charmed. This was the woman responsible for ruining my dream. I had to thrust my hands into my jacket pockets to control my temper. She was grinning at Erica like she was the nicest child she'd ever met. And my sister was happily smiling back, showing no sign of her usual psychopathy. Immi got in her car and Carolyn came across to us.

'Early,' she said, shrugging.

'Yeah,' I replied.

The five of us stood there, not saying anything more until another car appeared. The doors opened, and Wendy, Lucy, Amy, and Pete tumbled out. Pete was carrying a huge sleeping-bag.

'We don't need sleeping-bags, do we?' Wendy asked, the anguish in her voice suggesting that she'd been worrying about this all the way here.

'No,' said Carolyn, 'there's bedding at the cottage.' She looked at Pete. 'But it'll probably come in useful,' she said quickly. 'Maybe you'll decide you want to sleep under the stars.'

Pete dumped his sleeping-bag on the floor and sat on it. He reached into his rucksack and brought out a sausage roll, wrinkling down the cellophane before taking a bite.

'Bit early, isn't it?' Fuckpit asked.

'Breakfast,' Pete replied.

Wendy and Lucy both had small black canvas satchel-type bags. They looked too small to hold much, and I was surprised they hadn't brought more clothes.

The driver talked to Carolyn for a moment, and then got back in his car and drove off. Carolyn took out a clipboard and ticked off our names before asking, 'So who are we waiting for?'

'Perdita and Sheryl,' I replied, 'and Lola Doll.'

As I said this, the final car arrived and deposited the last three girls. Lola burst out first, carrying two large suitcases. She was wearing a yellow top and what looked like a tutu. Sheryl followed her, dressed more normally than usual in jeans and a baggy grey top. She carried a blue rucksack. As she approached us, I looked past her to take in the full effect of Perdita, whose colour-coordinated clothes drew attention from everyone. She was wearing a red-and-white striped top, a pair of red Capri pants, white socks and red baseball boots. Her brown hair was in its usual ponytail, held up with a red band. White fingerless gloves and a red vanity case completed the look. I smiled at her, hoping she'd come over to me, but she went straight across to Wendy. As I'd suspected, the rules were different when the group was together.

Sheryl shuffled across to stand beside my sister and me. I couldn't stop staring at Perdita, until she caught my eye and I had to look away. As Sheryl came close to me, I instinctively took a step backwards. It wasn't that I wanted to make her feel awkward, I just knew that if I was associated with her at this stage, the rest of the children would assume we'd become friends and avoid the pair of us.

We all watched the traffic, waiting for the minibus to appear. When it did, there was a sense of disappointment, as it was much smaller and less stylish than the cars that usually came to collect us. But as soon as Carolyn opened up the back doors, this was forgotten in our rush to bagsie seats. I was nervous when Lola grabbed Erica and got her to share a seat at the front, but couldn't stop them and was more worried about getting my own place on the minibus. I deliberately moved past Sheryl, shaking off her fingers and sliding in to the end of the back seat. I knew this position would be coveted, and there were two spaces beside me.

'Can I swap seats with you, Gerald?' Wendy asked me.

I didn't want to move, but knew I had to come up with a good excuse if I wasn't going to look churlish.

'Actually, Wend, I really want to sit by the window. It stops me getting sick on long drives.'

'There's plenty of other seats by the window.'

I was about to give in and get up when Perdita, to my astonishment, said, 'I've got some tapes I want to play Gerald on my Walkman, if that's OK, Wend.'

Wendy met Perdita's gaze for a moment, then sat down in front of us. Amy seemed troubled by this tension, and said, in an obliging voice, 'You can have my seat if you want.'

'No,' said Wendy, 'it's OK.'

She shuffled along as Pete sat next to her. Carolyn had gone round to the front and got in with the driver. I heard him ask, 'Are we ready to go?'

'Not just yet,' she said. 'One more to come.'

'Miss,' said Lola, 'is Nicholas Pennington coming with us?'

'No, he's travelling down separately. Along with a couple of my colleagues. Oh, and don't call me Miss. My name is Carolyn.'

We waited for five minutes. Immi appeared on foot, speeding up as she noticed the minibus. It was starting to get lighter outside. As well as her luggage, she was carrying a video camera. She came through the back door and sat with us instead of up front with the other adults.

'Can you make sure those doors are shut?' the driver asked.

She did, and we set off.

75

Wendy was ignoring Perdita, pretending to sleep. Perdita waited until we were on the motorway, then opened her vanity case and took out a tape.

'So what did you want me to listen to?' I asked her.

She smiled. 'I was going to try to convince you that the Beatles aren't shit.'

Still grateful for her earlier intervention, I was prepared to be mature about this. 'Do you have the *White Album*? I read in a magazine that that's the only good one.'

'We don't have the *White Album* any more. I made these tapes from my parents' record collection. When they were younger, before Mum started having her plays put on properly, they couldn't afford the house on their own and they had to have a lodger. And one day the lodger, who was a revolutionary communist . . . ' She gave me a careful look, to see if I understood. I pretended I did. 'Well, he gave the album to Jean-Luc Godard. Do you know who he is?'

I nodded, even though I hadn't a clue.

'He was going to use the music in a film. I don't know if he actually did, in the end, but we never got the record back.'

'Which one are you going to play me then?'

'It's up to you. I have *Abbey Road* or *Let It Be*.'

'I don't mind.'

'*Abbey Road*, then. That way I don't have to rewind the tape.'

She unwound her earphones and we pressed our heads together so we could have one each.

I was astounded Perdita was being so nice to me, risking ridicule from the girls I knew she wanted to befriend. Maybe it was her way of letting Wendy know that she wasn't going to be her lap-dog. I was happy to be used in this way, and hoped that Perdita would let me work with her when we reached the rented cottage.

As I listened to the music – which I liked, of course, but only really because Perdita did – I looked down the minibus, worried about my sister. I could see her doing Strawberry Patch to the back of Lola's hand, and worried Lola would start screaming. She was sitting near Lucy and also Fuckpit, who looked irritated to be stuck with the younger children. On the other side of the coach Immi was showing Sheryl and Jane how to use the video camera. It had taken a while to get past the traffic, and now the driver had reached a clear stretch of road, he'd put his foot down.

As the minibus speeded up, I closed my eyes and enjoyed the amazing sense of freedom that had only just swept over me. I was away from my parents, away from school, away from the draining sensation I experienced almost every day. I had a kind girl beside me, music in my ears, and was about to take part in an artistic enterprise that would stay with me for the rest of my life.

76

We arrived at the cottage just before midday. Nicholas Pennington was waiting for us, along with a stocky man in a blue shirt and cap, and a woman with gold granny-glasses and wispy blonde hair. The three of them were standing on the gravel drive as the minibus pulled up, and were dressed in waterproof clothing and Wellingtons. None of us was wearing anything like that, and I had a sudden fear that they were going to make us go on hikes and put me in situations where I would need all the equipment my father had forced on me the night before.

'Well,' said Nicholas, as we got out of the minibus and assembled in front of the house, 'Charlotte and Paul have prepared lunch so I thought we'd eat that and then start working as soon as possible.'

'Is it a cold lunch?' Immi asked.

'Yes,' said Charlotte, apologetically, 'sandwiches and fruit. We didn't know what time you'd arrive.'

'In that case, can we wait until the children have had chance to relax? I think they'd like to choose rooms, unpack and maybe even have a little rest . . . '

'OK,' said Charlotte, 'shall we eat at twelve-thirty?'

'Perfect.'

Nicholas looked displeased. 'I really was keen to get started. We have a lot to do this weekend.'

'And we'll get to it,' Immi told him. 'But the kids'll be much more responsive if you give them a little break.'

He didn't reply, turning round and walking back into the cottage. We gathered our belongings and followed him. The inside had been converted from its original design. The back part had two floors, but the front had been changed so that there was now just one huge room with a twenty-foot ceiling, perfect for our purposes. We went upstairs to the bedrooms.

'There are four bedrooms,' said Charlotte. 'A big one for the adults, and three smaller ones. It's up to you how you divide yourselves.' She looked at us. 'Maybe one room for the boys?'

Pete, Fuckpit and I went into the nearest room. It wasn't that big, and the four simple metal beds were close together. I took my bag from my shoulders and dropped it down on the mattress. Two minutes later, Sheryl appeared in the doorway and asked, 'Can I sleep in here?'

''Course you can,' said Fuckpit, and I was surprised to hear a salacious tone in his voice. I thought Sheryl was too plain to flirt with.

'Don't you want to go with the girls?' I asked.

She looked at the floor. 'There's no space in Lucy's room, and Wendy won't let me in with them.'

'That's a bit mean,' said Pete. 'Do you want to be in their room?'

'Not really,' she said. 'I'm happy here.'

Sheryl dropped her bag beside the bed, then took off her trainers and lay on the mattress. I wasn't sure whether I believed Wendy had stopped her sharing their room, and assumed she just wanted to be in with us. I was still worried she fancied me, but then I remembered her throwing the ball to Fuckpit on the first night of our improv exercises, and realised she could just as plausibly be interested in him.

Towards the beginning of this book, I wrote a bit about how as a child I had always imagined my life was being continuously broadcast on a pretend television station, and how in some ways writing this feels like finally playing a mental videotape of stuff I've been storing up for ages. But in the writing of this account, I have, up until now, ignored the existing physical documentation of this story. I'm not talking about the six televised episodes of *All Right Now!* that I no longer have copies of (they got lost along the way, and although it must be possible to find a recording somewhere, so far I've felt no urge to go looking), but rather the seventeen hours of videotape footage that various people shot during our weekend away. This I do have. Although it was originally recorded on Betamax tape and there was only one copy of the six cassettes stored at the production offices, I stole the tapes when we finished recording the series – knowing that otherwise they'd be likely to disappear – and have treasured them ever since, or at least, the VHS copy I made towards the end of the Eighties.

There was a time when I watched at least a few minutes of these recordings every night. About half the running time was taken up with professional-quality recordings of the improvisations and exercises that took place over this weekend. These bits were much less interesting to me than the other sections, which consisted of different members of our group walking round with the camera perched on their shoulder. These sections bear all the hallmarks of amateur video back before cameras got sophisticated enough to counterbalance their users' incompetence. Endless zooming, whip-pans, shakes, wobbles, whole sections where it's impossible to work out exactly what's going on. Sound that is never completely inaudible, but is always hard to follow, as conversations continue with no consideration of the camera, or the viewer who might one day be trying to make sense of these recordings. But in spite (or maybe because) of all this, I found those tapes endlessly fascinating, and the more I studied them, the more I managed to understand.

Eventually, however, I had to abandon this pursuit. It was impossible to cope with the sense of loss, and every night I went to bed feeling emotionally devastated. The tapes had taken on too much significance for me. So I watched them one last time and vowed never to take them down from my shelves again. That was a long time before I started writing this book, and to be honest, I'd always assumed that when I reached this stage of my story, I'd break my vow and reinvestigate the tapes. Now, though, I realise I don't want to, and that if I did it might even be detrimental to the construction of my story. Before I started writing I'd already selected all the events that seemed significant enough to be included, and seeing what actually happened again would force me to unstitch this account and fill it full of stuff that won't make things any clearer. What's on those tapes definitely influenced my initial decision of what to write about, but that seems OK as all it did was help bring the past into focus. And that's good enough, that's all I need, as I work out my own way forward.

We killed the half-hour before lunch lying on our beds and smoking Fuckpit's cigarettes (Sheryl took one; Pete didn't). The conversation was halting, with the four of us mainly muttering variations on 'Fuck, I'm tired,' or 'Do you think this is going to be difficult?' every couple of minutes.

Then Nicholas came to collect us.

'I trust you've all settled in.'

We trooped downstairs and sat around a large table where Charlotte and Paul had arranged our food. The sandwiches were simple: ham, cheese, or ham and cheese, a piece of fruit and a glass of lemonade. I sat between Perdita and Pete, eating and watching the adults.

'How d'you want to run this afternoon's sessions?' Carolyn asked Nicholas.

'Exactly as I said I would,' he told her, taking a small bite from his sandwich.

She nodded. 'Right. But what do you want us to do? Apart from supervise? I thought I'd take care of the video recording.'

He stared at her. 'Yes, that's fine. Charlotte, Paul and Imogen can participate in the improvisation if we need any adults.'

Immi looked shocked, her red head popping up. 'I can't act.'

'Nor can the children. Yet. That's what this weekend's all about.'

'Yeah, but . . .' she protested.

Nicholas turned to her, the force of his attention stilling her speech. 'I'm not asking you to do anything difficult. There won't be any real performance involved. That's for the next stage of rehearsals when we get the adult actors in. But I want the children to start thinking about their family groups, the relationships and the interaction, and for that we need you, Charlotte and Paul to step in . . . More as models than actors, a focus for their thought.'

Carolyn giggled. Nicholas and Immi glared at her. At the time, I remember being surprised that the producers weren't firmer with their dramaturge. But now I'm older and know about television – more from friends than from my own experience – it's obvious to me that at this stage, the producers had no real idea of what they were doing, and it was no doubt thanks to Nicholas that the idea turned into anything at all. I know that few programmes are commissioned without a year or two of pain, even if they are being made for the unexciting slot of just before *Highway* on ITV on Sunday afternoon, but I realise now that they'd probably got to this stage with their exciting concept, a fifteen-page treatment and an incentive from some well-meaning outreach department. They might even have been forced to take on Nicholas in order to have a professional on the project. Certainly he was the only one who acted as if there was anything at stake.

'Can't I handle the camera?' asked Immi.

'Sorry Immi,' said Carolyn, 'that's my job.'

After lunch we went into the large downstairs rehearsal space. Nicholas was walking on the balls of his feet, instructing us to form a circle around him. He led us through a few warm-up exercises – the pulse, followed by an improvisation where each of us had to add to the scene taking place – and then told us to separate into our two groups again. We formed these smaller circles and Nicholas placed a large rectangle of sugar paper in the centre of each. Both pieces of sugar paper had the word THEMES written in the middle in thick black marker.

'OK,' he said, 'now I want to start today by coming up with some possible themes for our programme. I need you to think about the people whose homes you've visited – them and their families – and I want you to write down a theme that occurs to you when you think about these families, or the person themselves. Does everyone understand what I mean by theme? It's an idea for the story, or a part of the story, a dramatic subject or topic that we can examine through improvisation.'

Everyone looked blank. But we still picked up pens and thought about what we could write. Erica wasn't involved in this, but sat happily alongside us. I sucked my pen for a moment, thinking of Wendy and Amy's mothers, then wrote down my theme. After a couple of minutes, our piece of paper looked like this:

PRIVATE SPACE   ISOLATION
              THEMES
BEING A TEENAGER   FEAR OF THE FAMILY
              SIBLING RIVALRY

while the other group had written:

TEENAGE REBELLION   MEAN SISTERS
              THEMES
                         SEEKING APPROVAL
      CREATIVITY   FREEDOM

Nicholas waited until we'd finished, then took the two pieces of paper and taped them to the wall.

'OK,' he said, 'yes, this is excellent. A lot of these themes naturally go together. For example, you could definitely link "being a teenager" and "teenage rebellion".' He took out a marker and found another rectangle of paper, writing TEENAGE ANGST at the top. 'And "isolation", "private space", and "freedom" sort of go together.' Underneath the first theme, he now wrote SPACE. 'And "mean sisters" goes with "sibling rivalry". Let's just call that SIBLING RIVALRY, shall we?' He wrote this down. 'What does that leave? From this sheet, we have "creativity" and "seeking approval". I think "seeking approval" probably fits with "teenage angst". So we don't need a separate space for that, but "creativity", yes.' He wrote down CREATIVITY. 'Which just leaves, on this sheet, "fear of the family". Now, who wrote that?'

'I did,' I said, worried I was going to get told off.

'I like that. Well done. So, let's see, what do we have? TEENAGE ANGST, SPACE, SIBLING RIVALRY, CREATIVITY and FEAR OF THE FAMILY. Yes, that's a jolly good start.'

He taped this piece of paper to the wall, and then said, more to himself than us, 'If we could think of one more theme, they could work as ideas for each episode. But maybe we won't construct the story like that. Let's see. I think the first thing we need to do is to work out our family, friendship and relationship structures. I think it makes sense to take advantage of the natural connections we already have, so Gerald and Erica, you can be the brother and sister of one family.'

I looked at Erica, who didn't seem concerned by this. The idea of being forced to spend the whole weekend working with my sister depressed me, so I said, 'I don't want to do improvisations only with Erica.'

'You won't, Gerald, don't worry,' Nicholas said in a surprisingly sympathetic voice. 'In fact, I think you definitely need a girlfriend, for dramatic tension.' He looked around. 'Any volunteers?'

I cringed. The room was silent. I looked over at Perdita

and smiled, trying to let her know that if she wanted to play this part it might be fun, and that I wouldn't read anything into it. But in spite of her friendliness on the minibus, she wasn't prepared to be that generous. Eventually, Sheryl said, 'If there's no one else . . . I mean . . . I wouldn't mind.'

'Good,' said Nicholas, before I had chance to protest, 'and Sheryl, you're an only child in real life, right?'

She nodded.

'So let's stick with that. Which means we have two families here. Wendy and Lucy, you're also sisters, right? So that's three separate families. What about the rest of you?'

Amy put her hand up. 'Can I be an orphan?'

Nicholas laughed. 'Why do you want to be an orphan?'

She shrugged. 'I thought it'd be interesting. And we already have a lot of different families.'

He considered this. 'That's true. But I'm not sure you should be an orphan. Maybe you could be in a care home.'

Wendy put her hand up. 'Can I be in care too?'

'No, you can't, because you've got your sister, but maybe someone else should be. A boy, perhaps? Robert?'

He smirked. 'OK.'

'Who does that leave? Lola, Pete, Perdita . . . '

'And me,' said Jane.

'Right. Pete and Perdita, stand next to each other.'

They did so. 'What d'you think, everyone?' he asked. 'Could they pass for brother and sister?'

'His hair's more blond,' said Perdita.

'Yeah, but that's often the case in real families,' Nicholas said dismissively. 'Actually, we don't want this to be all nuclear 2.4 families. Lola, you can belong to that family too. The three of you, two sisters with a brother in the middle. Pete, we can explore the problems of being a middle child once we get going. Now Jane, maybe you could be someone's cousin. I think, in fact, you should be the cousin of this family. I realise that brings a lot of you together, but I think a group of four will be good for improvisations.'

We stood there in our respective units: me, Erica and Sheryl; Wendy and Lucy; Amy and Robert; and Perdita,

Pete, Lola and Jane. He couldn't have arranged us in a less satisfactory way if he tried. Terrified I was going to be stuck with Erica and Sheryl from now on, I said, 'The groups will interact, won't they?'

'Yes, Gerald, of course they will, but not immediately. I want you to define your characters in those groups, and then we'll think about bringing everyone together. But first, I want each group to improvise a scene around one of the themes. Gerald, seeing as it was your idea, you three can do Fear of the Family. Wendy and Lucy, you do Sibling Rivalry. Amy and Robert, well, you might be able to do something with Space, right? And for the rest of you, I think Teenage Angst is a more inspiring topic than Creativity, isn't it?'

He didn't wait for an answer, instructing us to get on with our improvisations.

77

I think I'm making Nicholas Pennington more dynamic in this account than he was in real life. Maybe it's an accurate reflection of how he seemed that afternoon, as he got things going and showed us that we already had more to work with than we might have imagined. Like all creative people, Nicholas was a slave to his ego, and painfully aware of his artistic shortcomings. What I don't know is exactly what was at stake for him at this stage. Although the programme wasn't an unqualified success, it did increase his profile and reputation, and he was able to make a living doing similar television exercises for years after our show was forgotten. But I wonder whether he had other ambitions, and if he hoped to be recognised not for the novelty of the experiment, but for the quality of the scripts he eventually fashioned from our ideas. He was known as a dramaturge, having worked on a number of successful soaps and serials, but this was the first time he had been the sole scriptwriter. The publicity for the programme – more missing artefacts, packed away somewhere at one of my parents' homes –

made much of the fact that these were found stories, but he still insisted that he was billed as the sole writer at the start of each episode.

He came over to our group first. 'OK, Gerald, let's talk about your theme. Fear of the family. Where did that come from? Was it something you thought of when you visited Sheryl's house?'

'No,' I told him, 'Sheryl's parents weren't frightening. It was more . . .' I lowered my voice. 'Amy and Perdita's fathers. They seemed to intimidate their wives and daughters.'

I was talking to Nicholas as I would to a teacher, trying to impress him. It seemed to be working, and he said, 'Ah, so you didn't mean it to be as abstract as it sounded. In fact, what you're talking about isn't really fear of the family at all, is it? It's more fear *within* the family.'

'I suppose.'

'What about your family, Gerald? I remember at our first meeting you said that when you were younger your mother took you away from your father to be raised in a women's commune. Why did she do that?'

'I don't know.'

'Was she angry at your father?'

'She does get cross at Dad.'

'What about?'

I shrugged. 'His drinking and gambling mostly.'

'OK, that's excellent. Paul, can you come over here for a minute?'

Paul got up from where he was sitting with Charlotte and Carolyn. He looked annoyed, but still came across and stood near us.

'I want you to play Gerald and Erica's father. Now, Gerald, remember he doesn't have to be exactly the same as your father. We're creating a fiction, and trying to make everything more dramatic than real life. Are you frightened by your father?'

'No. Not really.'

'I didn't think so. But in order for there to be sufficient

tension in your story, I think you need to be terrified of your fictional dad. Do you ever have nightmares?'

'Sometimes. Not very often.'

'Are your parents ever in your nightmares?'

'I suppose they must be. I don't really remember.'

'OK,' he said, rubbing his temples, 'let's look at this another way. What's the scariest thing you could imagine about your parents? What would really frighten you?'

I closed my eyes and tried to answer his question. As I did so, I saw my father in one of his rare flashes of furious temper, after an afternoon of being wound up by my mother.

'I suppose the worst thing would be making my dad really, really angry . . .'

'Yes?' he encouraged.

'So angry that he wanted to kill us,' said Erica.

'Well, maybe that's going a *bit* far,' Nicholas replied, scared by my sister's bloodthirsty tone. 'We want this to be exciting, but let's steer clear of melodrama. How about we say that the dad's very short-tempered, because he's a heavy drinker, and jealous of his children's lives? Not so much over-protective as self-obsessed and bitter, because his life's not going the way he wants it to.'

'This is me?' asked Paul, smiling.

'You won't have much to do,' Nicholas said dismissively. 'The children will build their improvisations around you.'

Paul nodded. 'He sounds like a bit of a wanker, that's all.'

Nicholas scowled. I knew it wasn't the bad language that annoyed him, but rather Paul's flippant attitude towards the serious matter of our improvisation. He took a few deep breaths and then said, 'Sheryl, can you think of a scenario that would involve the four of you?'

She thought for a moment, and then said, 'Perhaps Gerald could be talking to me on the telephone, and his mum . . .'

'Let me stop you there,' said Nicholas. 'Don't get upset about this, it's not your fault, but there are several important do's and don'ts when it comes to constructing a dramatically satisfying scene. We can sort most of these out when we get to script stage, but there are one or two we might as well talk about as they arise. Telephone conversations aren't dramatic. They're tricky to do on television, and you'll mainly see them in silly situation comedies where the screen splits into two with an actor on each side. You'll rarely see people talking on the telephone in soap operas as soap operas are primarily realistic, and that kind of artifice reminds people that they're watching television.'

I put up my hand. 'Can't we do a realistic telephone conversation where you only see one side and don't know what the other person is saying?'

'If we were going to have telephone conversations in our drama, then yes, that would be the best way of doing it, but it makes more sense to avoid them altogether. Sheryl, can you think of a way of constructing the scene that doesn't involve the telephone?'

'Nicholas,' I interrupted, 'if we don't have any telephone conversations at all, won't people think that's unrealistic?'

'Well, Gerald, you have to understand that realism, in itself, is a dramatic convention. And because we're working within this particular convention, there are lots of things an audience doesn't need spelling out to them. For example, in realist dramas, you rarely see people opening and closing doors, unless there's a dramatic reason for doing so, like if a character is locked out of somewhere or is about to interrupt an illicit act, but this doesn't concern the audience. Someone walks into a room and the scene begins. That's a convention of realist drama. And the same is true of avoiding telephone conversations. We can get round your worries by having a telephone ringing in the background, which would be an almost-subliminal trick that we can play on the audience.'

He seemed to be enjoying explaining this, so I risked another question. 'Couldn't we put that stuff in? People opening and closing doors, one-sided telephone conversations? Just to show the audience that this is really real realism, like they've never seen before? I mean, this programme is supposed to be experimental, isn't it?'

'It's not "experimental", it's an experiment. And the

experiment takes place on the writing and acting level. The problem with your suggestion, Gerald, is that putting in that sort of thing wouldn't have the effect you imagine. People are so used to these conventions that they've grown to love them, and to disrupt them in the way you're suggesting would make people think you didn't know the conventions, and instead of looking new or radical, our programme would simply seem amateurish.'

I knew this was the end of the conversation. I didn't really accept Nicholas's argument – and don't to this day – but I didn't want to be the one responsible for making the programme look amateurish. I don't know why I was suddenly so interested in dramatic structure (at school I hadn't been at all bothered with questions of creativity, and being on television was much more important to me than any notions of storytelling), but something about Nicholas's dogmatic approach riled me, and brought out my inner pervert.

Sheryl came up with a different scenario that had me pretending I was taking my sister to the cinema and then secretly meeting up with her instead. She had my mother getting angry in the scene, and Nicholas interrupted her again to say, 'Sheryl, I thought we just decided that Gerald should be scared of his father.'

'But his father isn't scary. His father's really nice. It's his mum who's . . .'

'Listen, we're using your observations as a starting point. But if Gerald thinks he'd be more scared of his dad getting angry than his mum, then you have to respect that decision.'

Sheryl nodded, and Nicholas moved on to the next group to explain why what they were doing was wrong.

78

We spent the rest of the afternoon improvising. After we'd finished our first scenes, Nicholas made us perform them. The problem with our improvisation, he told us, was that it descended into a straightforward argument far too quickly. Conflict was fine, but too much fighting wasn't dramatic. It was a fair point: Paul, in particular, had been keen to turn the scene into pantomime, chasing me around an invisible settee. Wendy and Lucy's sibling rivalry improvisation was deemed to have the same flaw, although Nicholas was impressed with the verisimilitude of the girls' argument. The rest of us assumed the girls weren't acting at all, and were genuinely cross with each other. Amy and Fuckpit followed this with a weird, abstract, 'movement' piece that consisted of them hugging each other, looping their arms, and then pushing each other away. This infuriated Nicholas and he shouted at them, 'This isn't a school drama lesson, it's a realist soap opera. We don't want abstract movement exercises. I told you to construct a scene.'

Immi, who had not been needed by any of the groups, and was sitting at the back of the room with Carolyn, was shocked by Nicholas's aggressive tone, and said, 'I thought it was beautiful.'

Nicholas stared at her, then said, 'Be that as it may, this is not the sort of thing we want the group to be doing. Amy and Robert, stick to acting from now on, OK?'

They didn't say anything, but looked disappointed. The last four took their space and performed a scene with them sitting in a lounge while their parents had gone out, eating a pizza and talking. Nicholas liked this scene, but told them it was a bit meandering and lacked a dramatic centre.

'In general,' he told us, 'try to avoid scenes that are only conversation, with no dramatic motivation. This doesn't mean you have to argue all the time, but every scene should impart some information about the story as a whole. Think about what each line reveals about the character you're playing – well, yourself, I suppose – and why you would be saying these words to the other people in the scene.'

Nicholas made us think of a location where all the characters could meet. I remembered Perdita telling me about the teens-only nightclub she went to and suggested we come up with a fictional version of this.

'Yes,' he said, 'that could work. It's cooler than a youth club, and will give us something to use in the promos.'

Nicholas went outside with the other adults and left us to come up with a scene that could take place in this setting.

'I've got an idea,' said Perdita. 'Last year there was a scandal at the club when a girl pretended she'd been raped and a boy was arrested and then it turned out she was making it up and they had to let him go.'

'That sounds good,' said Fuckpit. 'I'll be the boy.'

'No,' said Wendy, 'it should be someone who looks innocent. Gerald.'

'Who should he rape?' asked Amy.

'He didn't actually do it,' Perdita reminded them.

'It should be you,' said Wendy. 'You should pretend he raped you.'

'I don't know,' she said, 'our characters are supposed to be close to ourselves, aren't they? That's not really something I'd do.'

'How about if you had a reason?' suggested Amy.

Perdita considered this. 'Yes, that could work. What about if Robert attacks you, Wendy? He doesn't rape you, he just gets a bit heavy-handed and you don't like what he's doing and you tell him off and he says something really horrible to you. This happens outside the nightclub, and I come out and find you and you're crying and you can barely speak and I'm saying to you, "Who did this to you, you must tell me," and you don't say anything so I go, "It was Gerald, wasn't it, Gerald did it," and because you don't reply I assume that's what happened and as you won't go to the police or tell anyone, I pretend Gerald raped me instead.'

'And he gets arrested,' said Erica eagerly.

'Brilliant,' Wendy replied, clapping her hands together.

We worked on this scene and then performed it for Nicholas and the other adults. Halfway through, he stopped us and said, 'What happens at the end of this scene?'

'You'll see,' said Wendy, 'we're just getting to the good bit.'

'No,' Nicholas said, 'just tell me.'

We told him. His response wasn't as positive as we'd expected.

'Children,' he snapped, 'this isn't *EastEnders*. This is a realist drama with sympathetic characters. Characters broadly similar to your real selves. We can't have Robert being some kind of violent psychopath and Gerald playing a suspected rapist.'

'But he's innocent,' protested Erica.

'I don't care. Jesus Christ.' He sighed. 'You're obviously not ready to work on your own. Let's start again.'

As the afternoon progressed, Nicholas started mixing up our groups and I got to do an improvisation with Amy and Robert. The scene began with me meeting Amy at the teens-only nightclub. Our interaction wasn't supposed to be romantic, but I had to start a conversation with her and then Robert was supposed to appear and get angry with me because he was protective of Amy. After an hour of improvising with my sister and Sheryl, changing groups had an instantly beneficial effect. Freed from the pressure of fending off Sheryl, I became, if not actually a different character, the best version of myself.

I suppose this is as good a place as any to write about my actual acting abilities. Before I got the part in *All Right Now!*, there were those 137 failed auditions, and the truth is, it was easy to see why no one could trust me even to chew gum on screen for seventy-five seconds. I was a wooden actor, a leaden presence, self-conscious and unable to convince. Nicholas couldn't teach me to surpass those limitations, but he did give me enough confidence to rise to the best of my natural ability, leaving the editors to handle the rest. Although it was impossible for me, at the time, to judge my own performance, none of the TV critics questioned my ability (they reserved their scorn for the precocious Lola Doll) and one or two even singled me out as the child most likely to go on to future screen success.

Still, that afternoon remains one of my most liberating experiences.

Five hours of uninterrupted improvisation made me forget my inhibitions, lose my nervousness, and develop an inner confidence that allowed me not to worry about how I seemed to the rest of the group. I could see the same thing happening to the others, as Fuckpit and Pete became less worried about seeming tough in front of the girls, Wendy and Perdita developed a quieter, more intimate manner, and the younger children became less intimidated, forming a comical team of four. What surprised me most was that Erica got so into acting that she forgot to be horrible, giving me a glimpse of the normal person she would one day become. I couldn't understand why she wasn't cross about having to perform with me and Sheryl, until I realised it was the first time I was interacting with my sister as if she was normal. Every now and again, I'd look at her and see something new in her face, a sincere pleasure at being taken seriously.

More embarrassing was pretending to be Sheryl's boyfriend. I tried to emulate Fuckpit's laid-back attitude, but I was terrified that if I didn't maintain a constant emotional distance, she might start thinking I actually fancied her.

The only two who hadn't relaxed were Jane and Amy. Nicholas noticed this and told them to stand together in the centre while the rest of the group sat down.

'OK,' he said, 'I want to return to an earlier exercise. This is just for you two, to help you have a stronger presence in the group. I want you both to take turns sitting in the centre while the rest of us ask you questions. The object of this is to define yourselves as characters, something I don't think either of you have quite achieved yet.'

Jane went first. I could tell she was uncomfortable, and worried that she was being criticised. I didn't realise how upset she was until she started crying. She remained composed while the tears ran down her cheeks, and it took Nicholas a moment to notice. Then he asked, 'What's wrong?'

'I'm no good at this,' she blurted. 'They shouldn't have picked me.'

'Don't be silly. You're as good as everyone else. You just need to relax, let more of your character come out.'

She exhaled, and tried to pull herself up straight. 'OK,' she said, 'what do you want to know?'

Nicholas started the process, gently asking Jane about her family and interests. I wasn't sure this approach was going to work, but she gradually relaxed, revealing more of herself than she had before. He let the rest of us question her for a while, and then said, 'Jane, I want you to promise me something.'

'OK.'

'From now on, I don't want you ever to feel ashamed. It doesn't matter what anyone's said to you in the past, this is the start of you becoming a star. Do you ever read interviews with film stars in magazines?'

She nodded.

'And you know how they act as if every little thing they think or experience is incredibly important?'

A shy laugh.

'Well, that's how I want you to see yourself. Don't worry about being called big-headed, you're going on television, that makes you better than everyone else. That goes for all of you, OK? Now, Amy, your turn.'

This was probably a bad thing to tell a room of fame-seeking teenagers. But it was wonderful to hear. Everyone in the group seemed to grow bigger. It was the final push we needed, and something that wouldn't have had the same impact if he'd said it back in London at the end of a session. We'd have gone home and told our parents and they would have laughed at us. 'You're not better than everyone else. What a ridiculous idea. Who told you that? The drama-turge? Nicholas what? He sounds like such a pseud.'

I've had a fairly non-elitist education. I went to the local infant, junior and senior school. The teachers came from red-brick universities, and it was always a foregone conclusion that I'd complete my education in a similar institution. No one ever told me I was particularly important, nor special nor clever. I was academically average. It wasn't until I started teaching at the language school that I witnessed the ease an expensive education can bring. And I'm convinced that the main reason students do well in such environments is not because of their actual abilities, but because they're told they're better than everyone else all along. They're in a blessed group, destined for greatness. A friend of mine who had a similar background to me, but then went on to Cambridge told me that on his first night there, the Master of his college gave a speech telling the students that they were now destined to go down in history, even if only because they'd attended this college. He tried to talk to the other people at the table about how strange this sounded, but they didn't understand what he was worrying about, having heard this sort of thing since they were born.

So this was the first time I'd been allowed to think of myself as important, and I'm sure the same was true of everyone else in the group. We weren't naturally privileged children, but did, I suppose, enjoy a degree of luxury: the freedom to believe we might have some acting ability, in the same way another child might think he's good at football, or could learn to play a musical instrument well enough to join a band. It was the same sort of ambition that someone like Geri Halliwell probably had when she started, a willingness to learn, and to be shaped. Maybe Nicholas understood this affirmation was all we were searching for, the reason we'd started going to auditions in the first place. His words united us, made us believe what we were doing was worthwhile. This sealed our bond, and became something that would last long after the end of this weekend.

79

After dinner, we were allowed to relax wherever we wanted, upstairs in our bedrooms or in the rehearsal space or kitchen. There was talk of going for a walk, but we pleaded exhaustion. The adults had a bottle of whisky that they shared between them. Fuckpit and Wendy tried to get slurps, but failed. Perdita went into the kitchen and asked if she could take the stereo up to her bedroom.

'OK,' said Immi, 'but be careful. It belongs to the cottage, not us.'

Perdita nodded at me and I followed her upstairs. Amy and Jane were already in the bedroom. The two of them had bonded after Nicholas had singled them out, and Jane had decided to swap bedrooms, not having liked being in with the younger children.

'Is it OK if we play some music?'

Amy nodded. Perdita plugged in the stereo and dragged her vanity case from beneath her bed. She looked for a tape. 'What shall I play?'

'Do you have any Bros?'

'No.' Perdita slid in a tape and pressed Play. *Like a Virgin*, side one.

Jane giggled, and asked Perdita, 'So what did you think of him?'

'Who?'

'Paul.'

Perdita smiled. 'All right, I suppose.'

'I think he is so *fit*,' said Jane. 'Especially when he was shouting at Gerald.'

'How was that sexy?' I asked, confused.

Wendy appeared in the doorway, drawn by the music. 'He's a stud.'

The three girls nodded. I waited a moment, and then said,

'But I still don't understand how him shouting at me was sexy.'

I felt privileged to be in with these girls, listening to their thoughts on music and men, but it was hard on my (at that time miniscule, anyway) ego. Although Amy, Jane and Perdita didn't have boyfriends, it was clear they didn't consider me eligible. It would have been worse if any of them had said they liked Fuckpit or Pete, but even Jane didn't seem interested in either of them. After a while, the conversation became more contemplative, and we talked about how alienated we felt from our families. Amy and Wendy were clearly more popular at school than the rest of us, and when we started moaning about our playground traumas, they drifted out of the room and went downstairs. Jane sensed that Perdita and I were happier talking to each other than to her, and she got up and left too. The second side of the tape came to an end, and Perdita replaced the cassette with music I didn't recognise.

'Who's this?' I asked.

She smiled. 'INXS.'

We listened to the tape for a while. It wasn't really my sort of thing, but I liked the crisp, rock sound. Perdita sniffed again, and said, 'My asthma's going crazy.'

I nodded.

'Gerald . . . You know when you came round my house?'

'Yeah.'

'Why did you ask me if I believed in God?'

'Because we were talking about Prince. And I wondered what you thought about his religious views.'

Perdita moved from where she was sitting and went across to the bed. She unlaced her baseball boots and took them off, then lay back on the bed. Then she said, 'But it sounded like there was something more personal behind what you were asking me.'

'Do you ever feel really, really lonely?'

'Gerald, I'm an only child. I feel lonely all the time.'

'How do you cope?'

'I live in my head a lot,' she replied. 'Music helps.'

'Do you ever imagine an audience?'

'An audience?'

'Watching you.'

She sat up on the bed. 'Do you?'

'I make up programmes for them.'

She smiled. 'Can you lock that door?'

'I don't think so. But it opens inwards, so I could drag the bed down against it. Why?'

'I thought you could lie here with me. But I don't want the others to see us.'

She got off the bed and I dragged it downwards. Then I lay beside her. I could hear the breaths moving in and out of her throat. Our bodies touched only slightly and the two of us kept very still. After a moment, I felt her reaching for my hand, and I let her hold it.

'But I still don't see what this has got to do with God.'

'OK,' I said, not wanting to be cryptic, 'this is what I mean: what's the point of living if no one knows what you're doing? I spend a lot of time alone, I like being alone, I sit in my penthouse ... '

'Your what?'

'Oh ... That's what I call my bedroom. The private penthouse.'

She laughed. But I wasn't hurt.

'I sit there,' I continued, 'listening to Prince and reading and drinking Coca-Cola and pretending my whole life is being broadcast on a secret television station. And although I know that's not true, I do think someone's watching me. Maybe God or people in Heaven ... '

'Oh God, Gerald, I'd be so terrified if that was true.'

'Why?'

Her fingers stroked mine. 'I'm shy, Gerald. I don't like being watched.'

As she said this, there was a loud bash at the door. I thought the bed would hold them, but they kept pushing until it was back far enough for Pete, Sheryl and Lola to pop their heads round the door and point a video camera in our direction.

'Whooooah . . . ' said Pete, 'and here you can see, in the next bedroom, Gerald and Perdita, who are clearly about to get up to no good.'

'Fuck off, Pete,' snapped Perdita, surprising me.

'So we were interrupting something,' he said in an insinuating tone, pushing even harder against the door.

We got up and let them in, magic moment destroyed before I had chance to say half the things I'd hoped to.

80

Late that night, when I'd entered the deepest part of my sleep-cycle, I dreamt someone was shaking me awake. When I eventually opened my eyes, I saw Perdita standing in front of me with a torch illuminating her face.

'We're going for a walk,' she told me.

'Who?'

'Me, Fuckpit, Amy and Wendy. Do you want to come?'

'OK,' I said, every blink painful. 'Can you see my trousers?'

She flicked the beam around until I'd located all my clothes. Then she turned away while I got dressed. I grabbed my bag and pulled out the torch and compass Dad had forced on me.

I followed Perdita out of the room. The others were standing on the stairs, ready to go. We walked down to the front door, shushing each other with every step. The noise of the lock and the turning of the handle was supernormal, and we all held our breath until it was clear the rest of the house was still sleeping. Then we ventured outside.

No one said anything as we walked across the gravel forecourt towards the lane that ran past the rented cottage. The moors spread out in every direction. I asked Perdita, 'Are we going to be able to find our way back?'

'Of course,' Wendy butted in. 'We'll just go in a straight line.'

This sounded risky. 'I've got a compass,' I told everyone. 'If we keep going North, it'll be easier to find our way back.'

I switched on my torch and checked the compass. As I did so, I saw that Perdita was wearing only a black nightdress beneath her coat.

'Aren't you cold?'

She shrugged. 'I didn't feel like getting dressed.'

We trudged across the muddy ground, not really heading anywhere, but following my compass. The five of us kept close together. I looked up at the moon.

'Did you girls sleep at all?' Fuckpit asked them.

'I did,' said Amy, 'these two didn't.'

'Hey, we're doing what we're supposed to be doing, finding out about each other,' said Wendy. 'We're just doing it at night, that's all.'

'You're going to be knackered tomorrow,' said Fuckpit. 'And there's no way they'll let you sleep in.'

'It's only making stuff up,' Wendy replied. 'It doesn't take that much effort.'

We carried on walking. Fuckpit made a strange noise with his tongue.

'What's that?' asked Wendy.

He smiled, but didn't reply.

'Oh, come on,' she said, 'I really recognise it. Is it from a film?'

'Ki-ki-ki-ma-ma-ma,' he said again.

'Tell me,' she demanded, 'what is it?'

'*Friday the 13th.*'

She laughed. 'Of course. I love those films.'

'Can we not talk about horror movies when we're going for a walk across the moors in the middle of the night?' requested Amy.

'*Friday the 13th* films aren't scary,' Wendy told her. 'They're more funny than anything. Everyone in those films is so stupid. Now, Freddy Krueger, on the other hand . . .'

'Who's he?' asked Amy.

'You know,' said Fuckpit, '*Nightmare on Elm Street.*'

'Oh,' she said, 'I haven't seen that either. I don't like horror films. Can we please change the subject?'

Amy did look afraid, as if she hadn't wanted to participate in this walk in the first place, and definitely wouldn't have come if she'd known this was the sort of thing we were going to discuss. I hadn't seen the films, although I knew Erica had, making Reggel's sister take the family video upstairs so she could scare her witless. It wasn't that I didn't want to watch them, just that all the talk about video nasties in the papers and on TV made me think that all horror films would be equally terrifying.

'So,' said Fuckpit, deliberately ignoring Amy's pleas, 'have you seen the new one?'

'*Friday*? Or *Nightmare*?'

'*Nightmare.*'

Amy came across and looked at my compass, deliberately dragging us away from Wendy and Fuckpit, who carried on talking behind us.

'I don't like seeing them in the cinema,' I heard Wendy tell Fuckpit. 'Every time I go to the cinema with Andy, he wants me to snog him, or give him a hand-job, and I always miss all the scary bits. Besides, it's much more fun to watch them on video. Late at night, with some friends . . .'

'Lovely,' whispered Amy. 'Those two were made for each other.'

'I thought she'd set her sights on Paul,' said Perdita in a similarly low tone.

'Yeah, but he's asleep. There's still time for her to talk Fuckpit into her bed.'

'Oh God,' I said, 'Sheryl'll be crushed.'

'Does she fancy him?'

'I think so.'

'I thought she fancied you,' said Perdita. 'She was pretty quick to volunteer to be your girlfriend.'

I ignored them. 'I love walking late at night. Don't you think the whole world's different when it's dark?'

'What is it with you and different worlds?' Perdita asked. 'Do you hate this one so much?'

'There are things I like about it. But I hope next time'll be better.'

'Do you believe in reincarnation?' asked Amy.

'No. I believe in different worlds. I think this time round is just a trial run where you get to select who you want to accompany you into the next world. And then that time round only the things you want to happen happen to you.'

'He doesn't really believe that,' Perdita told Amy. 'He's a ridiculous romantic.'

'I am happy at the moment,' I told them. 'To be honest, this weekend is probably the first time I've felt entirely happy in my whole life. Around other people, anyway.'

'What's that over there?' Amy asked.

There was a large red leather armchair beneath a tree. Not far from the armchair were a sofa and a coffee table. The furniture had been placed upon a rectangle of red carpet.

'Let's go over,' suggested Perdita.

'No,' said Amy, 'it's too weird. Something spooky's going on.'

We looked back at Wendy and Fuckpit, waiting for them to catch up. When they did, they stopped flirting and stood alongside us, staring at the furniture.

'I know what this is,' said Fuckpit. 'It's something Nicholas Pennington has set up for tomorrow.' He mocked our dramaturge's pretentious delivery. 'An aid for your imaginations . . .'

I shook my head. 'I don't think so. We've come a long way from the cottage.'

I was thrilled that everyone was taking this seriously. I didn't know why the furniture was here either, but I loved it when these sort of weird things happened. Part of me believed that we'd only come across this strange arrangement because I'd been talking about parallel worlds. My overactive imagination came more from my father than my mother. He was a big fan of *The Twilight Zone* and had once completely freaked me out by driving me thirty miles to the first house he'd lived in with my mother and telling me it was populated by parallel versions of us who'd lived different lives because they'd never moved.

'Well, it's only furniture,' said Fuckpit, walking towards it. 'Why don't we sit down?' He slowly lowered himself into the red leather chair. 'There you go. See. Nothing horrible's happening to me.'

Reassured, Wendy walked across and sat on the sofa. The rest of us took the remaining seats. Then Fuckpit said, 'Actually, I reckon I know what this is. It's a secret portal into Freddy's universe. What'll happen is, in a few minutes, we'll all become really drowsy, and then, when we fall asleep, we'll wake up in his dreamworld.'

'Can you please shut up?' barked Amy. 'I told you I don't like hearing about that stuff.'

'I'm sure it's nothing terrible,' said Perdita quickly. 'Someone probably dragged this furniture out here for a laugh.'

'It does feel like a dream, though, don't you think?' I said, reluctant to lose the sense of mystery. 'I wouldn't be at all surprised if I woke up and found myself back in bed.'

'This whole weekend feels like a dream,' said Fuckpit. 'Don't you think this weekend is so much fucking fun? I don't even mind all the acting.'

Everyone laughed. When it went quiet again, Wendy asked Perdita, 'Where does your name come from?'

'*The Winter's Tale*. It's Mum's favourite play.'

'It's such a pretty name. I wish I had a name like that.'

'Wendy's a nice name,' she said, 'it's got a really friendly sound. And it's sexy. I used to hate being called Perdita.'

Fuckpit took out his packet of cigarettes and offered them round. I took one again, although I knew I'd never be a genuine smoker. Somehow they made everything feel more adult, and I loved being included in this way.

I reached down and moved the torch, pretending I was trying to steady it, but really pushing it round so I could see more of Perdita. She looked cold, but confident, sitting back with her arms wrapped around her body. Amy sat between us, with Wendy perched on the arm of the sofa. Wanting to share my happiness, I said, 'The others are going to be so jealous when they hear about this.'

'They're not going to,' Amy said sternly.

'Why not?' asked Fuckpit. 'It's not school. They can't punish us.'

'Yeah,' she replied, 'but I couldn't bear being lectured by Nicholas. He's so pompous. Besides, there's no reason to tell anyone. We can save the showing-off till we get home.'

No one argued with her. We sat and smoked in the darkness. I felt so pleased to be included in this group, and was grateful to Perdita for inviting me. I hadn't been able to stop thinking about the five minutes we'd spent lying together on the bed, and wondering if it meant anything. All the sex-talk today had startled me – I certainly wasn't thinking of Perdita in this way, really only still in search of a first proper kiss – but it had also made me hopeful for the future, as if barriers I'd imagined would be in place for ever might soon be removed.

It was only because I saw the burning tip of her cigarette float through the darkness that I realised Wendy had got up and gone across to sit with Fuckpit in the red leather armchair. I nudged Amy, but she'd already noticed. Perdita turned and smiled at me, as the soft sound of them kissing became audible. For one terrifying moment, I thought Perdita was going to kiss me, and I realised I had no idea how to respond. I didn't even know if I knew how to kiss.

'I feel like a gooseberry,' said Amy, 'I'm going back.'

'You can't go on your own,' Perdita told her. 'We'll come with you.'

She stood up and pulled my hand. Feeling faintly relieved, I allowed myself to be led.

'Don't leave on our account,' said Wendy, momentarily disengaging from Fuckpit.

'It's OK,' said Amy, 'I'm about to fall asleep.'

'And you don't want Freddy to get you,' chuckled Fuckpit, before asking, 'Can you leave us a torch?'

'Take mine,' I said. 'Just chuck it under my bed when you get back.'

We got up and started walking back. I didn't bother checking my compass, as we all seemed to agree on the correct direction. As we walked, I found myself thinking of my sister. It was a minor triumph that she'd managed to go to sleep in a room with three other girls and not caused them any harm. I remembered what my father had said about how having Erica with me would make the weekend all the more special and I realised he was right. This didn't convince me of my father's innate wisdom, instead making me wonder if the problem with my family wasn't me or Erica, but actually my mother and father. I knew they were unhappy, but it never occurred to me that their characters might be cramped by their marriage, and that they, in turn, were attempting to restrict us. It was as if happiness had been outlawed in our home, on the grounds that if they couldn't achieve it, why should we?

We continued in silence until we reached the cottage, and then panicked when we realised none of us had a key.

'Well, one of us must have one,' I protested. 'We wouldn't have come out otherwise, would we?'

'Why didn't someone say something?' Amy asked.

'Wendy must have one,' said Perdita. 'I'm going to look for them. Gerald, come with me.'

'I don't want to wait here alone,' Amy protested.

'Someone has to,' Perdita told her. 'It would be stupid if we missed them coming back. You'll be OK here, we won't be gone more than a minute.'

Perdita took my hand and dragged me away. I let her lead me. She held my torch in front of her, shining it into the darkness. I was beginning to feel the weight of sleep, and only barely registered what was happening.

After a few minutes, I realised we were coming up to the furniture again. 'There,' I said, 'look . . . someone's sitting on the armchair.'

Perdita shone the torch across at the seat.

'Wendy?' she called.

It wasn't Wendy. It wasn't Fuckpit either. It was an elderly man in a grey overcoat and a flat cap. He smiled at us.

We screamed and ran.

81

The man turned out to be an insomniac farmer. He explained himself to Nicholas, nervously insisting that he had nothing to do with any missing children. When Wendy and Fuckpit returned twenty minutes later, they confirmed this, saying they hadn't seen the farmer and apologising for causing trouble. Wendy produced the front-door key and admitted she'd swiped it earlier in the evening. She confessed that the late-night jaunt had been entirely her idea, and said she'd made us accompany her. Nicholas stood there in his pyjamas with Perdita and me, his irritation outweighed by relief that nothing more serious had happened. I think he might have been angrier if he hadn't been so keen to get everyone back to bed. He let the farmer leave and we trooped back to the cottage.

I don't know whether it was because we'd disrupted Nicholas's sleep and he needed a lie-in, but things got off to a surprisingly late start the following morning. It wasn't until ten-thirty that we reassembled downstairs. The well-rested kids from the second bedroom – plus Pete and Sheryl – were much livelier than everyone else, eager to continue their improvisations. I think it was their excitement that made Nicholas alter his approach this morning, setting us an initial exercise requiring little input from him.

'On reflection,' he said, 'I think I was too strict with you yesterday. Because this weekend is supposed to be more about gathering stories than learning to act, I forgot that a lot of this will be new to you. For those of you who are finding this difficult, you should be aware that what I'm asking you to do is one of the hardest things in the world. Professional actors would find it impossible . . . Indeed, it would go against their very nature, which is why I don't want you to become professional actors just yet. But I realised last night that you do need some elementary training, so I'm going to start today with an improvisation exercise.'

This was Nicholas's excuse to play us an hour-long cassette of harbour noises. We had to pretend to be people whose relatives had spent the last year on the high seas and were due to return today.

'Just mill about,' he told us. 'You don't have to be yourselves today, so invent whatever personality you want.'

We did this for half an hour. I formed a group with Perdita and Wendy, who were pretending to be sisters. I told them I was a journalist, and that my father was on the ship. Nicholas, eavesdropping, liked this, and said, 'OK, in about quarter of an hour you're going to catch sight of the ship. When the ship returns, there will be a flag hoisted from the mast. If the flag is white, your relations are alive. If black, they're dead.'

The flag was black.

This prompted fifteen minutes of histrionics, with Lola Doll the loudest offender. Only Erica didn't seem that bothered, which, I realised, was probably exactly how she'd behave if the situation were real.

Nicholas seemed to have recovered by the end of the hour, and after this exercise we resumed yesterday's improvisations. He put the themes we'd come up with yesterday aside for the moment, and asked us instead to look at the notes we'd made when visiting each other's homes. We all had to choose a different member of the group and perform a monologue pretending to be that person. I wanted to be Perdita, but Lucy got there first, so I had to be Wendy. Sheryl was me. I didn't want Wendy to get angry, so I presented her as a strong independent woman. After I'd finished my improvisation, Nicholas said, 'Yes, Gerald, that was very good. I think we all got a clear sense of who Wendy is from your performance. And in order to use this knowledge to create drama, we will need to think of a situation that will force her to change her personality. Given how you see Wendy, can you imagine a situation that might make her vulnerable?'

I shook my head.

'Well, never mind. I'll work on that myself.'

Sheryl's impersonation of me was equally flattering, but I didn't read anything into this, knowing she wanted to be my friend. The only improvisation that was in any way insulting was Wendy's impression of Fuckpit, as she mocked his macho swagger. We all watched him while she tucked up her collar and struck poses, waiting for him to freak out. But he took the mockery in good sport. Wendy and Fuckpit had decided they wanted a romance in the programme, with Wendy apparently unconcerned about how her long-term boyfriend Andrew might react. I thought Nicholas might be cross about this change in plot, but it didn't seem to bother him. More dramatic material to work with, I supposed.

After yesterday, I was beginning to feel more confident and decided that as I was stuck with Sheryl, I might as well make the most of it. I still wasn't sure if I stood any chance of getting together with Perdita – in fact, I was a little scared about the possibility – but I had decided I would signal my suitability as a boyfriend through my scenes with Sheryl. That seemed more mature than sulking about the situation.

There was another relationship blossoming today, in some ways the most worrying of all. I couldn't tell when it had started, but it slowly became apparent to me that Pete and Erica were interested in each other. It seemed extraordinary that someone could fancy my sister, no matter how much nicer she'd become this weekend. But although I still knew little of love, I realised there had to be a reason for them wanting to do every scene together and chatting happily throughout every break.

Nicholas seemed to realise that we needed some more serious restrictions in order to produce anything substantial, and told us he would write outlines for the action in each of the six episodes before the next stage of rehearsal. By this time on Sunday afternoon everyone was exhausted and beginning to lose focus. He ended the session by presenting us with four more sheets of sugar paper and telling us to write down everything interesting that had arisen during the weekend. I scribbled down a few almost accidental funny exchanges, like when Pete told Erica that his dad had said 'You'll know when it's true love, son, because love hurts,' and Erica said 'Like this?' and kicked him. Then I recapped my pen and went upstairs to get ready to go.

Perdita sat next to me on the minibus. She handed me an earphone and we listened to her INXS tape again. Wendy and Fuckpit also sat together, as did Erica and Pete. I felt sorry for the people who hadn't fallen into couples this weekend, and looked to see how they had arranged themselves. Lola Doll had set up court with Sheryl and Lucy, both of whom seemed overwhelmed by her theatricality. Amy and Jane sat together at the back, not really talking to each other. The video camera had been abandoned, and everyone, even those in love, seemed keen to get home.

I had been expecting Shep to pick us up from the meeting-point, but as we arrived I noticed my father's car parked alongside the television company's transport. I felt embarrassed about the other children seeing my dad, and hoped he'd stay in the car. It didn't occur to me that anything might be wrong, and I assumed he was using this trip as an excuse to visit his mistress.

The goodbyes were brief. I grabbed my sister and quickly took her across to the car.

'Mum's here,' said Erica, surprised.

I looked through the windscreen and saw she was right. My mother sat in the passenger seat. We climbed into the back of the car.

'All right?' asked my father, starting the engine.

Erica and I were still full of excitement. We wanted to tell our parents all about our weekend away. But they seemed uninterested, reluctant to be shifted out of their heavy silence. Eventually, I couldn't take it any more and asked, 'What's happened?'

'We've got something to tell you,' said my mother.

Erica started crying. I looked at her, astonished. Did she know what was happening already? I was totally confused.

'OK,' I said.

'Your father and I have had a long conversation this weekend and we've come to a big decision.'

Oh, I thought, finally catching up, that's what this is about. They've given up on each other. I still didn't understand why my sister was crying. It had only ever been a matter of time.

PART VI

★

82

I started writing this book a year ago. I'm making a note of this here because when I first began this account I thought I would be giving you occasional updates about my current existence throughout, and now I realise it hasn't turned out that way at all. I've been totally overwhelmed by my material, and while my life hasn't been going badly, I've come to think of writing as a refuge, and only very occasionally feel the need to interrupt the action.

I was travelling into Central London on the tube today when three men got on and sat opposite me. They looked familiar and I immediately assumed they were actors. As they bantered with each other, I realised this assumption was correct. They weren't film or theatre actors, but performed in television commercials. One of the trio was more successful than the other two, although it sounded as if they often appeared together as a team. They joked about things that had happened on various shoots and I began to recognise the names of the products, and remembered scenes from the commercials they'd appeared in. It occurred to me that neither my housemates nor. I had auditioned for anything like this, and I wondered why not. I suppose the others were too ambitious, even though loads of genuine celebrities had started off doing this sort of thing. A friend of mine has a video of a short film she appeared in with Jude Law, called *The Go-Getters*, and it doesn't detract from his current fame to see him in this low-budget effort. And it sounded as if these men had a perfectly nice life, filming a commercial every other week.

After I'd finished *All Right Now!*, it took me a while to kick the television habit. We appeared as a group on various chat-shows, including *Wogan*, in the run-up to the initial screening, but even after the programme had definitely finished for ever, I still kept going a little longer. A woman who worked as a runner on *All Right Now!* went on to become a researcher and was always looking for someone who had experience of being on screen. I also continued auditioning, but without any success. So my only television appearances were the ones this woman wanted me to make. Initially, I went on as myself, on children's quiz programmes and comedy shows. Then, when she realised the audience no longer recognised me, she made me pretend to be different people. My most memorable performance was acting as a drug-addled teen on a medical health programme, an appearance that brought me so much recognition I was forced to give up on the game altogether.

I've spent the last few nights reading Victoria Beckham's autobiography, *Learning to Fly*. I'd been waiting for it to come out in paperback, and then to find it reduced somewhere. I was hoping for the same shivers of recognition I'd got from Geri's first autobiography, *If Only*, especially as there's only a few months' age difference between me and Posh Spice. There wasn't much – she seemed more insular, less aware of her surroundings than Geri – but the title of the book comes from the theme song to the TV programme *Fame*, and one of Victoria's formative moments was going to watch *The Kids from Fame* at the Albert Hall. Erica was the *Fame* fan, not me, but our whole family had gone to that show, along with every stage-struck kid I've ever met.

The reason this interests me is that so much of the art made by my generation – whether it's music, film, writing, videogames, web-design or fine art – refers to stuff we absorbed while growing up. Yesterday I went to a film preview and there were two well-known English directors in the audience. I started to wonder whether seeing this film would affect the projects they worked on next, and then I found myself wondering whether the films anyone made were a result of all the other films they'd seen. There's that old boring argument about how directors used to make films about their lives and now they make films about films, but that's not exactly what I mean. My question is, when lots of people see something that has a similar influence on them, does it push us all in the same direction and only emerge in the art years after the initial impact?

The other intriguing thing about Victoria making this *Fame* stage-show a central element of her autobiography is that for the next generation going to watch the Spice Girls in concert will probably be their similarly significant memory, offering the same distillation of ambition, the same love of showbiz, the same crystallisation of hope.

83

After the party, we didn't manage to get my bed back until nine o'clock. I spent ages trying to block out every bit of sunlight, then gave up and pulled the duvet high over our heads. The bed smelt of beer and the mattress was damp, but the possibility of sleep was too precious to abandon.

Sally stayed still in my arms until midday, when her wriggles became so vigorous that they woke me up.

'Sorry,' she said, 'I need water.'

'Me too. Can you bring me back some?'

She pushed away from me and got up. Sally was only wearing her underwear, and took her dressing-gown from the back of the door before leaving the room. I rolled over and surveyed the mess. It didn't seem too bad. There were sticky patches on the carpet and lots of empty bottles and cans, but no major damage. Someone had taken the jacket of one of my work suits out of the wardrobe and left it hanging over the back of a wooden chair, which struck me as odd, but it didn't seem harmed. Maybe they'd been impersonating me, or telling an anecdote that required them to be wearing a jacket.

Sally returned with two glasses of water. She handed me one and I asked her, 'How does it look out there?'

'Oh,' she said, 'not good. But I didn't see much. There's a man asleep on the stairs.'

'Which stairs?'

'Between your room and the kitchen. Your housemates are awake, by the way. They want us to go for breakfast.'

There were nine of us. Sally and me, Mickey and the TV woman (Sharon, it turned out), Tom and Darla (who'd got together last night), Lorraine and her policeman (Steve, I remembered) and Stan. We needed two tables at the greasy spoon. Sally and I sat with Tom and Darla, who, surprisingly, didn't look that mismatched as a couple. I remembered Darla being nice about Tom the first time they'd met, and considered the extra effort he'd made with his appearance since Sally started staying with us. Although I felt jealous that Darla had switched her attentions to Tom, somehow it seemed less upsetting than if he'd ended up with Sally. I thought back to the conversation I'd had with Sally in this greasy spoon last Sunday after our night at Darklands when she'd told me that Darla often arranged for her sister to steal her boyfriends. Some men, I suppose, would love that, but it wasn't my sort of thing, and I was confident Tom wouldn't be able to cope if he was passed on. But Sally had also said that there were some men Darla was genuinely interested in, and that these men tended to be on the perverted side. I didn't think Tom fitted this description, but then again, Sally had said I'd be surprised by the depths of perversity in even normal-seeming men. Still, Tom a pervert? It was hard to imagine him making that much effort, no matter how much he enjoyed *Red Shoe Diaries* on Channel 5.

'Who's that man on the stairs?' I asked Tom.

'Neighbour. From the left-hand side. He came round to complain every hour until about five, when Mickey let him in and he finished every half-empty can in the house, swimming cigarette butts and all. Eventually he threw up and passed out.'

'Is there anyone else still in the house?'

He shook his head. 'We threw them all out. I'll get rid of the neighbour as soon as he wakes up.'

The waiter brought us our breakfasts. We talked for a while about how odd it was to have complete strangers appear at your party, then quickly stopped when we remembered how close Steve and Sharon came to this category. Stan, too, had recently disappeared off with a woman he barely knew. So what was holding me back? Sally, obviously, but maybe it was time for the pair of us to have another conversation. Considering this, I reached into my jeans and pulled out Sophie's number.

'What's that?' Darla asked.

'Oh,' I said, 'nothing.'

Sally gave me a sideways look and I quickly stuffed the piece of paper back into my pocket, not yet ready to upset anyone. It wasn't any of her business, but I couldn't imagine her putting up with me going on dates while she shared my bed. And how would I explain it to Sophie? There was no woman in the world who'd buy that one. I had to think of a sensitive way of resolving this situation, and for that I needed a bit more time.

84

I didn't realise my mother would already have packed up her belongings. The hallway was full of cardboard boxes, blocking the way to the stairs. It was obvious that this hadn't arisen from one weekend's conversation, and it became clear she'd been planning it for some time. This made me angry, as it seemed further evidence of my parents' incredible selfishness. Erica and I had just experienced the greatest weekend of our lives: it was unfair of them to confront us with this on our return. Anger turned to fury when I saw my stereo among my mother's boxes. I turned round and asked her, 'Why are you taking my stereo?'

'It's not your stereo,' she replied in an even tone. 'I bought it, it's always been mine, I just let you keep it in your room. Now I want it back.'

'You selfish bitch,' I screamed, scuttling over the boxes and running upstairs to my room.

Retreating to our rooms was a tactic all my family used in arguments. Usually I got the best deal in these situations, as my room was by far the most luxurious, and I could happily hold out there for as long as it took me to calm down, or my parents to start worrying about me. But, I realised now, this was mainly because I had my music, and without it, my room's appeal was severely reduced. I couldn't keep still, and wondered how I was going to last the half-hour it normally took them to come upstairs. Fortunately, today Dad appeared after five minutes, rescuing me before I had the chance to crack.

'Come to the chip shop with me,' he said. 'I want to talk to you.'

He gave me a jowly, hangdog look, and I followed him downstairs. We went out to the car. It wasn't far to the chip shop – just beyond walking distance – and although he'd said he wanted to talk, Dad didn't say anything during the short drive. We both got out of the car and went in together. They needed to fry some fresh cod and we stood and watched the silent television on the corner of the counter as the batter sizzled.

When the food was ready, we took it back to the car. Dad didn't start the engine, but turned to me and said, 'Do you remember the other day?'

'Which day?'

'When you asked me for money to buy clothes?'

I nodded.

'Remember that I asked you for your loyalty and told you that you'd soon start having strange feelings about me?'

'Yes, but you said that would be in a few years' time.'

He looked away. 'This happened sooner than I expected.'

'What happened, Dad? What's going on?'

'I can't tell you, son. Not yet. It depends what happens tonight.'

'What d'you mean? Mum's leaving, isn't she?'

'That hasn't happened yet. There's still time.'

'Time for what?'

'Look,' he said, 'I can't explain now. I made a promise. But the promise was dependent on certain conditions . . .'

I didn't like the way he was talking. It sounded dishonest. So I shouted at him, 'It's because of you, isn't it? It's because of your affair.'

'Careful, son,' he warned me, his voice rich with restrained anger. 'You don't know what the fuck you're talking about.'

He was right. I didn't know what I was talking about. I *thought* I did, but I didn't. My parents weren't breaking up because of my father's affair. They were breaking up because my mother was also having an affair, an affair she refused to end. The man she was involved with showed up later that evening, after my parents had gone upstairs for one last conversation. I recognised his face. He had been one of the few adult males allowed into the women's commune. He rang the doorbell, and I answered the door to him, but he didn't come in. My mother asked me to help fill the van with her boxes and I was too stunned by what was happening to refuse. Erica climbed into the front of the van with my mother and they drove away.

My father and I sat at the table where we'd eaten our dinner, one of the rare occasions when we hadn't had trays on our laps in front of the television. He said his obligations to my mother no longer stood and that he would tell me the full story. I don't really know why, but as he talked I found myself inexplicably taking my mother's side. (Erica told me later that she had a parallel reaction, feeling sorry for my father while my mother explained why she was leaving him.) I didn't reveal my thoughts to my father, but he could tell his words weren't provoking the reaction he wanted and before long he grew exasperated and went out into the hallway for his coat.

'Where are you going?' I asked.

'For a drive.'

'Do you want me to come with you?'

'No.'

I heard the door slam, and didn't know what to do. In the space of a few hours, my family had disintegrated.

85

Tom went upstairs, woke our neighbour from his stupor, and asked him to leave. The neighbour avoided our eyes as he returned downstairs. After he'd gone, the nine of us went into the lounge. Mickey's DJ friends had dismantled their decks and disappeared with them early this morning. There was still a lot of mess, but it was mainly around the edges of the carpet, beyond where people had been dancing. There seemed to be several items of clothing, mainly black cardigans.

Tom found some bin bags and handed them out. We took different sections of the room and started clearing stuff away. In my small space I found an asthma inhaler, about fifty cans and bottles, a single woman's shoe, a used condom and three contact lenses.

I assumed no one would return for these lenses, and that they were probably irreparably damaged anyway, and flushed them down the toilet with the used condom. The shoe and the inhaler, I kept.

We moved on from the lounge to the rest of the house. In every room we found small scraps of paper and chunks of torn-off cigarette packet with a phone number and the words *Joel (Peep Show)* written above it. Someone had certainly tried it on with lots of people. When we'd finished tidying, Sharon and Steve said they had to go. The rest of us went up to the kitchen. Tom had discovered a six-pack hidden in his bedroom cupboard, so we sat and drank that while we filled each other in on everything that had happened at the party.

86

It was the first time I'd been alone in our house. I knew my father wouldn't return until the early hours, if at all. I wasn't sure whether he'd go to the casino or his girlfriend's house, and couldn't decide which would be worse. The house was too quiet. I turned on the television, then went back upstairs and found my Dictaphone, desperate to hear the voices of my new friends again. After listening to the Perdita tape for a short while, I convinced myself to call her.

I went upstairs to my parents' room and lay on their bed. I picked up the phone from the floor and looked at the clock on their Goblin Teasmade. Ten o'clock. Probably too late for me to call, but I didn't care.

Perdita's father sounded pissed off. 'Yes?'

'I'm sorry to be calling this late.'

'Who is it?'

'My name's Gerald. I'm involved in *All Right Now!* with Perdita. Would it be possible for me to speak to her, please?'

'She's gone to bed. She's got school tomorrow.'

I heard a noise on the line and then Perdita saying, 'Dad, it's OK, I'll talk to him.'

He sighed, and put the phone down.

'I'm sorry,' I said, 'I didn't mean to wake you.'

'It's OK. I wasn't asleep. Did you call for a gossip?'

'Not really,' I said, my voice wavering.

'Gerald? What's wrong?'

'I'm sorry, I shouldn't have phoned.'

'Tell me.'

'It's complicated. Your dad'll be cross with me for keeping you up.'

'Don't worry about him. He won't check on me. As long

as you're not disturbing him, he doesn't really care. Now tell me what's wrong.'

So I explained. As I talked, I thought of Perdita on the other end of the line in her bed and wished I was with her. She listened sympathetically and told me she expected something similar would happen with her own family soon. I knew she wasn't saying this to cheer me up, but I still doubted her. Perdita's parents, no matter how ill-suited, seemed more grown-up than mine, and at that moment, I couldn't see separation as anything other than an immature action.

We talked about my parents, and as I began to feel better, gossiped about Wendy and Fuckpit. I asked Perdita if she thought Wendy would tell her boyfriend what had happened.

'Not until she absolutely has to. There are lots of girls like her at my school, and they're all the same.'

'Do you reckon they had sex?'

'Didn't Fuckpit tell you?'

'No. Did Wendy say something?'

'Yeah.' Her voice lowered. 'She said she brought him off.'

'Oh.'

'What?' she asked. 'What's wrong?'

'Nothing.'

'Come on, Mr Coy, you're making me drag every last word out of you tonight.'

'I'm embarrassed to say.'

'What?'

'Well, what does that mean? She brought him off? I don't understand.'

'Gave him a hand job.' She said this with such sincerity that I wished I understood what she meant. Previously I'd always gone to my father with questions about sex (e.g. 'What's war, Dad?' 'War? Let me see . . . oh, no, son, that word's pronounced "whore" '). But at the moment I couldn't see myself ever asking him to help me again, and decided I would risk having Perdita think I was naïve.

'But what does that mean?'

'Hand job? God, you really don't know anything, do you?'

'No, but I . . .'

'It's OK, Ger, I think it's sweet. But maybe I shouldn't be the one explaining this. I feel like I'm corrupting you.'

'Please, Purr, I'm fed up of not knowing anything.'

Perdita sighed, and started talking, giving me my first real sex-education lesson. I felt worried her father would pick up the phone, but I remained silent. When she'd finished explaining, I asked, 'Are you still a virgin, Perdita?'

She sounded offended. 'Of course.'

'Who told you about sex? Your parents?'

'They told me the technical stuff. The kids in school filled in the slang. And books. Books are good. Have you read any Judy Blume?'

'No.'

'You should. She's a bit girly, but boys can read her as well. Although the most instructive . . .' She giggled, then rephrased. 'The best book is this book my mum's got called *The Hite Report*. It's lots of women who've answered questionnaires about sex. Reading that made me realise I was normal.'

'So do you do it, then?'

'What?'

'The touching yourself stuff. Girls can do it as well as boys, can't they?'

She went quiet, then said, 'Yes, Gerald, they can. But that's not the sort of question you should ask me.'

'Oh,' I said. 'I'm sorry.'

'I can't believe you've got me talking about this stuff. Even the tips of my ears are burning.'

I took this as a signal to change topic. Perdita seemed relieved not to be talking about sex any more, letting me ramble on. I was amazed no one checked up on her, but I supposed her parents probably didn't mind as long as she was already in bed. Even though I knew she found it wearing, I started talking about parallel worlds again, and how I wished there was one without any adults in it.

'Are you really serious about this?' she asked, eventually.

'I think so. It seems crazy that we go through our whole lives gathering experience we can never go back and benefit from. I find it really hard to believe that you only get the chance to live your life once.'

A voice came on the line. My father's. 'Well you'd better get used to it. As this world is the only fucking one that exists.'

He slammed the phone back down.

'Perdita,' I said.

'Yes?' she replied, sounding sad.

'I've got to go. I don't want him to catch me in his bedroom.'

'OK, Ger. Call me again some time. Promise.'

'I promise. Bye.'

I put the phone down and sprinted upstairs. Dad didn't bother me again, and although I was scared, I soon managed to will myself to sleep.

87

I called Sophie on Wednesday morning. I didn't tell Sally. In fact, I was pleased I'd managed to keep this from her. I knew she was growing tired of staying with me and it was obvious our arrangement couldn't last much longer. But I wanted to resolve this current phase of our relationship in a way that allowed me to thank Sally for her generosity rather than make her think I was desperate to replace her.

Sophie was surprised by my call. Although she sounded no more interested in me now than she'd been the first two times we'd met, she seemed open to the possibility of a date.

'How about this weekend?' I suggested.

'OK. Why don't you come round Friday night and we'll work it out from there.'

I called Sophie from home. The electrician the letting agency were sending round could only visit in the daytime, and

Mickey had decided that one of us should grill him with difficult questions. This was hardly my forte, but I was the one who'd taken least time off and was less likely to get in trouble with the Language School.

The electrician was due at ten, but arrived at eleven-thirty. I explained the problems we'd been having and pointed him to the main trouble spots. Mickey and Stan were convinced the electrics had got worse since Steve had broken into the secret room. Both of them really believed we had a ghost in the house who'd been angered by the weekend's disturbances. I had to admit, the place had got significantly noisier at night, although I put this down to our new human guests. Tom, Lorraine and I were getting fed up of their superstition, and had arranged the electrician's visit to stop them indulging such fantasies.

After I'd shown him round the house, he said, 'It's a miracle one of you hasn't had a serious accident. I can fix the shower room for you, but almost every room has something dangerous in it. You've got these tumbler-switches that are so old I've hardly ever seen them before, and they should definitely have a porcelain cover instead of a brass one. Hardly anything seems to be earthed. The best thing I can do is write up a report and give it to the letting agency.'

I knew Mickey wouldn't be happy with this result, but it seemed futile to argue with the electrician. He spent two hours in the shower room, then left. I caught a tube into work, just in time for the afternoon session.

So far, my housemates' romances seemed likely to last, at least for the immediate future. Except, that was, for Stan, and his mystery woman. That evening, I went into his bedroom and asked him, 'This woman you went off with . . .'

'Yes?'

'You never told me what happened.'

'We spent the week together.'

'Yeah, but are you going to see her again?'

'No, I don't think so.'

'Why not? Didn't it work out?'

'No,' he said, 'it's not that. She did something to me. Something I didn't like.'

Now this sounded interesting. Stan didn't like us coming into his bedroom, and I could tell he wanted me to leave him alone. As he was so tall, and prone to back problems, Stan had all his furniture specially made, and at this moment he was sitting in his large red leather throne, watching a video on his small television.

'What's this?' I asked.

'*The Custard Boys*,' he said, pressing Pause. 'What do you want, Gerald?'

'Well, come on, then, what did she do to you? Something sexual?'

'No, personal. Look, I really don't want to talk about it.'

'OK,' I said, 'I'm sorry. I'll leave you alone.'

'Thank you,' he replied, and carried on watching his film. I backed out of his bedroom. He had a number of coats and jackets hanging on a rack on the back of his door and as I went past I knocked off the suit jacket he'd bought during his time away. I reached down to pick it up and noticed two small Polaroids that had fallen out. Both pictures showed Stan posing with a naked chest and a spotted tie knotted around his neck.

'What's this?' I asked.

He turned round. 'She took pictures of me, Gerald, OK? Are you satisfied now?'

'Yes, Stan, sure, sorry. I didn't mean to upset you.'

He sat back down and I left him alone, feeling baffled but not wanting to cause him any further embarrassment.

88

Erica didn't come into school on Monday or Tuesday. I thought she might be off all week, but she showed up late Wednesday morning. I watched her walk across the playground from my classroom window, then put up my hand

and asked to be excused. As soon as I was outside, I called out to her, but she ignored me and went straight into a building on the other side of the playground. I ran after her, went through the building's double doors and found my sister's classroom. I knocked on the door and entered. My sister was sitting in the back row with her scary friends.

'Yes?' the teacher asked.

'I need to have a word with my sister.'

The teacher looked at Erica, who shook her head.

'Don't be silly, Erica. Your brother wants to talk to you.'

'I'll be in the corridor,' I said, stepping out of the classroom.

A moment later, Erica came outside. Her face looked washed-out and there were bags beneath her eyes.

'What's wrong, Erica? Why don't you want to talk to me?'

A tear appeared in her left eye. She wiped it away with her sleeve, but it was followed by several more.

'Did Mum tell you not to talk to me?'

She shook her head.

'Come on, Erica. We need to talk. Where are you staying?'

Erica turned round and ran back into the classroom. I left her, and walked back to mine.

89

I walked into the classroom and wrote *FALSE FRIENDS* in green on the clean whiteboard. This had always been my favourite lesson to teach, as it didn't involve memorising complex grammatical rules. Next I took a purple pen and wrote *rat, mail, eventual, Hell,* and *ramp*.

'Max,' I said, 'what does "rat" mean in your language?'

'Um, I think the English word is "advice".'

'Good. Nadine, what about "mail"? What does that mean in French?'

I was on auto-pilot. The class loved this kind of lesson. Normally we were encouraged to stop the students talking about their countries and cultures, as it distracted them from the task at hand. I was more lenient about this than the other teachers, partly because it was usually the most intelligent students who took an interest in their classmates' cultures, and also because I enjoyed picking up information along the way myself. But the 'False Friends' lesson was the only one where the students were actively encouraged to compare their native tongues.

Once the debate had got going, I found myself thinking about the night ahead. I had arranged to take Sally to the Lavender and was preparing to tell her that I wanted her to go home tomorrow. I hadn't decided whether I would let her know this was because I had a date. I thought I'd see how she responded first.

I caught the tube home with my housemates as usual. It was good to have Stan back with us, and we teased him throughout the journey. We walked back to our house from Oval tube station, and I went upstairs to my bedroom.

Sally was in there already, taking off her skirt. She looked at me. 'Sorry,' she said, 'I meant to get ready before you came home.'

'That's OK. Have you had a shower since the room was fixed?'

'I was just about to.'

I nodded, backing out of the room. 'I'll leave you alone then.'

It seemed mean to be taking Sally to the Lavender rather than somewhere in town, but the food was so good, and if she did react badly to our conversation, I wanted to be able to persuade her to come back to the house with me. She didn't appear to mind the unadventurous choice, and had even made an effort to look good, wearing a stylish black dress and a thin silver necklace I remembered her ex-boyfriend giving to her.

We ordered our food. The restaurant was usually crammed on a Thursday, but tonight it seemed quiet, maybe because it was still early. I asked Sally about her day and she told me her team had spent five hours deciding on the right pair of shoes for a model to wear in a commercial for a new woman's magazine.

'That's unusual, isn't it? Magazines advertising on TV?'

'Not really. Although it's mainly the new ones that have to do it.'

We talked about my housemates' new romances and I gave her odds on how long I thought each would last. After we'd finished our starters and two glasses of wine, I said, 'Sally, I've got something important I need to discuss with you.'

She smiled at me, the candlelight's illumination catching her neck. 'Yes?'

'I think it's time for me to sort myself out.'

'What d'you mean?'

'Well, you can't go on sharing my bed for ever.'

She laughed. 'I suppose not.' She looked away, then turned back to me, blinking. 'So when do you want me to go?'

'Don't put it like that. It's the right thing for both of us. You've nursed me long enough.'

She was crying now, although her voice was still composed. 'I could leave tomorrow morning.'

'Sally,' I said, 'this is silly. You're making me feel like I'm breaking up with you.'

She didn't say anything.

'You don't want us to have a relationship, do you?'

She shook her head, then got up and went down to the toilet. The waitress, who had witnessed all this, came across and asked me if we still wanted our main courses.

'I think so. Let me wait until she comes back.'

The waitress nodded and moved on. I worried about the impression I was giving her. Then I shooed this thought away, ashamed I was so self-conscious.

Sally returned from the toilet and sat down.

'We can cancel the rest of the meal if you want,' I told her.

'No,' she said, 'it's OK. I'm sorry. I'm not crying for the reasons you think. I just hate endings, that's all.'

'This isn't an ending, Sally, I promise. Why would it be an ending? It's just a stage.'

'Everything's just a stage, and then you turn back and wonder what happened and why you're not happy any more.'

I understood what she was saying, and took her hands in mine. 'We'll still see each other.'

'It's OK, Gerald. I said I'm fine. Just let me mourn this moment, all right?'

I nodded, and was careful about everything I said throughout the rest of the meal.

She moved out the following morning. On our last night together, we both cried and clutched each other with a ferocity I couldn't believe. We even started kissing and stroking each other, although we stopped short of making love, both aware that whatever we told ourselves, it would damage our friendship. She awoke before I did, and by the time I set off to the Language School with my housemates, she had gone.

90

Shep picked me up from my house. Since my mother had left, I'd stopped going round to Reggel's. My father had never been worried about me being in the house alone, and saw my mother's fears as a form of mollycoddling. I didn't feel as cross with him now, after he'd tried to make things up with me by buying me a new stereo. He also gave me a hundred pounds to spend on LPs, and, breaking my own private rule not to buy more than one record by any artist, I spent most of the money on Prince's backlist. I also bought the records Perdita had played on our weekend away, by the Beatles and INXS.

I still hadn't had a proper conversation with Erica. As I

climbed into the back of Shep's car, he asked, 'Where's your sister today?'

I told him my story. I had no idea whether my mother would want Erica to withdraw from the project. In a reassuring voice, Shep said, 'They've probably arranged for another driver to pick her up.'

This turned out to be true. Erica was waiting with the other children in the infant school we were using as a rehearsal space. Seeing Perdita again made me feel safe. She was wearing a long baggy red-and-white striped cardigan over a long red dress. Her appearance was less intimidating than usual and I just wanted her to hold me.

Nicholas arrived on crutches with his left foot in plaster. He was wearing a grey fedora, a blue shirt and brown cords. The rest of the adults followed behind him and Immi handed out his sheaves of photocopied paper.

'Hello, everyone,' he said, 'I hope you're ready to work. Tonight, and every night this week, is going to be much more intense than anything we've done so far. In a very short while, we're going to be joined by the actors playing your parents, and then we'll take a stab at sorting out the first episode. Can you all look at your pages?'

I stared at the first sheet. At the top was printed:

All Right Now! Episode One
Tour Guide: Amy

'Why am I a tour guide?' asked Amy. 'Do we have to have jobs?'

'No,' said Nicholas, 'that's not what that means. Although all of you will appear in the programmes for roughly the same amount of time, each episode will have one of you serving in the role of tour guide. What this means is that you will be the person who'll guide the audience through the action.'

'Oh,' she said, 'OK.'

'Of course,' he continued, 'not all of you will get to be

tour guides in this series, but don't worry, you'll get your chance when the programme is recommissioned.'

I thumbed through the sheets, looking to see who else got to be tour guides, but these pages only described the first episode.

'Can you all get back in your family groups?'

We did so. Nicholas sectioned off a large rectangular stage space. Then he asked everyone to sit down and went outside to find the adult actors. It was hard to fit on the too-small chairs and I was amused by how much I had grown since I was eight. I sat between Erica and Sheryl and waited to see what the people playing our parents would look like.

Nicholas came back in with four men and three women. The adults stood in the stage space and let the dramaturge arrange them. He gestured towards the first couple and said, 'You'll see that your characters have the same names that you do in real life. With the actors playing your parents, I want you to get into the habit of calling them Mum and Dad at all times. Amy and Robert, there will be one person who looks after you in the care-home and I want you to call him by his real name, which is Alan. Alan, can you step forward, please?'

Alan stepped forward. He was a large man in his late thirties, with a thinning head of blond hair. He was wearing a pair of blue jeans and a black shirt. I thought he looked cool.

'OK, and I have made one slight alteration to the set-up we devised at the weekend. Sheryl, you're still going to be Gerald's girlfriend, but you're going to take a while to start a relationship, so I've decided that you should be staying in the care-home with Amy and Robert. Can the three of you stand with Alan, please?'

They did so. Nicholas moved on to the next couple. 'OK,' he said, 'Gerald and Erica, these are your parents.'

We both looked at the two actors. I didn't know who had cast these characters and if their selection had been influenced by the work we'd done at the weekend, but it did look as though they'd taken my 'fear of the family' theme seriously, and chosen an angry-looking man and a timid wife. Our new mother glanced at us and reached for our fictional father's hand. I assumed she was doing this to make them look like a genuine couple, but the gesture upset my sister who got up and ran from the room.

'What's wrong?' Nicholas called after her.

'I can explain,' I said. 'Can I have a word with you outside, please?'

Nicholas held out his arm, gesturing for me to go ahead of him while he struggled with his crutches. Immi had taken off after Erica, and I knew she'd do a better job of comforting her than me. When we were in the corridor, he said, 'So?'

'Our parents have separated. They sprung it on us when we got back from our weekend away. Erica's been . . . very emotional about it.'

He nodded. 'What d'you think set her off?'

'The actors holding hands.'

'Gerald, do you think Erica would respond better if your parents in this programme were also separated?'

I considered this. 'I don't know.'

He jiggled round for a moment, trying to settle on his crutches. 'Can I give you some advice, Gerald?'

I nodded.

'Don't be afraid of emotion. I don't mean only in relation to acting. This is a big thing that's happened to you. I can see you're trying to package it off and push it away, and that will work, but only for a while. A far better way of coping is to approach the upset head on . . . to harness it and make it work for you.'

He was staring at me now, eyes scarily alight.

'My parents would be really cross if we talked about this stuff on TV,' I told him.

'Gerald, you won't be talking. You'll be using your emotions and creating drama. Your emotions are your property. No one can stop you expressing them in any way you see fit. If your family get cross with you, well, that's just because they're too ignorant to understand. Gerald, do you remember what I said before our very first exercise?'

I shook my head. He looked disappointed. 'What I said, Gerald, was that you'd come to take part in a difficult and painful process of transubstantiation. Do you know what that word means?'

'No.'

'Well, what it literally refers to is the moment in a Roman Catholic service when the Eucharistic elements – that's bread and wine, Gerald – are turned into the body and blood of Christ. The bread and wine still looks like bread and wine, Gerald, but it's been wholly converted. It may sound sacrilegious to use such a term in relation to what we're doing, but I do believe the principle is similar. When you act in this programme, you will be totally transformed. I'm not talking about you becoming Jesus, or even divine, but you will become a version of yourself that's not the same Gerald as the one who stands before me now. Do you understand what I mean?'

'I think so.'

'That's good enough for me. These are difficult concepts for anyone to understand, let alone a thirteen-year-old boy. But I want to squash all the squeamishness out of you early on. What you're doing here is more important than your life. It's more important than your parents' lives. What's happened to you, your parents' divorce, is a terrible thing. But it's also a gift. When you met me you stopped being passive. Now I have to show you how to exploit your talents.'

'Nicholas?'

'Yes?'

'Will you explain this to Erica too?'

He nodded. 'Not in the way I explained it to you, because your sister is different. It's obvious that she has no problem accessing her emotions. So I have to appeal to her intellect.'

I couldn't help laughing. Nicholas glared at me, and said, 'Your sister isn't unintelligent. Her mind's got a bit tangled up, that's all. I can save her, just like I can save you. Now go back inside.'

I did as I was told, returning to my empty seat alongside

Sheryl. Most people in the room, adults and children, looked blank or bored, but Perdita gave me a sympathetic, inquisitive smile. We all waited. Two minutes passed in silence before Immi and Erica came back in together, Nicholas hobbling behind them.

'OK,' said Nicholas, propelling himself back to the actors. 'Wendy and Lucy, can you come across, please?'

The two girls stood up. Wendy carried herself so confidently. She seemed more powerful than anyone else in the room, even Nicholas. I looked across at Fuckpit, and saw awe in his eyes. Nicholas pointed towards the next couple.

'Stand together,' he told them.

The next pair of actors looked too young to have a daughter as old as Wendy, although the physical similarity between the members of this pretend family disturbed me. Our pretend parents didn't look much like our real ones, or even Erica and me, but Wendy and Lucy's new parents were close enough in appearance to make me wonder whether they'd been cast with a photograph for comparison. Wendy's new mother had brown hair, loosely permed, a similarly round face, and blue eyes. Her new father had brown hair with blond highlights, and a neat brown moustache. His eyes were also blue, and his small nose was identical in shape to those of the two girls.

'Good,' said Nicholas, moving on to the last couple. 'Lola, Pete and Perdita, these are your parents, and Jane, your uncle and auntie. I've decided I'm going to take a little risk here and introduce one slightly melodramatic element. Jane, as we're moving away from strict autobiography in your group's story, I've decided to push things here, and make it so that your parents have been killed in a car crash. I know that's not really an original plot device, but I think it opens up interesting dramatic possibilities.'

These last two parents were the oldest. The father was tall, bald, and wearing a cheap grey suit. His wife looked more impressive than the other mothers, wearing sharply pressed trousers, a white polo neck and pearls. Her blonde hair was cut in a masculine style, and combed into a peak at the front. Her face was heavily wrinkled.

'So,' Nicholas continued, 'we'll start at the beginning. Can everyone sit back down apart from Amy, Robert and Alan?'

And so we started work on the first episode. Nicholas had mapped out fifteen main scenes, and tonight he videoed our improvised conversations to use for the development of his script. The episode began [scene 1] with Amy and Fuckpit in their care home with Alan. The two of them left this location and went to the teens-only nightclub [2], where we were all introduced into the action [3]. Nicholas had kept the scene we'd worked on at the weekend where I met Amy and talked to her and Robert got angry [4]. After this scene came a string of romantic connections: Wendy and Fuckpit [5], Erica and Pete [6] – I hadn't realised Nicholas had noticed this one – and me and Sheryl [7]. Nicholas stopped us here to tell us that while over the course of the whole series we would get the same amount of screen time, the division in each episode might be uneven. He also said that the chronology of action was not going to be completely linear, and that storylines might stop and be returned to later, allowing Nicholas to make sure we got the maximum amount of scenes out of our minimal action. So after scenes 8 (Lola, Lucy and Erica forming a comical trio) and 9 (Perdita and Jane mocking Pete about his interest in Erica) several characters were left at the teens-only nightclub, as Amy, Robert, Sheryl and I were persuaded to sneak away to Wendy and Lucy's house [10]. At the end of this scene [11], we were discovered by their parents [12], which would mean bad things for me in the next episode. I had a farewell scene with Sheryl [13] and then the last two scenes focused on Amy, Sheryl and Robert, showing them going home [14] and getting into trouble [15].

The session went surprisingly smoothly. Nicholas's main advice was to keep our dialogue focused and dramatic. Being videoed added a useful tension to the exercise, creating a serious atmosphere. It took about ninety minutes to get through our various interpretations of the fifteen scenes, after which we were rewarded with lemonade. Perdita came over and rubbed my arm.

'Hi, Gerald, how are you feeling?'

'All right.'

'What was the problem with your sister?'

'Oh, you know, about our parents . . . '

She nodded and sipped her drink.

'I really enjoyed our talk the other night.'

'Me too.'

I couldn't shake off a stiffness in the way I was responding. I think it was a delayed embarrassment about Erica's outburst, and a new awareness of the other children around me. Perdita sensed my awkwardness, and, after smiling at me again, walked over to Wendy and Robert. I went across to Erica and Lola. My sister gave me a defiant glare.

'Can I have a quick word with you, Erica?'

She looked at Lola. I was convinced she was going to refuse me again, but instead she came across to a quiet corner of the room.

'Are you OK?'

She nodded.

'What about Mum? Is she all right?'

'Yeah.'

'And that bloke from the commune? What's his name?'

'Dennis.'

'Is he nice to you? To Mum?'

'He tries.'

I was surprised by this answer. It showed an understanding I thought was beyond my sister. She was uncomfortable talking about this and I didn't want to make her suffer any longer, but there was one more question I had to ask.

'Do you think this is permanent?'

Her answer surprised me. 'Mum's going to contact you. Sometime soon.'

We walked back to the other children.

*

Shep drove Jane, Fuckpit and me home after the session. My house was in darkness.

'Jesus, Gerald, what is wrong with your family?' He looked at his watch. 'Well, don't worry, I've got a bit of time tonight. I can wait with you.'

I shook my head and pulled my key out of my pocket. 'It's OK. I have this now.'

'Good for you. Although I have to say I don't know what they were worrying about. You seem a lot more reliable than they are.'

'Thanks, Shep,' I said, opening the car door.

'Hey,' he said, 'do you want me to come inside with you for a minute? Check everything's safe?'

I thought about how messy our house had got over the last week. My mother was house-proud only in the sense that she rarely let anyone see inside, but since she'd gone things had got much worse. Not that Shep seemed fastidious. Why shouldn't I let him in? Dad wouldn't be back until the early hours and it would be nice to have some company.

'OK, Shep, thanks.'

He got out of the car, locked it, and followed me up the garden path. I unlocked the front door and we both went in. Ordinarily I barely noticed the smell, but with Shep beside me it seemed so strong that I wondered how he was able to breathe. He didn't say anything. I turned the lights on as we went, showing him through to the lounge.

'Would you like a drink?'

He smiled. 'Is your Dad a drinker?'

'You could say that.'

'So he might have some whisky somewhere?'

'I'll fetch it.'

'Thanks, Gerald, but only pour me a little bit, OK? Driving's my livelihood.'

Shep settled down on our sofa, rubbing his hands over the cushions. He stared at the television and I asked him if he wanted me to turn it on. He shook his shaggy head. I went out to the kitchen. There was a cheap wooden rack on the counter, grey blobs of superglue at every join. All the bottles were spirits. I pulled out the whisky and poured Shep a glass.

'Would you like any Coke?' I asked him. 'Or ice?'

'No, thanks, Gerald,' he shouted back.

I poured myself a glass of Coke and took Shep his drink. He sipped it, fingered the ends of his hair, and asked me, 'Is your Dad being OK to you?'

I sat down. 'He's doing his best.'

'But he's taking it hard?'

'Yes.'

Shep nodded. I was expecting another pep-talk, but, instead, Shep let himself sink deeper into the sofa and concentrated on his whisky.

We sat there in silence until he'd finished it. Then he put the glass on the table and said to me, 'I'll see you tomorrow then?'

'Yeah.'

'Don't stay up waiting for him. You've got a busy week ahead.'

He left. I watched him walk to the car, then shut the front door. I was getting used to being in the house on my own. This made the experience less frightening, but also less liberating. Frankly, I was bored, and astonished by how much I wanted my family back.

91

Everyone in our house knew about my date. This was my own fault. I'd shown off to Lorraine in the ten-thirty coffee break, and by the two-fifteen break she'd passed on this information to Tom, Stan, Mickey and all the students in my last afternoon class. Lorraine had been astounded that I'd kicked Sally out of our house, unable to abandon her theory that I secretly coveted my best friend's body. I think she even felt I'd been a bit callous, which surprised me, as she hadn't seemed that fond of Sally. Lorraine was also amazed I'd managed to move things on with Sophie since the night of the party.

'Why's that so surprising?' I asked, hurt.

'No, Gerald, don't get me wrong. I'm not saying you won't make out fine with her. It's just that, given the way she acted when we were in Bar Rumba, I'm surprised things have got this far.'

'You think she doesn't fancy me?'

'Gerald, let me give you some advice. Girls can fancy anyone. It's got nothing to do with who you are. It's all down to the way you act.'

'What's wrong with how I act?'

'You act strange. It's partly because you're so inexperienced, partly because of all the time you've spent in our house-of-no-fun, but mainly because, well, I hate to say it, but you just don't have the ability to get under a girl's skin.'

'Ah,' I told her, 'I switched that off.'

'No, Gerald, if you knew how to do it, you'd never switch it off. I mean, take me, I want to sleep with everybody. At least when I first meet them. I don't mean I'd actually go through with it, but I think about the possibility. I'm intrigued, if nothing else. God, I've even thought that about Tom, Stan and Mickey.'

'But not me.'

'No. And don't take it personally. It's just, you act like you don't give a shit what anyone thinks of you.'

'But that's an attractive quality. It intrigues girls, I know it does. Haven't you ever seen *Cat on a Hot Tin Roof*?'

She shook her head. 'It gets you to the first stage. And it's obvious you have no problem getting to the first stage. Sally, that girl Darla, Sophie, maybe. But you've forgotten how to take it further. You're arrested, Gerald. Don't you remember how you did it with your first girlfriend?'

'Did what?'

'Crossed over. Got intimate. Had sex.'

'Of course. I'm just taking things easy. Sally told me not to rush into a new relationship.'

'All I'm saying is, if you want to have sex with this

woman, you have to change your act. At the moment, she's toying with you. You're the mouse, Gerald. Mice don't get to have sex.'

I wasn't sure if this was strictly true, but nonetheless, I asked her, 'So what do I do?'

'Show her you're interested, but in a subtle way, so that she makes some kind of response. And then back off . . .'

'That's what I've been doing.'

'But you've missed the last part. Back off, let her panic, then rush in. It's all about female insecurity. Insecurity and reassurance. That's what you're not providing. The reassurance.'

I took Lorraine's advice seriously. I didn't get on that well with my housemate, but I respected her experience in romantic matters, and believed that she had an intuitive understanding of the female mind, even though her own was so strange. What she was telling me to do sounded manipulative, but I knew the beginning of relationships could benefit from such cunning.

By the time of our tube-ride home, all my housemates were discussing my date. Lorraine, Mickey and Tom enjoyed the subject because it allowed them to talk about their own new relationships; Stan because it gave him chance to make fun of me, reversing the usual order of things. For once, I was happy to let them mock me, as it only served to make me more excited about the night ahead.

I had decided I'd aim to get to Sophie's house for nine o'clock. She hadn't specified a time, but that seemed a suitably relaxed hour to arrive. Any later and she might start worrying about me, any earlier and she'd think I was a wimp. Choosing clothes had been difficult. I knew I'd looked too conservative in Bar Rumba, and too relaxed at our party, and needed to change my appearance for tonight. I let Lorraine loose in my wardrobe, hoping she wouldn't be too unkind. I'd expected her to insult everything I owned, but there were a few items that met her approval. Her selection surprised me. She picked out a fitted light brown jacket Ellen had bought me that I didn't really like and had hardly worn, a long-sleeved blue T-shirt that was too light for the weather, and a pair of Vivien Westwood jeans that I'd bought a couple of years ago on a whim and hardly worn since as they were slightly too tight.

'Now,' she said, 'don't you have any trainers?'

I shook my head.

'Can't you borrow a pair from one of the boys?'

'Tom and Mickey are two sizes smaller than me, and Stan buys his shoes from the circus.'

'OK,' she said, 'those'll have to do. But can't you at least give them a polish?'

After I'd had a bath, polished my shoes, and changed into the clothes Lorraine had selected, it was just after eight. Sophie lived in Finsbury Park. Allowing for the vagaries of travelling to what Mickey called 'the wrong side of London', I thought I should leave myself fifty minutes. The others were sitting in our kitchen, ready for their favourite Friday night television. I told them I was going and put up with a last few jokes.

On the way to the tube, it occurred to me that I should probably buy some condoms. This was a far more alien phenomenon than it should've been for a man my age. I'd only ever had sex with Ellen, and she'd gone on the pill before our first time, after a female friend had told her that the best thing about losing your virginity to another virgin is that you know you're absolutely safe having sex with them. And after that first time we decided that the experience was so wonderful we didn't want to explore any alternatives. I'd already told myself several times that my relationship with Ellen was over. Now I would prove it. Tonight I'd sleep with Sophie, and start my life again.

92

My father didn't come home that night. I took Shep's advice and didn't stay up, sensing that I'd have to cope with this sort of behaviour for a while yet. When my father was my age his mother died of cancer. His father binged for a whole year. My grandfather wasn't a gambler and had no interest in other women, so he'd stuck with booze, getting so drunk for days at a time that my father had to wait until he completely seized up and then nurse him back to health with soup until he was fit enough to start the cycle again. My father hadn't needed this sort of treatment from me, but it seemed likely that some kind of intervention would be necessary on my part, and I wanted to be prepared, ready to say the right thing.

My mother had sent Erica to school with letters for her teachers explaining what had happened, and there'd clearly been staff-room gossip, as I was getting a much easier ride than usual. Our school was suburban, and as many of the teachers had recently experienced their own marital problems, I wondered whether their sympathy had anything to do with their relationships with their own children.

I went home at four. There was no sign of my father, so I changed my clothes and watched children's television while I waited for Shep. He tooted from outside and I went out to the car. I climbed in the back. He leaned round and said, 'He didn't come home, did he?'

'No.'

Shep nodded and started the engine. We picked up Jane and Fuckpit and continued to the infant school. Nicholas was waiting for us, although some of the other children had yet to arrive. He handed me today's pages and I quickly checked the top sheet, amazed to see:

All Right Now! Episode Two
Tour Guide: Gerald

Nicholas had dropped hints yesterday that today's episode would be important for me, but I hadn't dared hope I'd get to be a tour guide so quickly. It seemed the perfect episode in which to be the centre of attention. People often missed first episodes, but by the second week there would have been reviews, adverts and publicity, and I'd be guaranteed a decent audience. I was so pleased with this arrangement that I didn't notice Perdita come up behind me.

'Congratulations,' she said.

'Thank you,' I replied, 'I'm sure Nicholas has only done it to be nice to me.'

'I don't think Nicholas could be nice if he tried. He obviously realised you were a strong enough character to carry an episode.'

'I'm sure you'll get one too.'

'I hope not. I prefer staying out of the limelight. How are you feeling, anyway, Gerald? Are things getting easier?'

I didn't like moaning, and didn't want Perdita to be constantly feeling sorry for me, but I couldn't lie to her, so I said, 'My Dad didn't come home last night.'

'Oh, Gerald, that's terrible. Are you worried about him?'

'He'll come home eventually.'

'Aren't you afraid he's had an accident?'

'He has places he goes to. It's not unusual for him to be out all night.'

Perdita gave me a hug. Everyone noticed, and I worried she'd be cross with me later. But I squeezed her back, grateful for the support. Nicholas hobbled to the centre of the room.

'As you can see, today's episode focuses on Gerald, and to a lesser extent, Erica. We're picking up from yesterday, so the first scene is Gerald and Erica getting home. Now, you'll remember that in the last episode, Amy, Robert, Sheryl and Gerald were discovered in Wendy and Lucy's house by Wendy's parents. Although the audience won't see it' – he stopped and smiled at me – 'Wendy's parents have called

Gerald's parents and they're waiting for him when he gets home. He's going to get in trouble not just for sneaking off, but also for leaving Erica alone at the club. Erica, you're still missing at this point . . .'

I'm hoping my attempt to adumbrate *All Right Now!* works without the visuals. It's the construction that's important to me, and the situations this fiction forced us into. The first scene of episode two had me in a position I would no longer face in real life because my parents were too worried about themselves to fret about me. It was oddly reassuring, being told off by a fictional father. This scene began with him questioning me alone, before my mother came downstairs and joined in. I hadn't yet had chance to talk to the actors and I didn't know if they had children of their own, but the way he talked to me made me think he probably didn't, as it felt as if he was making everything up rather than relying on his own experience.

'Right, Gerald's Mum, you're more worried about Erica,' Nicholas told her, 'so I want you to get really angry with Gerald, as if you're convinced something bad has happened to her and it's all his fault.'

The actress took Nicholas's direction seriously and started screaming at me, her melodramatic performance ensuring I could only respond or stay silent, pinned in a position where everything I said made things worse.

'Excellent,' encouraged Nicholas. 'Now, at this point, Erica, you come in, and Mum, you rush across and confront her. You're relieved, but the relief emerges as anger. And, Erica, you don't have to be timid. Respond exactly how you would in real life.'

The torrent of foul language that emerged from my sister's mouth quickly led Nicholas to intervene.

'No, let's try that again. I know you're only expressing yourself, Erica, but let's remember that this programme is going to be shown at teatime on Sunday afternoon. We have to exercise a little restraint.'

They had another go at the scene, and this time my sister

kept her swearing under control. They looked to Nicholas for instruction on how to end the scene and he told them, 'So we'll finish with the two parents going to bed, and the children being left alone. Then we have a new scene that's not on the printed sheets . . .'

The new scene was a conversation between our parents that I was supposed to eavesdrop on. When Nicholas described this scene he stared at me as if he thought he'd captured a reality I would recognise. But nothing like this had happened in real life. Maybe Erica had overheard this sort of talk, but I'd had no prior knowledge my parents were going to separate. I was going to explain this to the dramaturge, but knew how he would respond: 'I'm making real life dramatic, Gerald. Stories can't just be a stream of unrelated events. Scenes like this provide necessary narrative tension.' And he was probably right, so I performed the scene as he'd constructed it. After we'd finished our improvisation, Amy put her hand up.

'Yes?' Nicholas asked.

'I don't think you're getting Gerald's mum right. She's not the kind of woman to scream and shout.'

The actress looked offended. Nicholas looked at her and then back to Amy, telling her, 'Amy, you must remember that you only saw the public face of Gerald's mother. Gerald, do you think your mother is capable of behaving like this in private?'

I looked down at the floor. 'Yes.'

'Good. Let's move on.'

The rest of the episode was concerned with lighter matters. As punishment for my behaviour the previous night, I was forced to look after my sister as she teamed up with Lucy and Lola. Wendy and Lucy now had a pregnant cat in the story, and they sold (or promised to sell) kittens to Amy and Perdita. There was a big scene in Perdita's house where Pete reappeared and talked to Erica. I didn't think all this love stuff was realistic, but at least he kept in my suggested kicking scene. The tension in Pete and Erica's relationship came from them both being tough guys. Erica was the leader of her little gang, bullying Lola and Lucy. I don't know how much attention Nicholas was paying to themes and character development, but some nice subtleties had begun to emerge. Lucy had really come alive as a character, and it made psychological sense that she would be intimidated by Erica because she reminded her of her own sister, Wendy. Unable to gain acceptance from her own family, she was looking for respect from Erica, who used this weakness to control her. Fuckpit and Wendy were in this episode least, coming in halfway through to find Lucy and bring her home. The episode ended with Erica and me back at our house, as our mother packed her bags and moved out. This did upset me, although Erica was calm. Given how she'd responded yesterday, I found this astonishing, and wondered what Nicholas had said to her. I also wondered whether she'd told him this was how things had happened in real life, as I was surprised he'd got it so right.

Shep drove us home after the session. Jane and Fuckpit talked about who they thought would be tour guide tomorrow.

'I think it'll be you,' Jane told him, 'or Wendy. That's why you weren't in it tonight that much.'

'You weren't either.'

'Yeah, but I was involved in the action. And Nicholas won't want another episode that features Lola and Pete so heavily.'

'It won't be me,' he replied, 'because the first one was Amy. I reckon he's going to do a tour guide from each family group first. So you're probably right, it'll be Wendy.'

Shep stopped outside Fuckpit's house. He got out and walked up to his front door.

My house was in darkness. Shep didn't offer to come inside with me tonight. Maybe he had other things on his mind, or a late-night film to project. I unlocked the front door and went inside. My father had been home at some point this evening. There was a glass on the coffee table that hadn't been there earlier and when I went upstairs I saw his work clothes lying on his bed. I checked to see if he'd left me a note or some money, but there wasn't anything. I went back downstairs to the lounge and turned on the television.

93

Sophie lived on Blackstock Road. Her directions were idiot-proof and within minutes I had arrived at her home. I had to ring the doorbell for ages before she came down.

'Sorry,' she said, 'we had the music up too loud.'

We?

'It's on the third floor,' Sophie told me, leading the way. She was dressed to go out, apart from a pair of thick blue plastic flip-flops that I hoped she'd ditch for proper shoes. I'd had a panic on the way here that she might want to go to a club with a no jeans policy, but she was also wearing a pair, along with a black sparkly halter-neck. We reached her floor and she pushed open the door. Uncle C and Don were sitting in her lounge, talking about the music playing.

'It's this bit,' Don told him, 'do you hear it? The way the main sample gets quieter when you think it's going to go loud?'

'Yeah,' said Uncle C, 'wicked.'

Sophie didn't register my disappointment at seeing these two, asking me, 'Would you like a glass of wine?'

'Thanks.'

'I hope white's OK.'

'White's fine.'

I sat next to Don and nodded hello. He nodded back. Uncle C sipped his wine and said in a low voice, 'I didn't think we'd be seeing you again.'

'Oh well,' I replied, 'tough luck.'

Sophie came back in from the kitchen with my glass of wine. She didn't seem to notice the tension between us, and retreated back to the bathroom to finish her make-up. The CD stopped and Uncle C took a plastic case from his inside pocket.

'What's that, Uncle C?' Don asked, amused.

'Oh,' he said, 'just a little something.'

He got up from the chair and went over to the stereo. He changed CDs and pressed Play. The new music was jazz. Uncle C sat back down.

'Is this you?' Don asked him.

He grinned. 'Second set at the *Nightingale*. December 1987.'

'Where d'you get the CD?'

'A friend from the old days has bought himself a burner. He's making copies of all his tapes.'

'What do you play?' I asked.

He glared at me. 'Tenor sax.'

Sophie came back in from the bathroom. Don turned round and smiled at her. 'This is Uncle C's band.'

'Oh, I love this,' she replied, 'will you make me a copy?'

'This copy is for you,' he said. 'I got my friend to make duplicates of the best sets.'

I hate jazz. 'So is that where we're going tonight? A jazz club?'

'No,' said Sophie, 'didn't I tell you? We're going to a secret party underneath the arches at London Bridge.'

'London Bridge? It was hardly worth me coming over.'

'You wouldn't get in without us,' Sophie told me. 'Besides, Uncle C's going to drive.'

Uncle C grinned at me.

'Right,' I said, clutching my glass, 'so when are we going to set off?'

'Any minute,' she told me.

Don frowned. 'Let's listen to a bit more of Uncle C's band first.'

'It's OK,' he said, 'I have a CD player in the car.'

'Great,' I said, and it must have come out more sarcastic than I intended, as I got dirty looks from the three of them. I tried to make my face look innocent and started nodding my head and clicking my fingers as if I thought Uncle C's CD was the best thing I'd ever heard.

94

I looked down at the top sheet and saw Jane and Fuckpit had been right:

All Right Now! Episode Three
Tour Guide: Wendy

Wendy seemed nonchalant about Nicholas's decision. Lucy looked disappointed, sensing that if her sister got to be a tour guide that ruled out her chance this series. So far Nicholas had favoured the older children, and I wondered if this was a deliberate decision. He used the younger ones to provide the programme's humour, and gave us all the dramatic scenes, although so far there hadn't been that much serious action.

Nicholas seemed to have realised this, and started tonight's session by saying, 'Children, in this episode we're going to be tackling a very serious subject . . .' He glanced up at Immi and Carolyn. 'I've already had discussions about whether this is a suitable issue to address in a teen drama, but I think that as it's something that affects many children your age, we're actually providing a positive service in doing so . . .'

'What subject?' asked Wendy.

'Teenage pregnancy.'

'But aren't the stories in this programme supposed to come from real life? None of us is pregnant.'

'Yes, Wendy, that's true. But we're only using your real lives as a starting point. We have to have some stories that take off from reality. Otherwise the programme would be so boring no one would watch it.'

'So who gets pregnant? Me, I suppose.'

'Do you have a problem with that?'

'Yes,' she said, 'I don't want people to think I'm a slapper. If I do this in this programme, everyone'll come up to me in the street and think I'm easy.'

'No they won't. We've already established that you're in an exclusive relationship with Robert.'

'But what kind of slut doesn't use a condom? Or isn't on the pill at the very least? I don't even think it's accurate. Teenage pregnancy isn't that common.' She appealed to the rest of us. 'Do any of you have friends who've had abortions?'

It was typical of Wendy to think someone who didn't use contraception was a slut. But she'd made her point. None of us knew anyone who'd been pregnant.

'Who says you're going to have an abortion?' asked Nicholas. 'You might decide to have the baby.'

'That's stupid.'

'Well, no, actually you're right, you are going to have an abortion. But not in this series. Here we're just going to set things up.'

'I'm not going to do it. Why can't someone else get pregnant?'

'Wendy, it has to be you. There are only three romantic relationships in this programme, and the other couples are too young to handle this sort of material. Besides, this is your chance to shine. People will love this storyline, and we're going to be really sensitive about the way we handle it. You'll be a heroine, I promise you.'

At the end of the night's session, Perdita came over and said, 'Gerald, has your Dad come back yet?'

'No.'

'Then I want you to come home with me. I've spoken to my parents and they think it's a good idea too.'

'Think what's a good idea?'

'That you should spend a night with us. You can have dinner at our house, and sleep in the spare room. My dad will run you to school in the morning.'

'But it's miles away.'

'That doesn't matter. He always gets up early anyway, and he likes driving.'

'Perdita, that's really kind of you – and your family – but I'm not sure . . .'

'Gerald, I'm worried about you. Please come home with me.'

There was a reason I felt reluctant to take Perdita up on her kind offer. Although, thanks to my mother, I'd spent a lot of time in other families' houses, I was still nervous around people's parents, especially in this sort of situation. If Perdita hadn't told her parents why she wanted me to stay, I wouldn't have thought twice about accepting. But even thinking about having to explain about my wayward father again exhausted me. Just as I was about to refuse, Perdita took my hand and leaned over and whispered in my ear, 'I want to talk to you.'

Her warm breath made me shiver, and I was hers. She beamed up at me and said, 'We should tell the drivers.'

'Who's in your car? Is there enough space?'

'Me, Sheryl and Lola. It's OK. You can ride in the front.'

I nodded, and went over to tell Shep. He winked at me and said, 'Better hope your Dad stays away tonight.'

I didn't like his tone, but still smiled at him, glad he wasn't telling the producers about Perdita's plan. I looked at Perdita, who seemed to have sorted things with her driver. I waited until the children had started to leave, and then joined Sheryl and Lola.

'Are you coming with us?' Lola asked, her lisp less pronounced than when she was performing.

I went round to the front of the car and climbed into the passenger seat. Perdita, Sheryl and Lola got into the back. The driver looked at me and asked, 'Where am I dropping you?'

'Perdita's.'

He nodded, and started the engine. The car's headlights revealed the vehicles in front of us, slowly filing out through the infant school's narrow front gates.

Lola said, 'Wendy was good tonight, wasn't she?'

'Yeah,' said Sheryl, 'especially as she didn't want to do it.'

'Do you think that was genuine?' I asked. 'Or did she want to be persuaded?'

'No,' Perdita replied, 'she was serious. And she had a fair point. Every boy who watches this programme is going to have a crush on her.'

I shook my head. 'Not every boy.'

'What d'you mean?'

'When I see girls getting pregnant on *Grange Hill* or *EastEnders*, it doesn't make me fancy them. It makes me feel scared.'

She laughed. 'All right, maybe older boys . . .'

'Even so . . . it doesn't make a girl seem fanciable. It makes them seem like trouble . . . like they've lost their innocence and crossed over into an adult world.'

'Gerald, she's only pregnant in the programme. Not in real life.'

'But still, it does alter how you see the person. I reckon boys will fancy *you*.'

Maybe I shouldn't have said this. After I did, the whole car went silent. I knew why Perdita was embarrassed. I had no idea whether she had any romantic feelings for me, but my sense was that she didn't, and even if she did, she was evidently as shy as I was about such matters. What I didn't know at that time was that my comment devastated Sheryl, who, contrary to my earlier suspicions, didn't fancy Fuckpit at all, but had been in love with me since the day of our first audition, and although she was scared about me going home with Perdita, knew I had family problems, and thought Perdita was only doing this to be nice to me. But with that comment I had revealed that if I was interested in anyone it was Perdita, and that Sheryl would only ever be my fictional girlfriend. What Sheryl didn't know was that I was too scared to make any romantic overtures to Perdita, and that my going over to her house tonight was as innocent as it seemed.

When you're experiencing it, first love feels so shameful.

The memory of Sheryl and me sitting there nursing our crushes seems charming, but at the time it was terrible. And I think it was cruel of Nicholas and the producers to stoke our adolescent hearts. Adults have the same attitude towards children in love as they do to tormented animals, finding their pain amusing because it seems so small. Years later when we studied *Mansfield Park* for A-Level, I was the only one who didn't find Jane Austen's attitude towards theatrical entertainments exaggerated. I knew what she was getting at.

In the silence, I thought about being on TV, wondering if any viewers would fancy me. Because I'd always had my imaginary audience, I hadn't yet fully comprehended how things would change when the people watching were real. Television was such a big part of my life – I thought of my favourite comedians as personal friends, even though I'd never met them – that the idea of passing over to the other side of the screen suddenly filled me with fear. It was something I'd wanted for so long, but now it was actually going to happen, it felt like a strange sort of death.

I stopped myself panicking by thinking instead about how different it felt to be in this car. Part of believing that I was on TV all the time was that I only valued my own perspective, and I often forgot that other people existed independently of me. I was the only camera that counted. But at this moment I was struck by the realisation that there were all these other cars filled with different people driving home, and that the conversation in each one would be different.

The driver dropped off Lola. She said goodbye to us and went up the path to her house, which looked much more impressive than anyone else's.

'She's rich then?' I asked Perdita.

'You only just realised?'

'I thought she was precocious. And a bit more theatrical than the rest of us. But aren't we supposed to be children from normal backgrounds?'

'They didn't look at our parents' bank accounts. Normal in this case just means we're not from stage schools.'

I didn't reply, staring out of the window as the driver continued to his next stop. Sheryl got out without saying goodnight. I didn't know she was sad, and felt relieved to be alone with Perdita and the driver.

'I hope you're hungry,' Perdita's mother said as she opened the front door. 'Terrence has done a delicious *Blanquette de Veau.*'

I had no idea what this was, but Perdita made a face, so I doubted I'd like it. I hoped Perdita's family were the sort of posh people who wouldn't mind if you didn't finish your dinner.

Perdita kissed her mother's cheek and sat on a pink wooden box just inside the hallway, unlacing her black boots. Her mother asked us, 'Did it go well tonight?'

'It was all right,' Perdita told her.

'And Gerald, I understand you were the focus of the story yesterday.'

'Yeah.'

'Oh,' she said, 'you're just as bad as she is. You're both involved in this fascinating enterprise and neither of you wants to talk about it.'

Perdita's mother seemed different from the first time I'd met her. Maybe it was because last time she'd been writing and wrapped up in her own world and tonight she was making an effort, but I thought there was more to it than that. She hadn't behaved like this on audition day either. Something Perdita had told her mother had caught her imagination, and now she'd aroused her curiosity she resented it.

'So whose story was it tonight?'

'Wendy's. She's pregnant.'

'Goodness.'

'Only in the programme.'

'Yes, dear, I realise that, but still . . . How old is this girl?'

'Fifteen. She'll be sixteen by the time it goes out, though.'

'Nevertheless, it's a very brave topic to address. Was this

something you kids thought up, or did this dramaturge fellow . . . ?'

'Nicholas. Yes, it was his idea.'

'He sounds like a very interesting man. I suppose I'll get to meet him eventually. Gerald, has this given you an interest in acting?'

'I'm enjoying the improvisation,' I said. 'I don't know if I'll feel the same way when we're given scripts.'

'Yes, I suppose that will be quite different. Shall we go through?'

She led us to the dining room. There was a bowl of green salad and four plates on the table. A cat curled round my leg.

'Oh, Suzy,' said Perdita, reaching down to pick it up, 'don't pester our guest.'

'It's OK.'

'Suzy likes Gerald,' said Perdita's mother. 'Let's sit down.'

I took the chair opposite Perdita. Terrence looked older than Perdita's mother. His short grey hair stood upwards, coming forward into a V at the top of his forehead. He was wearing a short-sleeved blue shirt and smoking a cigarette.

'You don't mind if I smoke at the table, do you, Gerald? The girls have got used to it and now I can't break the habit. I'll put it out before we start eating.'

'It's fine.'

'Good. I thought as it's late we wouldn't bother with starters. There's dessert, though.'

'OK.'

'Do your parents let you drink wine, Gerald? I know you're under age, but we usually let Purry have half a glass, diluted with water, of course. If you don't think your parents will mind, I'll happily pour you one too.'

'My parents wouldn't mind.'

'OK,' he said, 'I'll bring dinner in.'

Terrence went into the kitchen and brought the food through in a large ceramic serving-dish. He doled out dinner and then gave Perdita and me our diluted glasses of wine. I waited until everyone else had started eating and then tasted my food. It wasn't as bad as I was expecting.

'Have more salad,' Terrence told me. He turned to Perdita's mother. 'Are you cold, Ros?'

'No,' she said, 'I'm fine. Why are you always asking me if I'm cold?'

'Sorry. How's the food, Gerald, do you like it?'

I nodded.

'That's great. I suppose it's been a while since you've eaten properly, right?'

Perdita glared at him.

'What?' he demanded. 'She's looking daggers at me because she made me promise not to ask you any questions. But you don't mind talking to me, do you, Gerald? I'm not being intrusive?'

'Terrence . . .' Ros warned.

'Gerald,' he said, 'it's up to you. If you don't want to talk about it, we won't talk about it.'

'I don't want to talk about it.'

Terrence looked frustrated, and dropped his fork. 'All we want to know is, are you OK? What's going on? Perdita tells us your father's been missing for several days?'

'He's not missing. He's just . . . not coming home at night.'

'So he's home during the day?'

'No,' I said, 'he's at work during the day.'

'So when is he at home? Is he at home now?'

'I don't know.'

'Dad . . .' said Perdita.

'What? The boy's father might be worried. I say we should give him a call. Let him know his son's safe. We don't want to be accused of kidnapping.' Terrence looked at us, waiting to see how we'd respond.

'It might be an idea to phone your father,' said Ros. 'Just in case he has come home.'

I shrugged. Terrence nodded, got up, and went over to the phone. 'What's your number?'

'It's written on the pad there,' Perdita told him.

I carried on eating my dinner. Terrence called my house. He let it ring. We didn't have an answerphone.

'No response.'

'Hang up then,' said Ros.

He came back to the table. 'And you're certain he won't be back tonight?'

'He usually comes back from work while I'm at the infant school. He changes out of his work clothes and then goes out.'

Ros asked me, in a soft voice, 'Do you have a number for your mother, Gerald?'

'No. My sister says she's going to call me soon.'

Terrence and Ros looked at each other. I didn't want their pity. They did, at least, seem to realise that there wasn't anything they could do.

'Let's have dessert,' said Ros.

After dinner, Perdita asked her parents if she and I could go up to her bedroom.

'What for?' Terrence asked.

'We have some stuff to talk about from tonight.'

'And you can't do it down here? Your mother and I are interested in what you're doing.'

'Dad . . .'

'It's OK, dear,' said Ros, 'you go upstairs.'

Perdita jumped up from her chair and we both left the room. We went up to her bedroom and I sat in her wicker chair. I heard Terrence shout, 'Leave your door open.'

She scowled and pulled it shut. Then she sat on her red bed and said, 'I'm sorry about my parents.'

'Don't be silly. You've met mine.'

'Thanks for coming home with me.'

'I'm glad you invited me. What did you want to talk about?'

She leaned back against her bedroom wall. 'I wanted you to be safe.'

'What d'you mean?'

'That night when you called me and your dad picked up the phone and swore at you . . .'

'Yeah,' I said, embarrassed.

'I know it's stupid. I know he's going through a hard time. But it really scared me.'

'My dad's not scary.'

'I'm not trying to criticise him, Ger . . .'

'No, I know, I'm just saying he's not a scary man. Really. He gets a bit angry sometimes, but that's only because he's lost. And it's easy to beat him in arguments. Your dad is much scarier.'

'But my dad wouldn't leave me.'

I didn't reply.

'Sorry,' she said quickly, 'I didn't mean that the way it sounded. Oh God . . .' she sighed in exasperation. 'None of this is coming out right.'

'It's OK.'

'I wanted you to be here. With me. I've been thinking about you a lot recently.'

'Me too, Perdita.'

'I don't know anyone else like you. I've never felt like this before. The things you say to me, when you say them, they don't sound deep at the time, but then afterwards, I find myself thinking about our conversations.'

'I do too.'

'And although you're a year younger than me, I've started thinking of you as a . . .'

'That's how I see you.'

She gave me a funny look. 'As an older brother, Gerald. You're like the brother I never had. And it seemed stupid that you weren't in my house. Especially when you needed me.'

I stared at her. An older brother? She wanted me to think of her the same way I thought of Erica? I couldn't believe it. Then I remembered my father, and realised this was 'only child' talk. She didn't realise how horrible it was really having a sibling. But even so, it seemed clear she wasn't thinking of me as a potential boyfriend.

'That's great, Perdita.'

'What?' she said. 'Did I say something to upset you?'

'No, of course not.'

'Are you sure?'

'Yeah, I'm sure.'

Perdita was eager to carry on the sort of conversation we usually had, but I felt too disappointed to make much of an effort. She noticed my reticence, but carried on anyway, hoping to inspire me with her own observations. I let her ramble on, trying to squash down my resentment. We passed the evening in this way, until Ros appeared and asked me to come with her so she could show me the bed she'd made up in the spare room. Perdita gave me a peck on the cheek and wished me sweet dreams. Feeling guilty about the way I'd behaved that evening, I stroked her hair and said, 'Thanks for rescuing me, Perdita.'

95

Sophie had been showing off when she said I wouldn't get into the party without her. There was no one on the door and as soon as we got inside everyone had to pay three pounds to get their hands stamped irrespective of status. This wasn't an exclusive party. But it was pleasant, and there were three rooms all playing music I didn't mind. I noticed a stage in the biggest room and asked Don, 'What's that for?'

'Dunno, mate. Shall we have a look?'

We walked across. A woman with bright red bunches and an Andy Pandy outfit accosted us with a plastic bucket.

'Spare change?' she asked.

'What's it for?'

'The actors. They're about to perform.'

Uncle C dug deep into his trouser pockets. 'Art should always be paid for.'

Dan and I threw a few coppers into the bucket. Sophie said, 'Put something in for me.'

'What kind of acting are they going to do?' I asked the woman.

'An alternative history of the rave movement in England.'

This was enough for me to want to walk off, but Uncle C

insisted we stay for at least the first scene. The actors came out on stage. Each of them was wearing PVC and carrying a plate of food.

'For years,' announced the first actor, 'the oppressive ceremony of Sunday lunch upheld the hegemony of the parental regime . . .'

The actors cast their Sunday lunches onto the floor. Plates smashed. Carrots, potatoes and chunks of roast meat splattered the stage.

'The rave scene destroyed the institution of Sunday lunch, encouraging ravers to stay in the fields rather than return to their families.'

Uncle C started moving towards the stage.

'Where are you going?' I asked him.

'To get our money back. This isn't art.'

Uncle C and Don tailed Sophie everywhere. I didn't blame her for this, but it was incredibly annoying. It was impossible to have a conversation without them chipping in, and reducing our interaction to inanity. On the dance floor, things were different. There she allowed her two friends to get annoyed as she favoured me, coming up close and looking in my eyes as we moved to the music. I knew there was something between us, but couldn't understand why she was making it so difficult. I assumed she probably had her pick of men, especially if tonight was anything to go by. Almost every man in the club checked her out at some point. And when they noticed me glaring back at them they nodded or winked as if to say, 'OK, mate, but we still don't understand why you're the lucky one.' I knew if any of these strangers were in my position, they'd be handling the situation with much more confidence. Desperate for a moment alone with her, I followed Sophie across to the queue for the toilet.

'Oh,' she said as I came up behind her, 'hello.'

'You don't mind if I chat to you for a bit, do you?'

She smiled. 'No, of course not. Are you having a nice time?'

'Yeah . . .'

'You don't sound sure.'

'No, I am . . .'

'Good.'

The toilet door opened and she went inside. Frustrated, I went back to join the others.

We left the party at four. I'd been ready to leave since one, but every time I nagged the others they said, 'Oh, come on, just another half hour.' No one had taken any drugs this evening (maybe because Uncle C was driving), but all three seemed to have inexhaustible energy, and when we got back to Sophie's, she said, 'Who wants to come up for coffee?'

I stared at the pair of them, desperately hoping they'd want to go home. But they both nodded, and Uncle C parked the car.

Sophie went into the kitchen to make the coffee. I was so tired, and knew it would be at least another hour before we got rid of her guests. Wanting to move things on, I said to Sophie, 'Actually, I'm really knackered.'

'Oh, Gerald, don't go to sleep yet. Have a coffee with us.'

She turned round and smiled at me. Maybe she was just being polite and would quickly get rid of her friends once she'd given them a drink. I'd been hoping her two sidekicks had invited themselves, and when they finally left she'd tell me how glad she was they'd gone. I sighed, and went back into the lounge. Don said to Uncle C, 'Let's listen to your CD again.'

He nodded and took it out of his pocket.

'Isn't it a bit late?' I asked them. 'What about the neighbours?'

'They're still awake. Listen, you can hear them playing drum and bass.'

'Oh,' I said, 'I thought that was a washing machine.'

Don put on the CD and we listened to Uncle C's band for a third time. Sophie said the music made her feel like getting stoned, and brought out a big bag of grass. I'd finally had enough, and told Sophie I really couldn't stay up any longer. Even if she did want to have sex with me, I knew I lacked the energy and wouldn't really enjoy it tonight. Besides, my expectations had diminished so greatly since setting out this evening that just sleeping alongside her would be reward enough.

'OK,' she said, 'the bed's made up in the spare room.'

'The spare room?'

'Yeah. It's only a futon, I'm afraid, I hope that's OK.'

'Fine,' I said, too tired to argue. All I cared about was sleep.

96

Terrence woke me at six. His fingers gripped hard on my shoulder, and I snapped upright. He could see I was startled, and held out his hands, trying to calm me.

'Relax, Gerald. The girls don't get up till seven, so we've got the house to ourselves. What would you like for breakfast?'

'I don't mind.'

'I think you're an English breakfast type, aren't you? Like me.'

'That sounds good.'

'Excellent. You have a shower, and I'll cook.'

I wasn't used to getting up early, but something about the manly, conspiratorial way Terrence had awoken me made all my sleepiness disappear. It was partly fear, and partly a desire to appear tough in front of Perdita's father. He left the spare room and I got out of bed. I'd slept in my underwear and felt pleased he'd offered me the chance to shower. My disappointment at what Perdita had said last night had coloured my dreams. First I dreamt I was in the teens-only nightclub and Perdita asked Fuckpit to dance instead of me, then I saw my mother telling my father she'd come back to our house if I was sent away, and, just before I awoke, I was on a life-support machine, and Perdita made the decision to turn it off.

I walked across the landing to the bathroom. This will sound pathetic, but the fact that I was about to stand naked in a place where Perdita was frequently unclothed was really exciting to me. I'd only recently begun to think of having an erection as pleasant rather than embarrassing, but today that engorgement felt wonderful. I took off my underwear and reached in to turn on the shower, wanting to get the water to the right temperature before climbing under the spray.

My breakfast was delicious. Terrence was proud of his culinary skills, and seemed delighted that I enjoyed his cooking so much.

'Do you do all the food then?'

He swallowed a small bite of tomato and said, 'Ros is a creative person. Creative people can't be trusted with cookery. They don't follow instructions, and get distracted.'

'But isn't cooking creative?'

'Well, yes, Gerald, yes it is. I'm impressed you realise that. Engineering is creative too. Christ, everything's creative if you do it right. Like your programme, for example. That's not just acting, is it?'

'You sound like Nicholas.'

'Do I?' This pleased him. 'Ros wouldn't like to hear that. She's built this man up into someone really quite special. Do you think she'll be disappointed when she meets him?'

He pointed his fork at me, a hopeful smile on his face. I stared at him, wondering about the secrets of this marriage.

'I don't know how interested he is in other people.'

He nodded, but this didn't reassure him. 'Sounds like they're perfectly suited.'

Terrence dropped me at school at seven-thirty. It was ridiculously early, so I went back to my house. There was still no sign of my father, but today I was relieved. The telephone rang. Thinking it might be Perdita, I went out into the hallway to answer it.

'Gerald . . . Oh God . . . Gerald.' It was my mother. She was hysterical.

'Mum? What's wrong? Why are you phoning so early?'

'I've been phoning all night. Gerald, I thought something terrible had happened. Where have you been?'

'Didn't Erica tell you? I stayed at a friend's house.'

'Which friend?'

'Perdita. She came to our house, remember? Her parents were really nice to me.'

'What? Where's your father? Put him on.'

'Um . . . He's asleep.'

'Then wake him up.'

Now I was stuck. Not wanting to admit I'd lied, I went upstairs, waited thirty seconds, and came back down.

'He's out cold.'

'He's not there, is he?'

'Yes. He's just asleep.'

'Then what time did he get in?'

'I don't know. I wasn't here.'

'It must've been after four.'

'It could've been. He has been staying out late.'

'But he's coming home?'

'Of course.'

'Gerald, I need to talk to you.'

'OK.'

'In person. When do you finish rehearsals?'

'On Saturday.'

'And when do you start filming?'

'Not for a couple of weeks.'

'Good. I'll call again next week. It's nothing to be worried about, I just want to explain some things to you.'

'All right, Mum.'

'There's one other thing.'

'Yeah?'

'How's Erica getting on with the programme?'

'Really good.'

'She doesn't have a problem with the other children?'

'Not at all. She's really changed, Mum. You'd be so proud of her. It's like she's a different person.'

I thought my mother would be pleased to hear this, but she didn't say anything. Although she wasn't as against *All Right Now!* as she'd been to begin with, I knew she remained suspicious of the enterprise, and I felt it was important to keep letting her know it was having a positive influence on me and my sister.

'Doesn't she tell you about it?'

'Only bits and pieces. And the things she does say worry me. It doesn't sound very controlled.'

'Oh, it is, Mum. Nicholas knows exactly what he wants to say.'

'I didn't mean artistically controlled. I meant, who's making sure you aren't being exploited?'

I laughed. 'This is the most exciting thing that's ever happened to me.'

'Well, Gerald, maybe that's how it seems to you. But you have to be careful. You don't realise the importance of privacy until it's gone.'

'OK, Mum, I'll be careful.'

'And tell your father to call me.'

'Is that how you're going to refer to him from now on?'

She pretended she hadn't heard. 'Goodbye, Gerald.'

My first lesson that morning was French. Our teacher, a hideously ugly Welshman, liked to set us inappropriate exercises about our personal lives. Today we had to write a letter to a French pen-pal describing our boyfriend or girlfriend (real or imaginary). So far I'd barely talked about *All Right Now!* in school, knowing that to do so would be to risk ridicule. Reggel and Francis were curious, of course, but until we started recording they weren't interested in hearing about rehearsals. But today I decided I would do the exercise as if Perdita was my girlfriend. They'd never met her, after all, and it would be ages before they saw her on television.

'If you want, you can make the person anonymous,' the teacher told us, 'or write about someone you wish you were going out with.'

Most of the class weren't going out with anyone, and I knew they'd take up the second suggestion. When it came to time to read out our letters, most of the imaginary girlfriends were barely disguised versions of Vicki Wade or Lisa Aland, while all the girls wrote about Jeff Paxton. When it came to my turn, I made sure no one could mistake Perdita for a fictional version of a girl in my class, immediately stating her name and how we'd met. I knew other people in the class would be surprised to hear I had a girlfriend, but I was amazed at the violence of my classmates' reaction.

'She doesn't exist!' shouted one.

'She's Snuffleupagus.'

'Now, now,' said our teacher, 'save the taunting for the playground.'

Do you like that? Not 'Don't tease Gerald, of course his girlfriend exists,' but 'Save it for the playground'. The moment the lesson ended, the whole class started up again, continuing the joke for the whole of morning break.

Jane and Fuckpit were also eager to tease me when we got picked up that evening.

'So are you going out now?' Jane asked me.

'No,' I said, 'it's nothing like that. We're just good friends. She sees me as a brother.'

'Oh, Gerald,' sniggered Shep, 'that's no good.'

I couldn't believe Shep was joining in too. 'Fuck off,' I told him. 'Fuck the lot of you.'

I took my photocopied pages from Nicholas and checked the first sheet:

All Right Now! Episode Four
Tour Guide: Lola

This was an intriguing choice, and I was pleased the younger children were finally getting some attention. I wondered whether Nicholas had the whole thing planned out, or was deciding on the structure as he went along. It was a sensible decision to switch focus at this point as Lucy, Lola and Erica had seemed especially bored during yesterday's session.

Although Lola was the tour guide, her main role in this episode was to provide support to her two friends, Lucy and Erica. Episode three had ended with Wendy confiding in her sister, telling her about the unwanted pregnancy. Erica was also facing emotional difficulties, having to deal with the aftermath of our parents' separation. Nicholas told Lola he wanted to look at what it was like to be the youngest child in a family of four, and to contrast this situation with Lola's role in her gang of friends. Additional tension was introduced with Lola's mixed feelings about her brother Pete's romantic interest in Erica. The main theme of the episode seemed to be Lola's questioning of her identity, and her search for a comfortable position for herself.

Nicholas had been generous to Lola. He'd given her a good story, and it was much less personally embarrassing than the plots Wendy and I had handled. Given that Amy's episode had mainly been about introducing all the characters, Lola probably had the best showcase so far. Unfortunately, she was the group's worst actor. Actually, that's not fair. She had a different performance style, one that revealed that by the age of twelve she'd already starred in too many school plays. She was good at double-takes, exaggerated facial expressions and impersonating animals. A first-year Dorothy who'd probably grow up into a sixth-form Rizzo rather than a Sandy. It was easy to see why the producers had chosen her, but harder to understand why Nicholas had given her this responsibility over Wendy or Erica.

My role in this episode was minimal, one small scene where I told Erica she was too young for a serious relationship and she shouted that I wasn't her father, and a scene where Wendy confronted me about Erica bullying her sister. I enjoyed the second scene more than the first, pleased to get an opportunity to square off to Wendy. I'd had far too many scenes with the younger children, and it was hard to get excited about acting opposite them. But fighting with Wendy was fun, especially as she genuinely appeared to lose her temper and started getting physical with me.

I was still upset about what Perdita had said to me last night, but had decided that rather than try to change her mind, I would use her trust to get as close as possible to her. I was young, the idea of having a girlfriend was still scary to me, and I now saw this relationship as an opportunity to find out about girls. I don't know if I would have felt this way if Perdita was interested in someone else, but for the moment at least, it seemed as if I was definitely the most important boy in her life, and that was all that mattered.

97

The clock-radio alarm went off at ten. I was still tired, but I could hear music playing in the lounge and decided to get up. Assuming Uncle C and Don hadn't stayed the night, this was my first chance to be alone with Sophie. I dressed and went into the lounge. Sophie stood in the middle of the room, ironing. There was no sign of her accomplices.

'Oh good,' she said, 'you're up. I was about to go and get breakfast.'

'Great. Shall I come with you?'

'No, don't worry. Why don't you have a bath? There's plenty of hot water.'

I sniffed my shirt. She laughed. 'You don't have to have one if you don't want to. I like having baths in the morning, that's all.'

'Do you have a towel?'

'There's one in there. And take your time. There's always a queue at the bakery.'

I nodded and went through to the bathroom.

I started the water running and sat on the edge of the bath, thinking about the time I'd been in Perdita's shower, and how exciting that had seemed. I didn't have those adolescent feelings now, but still felt the frisson I always experienced when I was in someone else's space. It was a real relief to be out of my communal house, even if only for a night.

I'm not the kind of person who plans things. I move from situation to situation, despising any sort of change and leaving everything until the last minute. This might have something to do with the women in my life. When I met Ellen I imagined our relationship would steadily grow stronger, and after we'd moved in together, I thought it wouldn't be long before we were married. But somewhere along the line something stalled, and I'd remained in the same position ever since. I admired Sophie's courage in deciding to live alone, and thought maybe if I could manage that I might be able to take control of everything else.

I stayed in the bath until Sophie returned, thinking that was what she wanted me to do. I towelled myself dry, and then put on her dressing-gown, going through to her kitchen.

'Oh,' she said, 'you're wearing my dressing-gown.'

'Sorry,' I replied, attempting a flirtatious tone, 'shall I take it off?'

'No, no, it's OK. You did dry yourself first, didn't you?'

'Yes, of course.'

'What do you want for breakfast? I've got normal croissants or *pain au chocolat*.'

'I don't mind.'

Feeling embarrassed, I sat down in the lounge and wondered how long I should wait before getting dressed. Sophie brought me in my plate and leaned over to turn on her stereo. It was Uncle C's band again.

'This really is a fantastic CD, isn't it?' she said. 'His band is absolutely brilliant. We saw them at the Jazz Café once.'

I ate my croissants.

'I'm in one of those really lazy Saturday moods when I don't feel like doing anything,' said Sophie.

'That's how I feel too.'

She smiled at me, her whole manner brightening. 'Really? Oh, I'm so glad. I've had such a hard week.'

'And we did stay up late last night.'

'Yeah, but that doesn't affect me. It's the job, I find it so demoralising.'

'What do you do, Sophie?'

'I work for a marketing company. It's so boring. Please don't ask me about it.'

'OK.'

It was hard to tell whether Sophie was acting differently because her friends weren't around or whether I got so irritated with Don and Uncle C that it affected the way I saw her. I'm trying to be totally honest in this account, and not worry about how I come across, but I realise that my feelings towards Sophie's friends possibly seem mean-spirited. All I can say in my defence is that they weren't just protecting the woman I wanted to fall in love with until I proved myself worthy of her; they were trying to make sure I gave up and went away for good. Nevertheless, I had a strong sense that she was equally frustrated with the way this date had progressed. I even thought I knew what she wanted from me. It was clear she had happily operated as part of this trio for some time. If anything was going to change, she needed me to challenge her current situation. This was a perfectly normal beginning to a relationship, where a couple has to negotiate how to deal with the other partner's friends, and work out just how far they have to separate themselves from the larger social group to survive as a couple. But I didn't want to do what she expected of me. I could see her friends loved her, and wouldn't give her up without a fight. Of course, I had enough self-awareness to sense that maybe this was a role Sophie had assigned them. They were her equivalent of my Sally, and at least they stopped short of getting into bed with their princess.

I went back into Sophie's spare room, took off her dressing-gown and put on my clothes. I'm finding it hard to explain my feelings for Sophie. It was a total instinct thing. I mentioned towards the beginning of this account how I think all relationships start with a Schrodinger's cat moment, and we were definitely still at the stage before the box was opened – so even though it seemed likely the cat was dead, there was still something that stopped me giving up and going home. I also realised that ever since I first met Sophie, my behaviour, character and attitude had been slightly off, and knew that the way I was coming across probably seemed a bit weird, and maybe even scared her. It was nothing compared to Don and Uncle C, but she was used to them. I had to relax, let her see me being normal.

Back in the lounge, Sophie turned and smiled at me, asking, 'Do you feel like getting a video?'

I smiled back. 'OK.'

We walked to Vid Biz. While Sophie browsed the new releases, I couldn't stop myself going to the Art House section to see if they had a copy of Perdita's terrible Canadian film *According to the Flesh*. I wasn't planning to persuade Sophie to rent it – I'd seen it twice, and both times it had made me feel sad – but this ritual was something I did every time I went into a video shop, which wasn't that often these days, as my housemates usually vetoed anything I wanted to watch. I don't know why I continued to do this. Maybe it was because it was as close as I was likely to get to meeting my old friend again.

'Did you want something arty?' Sophie asked, coming across. 'I don't mind. We can get stoned and try to work out what it means.'

'Yeah,' I said half-heartedly, 'OK.'

'How about this?' she asked, picking up a copy of a film called *The Ages of Lulu*. I'd never heard of it, and took the box from her. It was a Spanish film, and the synopsis made it sound like it might be sexually explicit.

'Sounds a bit dodgy.'

'Bad, you mean?'

'No, risqué.'

She laughed. 'That's not a problem, is it?'

'Not for me. If you don't mind.'

She shook her head. 'Shall we get it then?'
'OK.'

Sophie paid for the video and we started walking back to her flat. I think the main reason I was immediately attracted to Sophie was that she seemed so happy and confident. It was visible even from her movements on the dance floor. In spite of what Sally thought, I wasn't only attracted to manic depressives. What she said about me going round to the rooms of anguished girls at university was true, but not because other people's misery turned me on. I wanted to help them because I knew I was good at cheering other people up. My relationship with Ellen had worked because I was able to understand and appreciate the wisdom that came from her depressions, but in my heart I did want her to be happy. Walking with Sophie, I sensed a different sort of mind, one that worked in the same sunny way as Sally's or my sister's. But I still couldn't understand why someone so positive would have such worrying friends. When we reached the end of the road, she pulled out her mobile.

'Who are you calling?'

She looked amused by my question. 'Uncle C. He loves watching videos.'

'Oh.'

'What's wrong?'

'Can't we watch it on our own?'

'Come on, Gerald, it'll be much more fun with the three of us.'

I didn't reply.

'Well, I'll just try him,' she said, continuing to dial. 'He probably won't be in.'

I sighed and turned away, not wanting Sophie to see my expression.

98

Shep's headlights illuminated Perdita, Amy and Wendy, who'd wrapped themselves around various parts of the climbing-frame. The three of them hadn't spent much time on developing their friendship since Wendy had got involved with Fuckpit and Perdita turned her attention to me, but I felt pleased rather than scared to see them back together. I no longer felt intimidated by Wendy, and her attitude towards me had changed since Perdita had accepted my friendship. I got out of the car and walked over to them.

'Hi Gerald,' said Perdita, dropping down from her bar, 'Nicholas is late.'

'Where are the little ones?' I asked.

'Round the back. Exploring.'

Jane and Fuckpit came up behind me. Wendy held out her arms to Fuckpit and he darted across for a hug. A car and a minibus came through the school entrance.

'Here we go,' said Perdita, 'time to get started.'

My heart sank when I looked at tonight's pages:

All Right Now! Episode Five
Tour Guide: Sheryl

I hadn't speculated about who would be the tour guide today, but had assumed that now I'd had my episode, and Erica had featured prominently in the last two, I wouldn't have much to do until the grand finale. But it seemed that Nicholas thought there was still mileage in my story. I looked through the rest of the pages, wondering what the plot would be. One line in particular jumped out:

GERALD FINDS IT HARD TO COPE WITH THE FACT
THAT SHERYL IS FINISHING WITH HIM.

What? Not only did I have to cope with the embarrassment of the audience thinking that I was going out with Sheryl, but now I had to cope with them seeing her dump me. Sheryl seemed similarly surprised, telling Nicholas, 'I don't think this is very realistic. I wouldn't dump Gerald, I mean, if I was going out with him.'

'Yes, Sheryl,' said Nicholas, 'that might be true in real life, but as I keep trying to impress on you, this is a drama, and we need incident. Besides, don't worry about Gerald. I have plans for him.'

He winked at me. I knew he wanted me to be excited by this mystery, but I felt too tired to get up any enthusiasm. With school all day and these sessions every night, this had been a gruelling week. My early start yesterday hadn't helped, and although I knew it was silly, I'd started worrying about my father.

The episode began with Sheryl sneaking out of her house to meet me at midnight. Nicholas had a weakness for this sort of romantic situation, but it would work for our core audience, who turned out to be mainly in the ten-to-fourteen age group. This didn't strike me as significant at the time, but it was surprising how good Nicholas was at creating a world that children would identify with and envy, two qualities soap king Aaron Spelling said were essential for a successful show.

When we were improvising, anyone not involved in the scene sat and watched. Carolyn handled the video camera, and the rest of the group formed a usually attentive audience. Nicholas had told us not to play to them, but some children – Pete and Fuckpit especially – couldn't help clowning around for easy laughs. When we had drama lessons at school, we would perform scenes to each other, but that was after we'd had half an hour to devise them first. Improvising in front of a group was harder, although Nicholas's detailed, specific notes kept us in check, even sometimes giving us end-lines to work towards.

'This scene is a bit tricky,' Nicholas told us. 'For most of the episode, we're going to be relying on dramatic irony to focus the tension, but in this scene, Sheryl, you need to imply your dissatisfaction with the relationship to the audience without making it obvious to Gerald. Then we'll move straight on to the scene where you confess your feelings to Amy.'

I wasn't sure if Sheryl understood what she had to do, but it seemed Nicholas was instructing me to play dopey. This wasn't hard. I found doing romantic scenes with Sheryl so unpleasant that I performed with minimum commitment, the same way I'd only use the tips of my fingers to pick up a hot dish. Nicholas was pleased with the scene and I sat back with the group, allowing Amy to take my place.

When Perdita came over to me tonight, I thought she was going to invite me to stay with her again, but instead she said, 'Have you heard about Lola's?'

'No.'

'We're going to have a party there tomorrow. To celebrate the end of a hard week.'

'Lola's?' I said, surprised.

'She says her parents are really nice, her house is really big, and they let her do whatever she wants.'

Throughout the car journey home, we talked about Lola's party. Jane and Fuckpit had been in Lola's group to begin with, so both of them had been to her house and met her parents. I expected Fuckpit to be rude about Lola's family, but he sounded surprisingly respectful.

'All right,' I said, 'if her parents are so wonderful, how come Lola's like she is?'

'Maybe because her parents are so wonderful,' Shep suggested.

'She's spoilt, isn't she?' I said. 'You only think her parents are nice because they let her do what she wants.'

'Nah, man,' said Fuckpit, sucking hard on his Benson and Hedges, 'it's not like that. Her dad, he's really interesting. He's like a scientist, he's got this great position at some big company, and he's clever, y'know, not like other people's parents . . .'

'And her mum . . .' said Jane, sniggering.

'Yeah, Gerald, Jesus Christ. You won't believe how sexy Lola's Mum is. I almost came in my pants when I saw her.'

'Does she look like Lola?'

'She's his second wife. Lola's real mother died when she was little.'

'Oh,' I said, 'and how come we're not addressing that in our drama?'

'Don't be horrible, Gerald,' Jane told me.

'I'm not, I'm just curious why I have to do scenes about my parents separating, and Lola gets to have a story that's got no relation to her real life. Nicholas is such a bullshitter. He said this was supposed to be a different sort of drama, but it's not. It's just like a normal soap opera.'

'He is a bullshitter,' Fuckpit agreed.

'But real life was only ever supposed to be the starting point,' said Jane. 'You and Wendy have stories that are closer to reality because you're acting with your sisters. Our stories are different because we've got made-up families.'

'Yeah,' said Fuckpit, 'that's where you went wrong.'

Shep dropped off Fuckpit and Jane and continued to my house. Dad's car was in the driveway, and the house lights were on.

'So he came back eventually,' said Shep. 'Will you be OK?'

'Yeah. Thanks, Shep.'

He drove off and I walked up to my front door. My father was in the kitchen, making himself a huge cheese, onion and pickle sandwich. He didn't look especially depressed, and smiled at me when I came in.

'Hello, Ger. You just get in?'

'Yeah,' I replied, my voice cold.

'Do you want a sandwich?'

'No thanks. Dad?'

'Yes, son?'

'Where have you been?'

309

'Nowhere. We just kept missing each other.'

'But you haven't slept in your bed all week.'

He finished making his sandwich and lifted it to eye-level, gazing at it admiringly before taking a first bite. 'Yeah,' he said, his mouth full of bread and cheese, 'I know, but everything's OK. You don't have to worry.'

'Couldn't you have left me a note?'

'You weren't bothered, were you?'

'Well, yeah, actually. Mum phoned, you know.'

He put down his sandwich. 'When?'

'All Wednesday night.'

'What does that mean? Didn't you answer?'

'I wasn't here.'

'Why not? Where were you?'

'Where were *you*?'

'You know where I was, son.' He returned to his sandwich. As he chewed, a question came to him. 'If you weren't here, how do you know your mother was phoning?'

Your mother. He was doing it too.

'She called when I came back.'

'Did you tell her I wasn't here? I bet you did, didn't you, you little sneak.'

'No, Dad, I covered for you. But is this how it's going to be from now on?'

'Ger, I really don't know what you're upset about. I'm giving you your freedom.'

'What?'

'Look, you can do whatever you want. I don't care, OK? Stop thinking of me as your father. Pretend we're just a couple of mates sharing a house.'

His smile as he suggested this made it clear he thought it was the most brilliant thing he'd ever said. I sat opposite him, and he got up again and went back out to the kitchen.

'Want a beer, Ger?'

He rarely offered me alcohol, and I wondered how far I could push this.

'Yes please,' I replied, 'and can you do me a whisky chaser to go with it?'

I listened for his reply, but there wasn't one. When he came back into the lounge, he handed me a can and a small shot glass.

'Are you sure you don't want a sandwich?'

'Yes.'

'Do you want me to drive up to the fish and chip shop?'

'All right.'

'OK. Just let me finish my sandwich first.'

I opened my can of beer, and took a sip. Then I downed the shot in one. I could tell this amused my father. Perverse to the last, he raised the stakes.

'Ger, instead of fish and chips, how would you like a mixed grill?'

I laughed. 'You going to cook it?'

'No,' he said, 'I'm going to take you to my casino. They have a restaurant there. It doesn't do much food, but you can get a mixed grill.'

'How will I get in?'

'I'll sign you in as my guest.'

'But I'm only thirteen.'

'We go see eighteen certificate films together, don't we?'

'Yeah, but . . .'

'Relax, Gerald, there's nothing to worry about. No one'll realise you're under age. And besides, this place is very relaxed.'

He smirked as he finished his sandwich, still pleased with himself.

Dad was right. He didn't have any problem getting me into the casino. He flirted with the woman at the reception and after he'd written our names into the register, no one stopped us walking through. He gave me twenty pounds and directed me to the restaurant.

'No more drinks, though, OK? I'll let you gamble, once you've eaten, but we don't want you attracting too much attention.'

I nodded, and felt relieved. I was feeling a bit sick from the beer and the whisky, and felt pleased this part of the game was over. The restaurant was on another level, above the gaming tables. It had tinted glass windows and everything inside was a dingy brown colour. Although there was other food available, I trusted my father to have made the best selection and ordered a mixed grill. There were only two other people in the restaurant, an old man with a thick grey moustache, and at the next table, a woman in a nurse's uniform. She smiled at me. Terrified, I smiled back. She got up and brought her drink across to my table.

'Hello,' she said, 'I'm Elizabeth.'

I didn't know what to do. I felt convinced that if I started talking to her she'd kidnap me and I'd never see my family again. Come on, I told myself, be a man. If nothing else, this would amuse my father. I couldn't believe this woman didn't realise how old I was.

'Gerald.'

She tried to grip the corner of the chair opposite me. Her fingers slipped and I realised she was drunk.

'Are you here alone?' she asked, and I heard her strong Northern accent.

'With a friend.'

'Would your friend mind if I sat down?'

'He's a man. My friend,' I said quickly. 'But I'm not, y'know . . . '

She laughed. 'Neither am I.'

The nurse sat down. I wasn't brilliant at guessing adults' ages, but I thought she was probably in her twenties. She was drinking a cocktail, and there was pink sugar around the rim of her glass.

'I'm a nurse,' she said, and burst into laughter.

'I guessed.'

'Did you?' she said, finding this even more amusing. 'What do you do, Gerald?'

'I'm an actor.'

This sobered her up a bit. 'I thought I recognised you.'

Now I laughed. 'I doubt it. I haven't been in anything yet.'

'So you're an out-of-work actor?'

The disappointment was evident in her voice, and I should

have used this to get rid of her. But a stupid pride swelled within me, and I said, 'No, my show hasn't been on television yet.'

'Your show?'

'Yes.'

'What kind of show is it?'

'A soap opera.'

'Really?' she said. 'I love soap operas. We watch them all the time on the ward. *EastEnders. Coronation Street.* But I tell you what I really liked. *Albion Market.* I can't believe they stopped showing that.'

'We've got the same time slot,' I boasted.

'Honestly?'

'Well, almost. But that's one of the programmes we're supposed to be replacing.'

'*Albion Market* was great. It was so much less pretentious than *EastEnders.*' She smiled. 'I bet you're going to be a villain, aren't you? A sexy villain, a dark angel.'

I blushed, and didn't reply. The waitress came across with my mixed grill and placed it in front of me. Elizabeth licked some of the sugar from the rim of her glass. I started eating. She put her glass down and stared at me. I felt shy, and wondered if she wanted some of my food.

'You're young, aren't you?'

'Yes.'

'How old are you exactly? Eighteen?'

I pointed my finger downwards.

'Jesus,' she said, 'I've had too much to drink. I thought you were my age.'

'How old are you?'

'Nineteen. So, come on then, what are you, seventeen?'

'Thirteen.'

'Fuck off.'

'I am.'

'You're not thirteen. If you're thirteen, how did you get in here?'

'My dad signed me in.'

'The friend you came with is your dad?'

'That's right.'

'And where's he now?'

'Gambling.'

'Why would your dad bring you here?'

'I was hungry.'

She laughed. 'This is a horrible place to bring a child.'

'Why are you here?'

'I'm here to get drunk. It's safer than a pub for a girl on her own.'

'I thought you said it was a horrible place.'

'For a child.' She pronounced this word as if she was insulting me. But I didn't care. I knew I'd disappointed her.

'Elizabeth,' I said, 'I'm sorry if you think I tricked you.'

'I suppose all that stuff about you being an actor was made up?'

'No, it's true. It's just that most of the people in the soap opera are children.' I put down my fork. 'Will you help me play a trick on my dad?'

That night wasn't the first time I'd watched my father gamble. It wasn't even the first time I'd seen him play roulette, as he had a plastic wheel and baize he brought out on family Christmases. But it was the first time I'd seen him play roulette in a casino, and I was amazed by his method. I'd lost count of the number of long, detailed conversations we'd had about different stratagems for playing roulette (his favourite was one he'd got from a James Bond novel where you stick to red and black and double up on the colour that doesn't come up) and he was so convincing that I'd assumed his gameplay was so honed that calling it gambling was almost an insult. This perception had been backed up by the times he came home with large cheques. Now I realised that if he occasionally won big it was because he paid no attention to the amount he was gambling. Before each spin of the wheel, a flurry of chips whooshed from his hand and covered every inch of the baize. He even bet on zero every time.

'You're silly to bet on zero,' I told him. 'It hardly ever comes up.'

He placed a chip over that number. The croupier winked at me and spun the wheel. The ball dropped into the green ridge. I was shocked, and wondered if the croupier had total control of where the ball would stop. My father often talked about the role of psychology in roulette, stressing how important it was to make the croupiers like you and explaining how when they got tired certain patterns would emerge that you could exploit. But now I was seeing him in action, I had no idea whether this was gambler's nonsense or profound truth.

My father winked at me and slid across the chips he'd won from the zero bet for me to play with. I wanted him to think I knew what I was doing, but the only strategy I remembered was the James Bond one, so I stuck to that, waiting for Elizabeth.

She performed her role beautifully, coming over with the fresh cocktail I'd bought her and standing alongside me. She stayed there for a couple of spins, then turned to whisper in my ear. She kissed my cheek and slid a small folded piece of paper into my hand. I gave a slight nod, and she walked away.

'What was that, son?'

'What?' I replied.

'That girl. What did she give you?'

'I don't know.'

'Aren't you going to look?'

I opened my hand, and examined the paper. 'Looks like a phone number.'

'Hers?'

'Why would she give me someone else's phone number?'

My father didn't see the humour in this and turned his attention back to the table.

We left the casino at two o'clock. I had no idea how much money my father had won or lost, or whether he was up or down on the week. I'd won fifty pounds. Well, I had fifty pounds left of the chips my father had given me when we'd started gambling, and he let me keep it. I stood behind my father and after we'd both had our chips converted into cash, we went out to the car. I sat in the passenger seat. Just as my father was about to start the engine, a large black woman opened the right-hand back door and climbed in.

'My brothers, are you Christian men?'

I was too afraid to reply. I thought my father would make her get out, but instead he said, 'Yes. Don't worry. You don't need to convert us. We understand the evils of gambling.'

'No, my brothers, that is not why I am here. If you are good Christian men, like you say you are, you cannot desert me in my hour of need. As Jesus said, he that receiveth whomsoever I send receiveth me . . .'

'So Jesus sent you?' my father asked. 'Do you need money?'

'No, my brothers, I do not need money. I have to ask, because as you know, ask, and it shall be given you, seek, and you shall find . . .'

'What do you want?' my father asked, a touch of irritation entering his voice.

'I need a lift to Brixton.'

'Brixton? But that's miles away.'

'My brothers, I would not ask, if I was not in need.'

'Do you live in Brixton?'

'Yes.'

'OK,' said my father, 'I'll take you home.'

I couldn't believe he was saying this. I wanted to argue, but I was afraid of the woman, who had the ability to make scripture sound like a threat. I waited until my father pulled away from the casino before taking a closer look at her in the rear-view mirror. She was in her fifties, I thought, and dressed as if for church. She wore a large white hat with a floppy lace fringe, a dark blue dress, and was clutching her black handbag in her lap. I didn't understand why she was out so late, so far away from her home, but knew it wasn't my place to ask.

Having persuaded us to give her a lift, the woman seemed content to remain silent. I knew my father had decided to drive her because he did see himself as a Christian, although he hadn't been to church since the dark events of Erica's christening, and he was superstitious enough to believe that he'd genuinely been offered this chance to prove himself a good Samaritan. He was also an eternally optimistic person, and wasn't cynical enough to think it might be a scam.

It was a long drive to Brixton. I'd been feeling tired at the rehearsal, but the excitement of going to the casino had woken me up. Now I was sleepy again. I couldn't let myself drop off because I was convinced that if I did our passenger would pull a knife. I knew it was stupid to think this, but even at thirteen, I'd seen more scary films and television programmes than was good for me. I told myself that if the woman went to sleep I would too, but she remained stubbornly awake, clasping her bag and staring out of the window.

I examined the piece of paper Elizabeth had given me, wondering if it was her real phone number. Not that it mattered, as I'd never call it. After we'd been driving for an hour, my father stopped at a garage. The woman looked worried. Dad told her, 'It's OK, I'm just getting some petrol.'

She nodded. I unclipped my seat belt. Dad looked at me.

'I'll come with you,' I told him. 'I want a can of Coke.'

He shrugged, and the two of us got out of the car. Dad walked across to the pumps. I followed him. He looked askance at me, as if he was standing at a urinal and I'd come over to watch. It wasn't until I turned away that he started filling the tank.

'Dad,' I said, 'what are we doing?'

'A good deed.'

'How well do you know Brixton?'

He shrugged. 'I've been there.'

'So you'll know what to do if it's a trap?'

'Ger . . . don't be paranoid. Your mother's paranoid and that's caused us so many problems over the years.'

'Dad, you don't have to be paranoid to think this is a

strange situation. Why is that woman dressed the way she is? And what's she doing out this late?'

'What are we doing out this late? Who knows what's happened to her? She said she's in need. It causes us no difficulty to take her to Brixton.'

I realised my father was enjoying this small adventure. I wondered whether this was what he'd been doing this past week, driving around helping people and getting into scrapes. I also realised that tonight appealed to his *Twilight Zone* side, and that the way the woman had appeared out of nowhere was what made helping her so appealing to him.

I went into the petrol station's small shop and bought myself a 500ml Supercan of Coke, the kind they soon replaced with plastic bottles that somehow never seemed so appealing. I suppose it was endearing that my father had an adventurous spirit, and that it was helping him through this difficult time. I remembered one morning a few years before when I'd watched Uri Geller on a children's television programme and gone into the kitchen and bent all the knives and forks. My mother started shouting as soon as she discovered me, but Dad didn't get cross until he'd asked me whether I'd bent them with my fingers or my mind, and if I'd told him the latter he wouldn't have hesitated to believe me.

Dad paid for the petrol and we went back out to the car. He pulled out of the garage and continued driving. It wasn't long before I started noticing road-signs directing us to Brixton.

'Can I ask you a question? In return for the lift?'

'Yes, my brother, what's troubling you?'

'Am I going to Heaven?'

'Have you accepted Our Lord Jesus Christ as your Saviour?'

'Yes.'

'Then you will go to Heaven.'

'What about my character? Does it have anything to do with that?'

'Brother, can I give you some good advice?'

'Yes.'

'It's time for you to start going to church again. I know it wasn't your idea to turn away from the light . . .'

'How do you know that?'

She waved her hand. 'That's not important. But you should go to church. They have the answers you seek. Stop at the end of this street.'

He did so. The woman got out of the car. 'Thank you,' she said. 'You did a good thing tonight.'

I knew better than to argue with my father about what had happened. If he wanted to see it as a mystical experience, there was no point trying to persuade him otherwise. And maybe it would be good for him to start going to church again. He certainly needed something to calm him down. All that really mattered to me was that we had escaped this adventure unharmed, and it was safe for me to go to sleep.

99

Uncle C wasn't in when Sophie called him. I assumed this meant I was safe, but then she tried his mobile. He answered immediately, and after a short conversation, Sophie replaced her receiver and turned to me.

'He's doing a delivery in the area. He says he can be here in three minutes and not to start the video without him.'

Three minutes. That was all the time I had to communicate to Sophie how much I liked her, and to let her know that if she was up for it, I was definitely interested in the two of us having a go at a relationship. I looked at the light coming through her large window and tried to think of the right words.

The doorbell rang.

'That wasn't three minutes,' I said, 'it was barely twenty seconds.'

Sophie laughed and jumped up. 'He's always doing this. He likes to surprise me.'

'Let's surprise him by not answering.'

But it was too late. She was already halfway downstairs. I heard her open the door and then inhale sharply.

'Jesus,' she said, 'what happened to your face?'

'It's nothing,' he replied, 'I just got into a little scrape after I left here last night.'

'Outside my house?'

'Yeah, but don't worry, they won't be back.'

'There was more than one?'

'Three.'

'My God. I can't believe we didn't hear anything. You should have come back up.'

Uncle C entered Sophie's flat. I could see why Sophie had been shocked. He had a cobweb of cuts and dried blood across his nose and both cheeks.

'What the hell did they do to you?' I asked. 'Push a broken bottle into your face?'

'Something like that,' he replied. 'What video did you get?'

'*The Ages of Lulu*. Gerald thinks it might be risqué.'

'Well, let's hope so. Come on, Soph, put it on.'

The Ages of Lulu was risqué. Masturbation, orgies, three-ways, cunnilingus, transsexual sex and incest. If I'd been watching the film alone with Sophie, this would have been embarrassing, but maybe we could have started talking about sex and by the end of the afternoon might have ended up in bed. Instead Sophie and Uncle C got stoned and giggled through the whole thing.

I was trying to understand Sophie's relationship with Uncle C. His accusation that I always had to put a label on everyone had stung me, and I thought I could prove my open-mindedness by accepting him. It wasn't that Sophie's best friend was a man that annoyed me, or the fact that he was her relation. It was entirely his character that caused the friction.

By the end of the film, Sophie and Uncle C were so stoned that they remained comatose in front of the television. They sat watching a film on ITV, a Saturday afternoon matinee they found almost as funny as the video we'd just watched. The date was ruined. I wasn't going to sit around and wait for Uncle C to go because I knew he'd stay all day, all night and no doubt early into Sunday morning.

'Sophie,' I said, 'I'm sorry, I've got to go.'

She gazed at me. 'Really? Why? It's the weekend.'

'I know, but I've got some friends I'm supposed to be going out with tonight. I'm sorry, and look, thanks, OK, I had a really nice time. You too, Uncle C.'

He waved at me, unable to resist a smirk.

'Bye then,' I said. 'I'll see you around.'

As I walked to the tube, Sophie ran up behind me.

'Gerald,' she shouted.

I turned. 'Yeah?'

'Are you sure you're OK?'

'I'm fine.'

She looked at me for a moment, then nodded, and kissed my cheek. I felt furious, as much at myself as her. But by the time my train reached Oval, I was starting to turn the failed date into a comic routine for my housemates. Striding into the lounge, I threw the pack of condoms I'd bought on Friday onto the coffee table and launched straight into my story. It wasn't until I reached the part about us going to the underground club that I noticed the size of my audience. All my housemates' partners were there, as well as a group of Tom's actor friends. I pressed on regardless, my anger returning as I told my story. When I reached the end, they burst into applause. Instead of responding, I gave an exasperated sigh and went upstairs to my bedroom.

100

I awoke at two o'clock on Saturday afternoon. I couldn't remember going to bed and as I was still dressed, assumed my father had carried me in from the car. Last night's adventures were a dim memory. I got out of bed, went downstairs to the bathroom and started running the water. There was no sign of my father, so I thought I'd spend the time before Shep arrived getting ready. I still didn't have many items of clothing that weren't embarrassing, and the only way to look better than usual was to put what I did have through the wash.

I was really looking forward to tonight's party. I might not have had much experience of social situations, but I knew tonight was going to be exciting, maybe even as much fun as our weekend away. I thought back to what my father had said last night about how he wanted us to act as if we were a couple of mates sharing a house. I knew this was one of his confidence tricks, like the way he'd drive us places to stop us telling my mother about his mistress, but maybe it would be good for me. My mother had always been relatively strict, and as my sister had decided to be the rebellious one, I'd concentrated on being good. When I was young it had never occurred to me that this might be restricting my life. My mother wasn't timid, but she did have a few phobias, and preferred avoiding situations where she'd have to face them. Her biggest phobia was fire. When she was a child her school burnt down and since then she'd been troubled by nightmares about being stuck in the burning building. The nightmares were so terrifying that she refused to sleep unless the household bath was filled with cold water. She didn't need to do this any more, but still didn't like candles or people smoking in our house. The only time she got really scared was Bonfire Night, and every year she'd buy my sister and me a present instead of letting us have fireworks. I was fine with this, but Erica and my father – who both adored fireworks – would wait until Mum had gone to bed and then sneak into the school fields for their own private display. My mother's other main fear was crowds. She hated being surrounded by large groups, especially drunken people. This fear seemed sensible to me, and I didn't see my mother's worries as strange because they stemmed from anxiety about her safety, which struck me as a normal thing to be concerned about. But I realised now that because my father and sister were so reckless, I had stopped doing all sorts of things I might enjoy just so my mother wouldn't worry. These weren't to do with fire or crowds, simply social activities I had avoided because she was slightly overprotective. It was becoming clear to me that the reason I was so anxious about starting a relationship was because I knew my mother wouldn't let me socialise in the way couples usually did. If my mother had been at home, I knew she would probably have persuaded me not to go to Lola's party, although no doubt she'd realise it was futile to try to stop my sister. Not that I was going to use tonight to pursue Perdita – she'd made it clear how she saw me – but I could see a potential new future awaiting me if my mother didn't return home.

I had my bath, washed my clothes, and combed my hair, trying to use only a tiny blob of the toxic green hair-gel I'd bought from the local supermarket. Slightly floppy hair was always less embarrassing than being overslicked. I was ready long before Shep arrived, and when he rang the doorbell I had to wait a moment before opening so he wouldn't know I'd been watching for the window.

'So,' he said, as I got into the car, 'big night tonight.'

'The last episode, you mean?'

'The party,' he said, 'although I think it's a bit mean of you not to invite the drivers. We've been working all week as well.'

I realised he wanted me to joke with him, and said, 'Sorry, not my house. There's nothing I can do.'

Nicholas went round the room, handing out pages for the final session. As usual, I checked the front page first:

All Right Now! Episode Six
Tour Guide: Perdita

Surprised, I looked across at her. She was reading through the rest of the pages. When she'd got to the last one, her head came up and she beckoned me across.

'Have you seen this?'

'Yeah, I told you you'd get to be a tour guide. Congratulations.'

'No, I don't mean that. Look, here on the last page.'

I flicked through and saw:

PERDITA AND GERALD KISS.

The feeling this induced in me was partly like getting an A for an essay and partly like being told to do a talk in front of a school assembly. Nicholas had clearly registered my interest in Perdita, and had no way of knowing she didn't feel the same way.

'We can do this, can't we?' I asked her.

As nervous as this made me, I still expected to see Perdita smiling back at me. I thought she'd take my hand and tell me, 'Of course we can'. But instead, when her face didn't seem to answer me and I had to stare deep into her dark brown eyes, all I could see was fear.

'Perdita . . .'

'Gerald,' she interrupted, 'will you come outside with me for a minute?'

I followed her outside. We didn't stop in the cloakroom, but went all the way out to the car park. I could see she was terrified, and I didn't understand what I'd done to scare her.

'It's OK,' I said, 'I understand, it's only acting, I know it doesn't mean anything.'

She stared at me. 'I'm sorry, Gerald, it's nothing against you.'

'What isn't?'

'I can't do it.'

'Perdita . . . It's acting,' I repeated. 'I know you don't like me, but I don't like Sheryl, and I've had to play her boyfriend all week.'

'Don't like you?' she shouted. 'Gerald, I told you you're like a brother to me.'

'Is that why it's weird? Because you see me as a brother?'

'I already told you, it's got nothing to do with my feelings towards you.'

'Then I don't understand. Is it because it's embarrassing? This whole thing is embarrassing. All you're experiencing now is what the rest of us felt when we were tour guides. Remember that argument Wendy had with Nicholas, you thought that was silly.'

'No I didn't. I was the only one who said she had a point.'

'So that's what this is about, you're embarrassed about kissing me on TV? Perdita, I mean, my God, compare that to what Wendy had to do in her episode, or the stuff about my family that Nicholas has put in the story.'

'You don't understand.'

I didn't want to talk to her any more. 'I think you should speak to Nicholas.'

She looked at him through the window, then back to me. In that moment, she realised something, turned, and started running.

'Perdita,' I shouted after her.

But she was gone.

I went back inside.

'Where's Perdita?' Nicholas asked.

'She ran away.'

'Why?'

'She wasn't happy with her scenes.'

'Oh Jesus Christ. Immi, can you go out and find her?'

Immi headed outside.

Immi didn't manage to find Perdita. The team were worried she might have tried to hitch-hike and immediately called her parents. Terrence answered and told Immi that Perdita had called and was on her way home.

'Can you bring her back?' Immi asked.

'I'm sorry,' Terrence told her, 'she doesn't want to take part tonight.'

This made Nicholas so angry that he ignored the team's suggestion of letting one of them stand in for her and cancelled the whole session. The rest of the group were happy about this, pleased to be able to get to Lola's party early. I was too depressed to attend, and persuaded Shep to drive me home.

'What happened?' he asked.

'I'm sorry, Shep, I really don't want to talk about it.'

'That bad? OK, say no more, I'll get you home.'

'Thanks, Shep,' I replied. 'You're a good friend.'

'Happy to help. I remember what it was like. And if you feel like talking later, just let me know.'

I told him I would. He nodded and turned on the radio.

PART VII

★

101

It had been an annoying flight. I'd got stuck next to an old lady who played Super Mario Bros solidly throughout the nearly seven-hour journey, digging her elbow into my ribs every time she made the cartoon figure jump. Passport control wasn't too painful, but I knew I'd have to wait for Richard, who'd never been punctual.

Then I saw him, standing with the men holding up name boards by the entrance. He held out his arms and I accepted his embrace.

'Richard, I can't believe this.'

'I know, it's been ages.'

'No, that you're on time.'

He smiled. I noticed he'd grown a moustache and got a new pair of glasses with tinted lenses. Richard had always dressed as if he couldn't wait to become a fully-fledged academic, but he'd taken advantage of coming to America to further hone his image.

'Trading as a professional Englishman now, are we?'

He put a hand on my shoulder. 'Let's not start the insults just yet, OK?'

We didn't have to wait long for the Princeton Airporter. I put the suitcase on the seat in front of me and sat next to Richard.

'Tell me,' he said, 'what exactly did you do to Sally?'

'Nothing. Why? Did she say I did something?'

'Her exact words were "He's a fucking selfish sod and I don't care if I never see him again." '

'Really?'

He nodded. 'I can show you the e-mail when we get back. Did you sleep with her, Gerald?'

'No. We slept in the same bed for a while, but never had sex.'

'You slept in the same bed?'

'Yeah,' I said defensively, 'she was looking after me.'

'How does that work?'

'It was her idea.'

'Yes, she told me that, but I don't understand what either of you were doing. Are you sure there's not more to this?'

'Like what?'

'You can trust me, Gerald.'

'What do you think I'm hiding?'

'I've always known there was something between the two of you at some point. You just kept it quiet because you didn't want Ellen to find out.'

'Did Sally tell you this?'

'No one had to tell me.'

I shook my head. 'Richard, nothing ever happened between us. I've got no reason not to tell you the truth.'

'Well, maybe that's why Sally's so upset with you. You're too selfish to see that she's got a massive crush on you.'

'No, that's not it either. We had a long talk the night she stopped staying with me. She's sad because she feels a stage of her life is over. If she's angry with me, it's because I've started feeling better again.'

Richard snorted and sat back against the window.

'What was that?' I asked.

'Gerald, you know I love you and I'm really pleased to see you again, but you have to be careful about this bubble you live in. I realised it's a very reassuring defence mechanism, but it doesn't make it easy to be your friend.'

I sighed. 'I didn't mean that the way it sounded. I don't think Sally fancied me, OK? I think she wanted something else.'

'Like what?'

'Why are you still studying?'

'Huh?'

'It's nice not to have to make decisions, right? When I called Sally she dropped everything and took over my life for me. And I was really grateful. But we couldn't carry on like that for ever.'

'OK, Gerald, let me suggest an alternative possibility. Could it be that Sally did want to go out with you, but the way you turn everything into such a bloody drama put her off? She was probably too scared of the cosmic significance of making a move on you.'

I considered this. When Stan had made this suggestion to me, I had assumed he was an idiot. But because it was Richard, and he knew Sally almost as well as I did, I wondered if he was right. 'Oh God. Maybe you're right. What should I do?'

'Do you want to go out with her?'

'No.'

'Then spare the poor girl's blushes. Get the relationship back to normal as soon as possible. If you do it right, maybe the two of you can still be friends. But it means you'll have to put your ego aside and let her lead for a while.'

'OK,' I said, 'I'll call her as soon as I get back to England.'

102

I met my mother in the café of Bentall's department store. She bought me a Coca-Cola and the two of us sat at a table together. It was the first time I'd seen her since she'd left home. I cracked open my can and poured it into a warm glass. She sighed and said, 'How's your father?'

'He's OK. What did you want to talk to me about?'

'I wanted to make sure you understood this is only temporary.'

'You're coming home?'

'No. But it might not be long before you can come to live with me.'

'I don't want another father.'

She rubbed her face. 'I'm not talking about that. Don't make this hard for me, Gerald.'

'I'm not. Dad thinks I'm taking your side.'

'That's typical of him.'

'I'm not angry with you, Mum. I'm just not ready for a new family. I'd rather stay with Dad.'

Mum filled her cup with tea and added milk and sugar. 'Who put all this nonsense about new families into your head? All I'm talking about is you coming to live with me and Erica.'

'And Dennis.'

'Well, maybe not,' she said. 'Dennis is a . . . He's a friend. You've met him, remember, at the commune? He was all right to you, wasn't he?'

'He's not just a friend.'

'He's helping me out. It's hard to end a marriage all at once. I couldn't organise a place of my own with your father breathing down my neck. But now I've got time and space to find somewhere for the whole family, you, me and Erica.'

I didn't say anything.

'Don't you want that, Gerald?'

'No.'

'Then what do you want?'

'I want a mum and dad who live together, like all the other kids in school.'

This winded her. She sat back heavily in her seat, and said, 'You know how to hurt me, don't you?'

I didn't reply, thinking that it was unfair of her to act like I'd done something wrong. Then I noticed her tears, and said quickly, 'I'm sorry, Mum, I didn't mean it.'

Now she was silent. We finished our drinks and left the café. Outside, she gave me a twenty-pound note and we walked to different bus stops.

103

'What the hell is that?'

'Oh,' said Richard, 'he's called Silas. He's a Flat Coat Retriever.'

Silas was chasing his tail in the centre of Richard's small

apartment. Richard lived in a 'Butt Hutt', the colloquial campus name for the Butler Apartments, several rows of prefabs that formed a small shanty town at the edge of campus. These huts weren't an unpleasant place to live, but they definitely weren't the sort of shack you'd want to share with a dog.

'Is it yours?'

He shook his head. 'Heather's.'

'Who's Heather?'

'I'm not ready to tell you yet.'

'What?'

'It's a story for later. After several Sam Adams.'

'Have you broken up with Joan?'

He nodded. 'But I'd really rather tell you the full story.'

'Why didn't you let me know sooner?'

'It would've sounded strange as an e-mail. There was a series of events that ended with me breaking up with Joan. But I thought it'd be better for me to tell you face to face. And I will, I promise, after dinner tonight.'

It was hard for me to let this pass, but I knew the story would be better if he told it the way he wanted. The dog had stopped circling and looked up expectantly.

'Shouldn't you feed him?' I asked Richard. 'He looks hungry.'

'See boy,' Richard said, bending down to stroke him, 'Gerald does like you.'

I was sleeping in Richard's friend's room. She was an Italian-American graduate student named Linda who'd gone home for a friend's funeral. There wasn't any space in her wardrobe so I put my suitcase next to her bed.

'So do you have classes?' I shouted to Richard. 'Papers to write? Undergraduates to supervise?'

'Nope,' he replied, 'I've cleared everything. The only thing is . . .'

I went to the door. 'Yeah?'

'Well, Heather's in New York at the moment and she

wants us to go join her – in her apartment. I haven't really decided whether . . .'

'When does she want us to go?'

'Tomorrow.'

'Great. I'd love to spend some time in New York.'

'Gosh, that was easy. What do you want for dinner?'

We went to the Annex, an Italian family restaurant in a pine basement down from Nassau Street that had separate bar and dining areas. Richard spoke to a friendly head waiter and he took us to our table. I immediately felt at home, and happy to be in America. Looking through the menu, I was pleased to see the long list of steak, chop and veal dishes.

'My sort of place,' I said to Richard.

I didn't pester Richard for his story, letting him eat his dinner in peace. While we were eating, people kept coming up to the table to say hello. Most didn't stay long, and I noticed a brusqueness in the way Richard dealt with them. But he was so polite with the strangest well-wisher that the man pulled up a seat and sat alongside us.

'Adrian,' he said to this man, 'I'd like you to meet my friend Gerald.'

'Delighted,' said Adrian, in a fruity English accent. He offered me his hand and I shook it.

'Hello.'

'Oooh, you're English,' he squealed. 'Are you doing anything tomorrow night?'

I couldn't stop staring at this man, amazed he was Richard's friend. His blue blazer had unpleasant stains on both lapels, and his bright red hair stood up in ragged tufts. He had extremely pale, almost translucent skin, not that dissimilar to Stan's. There would have been something punk about his appearance except he seemed to be emulating an earlier generation of Englishman. If this was the sort of person Richard was hanging out with here, no wonder he'd changed his appearance.

'Sorry, Ade, we're going to New York for a few days.'

'Off to see Heather, eh?' he said, nudging Richard.

I realised that although Richard was being polite to Adrian, something about the man intimidated him. Richard had become a lot less strait-laced since moving to America, and I was pleased to see this flash of his old character. After Adrian had moved off, I said to Richard, 'What a clown.'

'Shsss,' he hissed, 'he might come back.'

'How do you know him anyway?'

'He's Heather's friend, not mine. But it's safer for me to keep in with him.'

'Safer?'

'Come on, let's go for a walk.'

We paid the check and I followed Richard. He seemed to be wandering aimlessly, so I asked him, 'Where are we going?'

'Firewood library.'

'OK.'

'Actually, that's probably a bad idea . . . Let's find a quiet alcove on the other side of the plaza.'

We walked across and found somewhere to sit. Richard seemed unusually agitated, and I realised it was time to hear his story.

104

I was working out how far I could push my father. I'd started calling him John instead of Dad, and yesterday had been brandishing a cigar when he returned from work (Dad was violently anti-smoking, having lost both parents to cancer). But nothing seemed to rattle him. I'd been certain loud music, which was something he really hated, would do it, but no: he pretended not to mind that either.

The house had become quite squalid before my father started tidying up. I had even come close to cleaning the place myself, but wanted to see how bad he'd let things get. Again, he avoided a drama. When my mother and father were both busy and the house got untidy, Mum would eventually freak out, calling the place a 'shit-heap', and shouting until we started clearing up. Now she was gone, Dad had started cleaning every weekend, giving me a few tasks of my own that I didn't mind doing as they weren't too taxing. (Not that he didn't try to cut corners wherever possible, serving dinner on paper plates to avoid washing up.)

The first time my mother had left home, five years earlier, I was eight. I'd been happy to go with her to the women's commune, because, as I told her at the time, 'You are my mummy and mummies are special.' I also associated everything that was depressing about our house with my father. He was at his most miserable at the time, probably as a result of my mother's threats to leave. There was one time when my mother had spent the whole day with me, helping me write and illustrate a small picture-book. When Dad came home he got so angry with me – I can't remember why – that he tore up the book. This was probably the cruellest thing anyone had done to me, and something Mum told me would never happen at the commune, where 'creativity is always encouraged'.

But when we got to the commune, the experience was terrifying. The women may have been enlightened, but their children weren't, and saw my sister and me as easy targets. When they attacked Erica, they got what they deserved. So I became the sole attention of their anger, often forced to run away and wait for an adult to find me. When my mother had been promoting the idea of the commune to Erica and me, she made it sound as if the three of us would be spending a lot more time together. But as well as living at the commune, my mother had a paid position there, and the women who showed up at all hours were so hungry for her attention that I soon discovered I was going to see a lot less of her than I did before.

Although I never wanted to go back to the commune, I was still upset when Mum took Erica with her instead of me. As I'd told my mother in Bentall's, I didn't want to live with Dennis, but thought I'd regret guilt-tripping her about wanting a normal family, knowing this wouldn't make her return home, and might encourage her instead to make plans which didn't include me.

I had worried about being left alone in the house with my father. But over the last couple of weeks we seemed to have achieved a new balance in our relationship. He no longer stayed out every night and since he'd started going to church, seemed to be slowly trying to curb his more excessive behaviour. And this will sound terrible, but there seemed much less stress in the house now there weren't any women around. Both my mother and sister seemed to thrive on creating their own special brands of aggravation, while my father and I much preferred a quiet life. He was a much nicer person without anyone baiting him, and I found that I no longer felt the anger towards him that I once had. At the time, I was upset that my parents were breaking up, but these days I feel grateful that I managed to avoid the usual family frustrations. As long as you've got a strong sense of yourself – something I've always had, and probably thanks to my parents – I think divorce, at the right age, can even benefit a child. Certainly most of the people I know who are really screwed up have parents who are still together. Adults always seem to find it easier to alienate their offspring in teams of two.

It still felt a bit lonely sometimes, and I was probably more melancholy than I remember in retrospect. If I hadn't had the filming of *All Right Now!* to look forward to, I might have fallen into a more serious depression, but as it was, I moped about and listened to music, filling my empty hours with fantasies of Perdita deciding she did fancy me after all. It was also during this time that I finally experimented with the possibilities Perdita had explained to me on the phone, which provided a strange kind of solace, evenings of distemper restoring my temper.

105

Richard waited until a group of students had passed, cleared his throat, and began, 'Joan doesn't like America. I knew that before I came here, but I thought that once she came out to Princeton and saw what it was like here and met some of the people from my department she might change her mind.

'After the first time she came here, it was obvious she didn't like anyone else in my department, and wasn't at all keen on living in Princeton. Someone once said that Princeton is the perfect place to do anything other than be in Princeton, and although that sounds cryptic, there's a lot of truth in that statement. You make your own life here – it really is somewhere with no distractions.

'Most people can cope with this. Some can't. In general, you know what I'm like, I don't mind it. But there are two problems that go with this territory. One is that you get a lot of thinking time. So if something's worrying you, like the future of your relationship, it's hard not to spend every waking moment obsessing about it. The other is that Princeton isn't like a normal university. People have worked so damn hard to get here, it's had a strange effect on them. So much studying doesn't make them clever, in a general sense . . . it infantilises them. There's a guy in our department who has terrible dreams about zombies every single night and he's twenty-nine. If anyone even mentions the word "zombie" in his presence, he starts crying.'

I chuckled.

'I'm serious,' said Richard. 'These people are like super-intelligent children, or the kind of oddbods who make a living from going on general knowledge programmes. They've been concentrating on their academic work since they were three years old and they all suffer from the delusion that there aren't enough hours in the day to get everything done . . . who knows, maybe it's not a delusion.

But these people are so eager to spend every waking hour in the library that they don't even stop to do their washing. You see people walking about the campus in their pyjamas and when you ask them what the hell they're doing they tell you they've run out of clothes. And, you know what I'm like, I'm not that sort of person. I can work for about six or seven hours straight but then in the evening I'm done for the day and I need a drink. But making a social arrangement with someone here is more difficult than getting a meeting with President Clinton. They'll happily meet you for coffee, or eat lunch in the canteen with you while they read a book, but at night they have one beer and paranoia sets in and they're back home for another few hours' study.'

'And everyone's like that?' I asked.

'Well, almost everyone, and therein lies my story. Once I gave up trying to persuade my grad friends to go out and drink with me, I started hanging out in bars alone. There are places where you can always find someone to drink with. One of these is the D-bar – D for debasement – but that's like a club that's only open to students, and I don't like drinking with undergrads because it reminds me of what I've lost.'

'What you've lost?' I asked, startled.

'Time, I mean. Innocence. Don't look scared. All I'm saying is drinking with undergrads depresses me. So I started going to the Ivy Inn, which has a few more locals than everywhere else and a different sort of atmosphere. I also went to Mike's Tavern and this Sports Bar that takes a while to walk to but is worth it when you get there.'

'Richard,' I said, 'were you going to these bars to pick up women?'

He shook his head. 'I was looking for friends, I suppose. Kindred spirits. The campus life can really get to you after a while. I wanted to find people who didn't give a shit when their papers were due . . . Fuck, I wanted friends who didn't write papers.'

I laughed, then quickly apologised. 'Sorry, Richard, I

don't mean to make light of this. I understand what you're saying.'

'Do you?' He stared at me. 'Good. Well, to begin with I was just looking for people to drink with, but there is this sort of sketchy undercurrent to some of these places ... Well, not the places, but there are some people who hover on the fringes of campus life ...'

'Like that guy who came up to you tonight?'

He nodded. 'Exactly. Oh God, Gerald, I'll stop dressing it up. You're right, sometimes I was looking for women. And that's how I met Heather.

'I was in the Sports Bar. It wasn't a game night so the place wasn't that full. There was a woman there, Heather, and she was sitting by the main large television eating a plate of hot wings. She was wearing a low-cut, almost backless white top and I couldn't help staring at this huge tattoo she had on her left shoulder. It was a tattoo of *The Little Mermaid*, and I couldn't help wondering what would make someone get that done. She had peroxide blonde hair with jet-black roots, and I was fascinated by her. I knew if anything happened it'd only be a one-night stand, but also that it'd be the best one-night stand of my life. So I ordered her a drink and sent it over. She must've asked who'd bought it for her because she sent one back, and after we'd been staring at each other for a while, beckoned me across.

' "Oh," she said, when I got close up, "I knew I should've worn my contacts." "Why?" I asked her. "Don't you find me attractive?" "Oh," she said, "I suppose you'll do." She kept winding me up all night and I put up with it because I thought I was going home with her. But then, just before the bar closed, she got out a coin and said, "OK, let's let fate decide." I tried to play along, y'know, asking, "Your place or mine?" But she said, "No, this is about whether you come back with me or go Macaulay Culkin." '

'And what happened?'

'I went home alone, feeling bitter and wondering whether it was a double-sided coin that she always used to get out of going home with people she didn't find attractive.'

'Were you still seeing Joan at this point?'

'No, we broke up shortly after her first visit. I'm surprised no one told you.'

'I suppose I don't really know that many of your friends, apart from Sally. Does she know?'

He shook his head. 'I don't think so.'

'So, when did you see Heather again?'

'In the library. She's a grad student too. She's doing a doctorate on the way women were educated in America during the early twentieth century. I was mortified to see her again, but she came straight over to me and asked if we could go for a coffee. I was still feeling pissed off, but she seemed to have changed her mind about me and asked if I was doing anything on Saturday. When I told her I wasn't, she asked me if I wanted to go to the Poconos to stay in a log cabin with her. I said OK and she told me she was planning to spend the evening watching the Tyson–Holyfield fight, and if I came the only condition was that I couldn't distract her. I promised to behave myself, and we went away together.'

He looked at me. 'Do you remember what happened in that fight?'

'Was it the ear-biting one?'

He nodded. 'That's right. Round three. Fight called in the fourth. You know I know nothing about boxing, but the point is, the fight was over quickly. It aroused Heather, but it didn't satisfy her. And she decided to take it out on me.'

I laughed. Richard didn't see the humour in his story, but it was so hard to picture him in the scenario he was describing. The idea of a woman using Richard to relieve her sexual frustration was very amusing, all the more so because he presented himself as an unwilling victim.

'I'll spare you the gory details. But something happened that night . . . Her energy, it had an effect on me . . . It's strange how good sex can bond people. I've definitely got better at it since I started seeing Heather.'

'I believe you. But why did you make your story sound so doom-laden? It's a good thing, isn't it?'

341

'Yes, but other people are a bit intimidated by Heather, especially as she's so different from Joan. I just wanted you to know how important she is to me.'

I nodded, and tried to look serious. This was hilarious. I couldn't wait to meet this woman.

106

Perdita reappeared for the read-throughs. Whatever had worried her before no longer seemed to upset her, and when we got to the end of the sixth script – which Nicholas had written perfectly well without the benefit of our improvisations – she was all ready to kiss me when our dramaturge said, 'No, don't actually do it now. It'll be better if you experience it for the first time in the actual performance.'

We started recording the day after the final read-through. By law, we had to do three hours of schoolwork every day we were recording, and today this was scheduled for after lunch. Shep arrived at seven and drove me, Jane and Fuckpit to the first location. We were filming the teens-only nightclub scenes first, in a real nightclub in Kingston, and Nicholas told me it would probably take three days to get all the scenes done. Over the last few weeks the group's excitement had started to wane, but now we were about to start recording, there was a fresh injection of adrenalin. Already the nightclub was filled with people preparing for the day's shoot. I expected them to pay attention to me – we were, after all, the reason they were here – but most of the crew had little time for any of us, as they were either busy with equipment or standing around smoking. I wasn't really interested in the technical side of the process, and although I would later be introduced to figures with cryptic job-titles like 2nd AD, I decided that I wouldn't study their movements too closely. The thing that seemed to interest everyone most of all was being given costumes and having their make-up done. Our costumes were normal clothes not dissimilar to the way we usually dressed. But everyone seemed upset with what they'd been given, so the woman in charge of costumes, who was rather taken aback by the violence of our reaction, said in a flustered voice that we could swap with each other if that would make us happy. This was fine for the girls, but as Pete, Fuckpit and I were completely different sizes, we were stuck with what we'd been given.

The three of us went to the gents' toilet we were using as a dressing-room and put on our clothes. Pete and Fuckpit moaned about theirs, but mine were by far the ugliest. I had been given a light blue jumper that looked like something a granny would wear, and a pair of green trousers my father might have admired. I also had a pair of black trainers that looked OK, but were too tight.

'Blue and green should never be seen,' laughed Pete.

'Fuck you,' I snapped back.

The make-up lady was doing the girls first. Perdita walked into the gents' toilet without knocking and approached me.

'I have to wait to have my make-up done, but come and talk to me.'

'I can't go into the girls' toilet, Perdita.'

'It's OK. Everyone's changed.'

'Yeah, but still . . .'

'It'll be fine. Don't be a wimp. Come on.'

I laced my too-tight trainers and followed her. I expected all the girls to shout at me as I went into their dressing-room, but no one said anything.

Lola was the one currently being made-up, sitting in a chair by the sinks. 'I want a proper dressing-room,' she complained, 'with light bulbs around the mirror. That's what I have at home.'

'You've got that at home?' asked the make-up lady, who seemed disturbed by this revelation.

'Uh-huh, and that's what we should have here.'

The make-up lady continued her work, ignoring Lola's boasts. I still regretted missing Lola's party. Even without Perdita's presence, it seemed likely I would have had a good time. Everyone had a story about some eccentricity of Lola's house or parents, or how Fuckpit and Wendy had got so drunk they threw up mid-snog.

Perdita pulled me to the back of the toilets, then made me go with her into one of the cubicles. She closed the door slightly, but didn't lock it, not wanting to attract the attention of the other girls.

'I need to apologise to you.'

'OK,' I said.

'I shouldn't have run away. I didn't think about how it would make you feel. Well, I did, but at that point I felt so desperate I just didn't care.'

'I understand.'

'No you don't. That was obvious at the time. And why should you? I can see how it might seem like an insult. Gerald, the reason I was worried about kissing you on TV was that I was scared about what my parents would think.'

'But your parents don't seem like they'd mind something like that . . .'

'I know, and they wouldn't. They like you – my dad especially, you seem to have really charmed him – and they understand about acting. It was me who minded. It's hard to explain. I was worried about having to talk to them about the scene, and having to tell them it wasn't my idea. I don't talk to my parents as much as I should. I told you before how shy I feel around them, and this situation just seemed likely to bring about a lot of unnecessary embarrassment. I kept picturing them having to explain to my grandmother, or our neighbours, or whoever watches the programme, and I could imagine the tone they'd take when they were explaining, and I just couldn't bear the idea of that.'

'So what made you change your mind?'

She sighed. 'I kept thinking how unfair I was being to you. It wasn't your idea to have a kissing scene, and maybe you feel just as awkward about kissing me.'

Perdita left the question hanging. I didn't answer.

'And it seemed silly that this was all a result of my timidity,' she continued. 'Like you said, my parents would understand, and it's no one else's business. These things only get to you if you let them, right?'

I hugged her. She smiled. 'We can do this.'

107

Richard sent me to get breakfast. When I returned, I tossed him his requested bag of bagels and sat down with my croissant.

'What's that?' he asked.

'What does it look like?'

'You don't eat croissants.'

I took a bite. 'Yes I do.'

'No, I know you, Gerald, you're a creature of habit, and as long as I've known you, you've never eaten a croissant for breakfast.'

I smiled. 'OK, you have a point. I'm eating this croissant to remind me of someone.'

'Aha,' he said triumphantly. 'Who?'

'A girl I went on a couple of dates with. I was hoping something was going to come of it, but things didn't work out.'

'This is a recent someone?'

'Almost immediately before I came here.'

'So this is why Sally is upset?'

'No, no,' I replied, 'I kept it from her.'

'And it's definitely not going to happen?'

I shook my head. 'But the problem's not with her. It's her friends.'

'What's wrong with her friends?'

I told him about Don and Uncle C. I made a big deal out of the story, trying to make it sound as important as his account of meeting Heather.

'OK,' he said, 'so those are her friends. What's she like?'

'The only way I can explain it is that she smelled right. I don't mean that in a literal sense, just . . . I don't know . . . there was something about her.'

'Is she pretty?'

'Yeah, but it's not that. I just had a sense that we were destined to be together. I can't explain why.'

'Well, in that case, if you ask me, it sounds like you gave up a little too easily.'

'Listen to you, the voice of experience. Just because I haven't spent the last six months looking for Ms Goodbar.'

He didn't reply.

It was still early. We'd both been awoken at sunrise by Silas, who'd torn about the apartment, yapping and turning noisy circles across my bedroom floor. Now we were both awake Silas sat silent, and the two of us were left with more morning than we knew what to do with.

'I suppose we could set off earlier,' said Richard. 'Heather won't mind.'

'OK,' I replied.

We finished our breakfasts and I went back into my room. I'd hardly unpacked, so it didn't take me long to get ready. I carried my case into the living room. Richard came out of the bedroom. He was carrying a stick, a pair of dark glasses and a dog harness.

'What the hell's that?'

'It's the only way to get Silas on the train. Apart from a carrying-case, and he'd go mad if I put him in one of those.'

'Where did you get that stuff?'

'Adrian gave it to me.'

'And where did he get it?'

'He stole it.'

'Who from?'

'A blind man, I suppose.'

'Richard, this is terrible. And so unlike you. I might have started eating croissants, but that's hardly the same thing as pretending to be blind.'

'Well, that's what I was trying to explain last night.' He looked proud. 'I've changed.'

'And not for the good, clearly. Can't you get in trouble for this sort of thing?'

'Why? It's not like I'm begging.'

'But it must be illegal. In fact, I'm sure it is. What if one of your undergraduates spots you? Or a faculty member?'

'Oh, I see them all the time,' he said nonchalantly. 'Most of them simply think it's a blind man who looks like me. And those who do know it's me think it's funny.'

'Richard, I have to say I'm really shocked by this. I don't think it's funny at all.'

'Relax, Gerald, it's really not a big deal. Once the tickets have been checked I'll take my disguise off.'

We walked down to the Wawa and bought some food and drink for the trip. I couldn't work out the ticket machines, which seemed even more complicated than the ones in London, so Richard did it for me. When we got on the train, he took my ticket from me and placed it in the strap at the top of the seat, a custom I didn't know about. We changed trains at Princeton Junction, and got on the New Jersey transit to Penn Station. From there, we caught a cab to Heather's apartment in the West Village. The cab driver didn't want Silas in his car, and I was astonished to see Richard ham up his blind man routine. This was truly out of character for my friend, who was usually one of the most ethical men I knew.

Heather let us into her apartment, which was on the second floor. Silas rushed at her and she fell onto the floor with him, happily rolling around with the dog, while Richard and I headed for the large green sofa. She jumped up from the floor and sat opposite us. I could immediately see that everything Richard had said about her was true. She had an intimidating quality, but this didn't detract from her femininity, and I was impressed that Richard had found such an exciting girlfriend. I didn't fancy her (I've never been the type to go after friends' partners), but I felt delighted that I would be spending time in her company. I hadn't disliked Joan, Richard's previous girlfriend, but there had been nothing exciting about her. She had been a female version of

Richard, intelligent, polite and good company, but rather too rigorous in her self-regulation. I'm attracted to people who have a strong sense of themselves, but if someone doesn't let loose once in a while, they can get a bit boring. And Joan was like that, always acting as if she was playing a part in a period drama. What I disliked most about her was the way she made Richard too cautious, as part of the fun of my friend was that although he saw everything – including me – as a potentially pernicious influence, he enjoyed being corrupted. Now Joan was gone, I sensed I was going to see another side of my friend's character, and as I was looking to have fun myself, this could only be a good thing.

108

I had been anticipating an epiphany when we started filming, but all that actually happened was that I realised most of the important work had already been done. Until this point, none of us had been taking the improvisation or rehearsals entirely seriously, each for different reasons, but in my case because I couldn't shake the words my father had said to me when I asked him if I could definitely be in the programme if I had the operation on my teeth: 'You know what these TV shows are like, Gerald. Nothing's definite until it's on air.' I knew this was true, and that even after the programme was recorded there was still a possibility that it might not be broadcast. But I had believed that the moment the cameras started recording there would be a change in atmosphere, a new awareness of the powers of creation bringing something tangible into existence. Now it had begun, however, the filming seemed almost an afterthought, a record of our experiences that couldn't quite match the magic of our primary interaction.

The director was significantly older than Nicholas or any of the production team. He had grey hair, which was Brylcreemed back from his forehead, and a blotchy red and purple face. He was wearing young clothes, a blue and gold tracksuit that had come from America and a director's baseball cap, red with a yellow insignia. When it came to my first scene with Amy, he let me do one take and then said, 'Gerald, I'm going to give you some advice here that will stand you in good stead for the rest of your life. It's something I once said to Bob Hoskins. The camera can always tell exactly what you're thinking. What are you thinking, Gerald?'

'I thought you could tell.'

'I can't tell. The camera can tell.'

'I'm thinking about the cameras,' I told him, thinking this was what he wanted me to say.

'That's perfectly natural. But it's giving you a strained, nervous expression. In this scene, when you're talking to this lovely young girl, Amy, all your thoughts have to be of her. Now, how do you feel about Amy?'

'I'm not sure.'

'OK. Let's look at the script.'


```
4. INT. TEENS-ONLY NIGHTCLUB. NIGHT.
GERALD notices AMY standing alone. He approaches
her.


                    GERALD
Is there another floor?


                     AMY
Only on regular nights. Is it your first time here?


                    GERALD
Yeah. I only came because my sister wanted me to.


                     AMY
Where's your sister?
```

I don't care. I'm avoiding her. What about you? Are
you here with anyone?

AMY

Yeah. Robert.

GERALD

Is he your boyfriend?

AMY

No. He's someone I live with.

GERALD

(shocked)
Live with?

AMY

Not in that way. I have a complicated family life.

GERALD nods. The two of them are interrupted by
ROBERT, who looks cross.

'OK,' said the director, 'now this is quite a cryptic scene we
have here. Nicholas, I think I'm going to need your input.
How exactly does Gerald feel towards Amy?'

'All the motivations have come from the children's own
improvisations,' said Nicholas, sounding a little flustered.

'Well, yes, OK, but neither I nor the boy seems to know
exactly what's going on here. Does Gerald have the hots for
Amy?'

'No,' said Nicholas.

'But this plays like a romantic scene.'

'He's flattered, of course,' said Nicholas, 'and pleased that
a girl's talking to him. It's not that he fancies her. It's more
oblique than that.'

The director looks at me. 'Do you understand what he's
saying, Gerald?'

I nodded.

'Well, you're a better man than I am. Let's try the scene again.'

109

'Octopi are so ugly they make squid look fuckable,' said Heather, taking a piece of sushi from our shared plate. 'Dontcha think, Richie?'

Richard didn't reply, gulping his Sapporo. He had been testy all evening, as Heather had pried my secrets out of me. He had been really shocked when I told them about Darla and Ronnie and my first experience with cocaine, a story that had delighted Heather. She'd spent at least half an hour detailing all her previous drug experiences before swearing that she'd given all that up since meeting Richard.

'Which doesn't mean I don't get cravings every now and again. Especially when I'm at one of Adrian's parties.'

'Is that that man who came up to us in the Annex?' I asked Richard. He nodded. ''Cause I have to say that he seemed like an idiot.'

Heather laughed. 'No one English ever likes Adrian. But that's what we think Englishmen are like. And it's easier to cope with Englishmen like Adrian than ones like you or Richard.'

'Why?'

'Because you're so intractable.' She looked at Richard. 'Is that the word I mean? Or do I mean intransigent?'

'There's not much difference,' said Richard. 'Anyway, we understand what you mean.'

There was a dismissive tone to his voice that clearly annoyed Heather, and she responded by leaning in closer to me.

'I'm not saying you should like him. But Princeton can be so fucking boring if you don't have someone sorting out fun for you.'

I thought about Sophie, and Don and Uncle C. Did they fulfil the same purpose for her?

'And you shouldn't take his web-site seriously.'

'What web-site?'

Richard rolled his eyes. 'Butt Hutt. He pays undergrads to appear on a web-cam, and let him take pictures of them.'

'Richard thinks it's disgusting and exploitative, which it is, but the thing about Adrian is that he can just get away with that kind of shit. Anyway, let's not talk about him any more. Do you have a girlfriend, Gerald?'

After we'd finished dinner, we went looking for a bar. The place we found was below street level, a thin empty place with a jukebox and a dartboard in the back. Heather was delighted by the dartboard, telling us we had to teach her how to play. There are certain songs that only really make sense when you hear them in America, and when Heather put 'For What It's Worth' on the jukebox it sounded sublime and I made her put it on five more times in a row. We stayed in the bar until early in the morning. As we were leaving a group of men were coming in to watch *Star Trek* on the TV behind the bar. I loved the fact that people were coming in at three to watch old television programmes, and wondered who they were. I tried to ask them questions, but Heather and Richard pulled me away, saying we'd had more than enough fun for one night.

110

I was surprised by the way Nicholas Pennington behaved when we started recording. I had expected him to fight the director on every decision, making sure the script got shot exactly the way he'd written it. But not only did he let the director make any changes he wanted, he also said it wasn't even that important that we got the words right, claiming that his lines were only intended as a template to keep the structure in place.

For his part, the director privileged Nicholas on set, giving him a prime position and asking him so many questions that the dramaturge frequently became embarrassed, saying his role had only been to facilitate the writing of the script, and that the real answers lay with us. I don't know if he was angling for more work, or whether he genuinely admired the director, but the two of them seemed to have a harmonious relationship.

They had two cameras going at once for most of the nightclub scenes, beginning with a single camera at one angle and then moving behind, sticking to the standard shot/reverse shot and not trying anything tricky. The director took time early on to establish what he called the visual grammar of the programme. He asked Nicholas if he wanted the shooting style to reflect the way the material had been composed, suggesting that it might be a good idea to go for long continuous takes to reflect the fact that the lines had initially come from improvisation. Nicholas shook his head and said, 'I want it to look like a conventional soap opera. If it's in any way different from a normal soap it's in the pace, and that will work best if it creeps up on the viewer.'

'OK,' replied the director, 'that makes things easier for me. You want the camera to observe the action rather than create it.'

Nicholas nodded.

I remember during that first week of filming I spent a lot of time talking to Perdita about dreams. I don't remember what I'd been reading, but in some book or other I had come across the concept of lucid dreaming. The book had been full of fanciful notions, but the two that especially interested me were that through careful training a person could learn to control their dreams, even down to their physical movements within the dream itself, and that if two people followed certain specific instructions, they could eventually share a dream. I can't remember most of these instructions, but I do recall that the first stage was that every night before going to sleep you had to stare at your palms and memorise every line. Perdita was fascinated by this, and the pair of us spent every evening quietly going over our scripts, talking on the telephone, and then staring at our palms until we dropped off. The possibility of sharing a dream seemed very exciting, and I really believed that if I could reach Perdita's subconscious she would understand that I was the one for her. It was also around this time that I first saw the children's film *Explorers* on video, which has a scene where the child characters find themselves in the same dream and discover what's wrong with the spaceship they've been trying to build, and only served to confirm the power of any action performed in dreamspace.

Over those first few days of filming, the director did attempt to shape our performances, telling us that although we were playing ourselves, we needed to heighten our acting style to make it seem naturalistic. He said that although in real life it took a while before you really felt you knew someone, for the purposes of our programme we needed to become recognisable types that the audience could immediately identify with. He hated it when we said anything that he saw as inconsistent with our characters, but instead of asking Nicholas to rewrite the lines, he made us improvise alternatives until we found the one that he thought sounded right. His favourites among the group were Lola Doll and Wendy, whom he considered more honest than the rest of us. These two girls were the most natural performers, able to achieve a simple immediacy that the rest of us found difficult. I could tell the director liked me, but he kept accusing me of over-thinking things and making myself look shifty.

He also had problems with Amy and Perdita. He told them they were holding back, but the truth was that they were just more subtle performers than Lola or Wendy. The younger children he tended to ignore, perhaps sensing that there wasn't much point in trying to teach them acting skills. Although we didn't have to watch the recording when we weren't taking part – in fact, Nicholas and the director preferred us not to hang around – I found myself staying to watch most of my sister's scenes. I felt proud of Erica, and thought she brought a sincere quality to her performance

354

that was missing from the acting of her two sidekicks in this episode, Lola and Wendy's sister Lucy. I thought about how miserable I'd felt when the producers had decided they wanted Erica to be in *All Right Now!*, and how adamantly I'd believed that it would be a terrible thing to let her take part, and realised that if I'd got my way not only would it have denied my sister an experience she was clearly relishing, but also that I might have completely lost contact with her. She was still reluctant to have much to do with me at school, but had come to regard the recording as a safe time, and was happy to talk to me here.

The producers kept telling us that we would find ourselves feeling odd bursts of energy during the recording process, and the adrenalin needed to get through the scenes might leave us over-stimulated or exhausted at different points in the day. Most of us were reliant on Coca-Cola, coffee and chocolate bars to keep going, and there was lots of trivial bickering. The two children who seemed most emotionally unstable were Wendy and Fuckpit. Wendy had just told her boyfriend Andrew that she wanted to break up with him, and was expecting a show of increased commitment from Fuckpit, who'd unfortunately chosen this moment to back off. Pete and Erica seemed calm by comparison, although their relationship – such as it was – looked like it was beginning to fizzle out. I was relieved by this, and hoped that it might soon dissipate completely. It wasn't that I was jealous of them, just that no matter how calm Erica seemed now, I knew there was no way Pete would be able to cope with her if any of her more psychopathic tendencies re-emerged, and it seemed safer if they separated before this happened.

111

I hadn't really considered what our sleeping arrangements would be when I first went inside Heather's apartment. I knew most people who owned property in New York could do ridiculous things with living space and assumed that there would be some panel that came out of the wall, or a hammock, or a switch that transformed the kitchen into a bedroom. Anything except the arrangement that was presented to me when we got back in the early hours of that morning. Richard, Heather and Silas all curled up together on a futon on the left-hand side of the room, with me on a sofa on the right.

'That dog's not going to wake up at dawn again, is he?'

'Leave him alone,' said Heather, 'he can't help being an early riser. And Richie will take care of him.'

'So I don't have to get up at six again?'

'Not unless you want to,' she replied. 'I'm going to sleep until my eyes pop open and won't shut again.'

'OK,' I said, 'I'll do that too.'

Silas started barking.

'Shssh,' cooed Richard, 'we're going to sleep now.'

Silas did wake me, but Heather and I complained until Richard attached his leash and dragged him off for an early morning walk.

'Think sleepy thoughts,' instructed Heather.

I did so and managed to get another couple of hours in.

Richard brought us all back breakfast. He winked at me as he tossed over a croissant.

'I will say something about having a dog,' Richard told me, 'you get to meet a lot of people.'

'Apologising to them after he's bitten them?'

'Silas would never bite anyone,' said Heather, in an outraged tone.

'No, but Gerald, you know me, I've never had any strong feelings about animals either way.'

'Poor Richard didn't have any pets when he was a kid. Can you imagine that?'

'You didn't have any either, did you, Gerald?'

'I had about seven hamsters. When I was really little.'

'Seven at once?'

'No, in a row. My sister kept killing them.'

'Oh, Heather, you mustn't listen to this. Gerald tells everyone his sister's a psychopath when she completely isn't. I've met her several times, and she's a perfectly nice girl.'

'She's nice *now*,' I protested, 'but she wasn't when we were young. And I didn't say my sister killed the hamsters deliberately. She was conducting a series of experiments. She put one in the oven to see if it could withstand heat, threw another out the window to see if it could fly. Hammy I to Hammy VII all suffered similarly ignoble deaths.'

'You called them all Hammy?'

'What's wrong with that?'

Richard shook his head. 'Anyway, my point was that dog people are a totally different breed of human being.'

'Watch out,' said Heather.

'No, I'm not being rude. I'm just saying if I'm walking down the street I rarely notice other people's pets, and even if I did, I wouldn't think of complimenting them, but whenever I take Silas out loads of people come up to me to talk about him.'

'That's because Silas is a beautiful dog, aren't you, boy?'

Silas licked her hand. She stood up and walked across to the corner of the room where she had a stereo and a huge stack of vinyl albums. She flicked through her collection and pulled out a record. I recognised the sleeve of *Accelerator* immediately, but didn't say anything, waiting until the record started and then shouting along.

'You know this?' she asked.

'Are you kidding? They're my favourite band.'

'Wow.' She looked away. 'Richard hates Royal Trux.'

'Only because he doesn't hear them properly. You like Ornette Coleman, don't you?'

'It's hardly the same thing,' he said snootily.

'Well, of course, because they're applying his concept of harmolodics to rock instead of jazz. But there's a lot to this band. You might not notice it on this album because it's a bit more straight-ahead than the others . . .'

'You're not one of those *Twin Infinitives* psychos, are you?' Heather interrupted.

'No, I mean, I admire it, but *Sweet Sixteen*'s the one that does it for me.'

'Oh,' she said, disappointed, 'I didn't buy that one because it got such bad reviews and now it's completely disappeared. Especially on vinyl.'

'I'll make you a tape,' I told her. 'I consider it my duty to spread the word.'

Richard was ignoring us. Heather noticed this and went over to give him a hug.

'So,' said Heather, 'what are we going to do today?'

'I need to look for a book at the Strand.'

'OK. Let's go there then.'

We went to Broadway and walked up. On the way, Richard tried to make the trip exciting by telling me how much I would like this bookshop.

'It's brilliant, but you can never find anything. It's a bit like Foyles, I suppose.'

I nodded, not really interested. I don't, as a rule, get that excited about bookshops, but I could tell that this was a trendy location. Most of the people scanning the imposing higgledy-piggledy shelves looked like students. I watched a woman with her head down in front of me, fingering along a row of spines. Her brown hair was in a ponytail and she was wearing a cream overcoat. She reminded me of Perdita, except that the last time I had seen her, in her Canadian film, someone had made her dye her hair blonde. She looked up.

'Oh my God,' she said, 'Gerald . . .'

I smiled. 'Perdita.'

She stood back and took a proper look at me before we embraced. I felt so pleased to see her. I pulled her close and held tight. As I released her, I noticed a man anxiously checking me out. He was shorter than Perdita, balding, and wearing a black V-neck jumper.

'Oh,' she said, 'Gerald, this is Eric Webster.'

I remembered Richard and Heather and looked round for

them. They were both observing us keenly. I beckoned them across and introduced them to Eric and Perdita.

'This is uncanny,' said Perdita. 'I was sitting in Eric's apartment last night wishing I had someone from home to play with. Outrageous. Be careful what you wish for.'

'Can we go somewhere and talk?'

Perdita looked at Eric, and then at Richard and Heather. None of them seemed pleased by this suggestion.

'Well, I really do have to look for this book,' said Richard.

'And we have that thing . . .' Eric told Perdita.

'OK,' she said, undaunted, 'what are you doing this evening? Eric has to check out *American History X*, and you could come with us to watch it if you wanted. We're going to the United Artists on Union Square. It's only a block away from here.'

'I know it,' said Heather.

'Let's do that then. We're going to the ten-thirty performance.'

Richard started protesting that he'd heard bad things about the film and wasn't sure he wanted to see it, but Heather said she loved Edward Norton and that seemed to decide things, although I could tell Eric wasn't happy.

'OK,' said Perdita, 'we'll see you there.'

112

Dad stood in his socks and pants, trying to iron a shirt. He'd had an appraisal yesterday, and it had gone badly. A few days earlier he'd made the mistake of telling one of his colleagues that his wife had left him, and the colleague had blabbed to management. Now he'd been told that his work was slipping, and if he didn't rectify things quickly, he'd get an official warning, something he was eager to avoid. When he'd asked them for evidence of his decline, they told him his shirts were creased.

'I've never had ironed shirts,' he told me that morning. 'You know what your mum was like. She hated housework.

They're picking on me for no reason. It's just like what happened to Dustin.'

Dustin was a colleague of my father's who'd been sacked after word got round the office that he was a transvestite.

'Gerald, let me give you some advice. When you grow up and get a job, never tell anybody anything. Human beings are horrible. They're truly, truly disgusting.'

I nodded. 'But it's not really relevant to me, Dad.'

'Why not?'

'I don't think I'll have the same sort of job as you.'

He looked up. 'Oh yeah? What do you think you're going to do?'

'Something creative,' I said.

He laughed. 'I think you'll find creative people are just as horrible. If not worse . . .'

'Yeah, but it's mainly men who are mean to you, right?'

'Why? Are you going to run a nunnery?'

'No, but I hope that I'll mainly be working with women. Like with *All Right Now!*'

'Right, so you won't face all the frustrations that normal people do. Well, that's brilliant, son. I'm really pleased for you.'

'There's no need to be bitter, Dad.'

'Jesus Christ, son, you have no idea how lucky you are having a father like me. Everything nice in your life is thanks to what I've done for you.'

'It was Mum who started me acting,' I said quietly.

'Yeah,' he said, 'but that wouldn't have counted for anything if you didn't have me to drive you to all the places you had to go to.'

'I know, Dad, and I'm grateful.'

He stopped ironing his shirt and stared at me, surprised that I'd dodged out of the argument. At that moment, Shep tooted his horn and I ran out the front door.

Until this moment, I hadn't felt any guilt about using my family as material for *All Right Now!* Nicholas's transubstantiation speech had silenced my conscience, and I did wholeheartedly believe everything he'd told me. But now my father was suffering at work, I worried that when today's episode was broadcast it would makes things worse for him. I understood that Nicholas was right, on some fundamental moral level, when he said that if my parents got cross about the way they were portrayed, it was because they were too ignorant to understand our artistry, but at the same time Nicholas had emphasised that no one could stop me expressing my emotions, and so much of what happened in Episode Two wasn't inspired by my emotions but my family's. I took out my script and looked through it again, thinking for the first time about how it would seem to my parents.

2. INT. UPSTAIRS LANDING. GERALD'S HOUSE. NIGHT.

GERALD stands by the door to his parents' bedroom. The door is open slightly and he is eavesdropping, undetected, on his parents' conversation.

DAD

So that's it then . . .

MUM

Don't make a big thing out of this. You know it's something we both want.

DAD

I never wanted this.

MUM

Oh, stop making it so heavy. I know you feel as relieved as I do.

When the actors had first improvised this dialogue, it had sounded so unlike my parents that I hadn't worried about how it might seem to them. But reading it now I realised it didn't matter. It was obvious the scene was about them, and the fact that they hadn't spoken these exact words wouldn't make any difference. In fact, I was certain that when they did see this scene they'd convince themselves that I really had been eavesdropping on them.

'You OK back there?' Shep asked me.

'Yeah. Just feeling a bit quiet.'

'Nothing wrong with that,' he said, and turned the radio on.

The location manager had found three empty houses in Vauxhall that we were going to use for all the family scenes. Today, the only people needed for the recording were my sister and me, and the two actors playing our parents. I had come to like some of the other adult actors, but had yet to bond with my fictional mother and father. The man playing my father intimidated me, mainly because his face was set in such a way that he always looked angry, irrespective of his actual mood. He was very dark, and turned up unshaven and wearing scruffy clothes that the wardrobe supervisors made him swap for a cheap brown suit and grimy shirts that did nothing to improve his appearance. The actress playing our mother was so timid that she was barely there, although she did have a strong, clear – but very sad – voice. I worried that they were going for a gritty urban realism in our scenes, and felt patronised that this was how they saw my family. I wanted to tell them about all the happy times, but knew Nicholas would only give me some spiel about how those sorts of scenes wouldn't be sufficiently dramatic.

Erica was already at the location, sitting in the lounge with Nicholas and the producers. Immi and Carolyn were drinking coffee.

'Hi Gerald,' said Immi, 'ready for today?'

I nodded. 'Looking forward to it.'

'Good.'

We recorded all our scenes that day, getting through the

action quickly. The episode's opening scene was the most difficult to perform, although I didn't have much to do in it. But my mother and Erica kept muffing their big speeches, and found it hard to keep summoning the required energy for retakes. I sensed that these scenes would prove more powerful than I'd imagined they would be, and worried they would have too strong an impact. We were moving so close to melodrama that the scene was in danger of becoming comic, and at first I couldn't understand why no one was commenting on this unintended effect. Then I realised that so much of this series flouted convention that there was a collective sense of relief at finding a scene with an easily identifiable dramatic intention.

Sharing the small house with a camera crew soon became claustrophobic. The director encouraged us to treat the house as if we were actually living there, and kept criticising me for not looking relaxed enough. I told him that I always felt tense when anyone around me was arguing, and I was behaving exactly as I would if the situation was real. He accepted this, and offered little further direction over the course of the day. We seemed to find our best rhythm mid-afternoon, although I wasn't sure whether this was because we'd started to get things right instinctively or because there was no longer enough time to do things over and over. Today our required hours of schoolwork had been post-poned to when filming had finished, and the tutor could see we were tired and went easy on us. For once, my sister and I had matching moods, and as we waited for the cars to take us home, even managed to have a normal conversation. I asked her how things were going with my mother, and she told me that she didn't think Dennis would be around much longer.

'He's not horrible, is he? To you or Mum?'
She shook her head.
'Do you think Mum might come home again?'
'I don't know.'
She asked about Dad and I told her some funny stories about the past few weeks. I knew if we talked for too long

we would start arguing again, and I was relieved when the cars arrived. I said goodbye to my sister and the tutor, and walked out to where Shep was waiting.

113

I opened this account by stating that I always prefer my friends when they're single. I stand by this, but there are some exceptions. Some people's partners improve their character, and this was definitely the case with Richard and Heather. I was trying to explain my thoughts on this matter to a friend the other evening, and he argued that most nice people had nice partners and bad people bad partners. But in my experience the fact that I like someone is no guarantee that I'll like their boyfriend, girlfriend, husband or wife. I think that a lot of people choose partners to answer some weakness they perceive in their own character. Strong individuals often choose partners who will force them to confront their own phobias and weaknesses. Weak individuals choose partners who strengthen their phobias and help them hide from situations that make them feel afraid or uncomfortable. The best relationships seem to be those where both partners have an equal, and opposite, distribution of virtues and vices. But all too often a person whose character you've whole-heartedly accepted will choose a partner who wants to change everything you like about them. Maybe I just know a lot of strong women and weak men, but most women I know won't put up with men like that, while many of my male friends have only really fallen in love when they've found someone eager to criticise them.

Usually I don't like it when this happens, but Heather seemed to have a positive influence on Richard. Something about Perdita had freaked him out, and as we went for lunch, he started trying to talk me out of our agreed assignation. I asked him how I could do this and he told me simply to not show up. It wasn't as if we were in regular contact; she'd soon forget about it. If Heather hadn't been here, I'd probably have had a serious argument with my friend. Fortunately, she soon helped smooth things over.

'Come on, Richard, can't you see he wants to meet this woman?'

Richard looked pained. 'Who is she to you, anyway?'

'Isn't it obvious?' Heather asked. 'It's someone he's got a crush on who he hasn't had sex with yet.'

I laughed, and said, 'She's a childhood friend.'

'Shit,' said Heather, 'I take it all back. You shouldn't meet up with her.'

'Why not?'

'Kid-sex is dangerous. It could destroy your life.'

I leaned on the table. 'It's not kid-sex. What the hell is kid-sex, anyway? She's someone I knew when I was thirteen. There wasn't any sex involved.'

'Was there any longing involved?'

I blushed. 'Maybe.'

'See,' she said, 'I knew it. These things can cripple you.'

'Surely it's better to confront them, though? What harm can come from me talking to her?'

'OK,' teased Heather, 'we'll let you keep your meeting. As long as you promise me something.'

'What?'

'Tell me you're completely over this girl. Tell me this will be a regular movie-trip and not the start of some mad doomed romance.'

'You two got together like that. Why can't I have some high emotion of my own?'

'We don't have a doomed romance,' Richard protested.

'I know, I didn't mean that, and anyway, I'm only mucking around. I promise you I'm not after anything more from Perdita than a nostalgic conversation.'

'Good,' said Heather, 'because her boyfriend looked pretty possessive.'

'You think that was her boyfriend?'

'Of course. Who else would he be?'

I nodded. She had a point. But I couldn't help feeling disappointed at Perdita's choice of man. Richard paid the check and we left the restaurant.

114

Wendy and Fuckpit broke up during the recording of Episode Three. She told Fuckpit her boyfriend Andrew had agreed to take her back if she ended her other relationship, and she'd been so impressed by his maturity that it made her realise that she was really in love with him, and that her brief fling with Fuckpit had been a case of 'sexual infatuation'. I don't know where she'd heard this phrase. Fuckpit was devastated, and he and I ended up having a fist fight. I'd like to say I was the victim of misdirected anger, but it's not true. I richly deserved the attack, having spent most of the day winding him up. I debated with myself about leaving this event out of my narrative, as it reveals a side of my character that isn't really in evidence through the rest of this account. The thing I find hardest to face when writing about myself is evidence of my past unhappiness. I'm an extremely optimistic person, and as a child one of my favourite coping mechanisms was to believe that every time something bad happened to me it meant something good would soon follow. This made me feel pleased when bad things happened because it meant I'd earned a future happiness. I only ever accounted the bad things, believing there should be more good in my life than bad. And because psychiatrists say that people with a sunnier outlook tend to lead happier lives, I think I managed to con myself into an almost permanent state of well-being. But there was one thing that caused me continued sadness throughout my childhood, a problem that was definitely connected to my relationship with my parents and sister, and became exacerbated during my time in the commune. This was that I tended to needle people when they were depressed, partly I suppose because I didn't know how to deal with their emotion, and partly because my mother had taught me to disdain the morose tendency in my father. I also occasionally found myself exploiting arguments between friends, in order to insert myself between them. This was a problem that became worse in the period after the end of *All Right Now!* but before I met Ellen. I don't know why I did this – it never worked out the way I wanted, and the two friends always got back together and blamed their initial argument, which I had had nothing to do with, on me. I realise now that I started picking on Fuckpit because I was jealous of him for having a relationship with Wendy when I'd failed to get together with Perdita. I don't know what I wanted from him – an admission, maybe, that he wasn't as cool as he pretended to be, that his nickname at school wasn't Fuckpit but Fuckwit, and he'd changed the consonant to make himself sound like a Lothario even though in reality Wendy was the first girl who'd ever been interested in him. But none of this was true. He was successful with girls. He'd done things I couldn't even imagine, things that at that time I never dreamt I'd get to do myself. It was frustration that fuelled the fight. I couldn't take a risk with Perdita so I was taking a risk with Fuckpit, and knew from the moment I started winding him up that there was no going back, that this would end in a fight, and there was every chance that I might be seriously hurt.

It wasn't as bad as it could have been. Fuckpit started the fight as we were walking towards the cars waiting to pick us up, grabbing me around the neck and turning me to face him. I swung back, hitting him beneath the chin. I realised this was dangerous, especially as my blow seemed to have no visible impact on Fuckpit. I thought to myself, here it comes, the broken nose, but he resisted the temptation to punch me in the face, instead hitting me as hard as he could in the stomach. Maybe my glasses put him off. I felt winded and sick; he could have moved in, but instead he hovered around me uncertainly, and I could see he didn't really want to hurt me. He didn't draw back his fist again until he saw Shep, running over from his parked car.

'Hey,' he shouted, 'stop.'

Fuckpit stepped back. I was so pleased to have avoided tears, knowing that if he'd gone for my face I would definitely have started crying. I looked up and wondered if I might even come out of this with some honour. The only person who'd witnessed what had happened was Jane, and she remained standing by the door to one of our fictional houses, uncertain what to do. Now that Shep had intervened, she came across, saying, 'Fuckpit started it.'

'I don't care who started it. I want to know what's wrong. Why are you two fighting?'

I started to say something, but didn't get far before Fuckpit, to my astonishment, burst into tears.

'Come on,' said Shep, taking him into his arms, 'come here.'

'I love her,' sobbed Fuckpit. 'I love her so much.'

'Ah,' sighed Shep, 'so that's why you're upset.' He looked at me. 'But what have you got to do with it?'

'I'm sorry,' I said, 'I've been winding him up.'

'Oh, Gerald,' he told me, 'don't take your troubles out on this boy.'

This comment annoyed me, but I didn't say anything, the four of us walking over to the car. I hated the implication that Fuckpit's misery was more justified than mine. I knew Shep must be someone who'd endured a serious amount of romantic trauma, and it made me furious that he'd identified with Fuckpit when he obviously had much more in common with me. Most of all, I didn't like the intrusion of adult understanding into our childish world.

Fuckpit sat in the passenger seat and I got in the back alongside Jane. I felt grateful to her for saying Fuckpit had started the fight, even though I knew she hadn't done so out of loyalty but because that was what she'd witnessed. Jane had taken longest to come to terms with the process of improvisation used to develop the initial scripts, but now the recording had started she was proving to be one of the programme's best actors. I didn't think Nicholas had given much thought to his decision to have Jane's parents killed in a car crash – it was an easy and inexpensive solution to a potential plot problem – but it lent an unexpected gravity to her performance. The wardrobe supervisor had been happy for most of the girls to exchange clothes freely, but after the first day of recording she'd become strict with Jane, giving her outfits that matched what she normally wore. The clothes looked as if they had been chosen by someone who couldn't decide whether to dress as an adult or a child, which seemed a perfect psychological response to her supposed emotional situation.

Four cast members from *All Right Now!* went on to further acting projects: Perdita, Wendy, Lola (who gained a useful notoriety from the critics who said they never wanted to see her on screen again) and Amy. Perdita was the only one who, after a long television apprenticeship, got as far as film. Wendy played the teenage daughter in *Second Time Around*, a short-lived ITV sitcom, and then after over a decade of occasionally cropping up on adverts, resurfaced a year or so ago in a small role in *Kiss* on Channel Five. Lola specialised in the annoying sister role in five years of children's dramas. Amy made only two small television appearances, one on *The Gentle Touch* and the other on *Juliet Bravo*. I envied my friends their success, especially when my parents implied that Perdita and Wendy had achieved something I'd failed at, but it made me wonder whether they had viewed *All Right Now!* as a stepping-stone, an extended audition. It could be that they simply had more ambition than me, but I felt the fact that they could go on to future acting jobs proved the programme hadn't had the same effect on them as it had on me. Oh, it's true, as I've explained, that I didn't give up on TV for a while either, but I didn't want fame; I wanted to prolong the emotional experience I'd had on *All Right Now!* Any craving for fame I had before taking part in the project disappeared with the first day of recording. My point is, when the talent scouts looked at the programme to pick out performers, they chose the ones who weren't giving their all, and avoided people like me and Jane. Maybe this was sensible, as we could never invest as much as we had in *All Right Now!* in anything else again.

Shep didn't refer directly to our fight, but slowly tried to get Fuckpit and me talking to each other again. When he'd calmed down, Fuckpit apologised to me and I said I was sorry for winding him up. Shep seemed satisfied by this, and allowed us to stop our stilted conversation and listen to the radio instead.

When I got home, my father was sitting on the sofa examining a small white postcard. I looked over his shoulder and saw he was looking at a biro drawing of a hangman's scaffold. The top of the scaffold was elongated to allow room for five stickmen to swing from the gibbet. Each stickman had his initials printed on his fat stomach, except for the last, who had a question mark instead.

'What's this, Dad?'

'The initials belong to people who've recently been sacked from the department.'

'And the question mark?'

'I suppose it's there to indicate that we don't know who's going to go next.'

'Who sent it to you?'

'I've no idea. Someone who thinks I'm going to be sacked, I suppose.'

He stopped staring at the card, and turned to look at me. 'Are you OK?'

'Yeah. Why?'

'You look a bit . . . worked up.'

I was surprised, and pleased, he had noticed. I decided to tell him the truth.

'I got into a fight.'

Although my father was a physically imposing man, and more than prepared to defend himself if the need arose, he always seemed scared of this sort of subject. This made me cross, especially as I imagined at this same moment Fuckpit was probably at home showing off to his father (an assumption that was far from the truth, I later discovered, as Fuckpit didn't dare talk to his father about fighting in case it acted as a trigger), and I wished Dad could do something other than sitting there anxiously waiting to hear what had happened.

'Right,' he said.

'I didn't lose.'

'Right.'

'Don't you want to know who I was fighting?'

'One of your friends, I assume.'

'Well, yeah, but . . .'

'Did Erica see you?'

'No.'

'But she'll hear about it?'

'Probably.'

'And tell your mother.'

'Relax, Dad, it wasn't serious. And everything's sorted now. The other boy started crying.'

My father got up from the settee. I could tell my story was upsetting him. Usually I would have pressed on, but tonight I decided to drop the subject.

'It really wasn't a big deal, Dad.'

'Good,' he said, wandering out to the kitchen. I realised that something I'd said had reminded him of his worries, or maybe he'd started thinking about the stickmen again. Eager to distract him, I asked, 'Is there anything for dinner?'

'Sure,' he replied. 'What do you want?'

115

We arrived at the cinema on time, but Perdita and Eric were already waiting for us. Eric had bought us all tickets. Neither Richard nor Heather had dollars on them, having intended to pay by credit card. Eric pretended he wasn't bothered by this, but I could tell it irritated him. I gave him the cash for my ticket, but didn't have enough for my friends.

'We can go to an ATM afterwards,' said Heather. 'It'll be OK.'

He nodded, and we went into our screen. The auditorium

was half full and we could have sat anywhere, but Eric headed straight for the back row.

'Did you have a good day?' Perdita asked, and I could hear something sad in her voice, as if she was struggling to make this occasion enjoyable enough to compensate for the possible personal cost.

'Yeah,' I said. 'We didn't do much.'

'Do you live in New York?' Perdita asked me.

'Oh no,' I said, 'Heather and Richard do, but I'm just here visiting them.'

'Well,' said Richard, 'I really live in Princeton.'

'Yeah, but Heather's here . . .'

'Some of the time,' she said.

'So how come you have to see this film?' I asked Eric. 'Are you a film reviewer?'

'Film reviewers see films before they come out,' he said. 'I'm a producer.'

'Don't producers see films at premieres?' Heather asked, sticking up for me.

'Sometimes. But I missed this one. Anyway, the big premieres are in LA. Although New York's a much more exciting film city these days.'

None of us knew whether this was true or not, so we didn't comment. Eric was filing right down to the far end of the row. I could tell Richard wanted to complain, but still felt guilty about not bringing money for his ticket. Perdita sat down next to Eric. I sat next to Perdita, and Heather and Richard sat next to me. Stuck for something to say, I told Eric, 'My sister's name is Erica.'

This didn't impress him, and he grunted. I said to Perdita, 'So you live in New York now?'

'Yes. At the moment.'

Eric glared at her. I ignored him. 'You know, it's strange. I keep forgetting that the last time we saw each other in the flesh you were, what, fifteen? I feel like I've seen you a lot more recently than that because I've seen you on TV and in that film. Although I realised the other day that I think I've missed some of your more significant appearances.'

She smiled. 'Oh yeah? Like what?'

'Well, I was out at a club with some friends – a weird club, in an art gallery – and I got talking to the owner, who invited me into his office and was totally fascinated by *All Right Now!* and looked it up on his computer . . .'

'On the imdb?'

'No, no, there's a fan-site, haven't you seen it?'

She shook her head.

'Anyway, it has listings for the other work everyone's done, and he was really impressed that you were in something called *When, Voyager?*'

'Oh, that,' she laughed. 'I make one five-minute appearance in one episode of a crappy British sci-fi programme and it gets me more attention than the rest of my work put together. I had to do an interview about it with some British magazine the other day, and I only did it on the condition that it couldn't go in the "Where Are They Now?" column.'

I knew it wasn't polite to ignore Eric, Richard and Heather, but there were only a few minutes before the screening started, and I worried that Eric would steal Perdita away the moment the film had finished. I'd meant to lead on to say that I was surprised Perdita had recognised me in the bookshop and ask whether I still looked the same as I had when I was fourteen, the last time we'd seen each other, but before I had chance, Perdita asked, 'How's your sister?'

'Good. Really happy at the moment. She mentioned you actually, last time we went for dinner.'

'Yeah? What did she say?'

I looked away. 'It's a bit embarrassing.'

'Oh, go on, Ger, tell me . . .'

'I've just split up with someone . . .'

'Really? I'm sorry to hear that.'

'No, no, it's OK. It wasn't serious.'

'Just an eight-year relationship,' Richard interjected.

'Eight years?' asked Perdita, looking at me as if I'd just told her about some rare tropical disease I'd contracted. 'God. With anyone I know?'

I shook my head. 'Anyway, my sister . . .'

'Yeah . . .'

'Well, this woman I used to go out with, Ellen, she suffered from depression. I did my best by her, but in the end I just don't think she wanted a happy relationship. I was a bit upset that we'd broken up . . .'

'I'm not surprised, after eight years.'

'And a female friend of mine, Sally, was looking after me, and Sally, I and my sister went out for dinner and Erica was explaining to Sally how going out with Ellen had changed me. She said the relationship had made me too serious and that before I met her I was much more hopeful. And when I said that wasn't true, she reminded me about all those silly, metaphysical conversations we used to have. She said we were proper soulmates and I shouldn't have been so shy with you.'

'Shy?' she said. 'Were you shy?'

The lights went down.

'Sh,' said Eric, 'the trailers are starting.'

116

For a while, my fight with Fuckpit had a strange effect on my relationship with Wendy. She'd stopped talking to Fuckpit, so, having not heard his side of the story, convinced herself that I'd been fighting for her honour. The result of this was that for the whole of the recording of Episode Four, Wendy, Perdita and I formed a close trio. This was my happiest time during the whole *All Right Now!* experience. Although the three of us had little to do in this episode, there were several delays and shifts of shooting order that meant most days we had to come to the recording locations and wait around. We didn't mind this, and although we weren't supposed to go off on our own, the production team paid little attention to us, even after our fight. I'd assumed I'd get in trouble with someone about that, but apart from the conversation with Shep, no one said anything. This surprised me at the time, but now I realise everyone was using the production for their

374

own ends, and as long as the scuffle was a one-off, no one wanted to take responsibility for disciplining us.

The atmosphere surrounding the recording was, for the most part, extremely relaxed. We were all working hard, the director was experienced, and the production team seemed pleased to have a programme that was definitely going to be broadcast. Perdita made me tell Wendy about the dream experiments, and for a while the three of us tried to meet in our sleep, although to be honest I didn't want anyone other than Perdita waiting for me in my dreams. One of our tricks was to all think about that red leather armchair and sofa we'd found in the woods during our weekend away, but all that happened was that Wendy had a nightmare about Freddy Krueger and I had one about the insomniac farmer. Wendy seemed a lot more serious since she'd got back together with her original boyfriend, Andrew, and her friendship with Perdita seemed to be deepening into something sincere and lasting. I valued every second I spent with them, but had an unshakeable sense that this situation wouldn't last long. I felt I was being given a glimpse of what my life might be like in a few years' time rather than experiencing something I could sustain now. Everyone had got much more mature since we started recording, and many of our conversations were about how difficult we found it to fit in at school now we had this new special experience of our own.

'Do you think you would watch our programme,' Wendy asked us in the middle of one of our walks, 'if you weren't in it and just read about it in a newspaper?'

'Definitely,' said Perdita.

'Really?'

'Yeah. I'll watch anything on a Sunday. My parents make a sort of buffet dinner and sit watching TV from the middle of the afternoon till the end of *Howard's Way*.'

'Don't you have homework?' Wendy asked.

'Yeah, but I get up early and do it in the morning. Sunday evening's depressing enough without doing schoolwork.'

'Wouldn't you watch our programme, then?' I asked Wendy.

'Well, it's a weird question, isn't it, 'cause it's hard to imagine yourself in that position. I think it depends. If I saw the first episode I'm not sure I'd carry on, because I think it'd seem a bit childish. Or say today's episode, with Lola and all the little kids. But if I saw your episode or my one, then I might watch it.'

I nodded. Wendy stared into space for a moment, then said, 'You two should definitely go out.'

I looked at Perdita. She didn't say anything. But I knew it wasn't my place to answer for her, so I kept quiet, praying she was considering this suggestion.

'OK,' said Wendy, 'something tells me I shouldn't have said that.'

'No,' Perdita replied, 'it's OK. It's not like that between Gerald and me. Is it, Gerald?'

'No,' I agreed sadly, 'we're more like brother and sister.'

'Not your sister,' said Wendy, 'she's a nutcase.'

'Yeah, but she's calming down a bit.'

'Maybe. Lucy's still terrified of her. Is she still going out with Pete?'

'I don't know. I was hoping it would fizzle out.'

'It probably has. Shall we go back?'

'Yeah,' said Perdita enthusiastically, 'I think I've got a scene coming up.'

We nodded, turned round, and started walking back.

117

It wasn't until the film started that I realised Perdita still smelt the same. I don't know what perfume she wears, and I only realised it wasn't her natural odour when she brought a bottle of it with her one day when we had to go on a local news programme. It surprised me that she hadn't changed her perfume in all the years since I'd last seen her. I'd assumed that was one of those preferences that would change as a person got older.

I knew as soon as the film started that I wasn't going to enjoy it, not because of the violence, but because it seemed likely to put us all in a bad mood and prompt arguments after the screening. There's an extremely violent murder towards the beginning of the movie – pumped-up Edward Norton stamping on someone's head – and Eric chose this moment to place his palm on Perdita's nyloned thigh. I knew the gesture was proprietorial, a warning to me, designed to make me feel uncomfortable. I also knew that Perdita didn't want him to do it. But he held his hand there and I couldn't stop myself from sneaking quick glances at it. Richard and Heather had disliked Eric immediately. I didn't think much of him, but I was prepared to suffer his presence for more time with Perdita. Now, though, I wished we'd found a different way of meeting up.

As the film progressed, so did Eric's hand. *Please Perdita*, I cried out inside myself, *cross your legs or take his hand away. You have to do something! He's trying to humiliate the pair of us. He knows I can see and you can't be enjoying having this done in front of your childhood friend while watching this nasty violent movie.* Perdita's skirt wasn't that long, and he was hiking it up now, hand like a horribly active rat between her legs. I could see her stocking-top and the clasp of her suspender belt. Eric noticed me staring and slumped down deeper into his seat. I realised, to my burning shame, that I had an erection and suddenly felt fearful that he was trying to get this response from me. I thought of Richard and Heather and their weird friend Adrian. Was this what was destined to happen to any of my English friends who came to New York, that they'd fall in with these strange deviants?

Eric took off his jacket and arranged it over Perdita's lap. He glared at me as if trying to imply that he was doing this to preserve Perdita's modesty, when I knew he really wanted to draw even more attention to his movements. There was no excuse for his behaviour. Most people gave up doing that sort of thing in their teens. It was so offensive. Why wasn't Perdita telling him to fuck off? I glanced round at Richard and Heather, wondering if they'd noticed what was going on. After Perdita and Eric had rearranged themselves, he started touching her again. I supposed Eric was doing this to prove he didn't care about me, didn't value his girlfriend's friendships and was going to rub my face in their sexual relationship. Perdita turned and muttered something to him. It sounded as though she was angry, but Eric ignored her. I made myself concentrate on the film, watching Fairuza Balk and trying to remember what children's film she'd been in, but couldn't help being distracted by the intensification of Perdita's breathing and the rise of her scent.

He was intent now, and the movements of his fingers definitely had a purpose. Was he doing this to prove something? That the physical was stronger than the psychological? Or that the psychological works in ways we don't want it to? Maybe Perdita's embarrassment, and her desire to resist what Eric was doing, would improve her orgasm? Who knew? Perhaps even the fact that this was happening in front of me would help her along. But I didn't want her to be subservient. I wanted Perdita to be defiant, to get back at him by unzipping my fly and stroking my cock, and then maybe in turn I could put my hand into Heather's knickers and start masturbating her while she wanked Richard. I watched Perdita's hand. It was hovering; she was trying to keep it out of Eric's eager view, and then she placed it surreptitiously on the side of my thigh. I realised as she did this that she was reading my mind, that this was as close as she could get to defying Eric, to letting me know that she understood what I was feeling. I moved my hand so my fingertips were brushing lightly against the side of hers. I closed my eyes, knowing that otherwise the unpleasant images on screen would be burnt onto my brain for ever. This was such a strange situation. I wanted to see it as a gift from God, but the unpleasant truth was that it was a gift from Eric, and it wasn't intended to be something I'd like. Or was it? His motives were unclear. He was in the film industry; maybe that sort of people were so corrupt that they did this every time they went to the cinema, like eating popcorn. Just another way to get slick fingers. I sat there with my eyes closed, wondering how long it would take. I felt as if I could feel Perdita's rising, from her breathing, her scent, and the stretch of her fingertips. He kept touching, and touching, and suddenly she was past the point where she could stop him, even if she wanted to. We were locked into this now. I opened my eyes and saw Perdita take her other hand and wrap it around her mouth. One . . . two . . . three . . . and then the sine wave, resisted so as not to shake the seat too much.

I got up and went to the toilet. As I was urinating, Perdita opened the door behind me.

'Gerald,' she called.

'Perdita,' I said, unable to stop my flow, 'what the fuck are you doing with that guy?'

'I'm sorry, Gerald, I didn't want him to do that.'

'What is this, Perdita? What are you getting me involved in?'

'Nothing,' she said. 'Please, Ger, I'm sorry. He's insanely jealous. He tries to act cool in public but he's been screaming at me all afternoon.'

She came right up behind me and wrapped her arms around my waist. It felt so disorientating still to be pissing while she held me.

'Gerald,' she said.

'Yeah, um, can you just let me . . .'

She chuckled and stood back. I finished off, shook myself, tucked myself back in, did up my fly and turned round. Perdita's cheeks were still pink from what had happened in the auditorium, and I felt a sudden rush of remembered attraction. Seeing her standing in front of me rekindled all my previous frustrated desire and I suddenly wondered what would happen if I tried to have sex with her here. She had changed her clothes since we had met in the bookshop, and was now wearing a long black dress beneath her cream overcoat, grey stockings and black leather shoes with a rounded toe and a raised heel. She'd released her brown hair from her usual ponytail and it hung loose over her shoulders.

She reached into her pocket and took out a folded piece of paper.

'It's my phone number. Please call me at one of the times I've specified there. I *have* to see you, but Eric can't know about it.'

I nodded, and took the piece of paper.

'You go back first,' she told me, 'so he doesn't realise we've been in here together.'

The moment for action had passed. I went back to my seat.

'You OK?' Heather whispered as I sat back down.

'Yeah.'

'Is she OK?'

'I think so.'

I looked back at the screen, realising that I had no hope of enjoying the film – although it was easy to follow, in spite of everything I'd missed – and all I could do was wait until it finished. Perdita retook her seat a few moments later, and Eric put his hand on her thigh once again, reminding me of his claim on her.

When the film was over, we all got up and left the auditorium together. Outside the cinema, Eric clearly couldn't wait to get away, and neither I nor Richard and Heather saw any reason to prolong the evening.

'OK,' I said to them, 'good night then.'

'Nice to meet you,' added Richard, polite as ever.

'Yeah,' said Heather, and we separated.

'What just happened?' Heather asked as we started walking back to her apartment.

'Which bit?' I asked.

'Did he have his hand up her skirt?'

I nodded. 'Working industriously.'

She whistled and turned a full circle, before dropping her shoulders back and saying, 'Oh my God.'

Richard quickly looked at Heather, and I felt sorry for

involving my friends in this. I doubted whether it was anything new for Heather, but I regretted bringing Perdita and Eric into Richard's life.

'Shit,' said Richard suddenly, 'we forgot to pay them for the tickets.'

Heather sighed. 'He looked like he could afford it.'

'It's nice walking here at night, isn't it?' I said, wanting to change the subject. 'I like walking around after midnight in London, but I'd probably only do it in the centre and then everything's always too busy. But it's perfect here. Quiet, but not intimidating.'

Heather shook her head. 'Don't change the subject. What's going on between you and your friend?'

'In what sense?'

'You didn't even try to arrange another meeting. I know you know you've got that guy nervous, and I can't believe you're giving up.'

'Can't believe?'

'Don't believe. What happened in the bathroom? Did you fuck her?'

Richard seemed astonished by this suggestion, and I enjoyed the suspense as they waited for me to answer.

'No,' I replied, 'she gave me her number.'

'I knew it,' said Heather, 'so what happens next?'

I sighed, and told her, 'I have absolutely no idea.'

118

So far I'd managed to ensure my physical contact with Sheryl had been kept to a minimum. When the director asked us to act more intimately with each other, I pointed out that the relationship was supposed to be coming to an end in this series and it would be good if viewers subconsciously picked up on this early on. The director was so pleased that we might be able to get a bit of foreshadowing into the story that he happily allowed me to follow this interpretation. My distaste for doing romantic scenes with Sheryl meant that the eventual break-up in this episode had a subtext Nicholas probably hadn't intended, although it was perfectly in keeping with his plot. It would now seem as if Sheryl was breaking up with me because she knew I didn't really love her, which cast me in a much less embarrassing light. I wondered whether the fact that I was really interested in Perdita would be obvious to the audience before the events of Episode Six. I acted in a very flat manner, trying not to give anything away, but was haunted by the director's insistence that the camera would pick up exactly what I was thinking. This seemed to be his only piece of advice, although he reformulated it in new ways every day. Today's variation was an instruction to think of the camera as a person watching everything we did with full knowledge of exactly what lay inside our hearts.

Sheryl and I had to spend a lot of time together during the week we recorded this episode. If I'd known how she felt about me, I might have guessed that Sheryl would choose this moment to ask me out. She knew I had feelings for Perdita, and maybe she'd worked out that Perdita didn't have the same interest in me. But after this episode we would see little of each other, and I think she worried that when I started doing romantic scenes with Perdita, she might change her mind about me. We were sitting together sharing a can of Coke when she said, 'Gerald . . . you remember what I said when Nicholas showed us this script?'

'What? About it not being realistic?'

She nodded. 'Yeah. I would never dump you.'

'I don't think it matters. It works out well in story terms.'

'No, that's not what I mean.' She swallowed. 'I'm saying you could trust me, if you wanted to give it a try.'

'Oh . . .'

She turned and looked at me, crestfallen. 'You're not interested then?'

'I'm sorry,' I said, and then I remembered a line I'd heard on a soap opera a few nights before. 'I'm not ready. I was in a relationship that didn't work out, and I'm not over it yet.'

This was a total lie – I'd never been out with anyone – but

it seemed to work. Sheryl looked surprised, but impressed, and no longer quite so sad. I had saved her from any potential embarrassment, although I suddenly realised that this would get back to Perdita. But who knew, maybe it would intrigue her, turn me into a proposition in a way I hadn't been before.

'So,' she said, 'should I go away now?'

'Of course not,' I laughed, and pulled her close to me, trying to hide the fact that that was exactly what I wanted her to do.

119

It took over a week to arrange my meeting with Perdita. I called her the morning after she gave me her number and waited for her to ring back; when she eventually did she told me that Eric would be busy the following Monday and asked whether it would be possible to meet then. I told her that was fine, which got me into trouble with Richard, who hadn't intended to stay in New York this long and now needed to go back and pick up some stuff from Princeton.

'Where are you meeting her?' Heather asked me on Sunday afternoon.

'I don't know. She's going to get back to me about that, but she sounds paranoid about being seen anywhere with me.'

'You could have the apartment for an hour or two, if you wanted.'

'Really?' I asked. 'That would be perfect.'

'What time will she be coming?'

'In the afternoon. Around two, I think.'

'OK.'

When I woke up the following morning Richard had long since left, but Heather was still sleeping on the futon opposite me. She'd tossed the duvet off her shoulder and I could see her *Little Mermaid* tattoo. As if she could tell I was staring at her, Heather opened her eyes and looked back at me.

'How old were you when you had that done?' I asked her.

'How old was I? Fifteen, I think. I was the most academically-minded little kid that ever lived. My parents aren't like that, and they were getting worried about me, afraid I'd burn out I suppose, so one summer they – literally – forced me to go to this kinda arty Summer Camp, just to get me to be more sociable, and I really, really didn't want to go, but when I got there I had such a good time. It was a total revelation, there were girls who introduced me to all these things I'd missed out on ... wonderful things like music and drugs and how to get boys interested in you. I assumed I'd never see any of them again, but some of the girls lived in Philadelphia, which is where I'm from, and we had these little reunions every now and again. And one time they all wanted to go to see *The Little Mermaid*, and I was really against it, it seemed so dumb going to watch a Disney cartoon. Now I suppose a lot of adults go, but back then nobody who wasn't a kid went to see children's films. But they kept insisting and insisting, and in the end I agreed to go, more because I wanted to see my new friends than anything else, and then the film ... Have you seen it?'

I nodded.

'And you like it?'

'Yeah.'

'Then you'll know what I mean. It's so enjoyable, and I had such a fantastic time, and the film came to symbolise something for me. Not to take myself so seriously, I guess. And a few months later I got the tattoo, to remind me that there's more to life than studying. Can you see me?'

I giggled. 'Not that well. I can see your tattoo, but the rest of you's a bit blurry.'

Heather and I had had a running joke about our contact lenses, mainly to annoy Richard, who claimed he would never give up his glasses. We'd spent ages in the bathroom, comparing solutions and plastic pots, and I had to admit that the American stuff was much better than mine.

I got off the sofa and looked round for my suitcase. Silas was sitting in it, resting his hairy bum on my clean clothes.

'Silas,' I snapped, annoyed.

'What's he done?' Heather asked.

'He's sitting in my suitcase. Fuck. I wanted to look smart today.'

'Shit,' said Heather, 'I'm sorry. I've got one of those sticky brushes to get rid of the hair.'

Silas sat there, tongue lolling. I clapped my hands together and tried to get him out of my case. Heather whistled and he jumped out and ran to her.

120

I'm not always the most sensitive of individuals. I can be confused by other people's emotion, and often laugh at inappropriate things. During the last week of recording, I was especially bad. I think it was because I was the only one who thought we'd get a second series. It was also because my story was only just beginning. Pete and Erica's relationship had fizzled out; Fuckpit seemed to have got over Wendy but the two of them were still barely speaking; Sheryl had asked me out and been turned down, but I had yet to force a conclusion to my flirtation with Perdita. Positive thinking: I had a vision of how this might all play out. The final episode, five more days of recording, ending with the conclusion I'd wanted all along: PERDITA AND GERALD KISS. Credits. The kiss does something to Perdita, all her doubts disappear, and we start going out. Series One goes out on TV and Series Two gets commissioned. We reassemble and this time the improvisations are pure joy. I've earned a respected position among the group; Perdita, Wendy and I are the cool kids, and in the second series our scenes are all light-hearted (apart from Wendy's pregnancy moments) and we do all these improvisations about the fun nights we've been having together. Mum and Dad are so proud of what their children have done that they decide to forget their differences and move back in together. Perdita and I alternate school with *All Right Now!*, which continues for another six series and then spins off into a major British movie. We get engaged, then married, have a kid, whom we love, and go on to have incredibly successful film careers, mainly working independently of each other, although we do occasionally do a project together, just for old time's sake.

It was this daydream that stopped me appreciating the other children's misery. Everyone else seemed to be in tears the whole time. Even Nicholas and the production team were upset, and I overheard Immi crying in the toilet. My response was to giggle and crack jokes constantly, prompting Fuckpit to snap, 'Fuck off, Gerald, you epileptic.' I don't think I appreciated just how unpleasant the others found their home life. Not that mine was easy. Dad might have calmed down a bit, but it was increasingly obvious that he was going to lose his job, and although at the time I didn't know it, this was the week my father committed his first act of fraud: forging my mother's signature on an application for an increased overdraft on their joint account, a relatively minor offence that would nevertheless begin the run of increasingly criminal behaviour that would eventually result in arrest and a short prison sentence. *All Right Now!* was important to me, but in a way I was looking forward to a break, being more used to reflecting on life than actually experiencing it. In fact, it's only really now that I truly understand just how desperate the other children felt about losing this outlet, because it's exactly how I feel about writing this account. I'm so scared about how bereft I'll be when I finally finish it. I've been going a bit crazy over the last few nights. Sophie's gone away and I've taken to sleeping with my manuscript. It's grown quite big now (although I use a large font and no doubt the book will shrink when it's put into proper print) and is heavy enough to hold in my arms. It sounds silly but it does affect my dreams, giving my subconscious permission to play with my past. Things have changed between Sophie and me since I started writing, and no doubt they'll change again when I finish. Maybe that's what I'm afraid of. I'm trying to package this stuff up, but some memories refuse to go quietly.

121

Heather left the apartment half an hour before Perdita was due to arrive. We'd had an enjoyable morning together and I was pleased Richard had found a girlfriend who was such good company. I couldn't understand why he'd been so keen to emphasise their sexual compatibility, and to suggest that this compensated for some defects in her character, because as far as I was concerned she seemed a great person all round. His behaviour reminded me of the nervous way my father sometimes introduced his girlfriends, as if he'd judged them through our eyes for us before giving us chance to make up our own minds.

She'd taken Silas with her, so I felt happy sitting in the apartment listening to Heather's CDs and waiting for my friend. I was running low on dollars and couldn't stay here much longer, but for the moment I was relaxed and enjoying my adventure. I hadn't been on holiday for ages, and was amazed at how good it felt to be away from my housemates. I had been spending so much time with them that I had developed a siege mentality, wondering whether I could cope with being away from them. But now I was here, almost alone, I realised just how oppressive their company had become. Running into Perdita again had made me reflect on the past few years, and I realised that what my sister had said to me in the Italian restaurant made more sense than I'd been prepared to admit, and my relationship with Ellen really had pulled me into a dark place. I know the first few post-university years are hard for everyone, but my father's arrest, and Ellen's failure to get into drama school and the subsequent deterioration of our relationship, had made me so desperate for a way out that I had accepted situations that

I should never have allowed myself to get into. Moving in with Stan wasn't really the problem – he was a good, loyal, and honest friend, and he had rescued me at a difficult time – but there was no real reason why I was working at a language school. It was marginally better than a call-centre, as at least the students stopped me from getting too depressed, but it was a stop-gap job I'd stayed in for far too long. While I'd been going out with Ellen I'd been fairly busy, and I stayed with her at her parents' house so often that I hardly thought about my room in our shared house. It had become a dumping-ground and occasional refuge. But I didn't live there in quite the same way the others did. They had a camaraderie I wasn't really part of, as I hadn't watched TV with them that much. Now Sally was gone, I supposed I could try to make myself more popular, but it made more sense to find a way of getting out of the house. Just thinking about the secret room, Stan's disappearance and the problems with the electricity exhausted me, as did the impossibility of ever having a private moment. Maybe my housemates' new relationships would bring our arrangement to a natural end. But what next? I had no plans for the future. Moving into a flat with Stan would be OK, but if the group split up I had no doubt he'd rather stay with Mickey and Tom than move in with me. What I really needed was someone to lend me enough money to make a fresh start. It didn't matter whether it was a bank, my parents or a friend. Of course, these weren't real options, but if I carried on living the way I was at present, I would never get the opportunity to discover what I really wanted to do with my life.

Perdita was early. I buzzed her in, then waited while she found the apartment. I stooped and looked at her through the peep-hole. Her hair was down and she was flicking the ends over her shoulders. I opened the door and we embraced. I was struck by how familiar her body felt, even though I had only hugged her once or twice before.

'Oh Gerald,' she said, 'I'm so glad we found each other again.'

'Me too. Come inside.'

She walked into the apartment. It smelt of dog. I wondered if Perdita had noticed, but didn't say anything, not wanting to bring it to her attention. Perdita went to the window, looked down into the street, then came back and sat down opposite me.

'You don't think he's following you, do you?'

'Not him. But it wouldn't surprise me if he'd paid someone else to. He probably doesn't have the money these days, although he could have a friend who's doing him a favour.'

I went across to Heather's desk and picked up a twenty-dollar bill. I offered it to Perdita.

'What's that for?'

'Richard had an attack of guilt about Eric paying for the cinema tickets.'

'Oh,' she said, 'I don't think he noticed you didn't pay him back, he was so pissed off. I'm really sorry about that, by the way.'

'It's OK. If you're OK.'

She nodded. 'I was more embarrassed than anything.'

'So what's going on?'

She looked away. 'Do you mind if we don't talk about that for a moment?'

'Of course not. Would you like a drink?'

'I'm OK. Are you still in contact with anyone from *All Right Now!*?'

'No. You?'

'I used to see Wendy, every now and again. But not for the last few years . . .'

I nodded. 'Are you acting at the moment?'

'Oh God,' she said, 'I might as well tell you. This is so tragic. Don't hate me.'

'I could never hate you, Perdita.'

'Eric's a producer. He's also a screenwriter, of a sort. He writes these low-budget, straight-to-video, softcore thrillers. Softer than softcore. I mean, they're not pornography, they're erotic thrillers. You know what I mean.'

I nodded.

'Well, he's written a couple that got him a bit of attention. There's a lot of this stuff now, and there are people out there, film students and writers for magazines like *Film Comment* or *Guerrilla Filmmaker* who study these films and look for people who are operating in the genre who do sophisticated stuff with the format. Have you heard of a director called Raul Ruiz?'

I shook my head.

'Well, he's got one called *Shattered Image* that we went to see a premiere of, and it's got photography by Robby Muller and a really intriguing plot, and basically, some people in the mainstream media started writing about this film and also other people like Gregory Hippolyte, and Eric is always mentioned in the same group, mainly for this film he co-wrote called *Candy Girl*. It even ended up getting shown at Sundance, and Mike Figgis sent him a postcard saying how much he liked it.'

'OK,' I said, 'so he's talented.'

'He's a fuckup. But when I met Eric I was still working. This was two years ago. As you probably already guessed, things didn't happen for me. In spite of what Eric told you the other night, New York isn't really a film town, and when I moved here from LA I was really kissing goodbye to my film career.' She stopped. 'Fuck it. Why can't I tell you the truth? It's because I'm so desperate to impress you.'

Perdita looked down at her hands. She was wearing a white suit jacket over a dark blue vest and a pair of dark jeans. She seemed so sad, and I wished I knew how to help.

'OK,' she said, 'the truth. I never really cut it, even as an English actor. I didn't have the training, because I'd always get enough work not to take time out actually to study acting. Oh, I could've gone to classes, but I'm lazy and as long as I could get by without them I was happy not to bother. But I did seem to have a career, of sorts, and one job usually led to another. My British TV work, such as it was, led to a Canadian film . . .'

'I saw it.'

'Did you?' she asked, surprised, and then remembered. 'Oh yeah, you mentioned it the other night. Well, one of the actresses I worked with on that film had a part in a proper Hollywood movie and I moved out there with her. We shared the same agent and she got me a bit of work, but it was never enough and I decided to move back to New York before I got myself into a really horrible situation. I was always intending to go back to England eventually, but I thought I'd just stay here until my money ran out, give myself time to mellow out. But acting, you know, is like a terrible addiction . . .'

I nodded.

'It's like gambling or something, and it's so hard to stop auditioning, especially as the people I was staying with in New York were also actresses. And, anyway, that's how I ended up appearing in this off-off Broadway play. It was this ridiculous psychosexual drama with lots of nudity, and one night Eric, who was a friend of the producers, came to see it. The producers were planning to take him out for dinner afterwards, hoping that he might option it. He asked them if they could get me to come to dinner. Of course I agreed and we went to this restaurant together. He made me sit next to him and turned on the charm . . . I know it seems unlikely given the way he's behaved in front of you, but he can be extremely seductive. All actors are insecure, and his non-stop flattery worked on me. I believed what he was saying because he thought the play was shit, and there was no way I could argue with that assessment, but that I had real talent. The producers were furious that I was getting all the attention, but Eric didn't give a shit. He made me leave with him and left the producers to pay the bill. I have to tell you that at this point I hadn't seen any of his films, and just knew that he was supposed to be a big shot. So he took me back to his apartment, and made me watch three of his films back to back. By the time the last one had finished it was four in the morning and I was really angry. He asked me what I thought so I told him the truth. The films were terrible . . . horrible misogynistic garbage, wish fulfilment, male fantasies, blah, blah, blah.

'And at first he was so shocked he couldn't reply. Then, after a while, he said, "You know what, you're right. But I'm going to change. I'll carry on writing and producing these films for the money, but at the same time I'm going to write a script for you, about you. You'll be my muse, and inspire me to write something wonderful. Only in order to do this, I need to know everything about you. And I mean everything. I need to know about your past, your psychology, your deepest secrets. But I also need to know how you would react in certain situations, situations you might feel uncomfortable in." '

'Perdita, what happened the other night, in the cinema, was that part of this?'

She nodded, and now the tears came. I was ready to go across and hug her, but sensed her story wasn't quite over.

'He's been doing things like that for the last two years. At first it was fun. I knew the script was going to be explicit, but in spite of what I said when I watched his videos, it was obvious he did have talent, and loads of actors have become famous in that way. Like, say, Nicholas Roeg and Theresa Russell. Except it wasn't about fame, it was about . . .'

'*All Right Now!*'

She looked up, shocked. 'Yes. So you do understand?'

'Of course. I've felt hollow ever since it finished.'

'Me too. And the reason I was never much of an actress was that it was never really acting for acting's sake that interested me. Playing someone else just couldn't have the emotional effect on me that playing myself did.'

'But at the time . . .'

'I know, I downplayed everything. And, understandably, that made you cross. But I didn't really appreciate how important the experience was going to be. You can only ever imagine a few steps ahead, right? It's not until later that you understand the route your life has taken.'

'That's exactly how I feel.'

'I can't get away from him, Gerald. I've given him

everything – he knows all about me. That's why he got so jealous when we met in the Strand. He made me get my mum to send me my teenage diaries and hand them over to him. He's filled hours and hours of videotape . . . he's got pictures . . . I can't do anything without him trying to record it in some way.'

'And what about the script? You said it's explicit?'

'Well,' she said, 'I imagine it's explicit.'

'You haven't read it?'

'He won't let me. Not until it's finished. But I don't think it'll ever be finished. It's just his way of imprisoning me.'

I went across then, holding Perdita while she wept. And after the tears we talked again. I was calm but insistent about my plan, and slowly she came round to it. I was careful and exact about what I was offering, having realised that Perdita didn't need me as a boyfriend but as someone to provide the service for her that Sally had provided for me. I had felt guilt about performing this role in the past, and even now Sally's words to me after my flirtation with Darla – 'You've got a Marilyn complex, Gerald. There's no point denying it. You like rescuing women. You think you can heal them' – were sounding again in my head, but I believed that this time I could help someone in a happy, healthy way. And more importantly, this would resolve my relationship with the first woman I'd ever been in love with, and free myself for the future. I don't believe in fate – life's too random – but I do believe that the best opportunities often arrive by accident, and living life well involves knowing how to exploit them.

122

On the last day of recording, I spent an hour in the bathroom cleaning my teeth before Shep arrived. Earlier in the week Perdita had made a gift to me of a small pot of Wild Cherry lip balm, and I now carried this in my pocket at all times. We had taken to massaging each other's shoulders during breaks in recording, and this morning we were especially gentle with each other, both feeling nervous about what would happen this afternoon.

It had been a while since we'd talked about the kiss. I knew she was nervous, but assumed that she'd had boy-friends before and at least knew how to do it. I was petrified I'd bite off her lip, or clash teeth, or reveal myself as ridiculously inexperienced. There was no one I could talk to about these fears, and I'd decided that I would just follow Perdita's lead and try not to do anything stupid.

Five of us were required for today's scenes: me, Perdita, Wendy, Lucy and Erica. The absence of Pete and Fuckpit stopped Wendy and Erica getting emotional, and there was a last-day-of-term feeling to these final hours of recording. We weren't having a wrap party, but there had been a small celebration the night before, and although we kids had been sent home early, the adults had drunk until daybreak and were all behaving sluggishly this morning.

Wendy, Lucy and Erica finished their scenes by lunchtime, and were allowed to go home. Perdita and I then had our three hours of teaching. The tutor, clearly bored, set us what she called a final exam, a three-hour practical criticism essay on 'La Belle Dame Sans Merci', which was far beyond either Perdita's or my ability to decode. (I mistranslated the last part of the title as 'without thanks', an error that led me into a complete misunderstanding of the poem.) After setting us this task, the tutor headed for the exit, saying she'd return to collect our papers at the end of the session.

'Will you mark them?' I asked her.

'Of course,' she said. 'I'll bring you the results this afternoon.'

'But it's not important?' I asked.

'Who knows what's important? Try your best, Gerald, you might find you enjoy it.'

She left us alone. I didn't understand what the tutor had been implying, but she made me want at least to have a try at the exercise. The two of us worked in silence for the first

394

half-hour, then, relieved to have something down on paper, started talking.

'Are they having sex?'

'What?' I asked.

'Here ... *She look'd at me as she did love, and made sweet moan.* That's them having sex, isn't it?'

'And she's ungrateful?'

'Or he is, probably.' She chewed the cap of her pen. 'I wish the day wasn't broken up like this. I'm really keen for it all to be over.'

I didn't reply.

'I don't mean that in a bad way. I just hate the way everything's so dragged out. I haven't been able to get sad like everybody else and now they're all acting like the programme's already finished when we've still got something substantial left to do.'

'Oh,' I said, 'Perdita, I forgot, I have got something important to tell you. You know you said that *Around the World in a Day* was influenced by the Beatles?'

'Yeah.'

'Well, it wasn't. I read an interview where Prince states categorically that the influence wasn't the Beatles.'

'Really?'

I nodded. 'Although I admit it doesn't sound like that.'

Even the producers had gone home when we came to record our final scene. Nicholas and the director were sitting in chairs watching us, and the director couldn't resist giving us a final instruction.

'OK,' he said, 'now we still don't know if we're getting a second series, and we don't want to disappoint people, so we have to invest this scene, and especially this kiss, with an incredible emotional significance. We have to make the viewer think that everything has been leading up to this moment. It has to seem like the best possible conclusion. Perdita, how do you feel about Gerald?'

'He's my best friend. He's like a brother to me.'

'That's not enough. This scene has to be pure focused

desire, from the pair of you. It has to be about love, lust, a whole future contained in this one brief intimate moment. Understand?'

Embarrassed, we both nodded.

'Good. Let's do it.'

```
42. INT. PERDITA's HOUSE. DAY.
GERALD and PERDITA sit facing each other.


                    PERDITA
I couldn't say anything before.


                    GERALD
Because of Sheryl?


                    PERDITA
Because of me. I wasn't ready.


                    GERALD
And now?


PERDITA and GERALD kiss.
```

123

Perdita handed Richard a lamp in the shape of an orange plastic bear.

'Are you sure you don't mind storing stuff for me?'

He shook his head. 'Although Heather's place is quite small, so I'll probably have to take some things back to Princeton. You can get in touch with me via Gerald when you want it sent back to England.'

Perdita started to thank him, then let out a small shriek. Oh God. I turned round and there he was, standing in the doorway. We'd planned this morning for days, and Perdita had insisted that this was the one time when Eric would be occupied elsewhere. He had made a habit of pretending to

396

go out and then reappearing unexpectedly recently, but this was a meeting Perdita had double-checked was definitely happening, with high-profile people who could give Eric lots of money. There was no way he'd miss a meeting like that.

Unless he knew his girlfriend was going to leave him.

'There's no way . . .' said Perdita. 'No way you could know.'

He laughed. 'You're not really surprised, are you?'

I didn't like being part of this. If I had had any doubt that my friend wanted out of this relationship, I would have left Perdita and Eric to their scene. But she reached for my hand, and I realised she was sincere. Now all I needed to know was whether Eric was serious about stopping her. I could have asked him outright, but I sensed it might be easier to sidle our way out of here. So I said, 'This is just acting for you, isn't it, Eric?'

He tilted his head, amused. 'Explain.'

'A conclusion to your screenplay. A bit of role-playing. You don't really want to keep Perdita against her will.'

'I'm not keeping her against her will. She's always been free to leave at any time.'

'So let us go.'

He rubbed his nose. 'OK. Maybe you're right. I'm playing a role. But it's not for my benefit. Perdita wants to stay. She just needs an excuse.'

She dropped her bags. 'You're insane. I'm desperate to get away from you.'

'Perdita, I know it's been hard. But this isn't the time to give up.'

'Give up on what?'

'On me. On you. On your acting career. You may think you want to go now, but the moment you walk out you'll regret it.'

'I don't care, Eric.'

'If you leave, I won't cast you. You won't even get to read the script. You'll see the film in the theatre and realise you kissed your one real chance at fame goodbye.'

'I'm exhausted,' she protested. 'There's nothing left of me.'

'That's how you oughta feel. I made you give me everything. Don't you want to see why?'

Richard pushed past Eric. 'She's coming with us. So you might as well say goodbye.'

'OK,' he said, 'if that's what she wants. But can you at least give us a moment in private?'

I looked at Perdita. She nodded.

'All right. We'll be in the lobby.'

Richard and I collected up Perdita's stuff and left the apartment. We walked down the corridor to the lift and got in together.

'Do you think he'll persuade her to stay?'

I shook my head. 'She's serious about this.'

'Good job we came early.'

'Yeah.'

The lift reached the lobby and we walked out. Although Perdita had taken trouble to introduce us to the doorman, he still looked at us suspiciously as we stood there holding her belongings.

'She moving out?'

'Going back to England.'

'Are you her relations?'

'Just friends.'

'Friends of Eric too?'

'Not really.'

He nodded, showing he understood.

When Perdita came down to the lobby she looked shaken but carried on as if nothing of import had occurred after we left them alone. I thought of Ellen, and the dark glasses she'd hidden behind when she and her father had come round to return my stuff, and I felt an increased respect for Perdita. Leaving Eric had to be more traumatic than leaving me, but she wasn't making a big deal out of it.

'Joe,' she said to the doorman, 'I'm giving you back my key.'

'OK, Ms Dawkins. Good luck back in England.'

Perdita shot a glance at me, and I shrugged apologetically. She came over to us and we left the building.

'He started the conversation.'

'It's OK, Gerald. I'm just glad to be out of there.'

We caught a cab back to Heather's apartment. Heather asked us if we wanted to eat before we set off.

'No,' said Perdita, 'we need something to do at the airport.'

Heather nodded. 'Then I guess that's it. It was good to meet you, Gerald.'

I kissed her cheek. 'First time I've envied Richard.'

She smiled. Richard gave me a hug. 'E-mail me when you get back.'

'Will do,' I promised.

'They're nice, your friends,' Perdita told me in the cab.

'Yeah,' I said, 'I've known Richard for ages. Well, not as long as I've known you.'

She laughed. 'I always thought I'd die of shame if I ran into you again.'

'Why?'

'Well, I wasn't exactly the most mature of adolescents.'

'Oh come on,' I said, 'neither was I. I'm not even the most mature of adults.'

She stroked my face. 'Thanks for rescuing me, Gerald.'

PART VIII

★

124

My father knew how excited I was. I'd spent all week flipping open the *TV Times* and checking the entry was still there. We had this habit in our house of running lines through anything we weren't going to watch and circling the few important programmes we didn't want to miss, and I had drawn a large red circle around *All Right Now!* as soon as the issue arrived. When the *Sunday Times* landed on the doormat this morning, I'd eagerly turned to the TV listings and found the programme was a 'Pick of the Day'. Although we'd appeared as a group on a few chat shows and had been interviewed by several newspapers and magazines, the last couple of weeks had been quiet, and my only continued connection with the programme was the occasional phone call to Perdita. There hadn't even been an advance screening for the cast and crew, and although we'd been promised tapes of the programme they'd yet to appear. But now at last the day had arrived.

Dad seemed to enjoy my excitement. He had started going to Evensong on Sundays, but today he stayed home. We had our lunch late and played poker while we waited for the programme.

We sat down on the settee with sandwiches as the adverts ended and a female voice announced the start of 'an exciting new programme based on the real-life experiences of a group of teenage children'. The first shock was the credits, an unpleasant arrangement of geometric electric blue and yellow, with our faces appearing one by one in the centre of the screen before being splashed by a messy blob of colour. The theme tune had synthesizers playing along with a brassy female vocal ('*All Right Now! All Right Now! Things were tough, but they're All Right Now! Times were rough, but they're All Right Now!*'). None of this seemed to bear any relation to the programme we'd made, and I gave my father a worried look, wondering what he was thinking. The credits ended and Amy and Fuckpit appeared on screen, standing in their care-home with Alan. It looked dingier than it had when we'd been filming and I remembered the director telling Nicholas that using less light signified social realism. At the time this sounded sensible, but coming after the garish opening graphics the effect was disorientating.

'There's Erica,' said my father as my sister appeared on screen. 'My God, she looks so normal.'

I laughed. 'You'll be surprised. She's much more mature in this.'

He looked sad. I realised he was thinking about not getting to see his daughter that often any more. For the first few weeks after Mum left, he was too consumed by self-pity to think about losing contact with one of his children. Then he was worried about his job, a concern that still troubled him. But now he had started to think about his future, and found new miseries. Personally, although I had grown closer to Erica during the recording, she was still too temperamental to be that good company, and I was relieved not to be seeing her every day. We would, in time, grow to be good friends, but for the moment I was still struck by how strange it was that a sibling is a person who's shared the most similar life and experiences to you, and yet is also the most difficult person to get on with.

Dad didn't say anything when I came on screen and from then on the two of us watched the first half of the programme in silence. As soon as the ad break started, the telephone rang. Dad got up and went to answer it. I lowered the volume so I could listen to the conversation.

'Yeah. She does, yeah. No . . . I agree. Yeah, it's good. Really? Yeah, yeah. OK. Sure. Bye.'

He came back into the lounge. 'That was your mother. She wants to come round next week so we can all watch the programme together.'

'Does she like it?'

'She thinks it's fantastic. Especially Erica.'

I wasn't offended by this, knowing that they were only impressed because they had lower expectations of her. Dad sat back down on the settee and the second half started.

'So what did your parents think of it?'

I could hear Perdita moving around on her bed. Her voice came louder down the line when she answered.

'Well, my Mum didn't think it was very well written . . .'

'But it's improvised.'

'I know, but she said she thought Nicholas could've done more with the material. My dad thought you were good.'

'Really? My dad said you were pretty.'

'Did he?' she replied, startled. 'This is so weird, isn't it?'

'I know. School is what I'm worried about,' I sighed. 'School is going to be hell.'

125

My house was empty when I returned. It was eight in the morning, so I expected the others to be up and preparing for school, but there was no one in the kitchen, shower room, or, I soon discovered, bedrooms. Unsettled, I went to my room and checked the answerphone and my e-mail. The answerphone had clearly been wiped several times while I'd been away, and there were only two messages left on it: one from Sally, and another from Sophie, asking why I hadn't responded to any of her earlier messages. This intrigued me, but it was too early to call her back. I'd been checking my e-mail on Richard's lap-top in America, so there was only one new message, which was from the language school asking if I'd be coming in today. I replied that I wouldn't, and went to bed.

I had never flown with anyone before, and I was amazed how much more pleasant it made the experience. Nothing seemed as bad with someone beside you, especially someone

I was so eager to talk to. I could cope with the delays, the turbulence, the crap food and worse movies, and didn't even bother trying to sleep. Midway through the flight, Perdita and I got up and went to stand near one of the exits so our conversation wouldn't disturb the snoozing passengers.

I suppose some of you are going to be upset that there isn't a swooningly romantic conclusion to my relationship with Perdita, but much as I love my friend (and we're still in regular contact), I just couldn't risk having sex with her. I knew this relationship was going to be important to me, and having just found Perdita, it was too early to lose her. Although we never discussed it, I assume she felt the same way. Maybe it's a conversation we'll have to have when she reads this book. I did consider writing a sex scene, consummating our love through an act of imagination, but it seemed too disrespectful. Look, I know people go to bed together all the time and still remain friends and any relationship can be salvaged if both parties are prepared to make the effort – and I realise that this is the second sexual relationship I've avoided in the course of this account – but there is definitely something inside me that takes over when it comes to this sort of thing. Maybe it's cowardice. I don't know.

Actually, it was probably the timing. You remember how earlier I talked about the Schrodinger's cat moments that precede most relationships? Well, I think the major factor in whether a relationship is going to work out is how and why it starts. If Perdita and I had got together, the whole relationship would have been underscored by our respective situations at that particular moment. I had just rescued Perdita; she was grateful to me. But her desire would have been predicated on the notion that she was exchanging a destructive relationship for a healthy one. And in spite of Sally's insistence that I had a Marilyn complex, I knew I'd soon get bored of playing Perdita's saviour.

But we did have a wonderful night together. The length of the flight allowed us to go through everything that had happened to either of us since *All Right Now!* Perdita told me about her parents, her boyfriends, her perfect moments. And I matched her stories with a verbal version of this autobiography. I told her how I understood what she'd been doing with Eric, and how it wasn't her desire to use art to make her life mean something that was wrong, but the way Eric had exploited this urge. 'Why is it so hard,' she asked me, 'just to live?' 'I don't know,' I replied, 'but I think Nicholas awakened a desire in us that needs to be fulfilled.' 'How are you going to do it?' she asked me. 'I don't know,' I replied, 'but I've been thinking about writing a book. That way it's all me, unfiltered by anyone else's perception or needs.' She nodded. 'That sounds like a good idea.'

When we reached Heathrow, we went to the luggage carousel together then through customs and out to the tube. Perdita was going back to her parents' house so she changed trains at Waterloo. We kissed, exchanged numbers and agreed to meet up soon.

I awoke at five o'clock when I heard the downstairs door slam. I dressed and went to see who it was.

'Stan. Where is everybody?'

'With their respective boyfriends and girlfriends. They all moved out when Mickey got electrocuted.'

'What?'

He put his bag down and rubbed his eyes. 'It was a loose wire in the tumbler switch in the kitchen.'

I felt a flash of guilt. Hadn't the electrician said something to me about tumbler switches?

'Is he OK?'

'He is now. In fact, it's all worked out brilliantly. Come with me.'

I followed him upstairs to his bedroom. He stepped over the junk on his floor and picked up an envelope from his desk. Then he came back across and handed it to me. The envelope was stuffed with fifty-pound notes.

'It's a thousand pounds. Lorraine wanted us to split your share between us but I told her it wasn't fair.'

'This is all my share? The whole lot?'

He nodded.

I was confused. 'My share of what?'

'Do you mind if we go into the kitchen and have a coffee? I'm exhausted.'

'Is it safe?'

'Seems to be.'

We went along the landing to the kitchen. I sat at the dirty table while Stan made himself a coffee. He asked me if I wanted one but I shook my head and took a Coke from the fridge instead.

'So?' I prompted.

'Mickey was fine, but the hospital kept him in overnight for observation. We decided to send Tom to meet the man who owns this house, after getting nowhere with the letting agency. Tom told the man we were going to sue him and he gave us the money instead. Tom said the man was really nice, and he was regretting letting the house and as soon as we move out properly – which we have to do in a month's time by the way – he's not going to rent it out any more, but spend some time doing it up properly.'

'Wow,' I said.

'Yeah. Oh, and he even told Tom the secret of the secret room.'

'Which is?'

'Apparently when the old lady died she specified in her will that the family wasn't allowed to sell the house, and that her grandson's bedroom must always be preserved as it is so he can stay in it at any time. The man said when the grandson's old enough they're going to give him the house.'

I nodded, and took the notes out of the envelope and folded them into my wallet.

I phoned Sally first, filling her in on Richard and Heather and my adventure in New York. I told her about the money and promised her I'd take her out for dinner sometime soon. I followed Richard's advice and made sure the rest of the conversation was all about her. I knew everything was OK when she started telling me about a man she fancied. Then I phoned Sophie.

'Gerald . . .' she answered.

'Hi Sophie, I'm sorry I didn't call you back. I've been in New York.'

'Oh,' she said.

'But I'm back now.'

'Right.'

'Sophie, don't take this the wrong way, but why are you calling?'

She went silent, clearly offended. Then she said, 'Well you left so quickly, and then you didn't call me.'

'I thought you didn't want me to call.'

'Why?'

'I don't know. Your friends don't seem to like me.'

'Gerald . . . the weekend didn't really turn out the way I planned it. Would you like to meet up again? Tomorrow, maybe?'

I wasn't sure, but said, 'Will it be just us?'

'Of course. I'll meet you at Leicester Square tube station. By the barriers, at nine o'clock.'

'OK. See you then.'

She hung up.

I spent the evening with Stan, watching one of his World War II films on video. I wanted to tell him about my adventure in America, but I could tell he wasn't interested so we watched the television in silence. After he'd gone to bed I went on the internet for a couple of hours and then turned in myself. Lying there trying to sleep, I found myself thinking of the secret room and how nice it must be to know you always have a childhood place to return to. My private penthouse was long gone, and neither of my parents had a room in their house for me. I envied the old lady's grandson, and hoped he was sentimental enough to keep this place rather than selling it for a ready supply of pocket money.

126

School *was* hell. The abuse started the moment I arrived in the playground. Usually I managed to avoid being bullied, mainly because although our school was only a tatty comprehensive, it had surprisingly large grounds, with plenty of places to hide. Reggel, Francis and I would simply head out to the furthest corner of the playing field, or hide under a prefabricated classroom to have our conversations. We managed this because most of the time we didn't draw attention to ourselves. Our classmates weren't that malicious, and had a lazy attitude towards picking on others, only really utilising this skill to preserve the pecking order. And this was exactly what I had threatened with my stab at playground celebrity.

Most of the abuse from boys centred on the fact that acting was 'gay' and only poofters would want to appear on TV. The girls concentrated on how ugly Sheryl was and how appropriate it was that we were playing boyfriend and girlfriend. The few children who had been in my French class when I said I was seeing Perdita pointed out how unlikely this was given that she was so pretty and I was a freak.

Still, the attacks weren't physical, and there were a few children (mainly from the years below me) who were impressed I was on television. More depressing, and surprising, was the envy of some of my teachers. They would make digs throughout my classes, saying stuff like 'Well, let's let our resident TV star answer this one.' I heard that Erica was suffering similar treatment, and it was making her more violent than ever. Eventually the two of us were called to the headmaster's office. The headmaster, who was the only teacher at the school to have been educated at Oxbridge, and a much more sensible man than most of his staff, told us, 'You two are in a very privileged position. It's wonderful to have achieved this sort of success so early in life, and you should be proud of what you've done. Especially you, Erica, achieving this as a first-year. And a young first-year at that. But a school is a very confined environment, and people don't like to be made to feel inferior. I'm not saying you're trying to do that – by all accounts you're behaving very responsibly, Gerald – but please try not to inflame the situation. OK, Erica?'

She nodded, and we were dismissed.

I've never asked my sister if she knew what was going to happen when our parents watched Episode Two of *All Right Now!* If she weren't halfway round the world in some unknown location I'd give her a ring now. I assume she probably didn't, but maybe she was the one who suggested to my mother that she should come to our house on the second Sunday, wanting to stir up trouble. I don't know why I hadn't realised how my mother would react. I suppose I'd been lulled into a false sense of security by her warm response to the first episode. No, that's not true. I was worried, but I hoped my parents would prove themselves by not being insulted by what they saw on screen.

It was a forlorn hope. By the first ad break my mother was screaming at my father, my sister and me, saying we'd taken outrageous liberties and demanding that I give her the phone numbers of everyone involved with the production of the programme, and all the other parents. I looked to my father, hoping he would take our side, but he was equally upset, although sad rather than angry. I was waiting for Erica to start shouting back, but she kept quiet, which infuriated my mother even more. As the programme ended, she shouted, 'I'm going to get this programme taken off the air. I can't believe you – my own children – would betray me like this.'

I went up to my private penthouse. Mum didn't stop me, already heading for the telephone. She was good on the phone – it was her medium – and I knew that although she really was very cross with us, she was also pleased to have a challenge as big as this to sort out.

*

My mother ended up staying at our house that night. I don't think this had been planned; it was an impromptu decision. I'd hoped the programme would bring my parents together, but had no idea it would happen like this. Erica told me later that during her phone conversations my mother had kept referring to our father, claiming he was equally outraged. I think she felt guilty about leaving him alone after that, and this was the beginning of my parents' handful of attempts to get back together before they finally gave in and got a divorce.

127

We went to Point 101, a peculiar but not unpleasant bar at the bottom of Centrepoint on New Oxford Street. It was Sophie's choice, after I had turned down her offer to take me to an illegal 'smokeasy' in one of the back streets of Soho. The bar reminded me of being in a departure lounge and brought back memories of Perdita. This made me feel warmer towards Sophie, and helped me get over the residual irritation I felt from the last time we met. But I couldn't resist asking, 'So where are Don and Uncle C tonight?'

She smiled. 'I didn't tell them I was meeting you.'

'Won't they be cross when they find out?'

'They're my friends, Gerald, OK? But they've got nothing to do with my relationship with you.'

We made small talk during the first few drinks. She seemed more nervous than the last few times I'd seen her, maybe because she wasn't stoned. I was glad we hadn't gone to the smokeasy. As I came back from the bar with the fourth round, she said, 'It's tipped, hasn't it? I can tell.'

I looked at the drinks, uncertain what she was talking about. 'What's tipped?'

'The balance. It's more on my side now.'

'What's on your side?'

'You're more relaxed. You don't want me as much.'

I should have reassured her. But the truth of her words had stunned me. She was right. I was calmer now.

'Sophie, why did you make it so hard?'

'Well, come on, Gerald, you were a bit weird.'

'I know. I couldn't help it.'

She smiled. 'Relax, it worked out OK. But I needed to know it was me you wanted. Not just anyone. A girl likes to be chased.'

'I can still chase you.'

'Relax, you've done enough. Shall we go home after this drink?'

I couldn't resist. 'Will Don and Uncle C be there?'

She hit me, then picked up her coat.

We didn't have sex that night. Sophie undressed to her underwear and we lay in bed together. It felt like the right thing to do, and different from sharing a bed with Sally. We talked a lot before falling asleep, and Sophie told me that she thought that whatever had happened in America had clearly made me more confident. And it was true. My past insecurity had definitely diminished, and I felt we were going into this relationship as equals. I was surprised that although she'd been the one who had had initial doubts, after our first night together Sophie was always the one who moved our relationship to the next stage. And any worries I might have had about marriage and babies when I started this book have disappeared during the writing, as I finally feel free of my more egotistical concerns and done with my past. When I started writing, Sophie gave me a photograph of herself to put by the computer to remind me how important it was that this book should lead to my current happiness rather than dwelling on old uncertainties. It also contradicts everything my dramaturge tried to teach me. If this were a novel, my dramatic destiny would lead me to Perdita. But, in reality, I found true love with a stranger I met in a nightclub.

128

My mother's campaign didn't really gain proper momentum until the broadcast of Episode Three. The first time she phoned other people's parents they weren't that responsive, understanding why she was upset but feeling smug that their own children hadn't betrayed them, and consequently being unable to rouse their own anger. But when Wendy's mother saw that her daughter was portraying herself as an unmarried mother she immediately phoned our house. This surprised me, as I'd assumed Wendy would have told her mother about this before the broadcast, and maybe slightly snobbishly, when I went round to their house, Wendy's mum hadn't struck me as the sort of woman who'd worry about this sort of thing.

'I told you I'd get this programme taken off the air,' my mother said when she came back into the lounge.

'Well, you haven't managed it so far.'

'Wendy's mother is going to phone the *Mirror* tomorrow. She thinks they'll run a story. And then that'll be it.'

This probably sounds as if my mother and I were being antagonistic towards each other, but it wasn't really like that. She seemed to have accepted, in her own odd way, that my sister and I had made an artistic decision, no matter how seriously she was opposed to what we'd done. And so it had become a battle between us. This was her way of expressing herself. Wendy's mother did call the *Mirror* the next day, and they did run the story. Middle pages. Check the archives. Wendy's mother and mine managed to persuade Amy's mother to be interviewed as well, even though her daughter had done as she'd requested and avoided having fictional parents at all. My mother didn't miss this, by the way, asking us, 'Why couldn't you be in the care home?'

'Nicholas said we had to have parents,' Erica replied.

'Nicholas, Nicholas, who is this bloody man? When I get my hands on him I'm going to string him up, I tell you.'

Mum was pleased with the article, and now convinced that the programme would have to be pulled. She phoned the producers every day, but they no longer returned her calls. When that week's *Sunday Times* arrived, I ran upstairs and dropped it on my parents' bed.

'Here it is,' I shouted, triumphant, 'still in the listings.'

Mum scrutinised the newspaper, unconcerned. 'They probably didn't have time to change them. But you wait. It won't be on.'

She was wrong. It was on, as usual. Now Mum was furious. This time she decided to fight fire with fire, and got herself and the other two mothers booked onto an afternoon chat show. The story was gaining momentum, and kept turning up in other newspapers and on the radio. Obviously I couldn't remember what it had been like when we did the mother-and-baby photo-shoots together, but Dad said he hadn't seen my mother so happy since then. I felt pleased to have given her this opportunity. I was more worried about my father, as his anger was more unpredictable, but he seemed to have resigned himself to the programme and got into the plot, no longer seeming at all upset.

The following Monday, the producers called me.

'Hi, Gerald,' said Immi, 'is your mum there?'

'Yeah. Would you like me to get her for you?'

'No, no, we're just curious. Do you know whether she's planning to keep up this campaign?'

'I don't know. She's still angry, but I think she's getting a bit frustrated that nothing seems to be happening. And she's a lot quieter this week.'

'Oh,' she said, disappointed.

'Why?'

'Because it's brilliant for ratings. Do you think she'd be prepared to do more radio and TV if she didn't know we were behind it, and we got them to contact her directly?'

*

Unfortunately, no matter how many interviews my mother gave denouncing the dramaturge and the whole enterprise, it wasn't enough to save the show. She was trying to kill it, but her complaining got us this close to being recommissioned. Erica and I were devastated. And my mother also seemed sad. She pretended it was because no one had taken any notice of her arguments, but I knew it was really because the spotlight had disappeared again, and we were back to the dissatisfaction of our normal daily lives.

Perdita was the only person from *All Right Now!* I continued to see after the show was over. We went to the cinema together, and for the occasional walk, throughout the next year, but as I was too scared to make my intentions known, our friendship soon fizzled out. On that shared flight from New York, Perdita told me that she often thought of me in the few months before she found her first proper boyfriend, and I felt the same way.

At least until Ellen came along.

129

It's early in the morning now, just before dawn. Tonight, like every night this week, I've stayed up writing. I no longer sleep with my manuscript. Sophie's back and growing impatient at the lack of time I spend with her. In preparation for this moment I've been reading up on famous authors and what they did when they finished writing their books. I'm sure it's a cliché everyone mentions, but my favourite anecdote was about Conrad finishing *Lord Jim* and then sharing a piece of chicken with his dog. I don't have a dog, but Sophie's been letting me off the housework since I started this book (and the mess has grown high around my desk), with the promise that I'll resume domestic duty when it's finally finished. It's tempting to spin this out for ever rather than go back to doing dishes, but a deal is a deal. I think I'll start by making her a nice cooked breakfast and taking it in with a flower and these pages on the same tray, a gift to my first reader, before this book, my life story, finds its way to the rest of you.

All Orion/Phoenix titles are available at your local bookshop or from the following address:

Mail Order Department
Littlehampton Book Services
FREEPOST BR535
Worthing, West Sussex, BN13 3BR
telephone 01903 828503, *facsimile* 01903 828802
e-mail MailOrders@lbsltd.co.uk
(Please ensure that you include full postal address details)

Payment can be made either by credit/debit card (Visa, Mastercard, Access and Switch accepted) or by sending a £ Sterling cheque or postal order made payable to *Littlehampton Book Services*.
DO NOT SEND CASH OR CURRENCY

Please add the following to cover postage and packing

UK and BFPO:
£1.50 for the first book, and 50p for each additional book to a maximum of £3.50

Overseas and Eire:
£2.50 for the first book plus £1.00 for the second book and 50p for each additional book ordered

---

BLOCK CAPITALS PLEASE

name of cardholder	....	*delivery address*
		(*if different from cardholder*)
address of cardholder	....	

postcode ....   *postcode* ....

☐ I enclose my remittance for £ ....

☐ please debit my Mastercard/Visa/Access/Switch (delete as appropriate)

card number ☐☐☐☐☐☐☐☐☐☐☐☐☐☐☐☐☐

expiry date ☐☐☐☐   Switch issue no. ☐☐

signature ....

prices and availability are subject to change without notice